Heart

Simon Morden

razor blade Press

Heart

This book was first published in September
2002 by RazorBlade Press,
108 Habershon St, Spoltt,
Cardiff,
CF24 2LD.

Heart is a work of fiction.
The characters and events described
are imaginary and any resemblance
to people living or dead is purely
coincidental.

Designed and typeset by
RazorBlade Press

Printed and bound in the UK

British Library in Publications Data.

A catalogue record for this book is available
from the British Library.

www.razorbladepress.com

Simon Morden

ISBN 0 9542267 0

Heart

Acknowledgements

To Jane, for translating:
To Richard, for reading:
To Sarah, Eleanor and Samuel, for letting me share the secret with them.

Let me not to the marriage of true minds
Admit impediments. Love is not love
Which alters when it alteration finds,
Or bends with the remover to remove:
O no! it is an ever-fixed mark
That looks on tempests and is never shaken;
It is the star to every wandering bark,
Whose worth's unknown, although his height be
taken.
Love's not Time's fool, though rosy lips and
cheeks
Within his bending sickle's compass come:
Love alters not with his brief hours and weeks,
But bears it out even to the edge of doom.
If this be error and upon me proved,
I never writ, nor no man ever loved.

Sonnet 116
William Shakespeare

Heart

Marianne Newton's story

Marianne Newton applied the last of her eyeliner. It was a tricky job; she didn't make her face up that often. When she did, it always took her far longer than she felt it ought, and twice as long as her husband thought it should.

"Come *on*, cherie! The taxi's going to be here soon!"

Marianne removed the kohl pencil from her eyelid and frowned. Robert wasn't being impatient; she was late, but it didn't help matters to know he was right.

"One minute, I promise," she called back through the bathroom door, down the stairs flanked with her pen and ink drawings, which Robert had framed himself, to the hallway where he stood. He was dressed like a penguin in his dark dress suit and best bow-tie, tapping the doormat with a leather sole.

She loved him, everything about him, from the premature bald patch in his red Highland hair to the blemish on the sole of his foot where he had stepped on a nail as a child.

She reapplied the cosmetic, the last half-centimetre joining perfectly with the first line. Done. She popped the pencil down on the edge of the hand basin and straightened her midnight-blue button-through dress. It swirled around her ankles.

"Ready or not, here I come," she said, sounding delightfully French, which she was.

Her shoes, flat strappy things, were on the top stair. She balanced herself on the banister as she slipped into them. The doorbell chimed. Robert grinned up at her, blew her a kiss and, still grinning, opened the front door.

He staggered back, blood staining his crisp white shirt like the blooming of a dark rose.

He stepped, stepped, fell to the glazed tile floor. A man wearing a tweed coat and black leather gloves strode in, pushing the door wide. He pointed his silenced automatic pistol in Robert's face. "Where is it?" he said.

Marianne froze, her second shoe half on. There was a dark pool collecting underneath Robert's back. Her mind went quite blank. For a moment, she couldn't even remember her own name.

The man with the gun lifted Robert by the throat, and walked forward until he pinioned him against the wall. He was joined by a second, more nervous colleague.

"Markham, hurry."

But Markham was quite content to take his time. He angled his gun down, down, and fired again. Robert's right knee shattered, and he screamed in anguish.

A gasp caught in her throat. Marianne still didn't move.

"We want it. You have it. Tell the bitch to give it to us." Markham pressed the long barrel against the bridge of Robert's nose.

Robert panted and swallowed. Despite the tearing pain in his shoulder, he turned his head and looked up at his beautiful wife. The gun moved with him. "Marianne, listen to me." He stared deep into her eyes, and she felt he was trying to pass her some of his love and deep regret. "Go get it. Go get it and run!"

He received a bullet between his red brows for his trouble. His body slid down the wall and sprawled lifelessly at the foot of the stairs. The remains of his head fell to his chest. He did not move again.

Marianne's marriage was over.

Markham touched the second man on the shoulder, pointed up towards her. "Get her."

Heart

The spell was broken: she bolted, and the two men vaulted the obstruction and raced up the remaining stairs.

Marianne was in the bathroom, door locked. She didn't stand with her back to the door, gasping – there was something too important to do than grieve now. She opened the airing cupboard door, reached behind the lagged hot-water tank and took hold of the sacking parcel that lay hidden. It was heavy, especially for little Marianne, and she dragged it out awkwardly.

There was a concussion from the door. It bowed inwards visibly, but held. It wasn't a modern fibreboard affair, but an original panelled door, solid wood as old as the house. She blessed it and the man who made it.

There was no time to unlock the window. Marianne hefted the long, thin rod of potato sacks and unbleached garden twine, and rammed it against the frosted window pane. The glass shattered and fell out on to the metal fire escape outside. She cleaned away the jagged edges with a brush of the bundle; some of the shards landed in the pile of dirty washing, others skittered across the tiled floor.

The door finally gave, splintering away from its hinges and falling inwards. The two men were greeted not with a cowering, snivelling woman who had just seen her beloved husband murdered in front of her, but an empty space for a window, a breeze against their faces and the tap, tap, tap of feet skipping steps on the fire escape.

She ran without her shoes. They flapped ridiculously and gave her less grip on the slick Kensington pavements than her bare feet did. She ran with a purpose: she knew where she was heading, to the nearest person on the list that she had memorised, she and Robert both. She

8

would have run, north, south, east or west a hundred miles to fulfil her mission.

Spring was turning to summer, the evenings were graced with light and warmth once more. There were people aplenty on the streets. She ran past them all, ignoring their curious stares. Nothing for her but the grave. They had found her, and the secret she had married into, and she knew her fate as sure as if she approached the gallows.

She did not resent it, any more than she resented her filthy feet and the ache in her legs. She would be with him soon, back with Robert.

It came sooner than even she expected.

She danced across a seemingly clear road when a speeding car struck her from behind. Sky and ground twisted and span as she was thrown in the air, loose like a rag doll. She had been hit so hard that she flew over the bonnet, the roof, the boot, and ploughed into the tarmac still moving forwards.

She tumbled to a halt. The hand that was wrapped so tightly around her prize was cut and bleeding thick rivers of red. She breathed, and pain like knives sliced her resolve to the bone. For the first time since her world had been torn apart, she cried out in terror and fear.

A woman looked into her eyes – one foreigner caring for another. The Arab woman knelt down and brushed Marianne's hairline with soft, strong fingers.

"You must not move," she said in good, accented English. "I will call an ambulance."

"Do not leave me! Help me!" Marianne tried to reach out her other hand and restrain the woman. But it would not move.

"Please, lie still!" She turned to someone else in the small crowd that was gathering. "Sir, make sure she does not move."

Heart

The dark face and black eyes were replaced by a different face.

It's him, it's him, sang a voice inside her head.

"Miss? Please just lie quietly. The ambulance will be here soon." The man visibly trembled as he spoke, and he rested one huge hand too gently on her shoulder. Eyes as blue as Arctic ice brimmed with emotion and shock.

"Do not fear," she found herself saying, "take it from me, a gift freely given and freely accepted. Take it and keep it close to you, and never give it up."

"I don't understand." The man put his hand to his forehead, just where his cropped white blond hair started.

"Closer," she said, and whispered in pain, "*Mon coeur.*"

The man leaned closer, moving his oversized body to lie on the hot, oily ground with her.

It's him, it's him.

"What I carry. Take it and go. Leave me and take it, because it is more important than my life."

"I can't leave you," he stammered.

"Listen," Marianne hissed. "You must do this for me, for everyone, or darkness will overtake us all."

With a supreme and final effort, she lifted what she held and pushed it at the man, and he had no choice but to accept it.

The Arab woman returned, and called out, "Please, a blanket, a coat for her."

Someone gave up their raincoat; it was draped carefully over her, leaving only her bleeding outstretched hand and her bewildered chalk-white face uncovered.

"Please tell him to go. Be my witness that I gave it to him freely and he accepted it."

The Arab put her finger to her lips and turned to the man still kneeling beside her, holding the long and heavy object wrapped in sacking and string.

"She wants you to go with it."

"I know." The man looked at the length resting in the palms of his hands. "I can't leave her like this. I need to know more before I just take it."

There was a commotion at the back of the crowd, now about six deep. The man and woman ignored it.

"Please," asked the man of Marianne, "What is this?"

"Go," she whispered with the last of her breath. "Go, before it is too late." Everything was receding from her: the sky, the faces, the pain. She heard the Arab woman say: "Her heart has stopped."

Her dress ripped open, from neckline to navel. Buttons span on the black road, gyrating chaotically but always slowing down. Hands folded on to her sternum and began to push rhythmically. Bright flashes of light accompanied each beat of the soon-to-be-ended dance.

"The ambulance is here. If you have the will to live, then do so."

Marianne exhaled and saw no more. Her body was lifted up, swung and turned. Straps tied her to a stretcher, but she was not there. She had gone, and it was dark.

Briefly.

Heart

Part I
Wednesday 9th April to Monday 19th May 1986

Chapter 1

Wednesday 9th April 1986
London

Torsten Neubauer's story

There was a large crowd. There always was. Those with cameras shot their rolls of film as if it were a new fashion. Tape recorders and notepads were brandished, notes manual and electronic taken down and used as evidence, twisted beyond recognition and stamped out in black and white.

Murder was the same in both countries, then. Neubauer had often spoken to gatherings like this and come away with the harsh brilliance of a hundred flashbulbs burnt into the back of his eyes. Curious that he'd never once been on the other side of the line that separated the mundane, common land from the hallowed ground of the crime scene. The fluttering tape marked the fundamental division in life: inside, the masters, those with the arcane knowledge and responsibility of justice; outside, the supplicants, those who demanded protection.

He moved through the ruck with ease, his slight frame slipping between the mainly stout English bodies to the front. He stood for a moment with the blue and white tape straining against his hips, feeling very much the stranger in the strange land. He was even being eyed with suspicion by one of the policemen with his ridiculous bullet-shaped helmet. It was odd, being on the receiving end.

He was beginning to feel uncomfortable. He patted his pockets and finally located the battered leather cardholder in an inside pocket of his ex-*Bundeswehr* olive green jacket. He opened up the cardholder to the officer in front, who let him through. He was inside, back on territory he was familiar with.

The house in front was no different to the others in the row. Terraced, three storeys and a basement, wide white-stone steps that numbered seven up to the blue-glossed front door. An opulent town residence for a rich man, in a street that quietly stated its position and wealth. But death had visited that home and marked it out for special attention. Two huge uniformed policemen stood on either side of the door. They looked down at Neubauer as he walked up the centre of the steps and between them.

All the time, he was soaking up information like a sponge.

The door had coloured-glass panels, cobalt blue, burgundy red, bottle green. None of these were broken and, to Neubauer's mind, they looked fragile. No forced entry. The door was ajar. He pushed it open. The hallway was dressed in glossy terracotta and the body lay at the foot of the stairs, sitting against the wall in the rigidity of death. The dress jacket and ruffled shirt had ridden up over the pale belly, and the piped trousers revealed socks patterned with diamonds.

There were three separate wounds. One to the right shoulder, another to the right knee, and what must have been the final shot: right between the eyes. There were hints of powder burns around all three entry points. There was blood; a lot of blood. It hadn't soaked into the sealed tiles, but had flowed across the floor, forming a black pool in which the body sat. He played it out. The victim opened the door to his killer; he knew him, or had at least expected him. Neubauer looked around for signs of a struggle. The pot plant on the telephone stand was intact, the bentwood coat-stand upright. No fight then; a shot to the shoulder. Pushed against the wall, the man had then had his knee shattered. Still held, he collapsed to the

14

floor; perhaps he even begged for mercy before the killer put a bullet through his brain.

That was how it was done. But the motive was what fascinated him. Why kill this man at this time? A contract? Revenge? Theft? Art, perhaps. Art was big business in Berlin, mainly Russian Czarist treasures smuggled out for American dollars. There had to be something worth stealing here.

Two plain-clothes officers brushed past him on their way to another room. Through a connecting door, he could see a white-overalled forensic specialist dust a Second Republic travelling clock for fingerprints. He put his hands in his jacket pockets, pulling the garment even more out of shape, and slouched over to the photographer who was repositioning his tripod for another salvo of motor-wound exposures.

"Hi," said Neubauer. "Do we have a name?"

"Yeah." The photographer's tie was flung over his shoulder. "Newton. Robert Newton. Married, no kids, worked in banking. That's it so far."

"*Danke,*" said Neubauer absently. He pointed to the stairs. "Can I go up?"

"Sure. Just don't tread on the stiff."

He took a five-step leap, and managed not to touch the banister or the body. He found himself alone, with all the noise and commotion below him. He moved carefully, taking every effort not to disturb anything. The victim was at the foot of the stairs. It could have been a drunkard's walk, or a deliberate act.

There were pencil drawings, carefully framed, leading up the stairs to the first-floor landing. Each one of a carefully, lovingly executed face that now lay pinned to the cold, grey corpse below.

He looked around the bedrooms. Only one was obviously in use; there was a box on the bed, with tissue paper spilling out over the edges, a box for women's shoes. On the dresser were a silver hairbrush and mirror, and an informal photograph of a happy, smiling couple against a lakeside shore. Robert Newton was in a kilt. A green waxed coat was drowning the slim, dark-haired woman under his arm. Nothing seemed disturbed.

The bathroom was a different matter. The door had been forced; the key was still in the reverse of the lock, but the wood torn away from the catch. A doorplate lay amid splinters on the chessboard-chequered floor. The glass in the sash window had been put out. The cupboard that contained the hot water tank was open.

Neubauer stepped around the glass shards that glittered prettily on the tiles, and leaned out of the window. The fire escape beckoned, and there was a blue satin shoe below, at the foot of the metal stairway. The majority of the glass was spread outside, not in. Someone had left through the bathroom window. He would suppose that the shoe on the ground matched the box on the bed. Robert Newton was married, and going out to dinner. Perhaps he was going with his wife. Perhaps he was going with his mistress, and this was her house.

He was still musing, when a self-important-looking man at the head of a phalanx of plain-clothes officers barged through the door.

"You. What are you doing?" The man's voice was one that was used to being obeyed.

"Inspector Torsten Neubauer, Berlin Police." When the man looked blank, Neubauer prompted him. "Interpol exchange? I was told you were expecting me." Judging from the welcome, he may have been expected, but not wanted. "You are Chief Inspector Arden?"

"Yes."

"I was at Scotland Yard. They said you were here. I came over."

"Let's see some ID, Neu-whatever."

"ID?" Neubauer's dark brows furrowed. He was a small, ratty man, with an uncontrollable mob of brown curly hair that always made him look like he'd been dragged through a hedge backwards. The photograph laminated on to his police card bore a distressing resemblance to reality.

Arden scowled at the West German eagle on the badge. "All right." He refreshed his mind with the unfamiliar name on the card. "Neubauer. Touch nothing. Disturb nobody. Ask no questions. I will talk to you when we get back to the Yard." He flicked the wallet back to the German, who fumbled the catch. On the third attempt, he fielded it and clutched it to his red-striped shirt.

"Sir?" It was a question.

"Just do what I say." Arden pointed his finger at Neubauer's face, earning him further dislike.

"Sir." Neubauer was more conciliatory. He eased himself from the confines of the bathroom. Arden could be heard saying something obvious inside. Murder was the same wherever; perhaps it was attitudes that were different. That was why he was here, to learn.

He leapt over the body on the stairs on his way down.

"D'you reckon I'm needed upstairs?" asked the photographer, who was folding away his tripod.

"I think so." Neubauer squeezed past the guards on the door, and skipped down the steps at the front of the house. If anything, the crowd had swelled. There were television crews trailing long leads back to their vans, and floodlights on high stands arrayed over them. As a concession, one reporter was standing inside the cordon, speaking to camera in short, serious sentences.

A woman in a long leather coat was scribbling industriously into a small notebook, every so often tucking a loose strand of hair behind her ear to stop it obscuring her script.

"Excuse me, Miss?"

"Yeah?" She didn't let the interruption prevent her rapid scrawl.

"You are police?"

"Uh-huh. DS Margaret."

"Margaret?"

She looked up, then down at Neubauer, her mousy-brown ponytail bobbing. "Margaret's my surname. Jessica Margaret. Who might you be?"

"Inspector Torsten Neubauer. West Berlin *Kriminalpolizei*."

"Blimey, the Interpol exchange bloke." She put her pen into the clip on the side of her notebook and extended her hand. "You spoken to Arden?"

"Briefly. He was busy, and said he would see me later."

"Arden has the grace of a rhino. Welcome to Britain." They shook hands. Margaret found his grip moist; Neubauer thought hers too masculine. "I'm supposed to be your liaison. Show you round."

"Make sure I stay out of Arden's way?"

She looked askance at him. "Just how good is your English?"

"Berlin is still an occupied city, Detective Sergeant. Out of three sectors in West Berlin, two armies speak English, and we also get English and American radio and television. If I do not understand something, I am not afraid to ask."

"So I'm not to worry about speaking too quickly?"

"Not at all."

She looked up at the house. "So what do you reckon?"

"About the murder? Am I supposed to have formed an opinion so early on?"

"I have. No reason for you not to have done, too. You're a copper." Margaret flipped her notebook back open and flicked through the pages purposefully.

Neubauer scuffed the ground with the toe of his shoe. It hadn't seen polish since it had left the factory; rather, it had built up a patina of dirt. "*Also*," he began, "Robert Newton either knew his killer or was expecting someone. Perhaps a taxi? He was going out to dinner, probably with his wife, who escaped from the house by breaking the bathroom window and running down the fire escape."

Margaret started to frown, but Neubauer continued unchecked. "As to why, that is a different matter. It could have been an arranged murder. Herr Newton worked for a bank, no? Perhaps he had angered someone powerful. Perhaps he had something worth stealing; if so, the thieves knew where to find it, because there was no mess. Perhaps it was, how do you say, faked. Wife kills husband, pretends to run away, afraid. Or wife's lover kills husband."

"Or husband's lover."

"Why is complex, like people. The universe is predictable, mechanistic thanks to Copernicus and Galileo. People are not." He smiled his wide weaselly smile, all teeth and glistening gums.

Margaret stood in her flat-soled shoes and regarded Neubauer closely, not sure what to make of him. "For someone who wasn't sure whether any opinion was appropriate, you seem to have some definite ideas."

"A habit. I think too much. What was your thinking?"

Margaret consulted her notes. "I'd go for the wife or a lover. Most people are murdered by someone they know, and it's normally the spouse. Find the wife, and we'll have our answers."

"You are reluctant to draw conclusions."

"I'm only a sergeant. I'm not paid enough to have conclusions."

"So, what *do* you do, Detective Sergeant?"

She held up her pen. "I take notes, Inspector."

"Good! So come. Let us make some notes. Would you like to follow me?"

"Where are we going?"

He dipped under the blue and white police line and pushed his way through the throng. A couple of hacks shouted some questions at Margaret; she told them impolitely to go away.

Out of the knot of bystanders, she fell in beside Neubauer.

"Is it the same in Berlin?"

"Yes. We keep more order, but yes, it is the same."

"What's it like?"

"Berlin? It is a city with a wall. Most of the time, you do not remember that there are five Divisions of Soviet tanks ready to occupy your streets. But they are there. Did you know that the Wall is built slightly back from the border? Even to touch the Wall is to enter a foreign country. There are doors in it, and the guards can come out and snatch those painting the Wall. We have to stand and watch because it is their right." He turned right at the crossroads, following the block round. "Berlin is beautiful, a place of freedom. But there are buildings that we cannot make new because their outside wall is East German. So there they stand to this day, with bullet and shell holes."

"Sounds like Tower Hamlets," said Margaret.

They turned right again. The entrance of the courtyard at the rear of the houses beckoned. The area was heavily in shadow, and even on that cloudless day, the sun had to set. "Here. See, up there? That is the bathroom window." He pointed it out to Margaret, who instantly began to sketch and describe it in her book.

Neubauer slowly walked into the yard, scuffing his feet on the smooth granite cobbles. His eyes searched the ground closely, stopping when he reached the foot of the fire escape. The strappy shoe lay sadly on its side. He pivoted, his hands on his hips, and turned to face the way he had come. He strode briskly back to Margaret.

"Sergeant?"

"Technically, we have no jurisdiction over each other. I'm not your subordinate, and you are not my superior."

"Correct."

"Call me Jessica, and I'll call you Torsten."

"*Also.*" He made a curious half-bow. "Yessica, come and see." He took a step back and knelt down beside an overflowing rubbish bin. "A shoe, new, never used. The gold lettering inside is not worn. Perfect. There is the other by the fire escape. It is a woman's shoe, unless fashions are different here."

"Don't be daft."

"I was making fun. Never mind. Yessica, could you run in such shoes?"

She unselfconsciously got down on her hands and knees. "Not really. Perhaps some women could, but not me." There was too little heel; it would flap uncontrollably.

Neubauer straightened up. "Size five. Is that small? We measure shoes differently in Germany."

"Fairly small."

"I think that Frau Newton is quite small too. These are her shoes, and they come from a box on her bed." He smiled the same wet smile as before, and it was just as unattractive the second time. "It is like Cinderella."

"You think she ran?"

"I know she ran. Down there, across here, kicking her shoes off as she went. And then ... where would a woman in her evening dress and no shoes run to?"

"Back to the Ugly Sisters?" She brushed her hair behind her ear again.

Neubauer laughed. "Excellent! Come, Yessica. You can tell Chief Inspector Arden what you have found."

Chapter 2

Wednesday 9th April 1986
London

Gideon Smith's story

Gideon Smith stumbled across a train home at King's Cross. He had enough wit about him to find himself an empty seat, facing forwards in a group of four around a table. He sat while the carriage filled up around him.

Everyone had a bag. They stowed them in the overhead racks, between and under their seats and, when there was no more room, in the luggage bay near the door. Gideon had only the long bundle of string and sacking in his twisting fingers, and he held it clutched across his body.

He knew that she was dead. He knew it was so the moment the Arab woman had torn her beautiful dress apart and pressed her brown hands down on her translucent white sternum. He closed his eyes and saw the cascade of little fabric buttons arcing through the air. He saw the jewel-like tattoo between her breasts, red, blue and green diamonds around the head of a tapering black line. He saw it all, and he would never forget.

He remembered standing and mumbling to himself: "Don't die. Please don't die." He remembered looking imploringly at the faces around him, each with their mixture of fascination, pity and ineffectual goodwill.

He remembered the shove in his back, and his turning around, with all his frustrated grief and anger at boiling point.

Hard, passionless black eyes had met his watering blue ones. Gloved hands had wrapped themselves around the package freely given, and pulled. "This belongs to us," the man in the tweed coat had said.

Gideon Smith, six foot four in his stockinged feet, had kicked out twice. One blow connected with each unprotected shin. He had followed them up with a knee straight to the groin. The man's breath had whistled out of his throat as he fell.

He remembered the voice that came from nowhere and talked directly to him alone: run, run, run as fast as you can.

He had obeyed, even as another hand tried to take hold of his arm. He scattered the circle of onlookers in his wake and, once free, had put his head down and sprinted. He had left his nameless and unnumbered assailants behind him, and left a woman cold and broken on the road.

By turns, he had found himself at the station. That part was blank. He didn't know London, and couldn't imagine how he'd arrived at the one of the few places he recognised. He opened his eyes again, and the train was moving. It swept out of the station into bright sunshine.

The conductor announced the train's departure time, welcomed the passengers aboard, and read out a list of destinations. Gideon half-heard Doncaster mentioned, but he was still thinking about the woman.

Her first words to him had been "Do not fear." Gideon had very little to fear from anyone. He was fast, strong and useful in a fight on or off a rugby pitch. His size was intimidating. His crooked nose and thick neck deterred all but the most ferocious. Yet she had said, "Do not fear." Why? His brows knitted together in a frown.

Perhaps she had said it because other people might think he had stolen from her. To be accused of robbing a dying woman; that would be something to be afraid of. She had said to the foreign woman, the Muslim, "Be my witness." In her last moments, she had thought only of Gideon's safety and well-being. He loved her for it.

Perhaps it was the package itself. Underneath the brown hessian and string there could lurk horrors unknown. He squeezed with his hands, and reassured himself that he felt an object solid and inanimate.

Gideon turned his head and watched the suburban landscape speed by. His eyes blanked out, and he let the constantly changing image flicker on his retina without the signal ever reaching his brain.

She was dead, and he had seen her die. He didn't even know her name.

His trance was broken by the murmuring of the ticket collector working his way down the carriage. "Tickets, please" and "Thank you" chanted the coal-black conductor, fine in his dark blue uniform with red piping. His clipper took odd shapes out the edges of the red and green card tickets.

Gideon searched his pockets. In his wallet he found the return portion of a Cheap Day Return from Sheffield. He stared at it. He'd bought the ticket that morning; he'd travelled down to London, and now he was on his way back. For the life of him, he couldn't remember why.

"Sir, your ticket?"

Gideon started. The conductor was holding out his hand and spinning his clipper like a six-shooter.

"Sorry." He was clipped, and the conductor moved on. The businessman next to him looked at him strangely. Perhaps it was the way he looked: hard and threatening. The man in the suit had not chosen to sit there, but a change in his schedule had forced him from his booked seat on the earlier train. He shifted uncomfortably, and concentrated on the share movements in his pink newspaper.

Gideon stared at his reflection in the double-glazed window. His *doppelgänger* frowned unpleasantly. He'd booked a day's precious holiday from work. He'd planned the trip, yet as far as he could recall, he hadn't met anyone or gone anywhere specific. He'd ridden the tube using a one-day pass. He'd rumbled through the bowels of London, finally emerging at Hyde Park. He had wandered under the trees and thrown bread to the ducks on the Serpentine.

Then he'd walked down into Kensington, along Cromwell Road past the gothic red-brick façade of the Natural History Museum. He had looked up at the traffic lights, seen a dark car speed ludicrously through on red. He had been too far away to save her and was forced to watch open-mouthed as the woman in the long blue dress flailed hopelessly in mid-air.

The creeping realisation was that he'd done nothing all day.

Perhaps, thought Gideon, I'm going mad. He stretched his fingers and cracked his knuckles. He contemplated the contents of the sacking. The first stirrings of curiosity turned in his belly.

"Excuse me," he said to the man on his right.

The businessman sighed, and got out into aisle to allow Gideon to slide himself along. The central arm on the double seat folded up. It allowed someone of his size to strain and squeeze his way out.

"Thank you." He extracted himself like a cork from a bottle. As he stood up, swaying slightly from the motion of the train, he felt a stiffness in his calves. The shoes he was wearing weren't made for running, and he had run long and hard. He stretched his legs as he walked to the toilet, where he locked himself in.

It was early in the journey. There were no piles of paper lying in pools of foul water that slopped across the floor, and there were still towels in the dispenser. He closed the lid of the toilet seat and lowered himself down, wedging himself with extended feet. He laid the wrapped parcel in his lap, and examined it.

It was long, four and a half feet from end to end. It was rigid and heavy, wider at one end than the other. He plucked at the knotted string. Whoever had tied it had meant for it to stay tied for a very long time. Gideon's fingers weren't designed for such close, intricate work and he realised his limitations. He fished out a small penknife from his jacket pocket, and began to tease the first knot open with the tool meant for getting stones out of horses' hooves. Cutting would have been quicker and simpler, but he would then have had to retie the string using a foreshortened length.

It took him a quarter of an hour of eye-straining work, but eventually the five pieces of twine were undone and stored safely on top of the toilet paper dispenser. He unrolled the hessian, and the outline of its contents grew clearer. Faded on the outside of the sacking was the War Office symbol: black arrow, and two initials: WO.

He opened the sack, and reached in. It was cold. He worked it free, and held it up to the light. He was holding a sword. He almost dropped it in surprise, but he had a safe pair of hands and the second it started to fall, he snatched it up again. He rested it across his palms.

The sword was bright shining steel, fluid like mercury, as polished as a mirror. The grip was of a leather deeply tanned to dark red, and the guards either side swept outwards for a hand's breadth. Set in the pommel was a ruby-red stone the size of an eye, held fast by a scaled eagle's foot of metal. A blue gem was caught in a net of filigree on the first solid guard, and a green jewel was grounded in a cup on the second that almost swallowed it up. None of the stones were cut or faceted, but had been polished so smoothly they glowed with inner fire. They were clear and rich, flawless and priceless.

The blade was arrow-straight, tapering a few inches from the end into a keen point. There was writing along its length, either side of the single raised rib. He turned the sword over, and there were similar marks on the other side. It was in no language Gideon recognised. Even the letters were unknown. They looked like a series of waves on an ocean, and the marks of dots and bows above them like foam.

Gideon had never held anything so beautiful in all his life. The line and form were perfect. It looked new, burnished so bright. But it felt old. He curled his hands around the oval of the grip, and found there was just space enough between the red jewel and the square knot of metal on the guard. The sword balanced itself, and he swung it in a slow arc. It moved like a diving hawk, clean, swift and powerful. Unstoppable, even.

But the cramped confines of a toilet cubicle in a northbound Inter-City 125 was not the place to practise.

Reluctantly, Gideon hid the sword back in the sacking and rolled the excess over until it resembled its previous appearance. He dragged it this way and that, then retied each knot as carefully as he could. He carried it back to his seat, and received a highly curious stare from the businessman. He'd been in the toilet for half an hour.

Gideon ignored the raised eyebrow, and hunkered down, resting his head against the upholstery. The train rocked him like a pendulum, lulling him to sleep. Before he finally succumbed, he folded both arms over the sword and squeezed it between his knees. Now he knew what he'd been given, he held it even more tightly to himself.

Wednesday 9th April 1986
Sheffield

Home: the slightly shabby rented house he shared with Nick. The wallpaper in the hallway was starting to lift at the junction with the sludge-green skirting board. The carpet had seen better days, some fifteen years ago. The air smelled damp and mushroomy.

It was cheap, though, and let them spend their money on more important things.

"You in?" he called. There was no reply, which suited Gideon's purposes for the next few minutes. He took the stairs two at a time, and nudged open his bedroom door with his shoulder.

It wasn't so bad for a bachelor. Most of the dirty clothing was in one pile, and the only disgrace was the pyramid of beer cans on the dresser. He wrestled with his gothic Edwardian wardrobe, and finally prised open the door. The sword went in, one end resting on his second-best suit, the other in the heel of one of his black shoes.

"Take it and keep it close to you, and never give it up." That's what she'd said as tried to force the sword on him.

The urge to hide it was strong, almost compulsive. He didn't wonder for a second if he was doing the right thing. He knew it with cold certainty. Gideon closed the door on it, and started for the landing.

The front door slammed. He checked his watch, and surprised himself at how late it was.

"Gideon?"

"Up here," he called. "If you're going to the kitchen, I'll have a beer."

"Good man."

Heart

He was sitting on the settee before Nick appeared, each hand holding a refrigerated can of bitter. Nick tossed one to him, and threw himself into the single armchair. They cracked the ring-pulls and swilled the froth spurting from the openings simultaneously.

"Ah, that's better." Nick loosened his electric-blue tie, and struggled one-handed with his top button. He nodded at the blank screen of the television. "Anything on?"

"Search me." Gideon ripped the ring-pull away completely, and tipped some of the contents of the can into his mouth. After he swallowed, he asked: "Out with Gill?"

"Aye, lad. A fine woman she is too."

"Not back with you?"

"Not tonight. She's got an early shift, and she complains I wear her out." Nick smiled a dirty smile, and brushed his dark hair away from his eyes.

"Nick?"

"Uh-huh." He reached over to the coffee table for the newspaper, and rustled through it for the TV listings.

"Did I say where I was going today?"

"No," said the newspaper. "Didn't you go to work?"

"I took a day's holiday." To Gideon, it sounded even stranger spoken than it had done just thought.

"Go anywhere nice?" Nick folded the paper back up and stretched out to the TV set. The dense muttering of a crowd, and the sound of a leather ball being struck underlay the serious business of commentating.

"London," said Gideon. "I went to London."

"What for?"

An Arsenal midfielder hoofed the ball high from inside his own half towards the Leeds goalkeeper. A defender collected it and looked around for someone to pass to.

"Didn't I say?"

"No." The defender slipped it to the left wing, and received it back straight away. Nick, still staring at the screen, furrowed his brow. "You all right? Didn't get a knock on the head on Saturday, did you?"

"It's Wednesday; it would have shown before now."

"If you say so." Nick leaned forward, and with a little dig of his fist, urged the Leeds forward on.

Gideon would get no further meaningful conversation from his friend until after the final whistle. He lay his head back into the dusty confines of the sofa and finished the beer. The Leeds attack faltered and broke down against the Arsenal back four. The ball was knocked back into the centre circle, and a red-shirted played scythed down an opponent. The commentator suggested it was a robust tackle; the referee disagreed and, to a cacophony of noise, showed a yellow card to the offender.

"I think I'll go to bed," said Gideon.

"Sure," said Nick, distracted. "'night."

He padded upstairs to his room, and shut his door firmly behind him. He went straight to the wardrobe and took the sword out. He picked it up, felt its weight and the way it filled up space. It was not just an object, it inhabited where it was. He needed to see it again. He sat down with his back to the door and started the laborious task of releasing it from its fibre prison. He stopped after every knot to flex his knuckles, then continued.

When it was done, Gideon put the sword across his knees and marvelled at it. It was more glorious than when he had first gazed along its mirrored length. He ran his index finger down the spine to the tip and tentatively tested the point.

Heart

It was sharp, but reluctant to cut him. The edges were fine, bevelled, ground and polished to a keen line. It was a blade that would keep splitting wood, leather, metal and bone with one screaming swing after another.

He took it by the hilt and held it up. His reflection was not his. A dark-eyed scarred face bellowed a blood-freezing challenge through a wild, foam-speckled beard. Then it was gone, hacked off its neck in one massive blow. The surface of the sword glossed red.

Gideon leapt a clear foot in the air, every muscle in spasm. The sword fell back across the floor with a metallic clatter.

He sat sprawled against the door, panting for breath and suddenly wreathed in cold sweat. He simply did not believe his eyes. He listened to his accelerated heartbeat and the roar of a goal filtering up from the TV. Nick hadn't heard, or had chosen to ignore, the crashing above his head. He cursed an over-active imagination.

Tentatively, he reached out and pulled the sword back on to his lap. It shifted as his knees moved, and he saw the image of the dead woman he'd left on the street.

"Don't be afraid," she said.

Gideon shut his eyes and snapped his head away.

"Don't be afraid," said her voice in his head, clear as a bell, soft as a lover's whisper.

He knew then that something was seriously wrong. He dare not think the sword was haunted. That would mean he would have to get rid of it, and she had told him that it was more important than her life.

It was just him. Post-traumatic stress. Shock at seeing someone so young and beautiful die in front of him. There were plenty of reasons for seeing things that were not there, hearing things that could not be.

"Don't be afraid."

32

Gideon wasn't afraid. He was strong, inside and out. He was wary and wise. He was fine, just fine. The trembling in his hands was nothing. The fluttering in his stomach was hunger. He stuffed the sword back into the sack and rolled it up. He searched around his room, looking for somewhere to keep it out of sight. He ended up taping it behind his wardrobe, using the electrical tape he used to keep his socks up while playing rugby.

That night, his dreams were a zephyr, a suspiration of sighing. He remembered nothing when he woke in the morning.

As he left his room after dressing in his jacket and tie, he slipped his fingers in the gap between the wardrobe and the wall. He touched the sacking.

"I'm not afraid," he told himself.

Chapter 3

Wednesday 9th April 1986
London

Torsten Neubauer's story

The shoes were sealed in plastic bags and carted off by Forensics.

Back at what everyone referred to as "The Yard", Neubauer was issued with a visitor's pass and given the paperwork that his Embassy had arranged to be hand-delivered the previous day. Arden had called a press conference, and every officer on the case had been called away to make him look more impressive. Neubauer sat at Margaret's desk, writing the same information on three separate copies of the same document, using his neat, cursive script. He doubted that anybody would ever read what he'd written, and he was tempted to put down something outrageous.

He was prevented by the return of Margaret, who looked over his shoulder at his efforts before rewarding him with a coffee, "Black, no sugar." She grimaced. "How could you?"

"Habit. My parents drank it like that." He placed the mug perfectly within the circle of a stain made by an earlier drink. "And the press conference?"

"Arden got on the telly, so he's happy. The press have their story, so they're happy. We've got the case good publicity, so we should be happy. The shoes went down well. Arden's now convinced himself that he found them."

"We know different." He observed the other officers in the incident room making phone calls. "What is happening now?"

34

"They're searching for the wife. They're going through their address book, and other associates."

"And what are you doing?"

She sat on the edge of the desk, and looked uncomfortable. "I'm looking after you."

"Chief Inspector Arden has given you this job. Does he not like you?" Neubauer drank some of his coffee, which was a foul, watery, machine brew. His office had its own percolator.

"No, I suppose he doesn't. He doesn't like women. It's a good job I'm not black."

"Arden does not like foreigners? That could be difficult. I am here for three months." He stared at the large map of London pinned to the wall. It looked wrong, alien, British. "Has anyone tried the hospitals?"

"This soon? Why?"

"It occurs to me that after several days when we are concerned for Frau Newton's safety, she will be precisely where she had been since today. She may have no identification with her. If she was prepared to lose her shoes, she may have lost her purse too."

Margaret pulled open the bottom drawer of her desk and hefted a copy of the *Yellow Pages* on to the desk. "Try under 'H'."

Neubauer gratefully abandoned his form-filling. Opening the book, and shuffling through the thin leaves, he found a depressingly long list. He started dialling.

"Good evening. My name is Inspector Neubauer, and I am calling from Scotland Yard. We are trying to trace a missing person. A name? Marianne Newton." He spelt it for the receptionist. "No? Have you any, any ..." His German/English dictionary was with the rest of his luggage, at an Embassy-owned flat in somewhere called Kensington. "Bodies without names? Unidentified, yes, thank you. Yes, certainly, I will wait." He picked up a biro

Heart

from Margaret's green plastic pencil holder and laid it on top of a pad of Metropolitan Police notepaper, then found the pen he had been using under the telephone book. "Describe her? One metre sixty, sixty-five kilos. Sorry, can you convert? I do not have my calculator with me. Hair, dark brown; brown eyes. Yes, female. Size five feet. No one like that? Good. I am not disappointed. Thank you for your help."

And so on down the list.

Until: "You do? Hit and run? I am sorry, I am unfamiliar with the term. Car accident? She was on foot, yes? At what time? Admitted at seven fifty-seven. May we come down? Yes, there will be two of us – myself and Detective Sergeant Margaret. Thank you. Goodbye."

He put the phone back on its cradle, and saw Margaret by the big map.

"Yessica."

"Yeah?" She continued looking up at the map. "She's out there somewhere."

"She is. Where is the Royal Free Hospital?"

It took her a moment to find it, then she pointed it out.

"That is where she is. Dead on arrival at nineteen fifty-seven. A car accident, they say. I have told them we will come and view the body."

"Torsten, I thought you were supposed to be observing."

"And you are supposed to be looking after me. Come, they are expecting us."

Margaret grabbed her coat from the back of her chair, and looked around nervously.

"Are we not going to tell anybody?" asked Neubauer.

"No we are not. The last thing Arden wants is a woman and a Kraut saying they've found another body."

36

She placed a hand on his back and hurried him from the room. "We'll tell him if it's her, and not before."

They trooped down the stairs to her car, a red Escort. She unlocked her door, then leaned over to let Neubauer in. As he fastened his seat-belt, he commented, "I am unused to this."

"What?" She kicked the engine into life, and pulled away from the kerb.

"Driving on the wrong side of the road."

He was in a state of shock by the time they arrived at the hospital. Margaret got him a cup of coffee from the automatic dispenser – the WRVS was closed – and hoped it would calm him down. At least her passenger had stopped muttering obscure and incomprehensible expletives about halfway through the journey. He had lapsed into a sort of stunned silence that she associated with battle fatigue.

"*Danke*," Neubauer said, reaching up his sweaty hands for the coffee. He sniffed at it, made a face, but drank it all the same. Slowly his heart rate approached normal. The sound of vigorous vomiting could be heard from one of the curtained cubicles. He looked around for Margaret, worried that someone might try and treat him.

She was at the Admissions Desk, showing her warrant card to the charge nurse. He picked up a phone and dialled, talked briefly, then pointed Margaret back to the bank of seats occupied by the wounded, the mad and their friends. She narrowly avoided being run over by a trolley being propelled at high speed by two blood-spattered ambulance men. Neubauer failed to see who or what required such haste.

"Someone from the mortuary will be up soon." She smiled gleefully. "Feeling better?"

"*Ja, ja.* The experience was interesting. I will get used to it." He finished his sour drink and briefly pinned the rim of the plastic cup between his top lip and his nose, where he wiggled it up and down. The vomiter had finished their re-emetic marathon, and there was relative quiet. He let the cup drop back into his hand. "Is this busy?"

"It's only Thursday night. It's twice as bad on Friday and Saturday. Drink, drugs, glassings, knifings, car smashes, suicides. All a bit sad, really. More often than not, you'll find some CID down here trying to sort it out."

"Detective Sergeant Margaret?" The speaker was a mild man in his fifties, with a bleeper poking from his top pocket. His white coat had some unnerving stains patterning the front.

Margaret sprang to her feet. "That's me."

"Doctor McPherson." He wiped his hand on the back of his coat, then thought twice about shaking hands.

"This is Inspector Neubauer from Berlin."

"*Guten Tag, Herr Inspektor. Wie geht es Ihnen?*" McPherson said with a grin.

Neubauer was caught off guard for a moment. He'd understood that the English were poor linguists. McPherson was Scottish. "*Es geht mir gut Herr Doktor. Und Ihnen?*"

"*Ich bin müde. Es gibt zu viele Leichen heute. Veilleicht haben wir etwas, was sie benötigen.*"

"Knock it off, you two. I don't even have O-level French."

McPherson acted like a naughty schoolboy caught passing notes in class. "Apologies, Detective Sergeant. You'll want to see the body now."

"If we can." They fell into step behind McPherson's long strides. "By the way, Torsten, how many languages do you speak?"

"German, English, good Russian. Some French. A little Turkish, Greek, Spanish, Italian. That is about all."

38

"Haven't you got anything better to do?"

"Germans have always liked foreign travel."

"Very funny."

"Not everybody in the world will speak your language. You English rely on the Americans to spread their culture, and it makes you lazy."

Margaret scowled. "A good job I've stayed in this country then."

McPherson pushed open the door to the mortuary. The body lay under a white sheet in the centre of the stainless-steel sterile room. Formaldehyde was the dominant odour.

"We wheeled her out especially. Igor, the cover, if you please."

A young man with long, lank hair, unfolded himself from a metal-framed chair in the corner. He had the unnerving appearance of a cadaver himself, with deep-set dark-rimmed eyes. He nonchalantly flipped the sheet away from the body's face, and took a step back. He watched Margaret's reaction, which was guardedly neutral.

In repose, she looked like she had been carved by a master mason from finest alabaster. She was cool and refined, distant, very French, very Celtic: pale skin, hair bark-brown and copper-fine.

Neubauer moved forward slowly, almost reverently.

The other side of her face was less perfect, lined with red stripes, black grit impregnating the wounds. An abrasion from the road surface. Her hair was a halo of dark curls, still damp from the bath she had enjoyed while still living.

"Pretty," said McPherson, "Someone will miss her."

"Not her husband."

Heart

"No?"

"He was shot dead just before." Neubauer made his lips go thin. "How did she die?"

"We haven't done a post-mortem yet. We were waiting for an identification and a next-of-kin."

"But?" He leaned over her, imprinting her face in his mind.

"She was hit by a speeding car. Massive internal haemorrhaging, haematoma, collapsed lungs, shock. Any of them will kill," explained McPherson. "Most of her bones are broken. Despite the dead on arrival label, she would have been unlucky to hit the road conscious, let alone alive."

Margaret pulled a photograph, already creased, from her pocket, and compared it with the face in front of her. "It's her. Marianne Newton."

The pathologist picked up a clipboard and wrote down the name. "You're detectives. Perhaps you can tell me about this." He passed the clipboard to Igor, and pulled the sheet slightly further down. Margaret began to feel uneasy.

Between the swell of Marianne Newton's breasts, just over the sternum, was a picture-bright tattoo. Red, green and blue diamonds, glowing under the sharp theatre lights, clustered around the head of a tapering streak, densely black.

"I've been working in here for thirty years. I've never seen one like it."

"What is it supposed to be? A cross, perhaps?" Neubauer started to reach out to touch it, then realised it would be singularly inappropriate.

"Perhaps." Margaret turned away. She was disturbed, and couldn't tell why. It wasn't her first dead body. It wasn't going to be her last. She felt a weight lie on her, and start to crush her gently. "We've seen enough. We'll try and find some family for you."

"Thank you, Detective Margaret."

Neubauer was deep in thought. "Doctor McPherson, could she have been murdered?" He stuffed as much of his hands into his pockets as he could.

"Certainly." McPherson's eyes followed the trolley as Igor wheeled the body away to cold storage. "If the murder weapon was a motor car."

There was a bitter taste in Neubauer's mouth. "Death is odd, is it not?" He pulled the car door shut and belted himself in.

"Why odd?" Margaret cajoled the car to life with judicious use of the choke. "Dead's dead and that's it." She felt none of the bluster that she spoke.

"You think so? Marianne Newton lies in a hospital, cold and still. But she lives on. We ask so many questions about her, and only she can answer them. Why did she run? From who? What was going on in her life?"

"That's detective work, not speaking with the dead."

He sighed. "In this country, perhaps, sergeants are not paid to think. They do the dirty work, the interviewing, the driving around, the taking of photographs. Tell me, what rank do you have to be to have ideas?"

Margaret had just engaged first gear. She slipped the clutch and stalled. "If that's supposed to be a joke, it's not funny!"

"What do you think, Yessica? I want to know."

"All I'm thinking about is how I'm going to explain to Arden what we were doing here when I should have been keeping you away from everything." She hit the steering wheel with her hands and sagged back in her seat.

Neubauer nodded slowly. "Ah. I see now. The cat is out of the bag, no? I am sorry for you. In Germany, I believe it is different."

"Torsten ..." She belatedly covered her mouth with her hands.

"You were doing what you were ordered to do. You are a police officer, and you have people above you. But we have a history of people doing what they were ordered to do, and we hope never to repeat that history. It starts like this, you know. I am nothing. Just a stupid *Auslander* who can be obstructed to no great consequence. But then you lie to court, lie to protect yourself, lie to protect others. You are better than that. You should not be afraid."

"Now that you know, what are going to do?" She started the car again, and pulled out into the flow of traffic outside the hospital. "I could kill Arden. Look at what the bastard has made me do. Torsten, I'm sorry. I can't even keep a secret, can I?"

Neubauer braked with his feet as they came up behind a bus too quickly for his liking. "You should be proud of what you do. You should do things that make you feel proud. I think that you should make a decision to do what is right."

"Arden's my Chief. Promotion depends on his say-so. I do the graft, and maybe one day I'll make Inspector."

"He will not always be above you. You are too anxious."

"Ambitious, please."

"Sorry."

Margaret ran an amber light and Neubauer put his hands over his head.

42

"*Mensch!*"

"I'll tell Arden what we've found. Maybe we can make a go of this." She changed the subject, worried that her bravado might give out. "Where are you staying?"

Neubauer recovered some composure. "I have an address in, where is it?" He fished out a crumpled piece of paper. "Kensington? You know it? I believe it is close to the Embassy. Will it be nice?"

"I'm sure. I'm back to sunny Hammersmith after we clock off."

"So you are going to tell Arden?"

"I'll stand up to him. Just this once."

Neubauer was alone. The embassy flat was furnished to a high standard, and its front windows overlooked a park with huge green leafy trees that rustled gently in the night breeze. His suitcase was unpacked, his clothing and personal effects were put away. He smiled at his own efficiency.

He took his mug of coffee over to the phone, and dialled international from the comfort of a well-upholstered, high-backed sofa.

"*Guten abend, Esther. Wie gehts?*"

"*Torsten! Ist etwas nicht in Ordnung? Was kann ich für dich tun?*"

["Yes, yes. Everything's fine. I'm calling because I wanted to hear a familiar voice."

"You don't normally get lonely. What's the matter?"

"It's very different to how I expected. They work differently. They behave differently. I am a little uneasy, perhaps, about how I will get on."

"They are different, Torsten. They're British. They live on an island. Berliners are different from other Germans. Why did you expect otherwise?"

"No reason. I'm just nervous. I've no real role here, have I? My liaison is a sergeant, which I assume is an insult, and Chief Inspector Arden is apparently a xenophobic misogynist. Fortunately, he is too busy to see me."

"Poor Torsten. Still, in three months' time it will all be over. It will be business as usual. But you are there to learn, no?"

"I don't think so. I'm here to teach these people that Germans aren't so scary after all."

"They picked the wrong man to send, then."

"Sweet of you to say so. I don't look like a stormtrooper."

"It's your mind that's scary. You'll run rings round those English flatfoots. What's this Sergeant like?"

"Arden's probably done me a favour. She's the brightest of them all."

"She?"

"Esther, you old gossip. Arden doesn't like her because she's a woman, so he assigned her to baby-sit me and keep me away from anything interesting. Not that it's worked so far. I got to New Scotland Yard, and discovered that they were all out at a murder investigation. I had nothing better to do, so I had a look around myself."

"You didn't touch anything, did you?"

"I tried. I could never resist those first moments when everything is still warm, hardly stopped moving."

"So who was it?"

"A banker and his wife. Several things are odd, mind. Do you have a pen and paper?"

"Do I ever answer the phone without them?"

"I want you to draw a diamond at the top of the sheet, another below to its left, and another below to its right. Okay? Then a line, thick at the top, tapering to nothing, directly underneath. Done that?"

"Yes. What is it?"

"You've the encyclopaedic knowledge of obscure facts. I was hoping you could tell me. One of the murder victims had this tattooed on her breastbone."

"It looks like a cross. Stylised, but a cross all the same."

"That occurred to me, too. Esther, this isn't urgent..."

"... but you want your faithful bloodhound to poke her nose around and see if she has any information."

"You're a gem. It's not urgent. It's a problem for the British police, not me. I just thought that if you could work out what it was, we would score another great victory for the Fatherland over the ignorant Britishers."

"You're terrible. I have no doubt that I'll read of your arrest in the international section of the newspaper. So, did you call me to ask this favour, or are you genuinely lonely?"

"I'm afraid that I will be lonely. Jessica is about the only person I've spoken to all day at any length. How's Pieter? Is he coping without me holding his hand?"

"I heard him saying to Rolf this morning that he'd got shot of that officious git for a whole three months. Who could he be referring to?"

"Just because he has no discipline and no respect. But you're making that up, of course. Pieter would never call me a git. Give him my regards, and tell him it'll be back to normal sooner than he thinks."

"Of course I will. It's late, Torsten."

"Which is a polite way of telling me to get lost."

"Polite? Go to bed, Neubauer. Go to sleep. Or have you drunk too much coffee?"

"I have in my hand the first decent cup of coffee I've had all day."

Heart

"Well, don't think too much, then. It's bad for you."]

"*Gute Nacht, Esther. Schlaf gut.*"

"*Danke, du auch. Schick' mir eine Karte.*"

"*Ja, ja. Grusse von London. Tschüss, Esther.*"

He slowly replaced the handset, and finished his coffee in contemplative mood.

Chapter 4
Thursday 10th April 1986
London

Torsten Neubauer's story

The next morning, Margaret arrived late to find Neubauer at her desk, his feet up on the stationery pad, drinking yet more machine coffee.

"Feet off." She dumped her bag next to her chair. "Interesting reading?"

"*Ja.*" Neubauer flicked his shoes away and passed her the autopsy report of Robert Newton. "What did Arden say to you?"

"He said little, which spoke volumes. I think if he takes the credit for everything we do, he's happy." She leafed through the pages of the report. "If we make waves, he could make life impossible for me and very boring for you. I think we ought to be satisfied with that." She reached the post-mortem photographs and stopped. "I'll be damned."

"The Newton Cross makes another appearance."

"It looks more faded than hers." She separated the photograph from the file and held it up to the light. "His is older."

"A guess: hers was done when they married. Say, six years ago? I have seen many tattoos before. The Russian *organitskaya* have a liking for them. Tattoos are strange, do you not think? They are permanent. A mark of both alienation and belonging." Neubauer looked around on Margaret's desk for another folder, nearly tipping his coffee over himself. "There is something else, too. Perhaps it is my English that is poor and I do not understand what is being said."

Heart

"Get to the point, why don't you?" Margaret had got up late, and was caffeine-deficient.

He finally found what he was looking for. "*Hier sind sie.* Interview statements. They do not tell us anything."

"Even in Berlin, I'm sure people don't like talking to the police."

"That is so." His finger traced down the photocopy of the first statement, following the handwritten words of the interviewing officer. "But this, this is different. For example, Joseph Jones, painter and decorator." He paused to work out what the phrase meant. "He was working in the front room of the house opposite. Opposite! He had a clear view of the Newton's front door. He saw the car pull up, and then what?"

"What?"

"Nothing. He saw nothing."

"He turned away."

"He was painting the windows. He was looking at them the whole time. He saw no people get out of the car, no guns, no shots. He should have seen everything."

Margaret pulled the sheet of paper from his fingers and glossed it. "Things get missed."

"The man can remember nothing until the taxi arrives. He remembers that very well. So, the best witness saw only a black Jaguar car. What about Michelangelo Trabioni, waiter? He was walking down the street on his way to work. He also saw the black Jaguar park outside the Newtons'. He asked to give a statement after he heard the news on the radio at the restaurant. He is not a man who does not want to talk to the police. He is upset that he cannot remember. But he cannot. Neither can the other two witnesses. As they look at the car, they forget." He passed the rest of the file to Margaret. "Do you not find that, what is the word, odd?"

48

"Granted it's unusual. Someone will interview them again, and perhaps they'll remember."

"Perhaps. The shooting of Robert Newton took place at nineteen twenty. We have four statements. None of them can remember anything except seeing a black Jaguar pull up. None of them report shots being fired, or the car driving away. At nineteen thirty, a taxi driver, booked by Robert Newton himself, arrived and found the body. The Jaguar was not there then. He was due to arrive ten minutes earlier, but was late. The witnesses' statements are full, but they cannot, despite themselves, remember. Which, by coincidence, is what happened in the street where Marianne Newton was run over."

The file was on the floor. He dusted off the bootprint from its cover, and opened it out. "Nineteen thirty seven, a telephone call was received by the ambulance control, reporting a woman on foot being hit by a car. A police car is sent also. The officers arrive just after the ambulance. They ask if anyone saw what happened. Twenty, thirty people say they saw the woman hit by a black Jaguar. But no one can tell them anything else about the car."

"This is stupid." She took the file from him. "This Arab woman who rang for the ambulance. Sanaa Al-Khulfi, wife of a Yemeni trade delegate. She was first there."

"Yes. But her statement is incomplete. It does not say anything about what happened after the car hit her."

"Should it?"

"I think so. You see, I remembered something last night. There was a hot water tank in the bathroom. The door was open. Now, imagine: your husband has been shot dead in front of you. You run from the house. Perhaps you are upstairs already. The fire escape is your only way out. Why then do you stop to open the door to the hot water tank."

"Airing cupboard. It's called an airing cupboard. It was open already."

"*Also*. The bathroom door would not open fully with it already open. It was opened once the door was closed. There was something in the airing cupboard. Marianne Newton took it with her." Neubauer stood up and searched his pockets for an address. "Perhaps, she still had it with her when she was killed. I think we should ask Mrs Al-Khulfi." He produced a piece of paper with directions to the Yemeni Embassy scribbled on it. "She is expecting us at ten o'clock."

"Torsten, have you seen Arden yet?" Her voice was heavy with meaning.

"When you say 'seen', I suppose you mean, have I had a meeting with him?" Neubauer collected the file from her desk and nestled it under his arm. "Not as such, no."

"Don't you think you ought?" Margaret looked to the windows that lined the corridor. Arden's office door was visibly ajar. "I don't think we can go rushing on ahead like this."

"Yessica, I do not understand you. We may have a double murder and you will be the one who makes the connection. I cannot believe that there are very many black Jaguars, even in London. Besides," he smiled, "what would he want to talk to a Kraut for?"

She picked up her bag again and slung it over her shoulder. "You are going to get me into so much trouble, I can't begin to imagine it all."

On a strangely hot day, they met Sanaa Al-Khulfi in a cool drawing room at the Yemeni Embassy. They had coffee served in Arab fashion: strong, black and very sweet. Margaret hated it at first taste, but bolted down a couple of the tiny cups out of duty. Neubauer, used to hanging around in cafés frequented by Turkish immigrants, enjoyed the bitter-sweet taste. He was also good at the small talk that seemed to approach subjects at a tangent and skim off again before reaching any definitive statement.

The short woman in a dark dress and white headscarf spoke good English. She didn't need the interpreter that hovered as wallpaper. She poured the coffee herself. Her fine, dark features still bore a troubled look from the previous day's events.

Neubauer saw Margaret's difficulty with her drink, and turned her thimble-sized tumbler upside down on the silver tray. He himself was offered, and accepted, a third serving.

Margaret explained who she was, who Neubauer was, and why they were both there. "You don't have to answer any of our questions if you don't want to. You have full diplomatic immunity. But we'd like to know what happened yesterday."

Mrs Al-Khulfi frowned. "I am happy to answer your questions. But I have already given a statement to one of your officers."

Margaret looked at Neubauer, and bit the bullet. "I know. We have reason to believe that something other than a car accident killed Marianne Newton."

"Is that her name? I did not know."

"You said that she was hit by a black Jaguar."

"Yes. It was going too fast, I am sure. It happened so quickly. It hit her from behind and it was gone." She gripped her hands as she spoke, remembering uncomfortable thoughts. "You know all this."

Neubauer coughed gently. "If I may?"

Mrs Al-Khulfi nodded her assent.

Heart

"You said at the end of the statement that you called an ambulance after realising how seriously Mrs Newton was injured. When you returned, was there anyone else with her?"

"There was a passer-by, a man. I had told him to look after her while I used the telephone."

It was Neubauer's turn to frown. "It is not in your statement. Did you tell the officer this?"

"Yes, I believe so. Perhaps I did not."

Margaret already had her notebook out, pen poised.

"Please," coaxed Neubauer, "if it would not be too much trouble, could you tell us?"

And she did.

"This man," she said, "he was tall, big, like a Viking. He cried over her when he realised that she was dying. She gave him something that she was carrying, and she told me that I was her witness, that she had given it to him freely, and that he had accepted it freely. I do not understand what she meant."

She bowed her head, and Margaret had to prompt her.

"With her last breath, she told him to go, take it away. Her heart stopped. I tried to revive her, but *inshallah*, she was dead. It was her time."

"And the man?"

"He had gone when I looked up again. There was a crowd around us. He was not there."

Neubauer leaned forward, intense concentration on his face. "What did she give him? What was more important than her life?"

"I do not know. It was a ... something, wrapped in a sack. Long, heavy. It was tied up with string." She threw up her hands. She did not know, and she was frustrated by her lack of knowledge.

52

As they left the Embassy, Margaret turned to Neubauer and said with feeling, "Torsten, what the hell is going on?"

"I am afraid I do not know. 'I give it to you freely.' What do you suppose it was?"

"It was whatever was worth killing both Robert and Marianne Newton for. But Arden's never going to buy this. We've no evidence, no witnesses who can say anything meaningful, and the man who has the key has vanished."

Neubauer stopped, and looked up at the trees that lined the road. They were full, green, swaying gently in the breeze and robbing the hot blue sky of some of its fierceness. "What would be so precious that you would have to hide it out of sight, but you give away to a stranger as the last act of your life? A riddle, no?"

"It must be worth a fortune."

"Or nothing at all. It could just be very important."

They reached the car, and Margaret slapped her hands on the blistering hot surface of the roof. "What a mess."

"*Also.* To cheer you up, I am invited to an Embassy party tomorrow night. The invitation says '*Herr Inspektor Torsten Neubauer und ein Gast*', but I have no guest. Since you are the only Englishwoman I know, would you come?"

She stared at him askance. No one ever asked her out, and her reply was carefully guarded. "I don't know, Torsten. Everybody will be important or German, and I'm neither." She unlocked the car door to cover her confusion. "Besides, I don't have a thing to wear."

He laughed. "And I have?" His clothes were badly fitting and cheap. Even the Army didn't want them any more. "Please, Yessica? You would enjoy it, and I do not think that you go to many parties that are not police?"

"No. No, I don't." In fact, she couldn't remember the last time that she had gone somewhere and met a roomful of people she didn't already know. She opened the door. "Okay. What time?"

Chapter 5
Thursday 10th April 1986
Sheffield

Gideon Smith's story

Gideon habitually queued at the bus stop at the end of his street, standing with his head down and more often than not nursing an injury or a hangover. This morning, he uncharacteristically raised his eyes to inspect his fellow travellers. There was a woman in a paisley headscarf in front of him, swinging her faded Silver Jubilee shopping bag against her legs. Before her in the queue was a man in a smart suit, tapping his left shoe arhythmically on the pavement while scanning the headlines on a folded down copy of *The Times*. Behind him was a bleach-blonde shop assistant, already in company uniform, noisily chewing gum and jangling her change in her painted-nailed hand.

Everyone of these people had secrets. Perhaps they had secrets bigger and better than Gideon's, but would any of them have received a sword from a dying woman who told them to take it, go, to do it not just for her, but for everyone? Would they have dropped it again when she told them that darkness would overtake them all if they didn't do as she said?

Gideon had made the choice after very little conscious thought. He'd taken the sword to please her, because she was beautiful and in pain. On reflection, it hadn't been a wise choice on her part, but as she'd died moments later, she'd been pressed for time. Gideon was the best she could manage.

So he thought.

The bus arrived. He paid the driver, took his ticket, and in a change to his normal routine, went upstairs on the double-decker, and sat at the very front. He used to do that all the time, from when he was ten and allowed to travel on public transport on his own. He couldn't remember when he had stopped racing to the front, and sulking if the two bench seats were already full. Fourteen, fifteen, maybe; when he had started to grow into the man he was now.

The windows downstairs were bespattered with sufficient layers of dust to render them opaque. In contrast, upstairs was a conservatory, and he was reminded just how green Sheffield was. The trees by the sides of the road were bursting with new life, and the sun sliced through the foliage to dapple the ground beneath.

The bus sailed down West Street and through the city centre. Gideon watched the pubs roll by. He knew the interiors of most them intimately, and could have told tales about each of them if he'd been in any state to recall the next morning what had happened. The rugby team drank heavily and danced chaotically until they were poured out of the door of a nightclub.

Gideon's stop neared. He swung himself down the stairs, pausing to stab the bell button with his thumb. He stood in the aisle, crouched down as anyone over six foot had to. The brakes squealed and the door wheezed asthmatically. He and two others stepped down to the pavement. One went left, the other right. He went straight on, through the glass door with the gold lettering: Pickett McInly – Accountants.

Gideon Smith was an accountant, and good at his job. It suited him because he found he didn't need a high degree of initiative, but a quiet methodical way of working. He could follow the rules as long as he could remember them, applying this formula to one file, that procedure to another. The bonus was that he was entirely ambivalent about his chosen career. He could have been stacking shelves in a supermarket or working as a street cleaner, but they didn't pay as much or leave him the free time he needed to train, play and drink. He neither hated his work, nor did he love it. Most of his colleagues shared his view; they clocked on in the morning, did the graft and said thank you very much for the monthly wage slip.

He waved at Jean on reception, and nodded at Eric as he passed him on the way to his desk in the open-plan office. Eric scowled at Gideon; he lived and breathed double-entry book-keeping, and wondered why anyone would take a day off from VAT returns. Gideon flopped down in his sprung chair and inspected his in-tray. He took a deep breath, and began opening yesterday's post.

Yesterday had been a hundred and fifty miles and a lifetime ago. He looked at the files balanced on the corner of his desk, some of them book-thick. He stared at them for five full minutes, wondering if he ought not just get up and walk out again, and come back tomorrow when he was in a better state of mind.

"A penny," said Eileen, as she popped another seven envelopes into his tray.

Gideon blinked. "Sorry?"

"For your thoughts." The office junior grinned coquettishly at him, head tilted towards one shoulder.

"Doesn't matter." He sighed as he flicked through the new arrivals. Eileen was still standing before his desk, swaying like sea-grass. "Was there anything else?"

"Good holiday yesterday? Go anywhere nice?" Her voice was gently Scottish, warm and soft, capable of teasing a winkle from its shell. Once she'd got her gossip, she'd impale her confidant on a pin and watch them squirm.

"Other people would like their post, too, Eileen."

Heart

Gideon breathed a silent prayer, thanking God for Eric's huffiness. Eileen pouted and tottered away on her high heels.

He worked solidly until eleven, when they all stopped for quarter of an hour for a cup of tea and a biscuit. It was one of Mr McInly's traditions; the tea trolley was wheeled to the centre of the office, and the workers collected their drinks. The managers emerged from their offices to talk with their subordinates, and the juniors found a chance to ask their seniors for informal help.

Gideon took his mug back to his desk and took off his shoes. He found his feet sore and wanted to cool them down. He groaned inwardly as Eileen stalked across towards him, intent on her prey. He looked around for an escape route, but it was too late.

"So what did you get up to yesterday, Gideon?" She'd stopped calling him Mr Smith within five minutes of entering the building. The only surname she ever used was that of McInly. She pushed his files on to his writing pad and perched on the empty corner, settling in for the duration.

"Nothing much," said Gideon tersely, even though he knew she wouldn't let him get away with just that. He bit sharply on his biscuit and ground it to crumbs between his teeth.

"Come on, where did you go?" She opened her split skirt and smoothed her stocking top. She was only seventeen, and already she was having an affair with Gerald Potts. It had made for a very awkward situation when Mrs Potts came to the Christmas party. Everyone nodded and smiled like nothing was going on. Eileen was young and pretty, and she didn't care one jot about Mrs Potts, or even Potts himself. Gideon wondered if he knew. She pressed him further, and leaned forward towards him: "Was it a woman?"

Simon Morden

He looked down her deeply cut blouse at her
barely constrained breasts. All his eyes wanted to see was
a cluster of three coloured diamonds around the head of a
tapering black line. He suddenly despised her bleached
blonde hair, her perfect too-wide smile, her easy sexuality
flaunted like a banner. The colour of his eyes when near-
white with ice. His voice was even, too controlled. Anyone
with half an ounce of common sense would have backed
away, apologising. "Eileen, leave me alone."

"Come on," she cajoled, and flicked at her hair.
"You can tell me."

He slammed the last fragment of his digestive
between his desk top and his palm, turning it to dust. He
was half out of his chair, and nose to nose with Eileen.
"Take them away and get them out of my face!"

Her smile started to slip, like a string of pearls cut
at one end. She sat up slowly, her hand clutching at the
collar of her blouse. Gideon's attention was drawn past
Eileen. Everyone was staring, cups poised at lips, dunked
biscuits collapsing to the carpet in soggy lumps.

"You, you can't speak to me like that." Eileen's
voice had gone hoarse with shock. "How dare you!"

His eyes travelled back to her, and he locked his
will with hers.

"I dare because I earn my keep here. You're here
because you're in and out of bed with Potts every chance
you get." As her jaw dropped, he stoked the fire with his
opprobrium. "You know bugger all about filing, you can't
operate the phones without diverting calls to Doncaster,
and you make a shite cup of tea. My life is my business,
woman, and I don't need some Scottish tart sticking her
tits into my face trying to get out of me that I saw someone
die yesterday. She's dead and you're alive, and I wish to
God Almighty that it was the other way round."

59

Heart

Gerald Potts was standing in the corner of the office. Even from Gideon's desk, he could see a vein on his temple throbbing.

"Mr Smith?" Potts shouted. Eric's teacup rattled in fright.

He looked around the sobbing mess of Eileen to Potts. "Mr Potts," he said, as if he had been asked to pass the salt at dinner. He stood fully, and dusted the biscuit debris stuck to his hand on to the floor. The tight knot of tension he'd been feeling melted away. He wasn't afraid. "You want to see me?"

"My office, Mr Smith." Potts turned and walked swiftly away. Eyes went from him, back to Gideon, to the slamming door, back to Gideon, like a slow-motion tennis match. There was the hush of collectively held breath.

Gideon pushed back his chair and headed after Potts. He ignored Eileen and felt no remorse. When he walked the brief distance down the corridor and into Potts' office, he found that Potts had been practising his lines. The manager stood facing the window, his thumbs hooked around his jacket lapels.

"Come in, sit down and shut up. You will apologise, Mr Smith. You will apologise to Eileen. You will apologise to the rest of the staff that had to listen to your tirade. You will apologise to Mr McInly, who will undoubtedly hear of this incident." He turned with a sneer painted on his face and delivered the final blow with high-handed mock mercy. "And you will apologise to me."

Contrary to orders, Gideon was still standing, leaning against the back of the chair in which Potts had presumed him to be sitting meekly. "Shall I apologise to your wife too, for pretending that you're not doing Eileen?"

"Doing Eileen?" Potts moved from the moral high ground to the slopes of doubt.

60

"What else would you call it? It's hardly making love. Sweaty gropings in the stock room, working late with your office door locked, being on the sick at the same time? You're hardly discreet, Potts. Everybody knows. I don't know about McInly, but he's no fool." Gideon span away bewildered. "God, man. How long has Eileen been here? Six months? How long have you been married?"

"Sixteen years." Potts felt his knees start to buckle.

"You do Eileen, then go home to your wife. She trusts you, you bastard, and this is what she gets."

Potts was white. He found his way into his executive leather chair. He'd had sex with Eileen in that very chair only last night. "Everybody knows. Everybody. That's not true, is it?" He was clutching at straws.

"You poor, mixed-up bugger," said Gideon, almost kindly, and sat down opposite him. His frame crowded the chair and made it creak. "She's taken you for a ride, and you're blind to it. It's a joke we all talk about. Even the cleaners."

Potts was halfway to putting his face in his hands when there was a gentle knock at the door. It opened without waiting for a reply. The severe and imposing figure of McInly appeared behind Gideon.

"Gentlemen? I'm not interrupting anything, am I?"

Potts looked like he was about to faint. He made it to his feet entirely on automatic. "Mr McInly."

Whether he was about to speak a complete sentence, or he was just expressing his surprise at being able to recognise the senior partner was immaterial. He was cut abruptly short. "Mr Smith, if I might see you in the conference room for a few moments? Mr Potts, have you any appointments this lunchtime?

Heart

Potts fumbled his way through his desk diary. "No, Mr McInly."

"I shall expect you in my office at half past twelve."

"Yes, Mr McInly."

"Very good, Mr Potts. Mr Smith, if you please."

Gideon followed McInly to the conference room, wondering if he was about to lose his job or receive a medal for gallantry. The room was cool, painted with muted shades of grey and lit only with indirect lighting. The table was an immense oval of black ash. McInly pulled out a chair, but sat on the table. His black shoes, polished to a brilliant shine, rested on the fabric of the seat. He was trying to put Gideon at ease.

"Gideon, Gideon. What happened?"

"I lost it." He took a chair for himself and slumped into it. "Any other day, I could have taken it. Today, no. Eileen picks and pulls at you until you tell her what she wants to hear. I wanted her to realise how much I resented her questions, and I bit back. Once I started, I didn't stop." He shrugged. "Sorry, Mr McInly."

McInly picked out a fountain pen from his top pocket and tapped his upper lip with the cool metal barrel. "Does everybody really know?"

"About Mr Potts and Eileen? The only person who doesn't is Mrs Potts."

The motion of the pen became slower, more deliberate. "Oh dear. Then I suppose something will have to be done. Thank you for you time and your honesty, Gideon. You may return to work."

Jean was waiting for him when he returned. "That was brief. How did it go?"

"He didn't sack me. Not straight away, anyhow." He looked around. "Where's Eileen?"

"One of the girls took her to the ladies to tidy her up a bit. Gideon, I think you went a little far, wishing her dead. So she's behaved badly ..."

"You called her a trollop last week."

Jean carried on despite his interruption. "You're not to judge. You don't know everything about Eileen. Mr Potts is a different matter; he should know better."

Gideon brushed the last crumbs from his desk, and poured the now cold mug of tea into his pot plant. "That's the way I feel. She's screwing up people's lives while others more worthy end up being snuffed out in a moment."

"You said you saw someone die."

He shut his eyes, and remembered it was only yesterday. "Run over, right in front of me. Jean, she was beautiful. She breathed goodness."

Jean laid a pale hand ridged with age on Gideon's shoulder and patted it. "Perhaps, Gideon, perhaps." She went back to reception, leaving Gideon to struggle with his concentration.

Each time he thought he'd succeeded, he blinked and saw two brown-skinned hands closing over a bright tattoo. He looked up just the once. Potts was walking like a zombie towards the foyer. His vacant gaze crossed the office and went through Gideon. The doors swung shut, and Gideon went back to his work.

Friday 11th April 1986

He learned his fate on Friday. He was offered a transfer to the new office in Newcastle upon Tyne. It was a promotion, but McInly made it clear that it was the only job in the firm that Gideon would be offered. Potts was staying, as was Eileen, although she'd been warned off the older man. She'd already typed up her résumé in company time.

Gideon had been handed the rough end of the deal, and everyone knew it. They commiserated with him, and sympathised with his position, although not sufficiently to tell McInly he was doing the wrong thing.

"Newcastle? What's in Newcastle?" He held McInly's letter tightly in his fist.

"Brown ale and a football team?" hazarded Jean. "Coal mines and shipyards?"

"Not any more there aren't. All that's left are a lot of short grubby people with funny accents." He threw the letter down on his desk and contemplated throwing his pot plant through the window. "Why me, Jean?"

"Because, Gideon, Mr Potts is too good at what he does to move him. Eileen is unsackable; she'd take Pickett McInly to the cleaners in front of an industrial tribunal. You, on the other hand, are the cause of all McInly's woes. As soon as you said we knew, he had to do something. He couldn't move Gerald or Eileen, so he chose you."

The yucca stared him down. "That explains why, but why?" His frustration grew more diffuse, less directed at specifics and gave him a general feeling of dissatisfaction.

"So that nothing like this will happen again," said Jean. "You're the scapegoat, Gideon. It could have been any of us, but it was you. We won't step out of line again."

"And if I tell him I won't go, he'll sack me. I've no choice, have I?"

Jean smiled sadly. "Not if you want a job. Take it, Gideon. It's a new start."

"But I don't want to leave. I like it here."

"We'll miss you."

Everything had changed, and was about to change further. His life was becoming unrecognisable. "I'm from Yorkshire. I belong here."

"We'll give you a good send-off. Something to remember."

Gideon sat at his desk, and already it looked foreign to him. "Sure. What am I going to tell Nick?"

Heart

Chapter 6
Saturday 3rd May 1986
Sheffield

Gideon Smith's story

The iron was still hissing steam as Gideon put on his crisp white shirt. It was warm on his back. His fingers fumbled with the buttons; the shirt was still fairly new, and the buttonholes tight and difficult.

Nick stood by the door, tapping his heel impatiently on the skirting board. "Gideon, you're going to be late for your own leaving do."

"I'm coming, I'm coming." He threaded his cufflinks through with the aid of his teeth, then tucked his shirt into his suit trousers. He cinched the belt and zipped the fly. "Where's my tie?"

Nick slipped it off the hanger swinging from the back of the door. Gideon positioned himself in front of the mirror above the fireplace and did the knot tight up to his Adam's apple. He turned to find his jacket held out for him. He threw it on.

"Now," said Nick. "we're leaving."

"Wait. I haven't got my wallet."

"You won't need it; you're not buying a drink all night." Nick propelled Gideon towards the hallway. As he passed the telephone table, he flicked Gideon's keys at him. "Put them somewhere safe."

Gideon made to swallow them, then put them in a trouser pocket.

"Nothing safe about your bowels, matey." Nick hauled the front door open, and pointed to the waiting taxi as he started to lock up. "Tonight's going to be a good night; one of the best. We are going to get you so smashed that it'll take you a week to sober up."

66

"I'll enjoy it," said Gideon, getting into the minicab.

"Enjoy it?" Nick followed him in. "You'll be lucky if you remember it. West Street please, driver."

The taxi pulled away from the kerb, and Gideon looked at his friend. With sadness he realised that he knew all about Nick, but didn't really know him at all. The reverse was also true. They talked, they joked, they got drunk together. They shared the same bathroom, but not each others' lives. He wondered if that was always the way between men.

On the taxi flew, racing through amber lights, past all the familiar landmarks of the past seven years. He'd come to university, and like so many people, stayed on after graduation. It was strange to think that this would be his last Saturday night in Sheffield as a resident. He gazed out of the car window at the place he called home until Nick leaned forward and asked the driver to pull in opposite one of the pubs.

They were the last to arrive. Half the office were there, even McInly, who graciously bought a round of drinks for everyone and then bowed out. He shook Gideon's hand, told him that he expected to hear only good things from Newcastle about him, and wished him well. Gideon returned the gesture ambivalently.

Ten of his rugby team, with wives or girlfriends, had turned up to see Gideon off in their own inimitable fashion. There was raucous laughter and shouting that threatened to break into lewd song. A full pint glass was pressed into his hand. "Down your neck, Gideon lad."

Gideon braced himself, head slightly forward, legs shoulder width apart. He drained the glass in one, without swallowing. Roars of approval greeted his feat, and he swayed under the backslapping and punching. He caught sight of Jean, who shook her head, smiling in disbelief. He winked at her, saluting her with the empty glass still cascading with foam.

The glass was pulled from his hand by Gilly, and a double whisky put in its place.

"Hi," she said. She stretched up to kiss his cheek, and her black lace dress strained dangerously. He caught the scent of musk in her dark blonde hair.

"Thanks for coming." He smiled awkwardly at her.

She smiled brightly back. "Good luck, Gideon. Thanks for looking after Nick."

He raised his new drink to her, and tossed the spirit down after the beer. Her image shimmered and blurred, then resolved more beautiful than before. But she'd seen Nick first, not him.

There was more beer after that, and faces crowded in on him, wishing him all the best in his new job, clasping his hand in theirs and pumping it good-naturedly. The women kissed him on the cheek, or on his lips, depending on how much they'd drunk, and Nick was forever scrubbing his skin free of red lipstick.

In the way of these things, someone decided it was time to move pubs. Glasses rattled as the remainders of drinks were guzzled with intemperate haste. With the rugby team to the fore, they belched their way to the door. The cold air hit Gideon like a hammer. He gasped and reeled, and was caught by the solid arms of the prop forward.

"Steady, old man."

"I'm fine. Just let me find my feet." He struggled to vertical, and weaved his way to the next bar. He was sat down and given whisky.

Jean squeezed in next to him. "Gideon, are you all right? I thought we'd lost you there." She sipped from her port and lemon, her third of the evening.

He took a deep breath and tried to look at his watch. He couldn't quite focus. "I'll last the evening out, don't you worry."

"Quarter to ten," she said helpfully.

"The night is yet young. We'll be off to a club, I reckon." He did feel a little groggy. It would pass. He'd eat some crisps and peanuts, and he'd carry on until the small hours.

"I don't think I'll be joining you. I'll let you bright young things party the night away."

"Come on, Jean, you're not old." He was slurring, but he was happy.

She laughed, increasing Gideon's pleasure. "You say the sweetest things. I'll be off home to Alec while you're tripping the light fantastic."

"You're a good woman, Jean."

"I'll save that for my gravestone. But you're a good man, too, Gideon Smith, if a little drunk."

"You call this drunk? You've seen nothing."

He was true to his word; he stayed the course. But by the time they reached the club, Gideon could barely stand unaided. There were considerably fewer bodies than had started out that evening, too. After the last pub, there had been an orgy of drunken vomiting in an alley. Taxis ferried the fallen away to Valhalla.

Inside the club it was as dark as night, lit by explosions of light and shaken by barrages of noise. Gideon was helped into a seat next to the dance floor and given another drink. Some of his group joined the throng on the crowded dance floor and gyrated away to music so loud it had been reduced to the pounding of the bass beat.

Nick slid along the seat next to him.

"All right, Gideon?"

"Good, good," yelled back Gideon. His eyes looked at the dancers without focusing. "I'm sorry I'm leaving, You'll have to find someone else to share the rent."

"I've been thinking," shouted Nick as intimately as he could. "I'll ask Gilly to move in with me. It's about time I did. A bit more commitment. See how it goes, you know?"

Gideon nodded, and gave him the thumbs-up. "You're suited."

"I haven't asked her yet. It's waiting for the right time. I mean, what if she says no? We won't be able to carry on the way we did before. It's a big decision." He lunged for his pint, and slopped some over the lip on to the already wet table. He tried a second time, and connected correctly with the drink.

"Here she comes now. You could ask her tonight."

"I can't. I'm pissed. She'd not believe I was serious." Nick wiped the foam from his mouth. "I'll do it tomorrow."

Gilly sat next to Nick, pressing her side against him. They started kissing, and Gideon looked away. As his eyes grazed the dancers, he saw a figure gliding in and out of the heaving mass. Her head was down, and she seemed to concentrate on her footwork. Her arms were straight and her hands clasped behind her back. She was skipping in a pattern only she could discern, her bare feet stroking the floor with the lightest of steps.

She wore a silk dress of deepest blue, and it floated like a cloud around her legs. As she swung in front of Gideon, she held out her hand, then span away. She looked over her shoulder at him, her dark hair brushed away from her face for a moment. She smiled and beckoned, mouthing, "Don't be afraid."

Gideon stood up, very slowly, unsure of the ground beneath his feet. The woman disappeared from view, only to reappear in the dead zone in front of the speaker stacks. She was trapping light beneath her feet wherever she touched the ground.

Nick came up for air and tugged on Gideon's sleeve. He shook him loose and began to edge out from behind the table.

"Gideon?"

"It's her," he said in disbelief, his words lost under the cacophony of the club. He lurched forward; the dancers parted before him and closed seamlessly behind. He was lost in a boiling sea of bobbing heads and twisting limbs. He moved forward towards the DJ's stage, and she was still dancing, alone and to a different tune.

She smiled again when she saw Gideon approach. Her skin was sheened with glossy sweat, and strands of her hair stuck to her face. She slowed her dance, and grasped the hem of her dress. She curtsied to him in strange formality.

"You're dead," said Gideon. "I watched you die."

There was no way she could have heard him; the sound from the speakers had whited out his ears. She held out a porcelain hand to him. Her voice rang in his head as clear as a songthrush. "Dance with me." Her fingers were reaching for his. She touched him, and she was real.

A hand grabbed at his jacket, and he turned involuntarily. Gilly, a worried look on her face, tried to pull him back to his seat. He wrenched himself free and lifted his hand, grasping.

She had gone. His head swivelled so fast as to make him dizzy. She was nowhere to be seen. He cried out in pain, and no one heard him. He'd felt her hand, she who was almost a month dead. She would have had warm breath, too, and a heart beating under her dress, just below the tattoo. She was too real to be a ghost. Gideon stood, dumb and bewildered, then allowed Gilly to lead him meekly back to his seat.

Nick was lying face down on the table. Gilly shook his shoulder, shouting at him to wake up. He slid under the table to the floor to join the spilt beer.

"Gilly?"

"He's passed out." She raised her eyes to heaven.

"What did you expect, the amount he's drunk?"

She poked Nick with the toe of her shoe, none too gently. It elicited no response. Gideon got awkwardly to his knees and dragged Nick out by his arms. He was completely limp. His eyes had closed and his mouth had opened; he looked like a blind fish.

Gilly bent down next to him. "Nick? Nick? Gideon, slap him or something."

Gideon patted his cheek with the flat of his hand, once, twice, three times. "He's just had too much."

"Is there a problem?"

Gideon looked up, and a tuxedo-wearing bouncer was leaning over them.

"Passed out."

"I think you ought to take him home, don't you?"

"Yeah, probably."

Gilly shook her head slowly. "We'll take the useless idiot home."

Gideon checked his watch, and slowly read the time off it. It was only a quarter past twelve. He felt a tug of conflicting desires.

"I can't do it without you, Gideon. I can't lift him."

"You're right." He pulled the beer-sodden form upright, put one arm under Nick's armpit, and locked the other arm up over his shoulder.

"You going?" someone asked.

"Aye. Nick's a bit worse for wear." Gilly was saying her goodbyes, too. "I'll see you around."

"Have a nice life, Gideon Smith."

He dragged Nick out to the taxi rank. Gilly had already commandeered transport, and was holding the door open for them.

"I'm really sorry, Gideon. I'll have something to say about this in the morning. Ruining your evening like this. It's shocking."

As Gideon laid Nick out on the back seat, the driver muttered something about kids. Gilly got in the front passenger seat, and gave Gideon's address. The driver leaned over and started his meter, the bright green numbers flicking over as he drove through the city streets, filled with revellers and speeding taxis.

Gideon was half asleep himself when they pulled up outside the house. He drowsily manhandled Nick to the front door, and fumbled for his keys. He dropped them, and decided to wait for Gilly to finishing paying the fare.

"Sorry."

"Butterfingers." The keys were gathered up and Gideon pulled Nick over the threshold.

"Stick the kettle on, love. I'll get him upstairs."

Nick's shoes bounced up every riser and, despite himself, Gideon was glad to lay him out on the double bed.

"You're a dead weight, lad," he said. He pulled off the shoes, undid his trousers and tugged them free. He wrestled with the jacket, tie and shirt, and left them in a pile on the floor. He pulled the duvet over him, and turned the light out.

Gilly had made them both coffee.

"He's in bed." He took a pint glass from the sink drainer and filled it up from the tap. He chugged half of it down, and wiped his mouth with the back of his hand.

Gilly was sitting on the edge of the table, swinging her legs and showing her stocking tops. She smiled at Gideon, and shook out her shoulder-length hair. "I can't apologise enough. Your big do, and Nick goes and ruins it. I wish I could make it up to you somehow."

Gideon leant with his back against the sink and watched her. He didn't think she could know how much he was tempted.

"I'm really angry with him. I'm at the stage where I just don't care what happens. And it would serve him right."

He watched her play with her hair, brushing her open lips with a snake of strands. He wished he was that drunk, so that he wouldn't have to make any sort of decision. He had to say something. "He's a good friend."

"Perhaps he is, but you're not the one out for the count in bed. What's a girl to do?" She stopped fiddling with her hair and rested her hands on the very tops of her thighs.

He could have taken his cue. He could have accepted the invitation, bedded her, and woken up the next morning with a thick head and little remembrance. But he didn't. Tomorrow, Nick would ask Gilly to move in with him, and it would ruin everything if he found out what had happened that night.

"Gilly, look. Thanks for the coffee. I'm going to bed now. I need my sleep."

"I'll come up too."

"Don't wake Nick."

"I don't think I could, but I don't have to try, either."

Gideon cursed himself. He ached with a peculiar longing for her. Not for any woman; just her. "Goodnight, Gilly."

He slept alone.

Sunday 4th May 1986

And woke to the sound of desperate and frantic screaming. It took him a while to come round, and another few moments to realise what the noise was. He sat up, and his brain grated inside his skull.

The screaming went on and on and wouldn't stop. It was coming from across the corridor. The alarm clock read 09:37, and it flashed the passing seconds out.

It was Gilly screaming.

Quickly, he clambered from the bed, tossing the duvet to the ground. He grabbed his dressing gown as he flung open his door, and threw it on as he made the two steps to Nick's room. He charged the door. Gilly was kneeling up in bed, her naked body shadowed by the curtains. Her mouth was wide and fixed, and she just kept on screaming.

"Gilly?"

She didn't turn to him. Instead, she pointed one trembling finger at Nick and wailed her banshee wail. Tears poured from her eyes and her pale flesh shook.

He turned on the light, and saw Nick. He was lying, arm outstretched in a most uncomfortable position, neck twisted up off the pillow. He approached the bed and touched Nick's extended hand. It was rigid. The skin was grey and cold to the touch. Gideon jerked back.

"Oh shit. He's dead." He took another step away. "He's dead, Gilly."

She sounded like she was choking, she was crying so hard.

75

Heart

He took hold of her shoulder. As his fingers touched her, she snapped back with such violence that she slipped half off the bed. Between her laboured gasps for breath, she growled: "Go away."

"Gilly, he's dead!" Gideon extended his grasp and caught her around the wrist.

She fought him furiously, clawing at his face with her free hand, kicking out with her knees and feet, her struggling so frenzied that he let go with surprise. She fell to the floor at his feet and wept freely. He picked her up without further protest. She was as light as a feather, cradled in his arms. He put her in his bed, and covered her gently with the duvet.

"Stay there, Gilly. Just stay there."

He ran down the stairs, almost tripping himself with his dressing gown cord. He snatched up the telephone and dialled 999. The answer was almost immediate, too quick for him to think.

"Which service do you require?"

"I … don't know."

"Hello? Caller? What is the nature of your emergency?"

He heard himself say. "He's dead. Dear God, he's dead."

"Putting you through to the police."

Gideon leaned on the wall and slid down it, not stopping until he was sitting on the threadbare carpet. He heard the operator give his phone number and address to the police telephonist.

What am I going to say?

The autopsy revealed that Nick had died of a slow haemorrhage in the brain. A great ball of blood had swollen up and pressed against the convolutions of his

76

frontal lobe. The pressure had first disabled him, then killed him.

The Coroner told Gideon and Gilly, and Nick's hollow-eyed parents and brother and sister, that the alcohol he had consumed had masked the symptoms. He could have been treated. He could be alive.

And worst of all for Gideon, the sober-suited man informed him that Nick had been dead for over nine hours before the paramedics had shrugged their shoulders and shrouded the body with a clean sheet. He'd been dead when Gideon carried him from the nightclub. He'd been dead when stripped of his clothes and put to bed. He'd been dead when Gilly put her arm around him, pressed herself against his back and slipped into unconsciousness.

She hated Gideon Smith.

Chapter 7
Monday 5th May 1986
London

Torsten Neubauer's story

"Neubauer. A word, if you have a moment."

The voice was unfamiliar, and Neubauer looked up from the ballistics report he was inspecting. Arden was standing at the door to the squad room, appearing slightly crumpled, slightly sweaty, slightly worried. Nothing that he could put his finger on, just a vague air of decay that was hanging around the Chief Inspector like a bad odour.

It was the first time he had spoken to the German since they had encountered each other in the Newtons' bathroom.

"Of course, Chief Inspector. Here, or in your office?" They were not alone. Three other officers were bent over their desks, studiously ignoring the exchange as if their lives depended on it. They probably did; Arden's reputation was of a spiteful man who did not forget, or forgive.

"My office, I think." Somehow he could not bring himself to say please.

"Certainly." Neubauer got up and followed Arden down the corridor to his nameplated door. When he was ushered in, he found that there was a strangely spartan feel to the room. There was a desk with a telephone. A bookcase with six books on it. A locked filing cabinet. A chair behind the desk, a chair in front. That was it. Nothing on the walls, nothing on the wide window ledge that looked out over the London skyline, no photographs, papers, notepads, anything to indicate that Arden did any work in his office at all, or had a life outside it.

Neubauer's office was a clutter of organic chaos. He knew where everything was, could point to a particular pile of haphazard files and name every case therein. His office was a greenhouse. Arden's was a freezer. It was chillingly peculiar.

"Shut the door, Neubauer." He called him *Newbower*, perhaps taking delight in mispronouncing the name, but not showing any joy at all. Arden took the seat behind the desk, sat upright in it, moved the white telephone slightly to its right.

Neubauer did as he was asked, and took the other chair unbidden. In the same way he nominally outranked Margaret, Arden outranked him. But there was no jurisdiction, and he was a guest! Arden should be extending him respect and courtesy. Instead, he felt threatened.

For good reason, it transpired.

"You're taking an interest in the Newton case. Very commendable."

"Thank you. I am enjoying assisting Sergeant Margaret in her investigations."

"There are, however, limits to what you can and cannot do. You will stop me if I'm going too fast for you."

"Have no fear of that, Chief Inspector." Neubauer was wondering what Arden was building up to.

"I have it on good authority that you have been questioning witnesses. That, I'm afraid, is not appropriate. You are here to observe only."

"As I said before, I am enjoying assisting Sergeant Margaret. She is a most diligent detective and an asset to your department."

"Have you been questioning witnesses?"

"Chief Inspector, I am a curious man. Sometimes, questions just appear. I cannot help myself. So, yes, I have asked questions of witnesses."

Heart

"That is not your role."
"Perhaps I should write them out, and Detective Sergeant Margaret can ask them for me."
"I don't want you asking questions of witnesses." Arden's delivery was dispassionate, almost unconcerned. Neubauer suspected that he could be a demon if provoked; overcontrolled people made him nervous.
"You have made yourself clear on that point, Chief Inspector." He smiled his wettest, most toothy smile. He hoped that Arden would dislike it intensely. "Anything else you need to explain to me?"
"There is more to British policing than just this one murder. You should expand your horizons."
"I have three months. I am sure my liaison officer will arrange something for me once the murder of the Newtons has been solved. I am looking forward to an excellent education."
"Yes. As long as we both know where we stand."
"Of course, Chief Inspector."
"You can leave that report with me."
Neubauer looked under his arm. He had picked up the ballistics report and carried it in with him.
"The facts of the case should not concern you. You are here to study our methods only."
"That is clear, Chief Inspector. Perhaps I can return this to you when I have finished reading it. I am, as you say, studying your methods. They are most interesting. I am sure you would not want to leave any gaps in my knowledge." Neubauer's contempt for the man was barely hidden. If Arden took offence, so what? The Embassy would back him. He came highly recommended.
Arden relented. "Whatever. We have a saying here in England: keeping your nose clean. You'd do well to understand what that means."

"I will go and look it up the moment I get back to Sergeant Margaret's desk. If that is all, I have some reading to do." He patted the file, and wondered what was in it that he was missing.

"That will be all for the moment, Neubauer." Arden should have bent his head over a file. But there was no open folder, no pile of papers for reading. He just stared at the opposite wall, and waited.

Neubauer smiled again. "Thank you for you time, Chief Inspector." He left, clutching the report to his chest.

Margaret was waiting for him when he got back to her desk. "You've been to see Arden."

"Yes. He is a strange man. He does not want me to look at the Newton case."

"He doesn't want me to show you anything, either. If you transgress the rules once more, I'm off the case." She looked dark, like a thundercloud.

Neubauer looked over his shoulder, to check for eavesdroppers. "What did he say? Is it that he does not like you, that he does not like me, or that he thinks we make him look stupid?"

"What does he want? What is he after?" She started to look around for something to hit. She was furious. Neubauer could see a bad end to her career if Arden happened to walk in. He had to get her out of there.

"Come. We need to walk." He put down the file and grabbed her arm, steering her down the corridor before she could gather herself enough to blow up at him in public. He spotted an empty interview room, directed her in and slammed the door shut behind them.

"What does that bastard want from me? Tell me, Torsten, what is he doing? Is this spite? I should just tell him that I'm not having this! He is interfering and I won't have it!"

Neubauer sat down in the only chair. "That would be a mistake. You would spend the rest of your life writing speeding tickets. Arden is not worth so much passion."

She kicked the door, then struck it with the palm of her hand. The thin hardboard face of the door now carried two dents. "Why?"

"I do not know. He wants me out of the way. He wants to make you angry so that you hurt your own job. He is only one man. He will not always be over you. I ask you not to do something that you regret later. We can always follow the rules."

Margaret sat on the floor. "Arden's rules, which he makes up as he goes along. There's nothing I can do, is there? This is so bloody frustrating." She was still angry, but now her fury was directionless and less distinct. "I thought we were getting somewhere."

"Perhaps that is the reason. His pride has been hurt. He must control us. *Also*. Let him. He cannot win."

It took thirty minutes to distract her enough to calm her down. Margaret tidied her desk and discovered that the ballistics report had gone. The Newtons had moved on and had left her behind.

Monday 19th May 1986

The reading of the will was two weeks later, in the cramped offices of an ancient and reputable firm of solicitors. Everything smelled of probity and dust. Margaret and Neubauer were shown into a dimly lit room with heavy red flock wallpaper and yellowed ceiling. They had wondered if Arden would send anyone along officially. If he had, they never showed.

Dominating the room was a gothic table in wood so dark and old that it resembled black marble. Chairs were tucked under the table, and it left just enough room to squeeze sideways around it. Three people – two women and a man – huddled in a corner, talking very quietly and secretly to each other. They viewed the newcomers with deep suspicion, casting frequent sideways glances in their direction. The temperature of the room dropped a few more degrees.

After ten minutes, an old man with no hair and egg on his old school tie shuffled in, and took his place at the chair nearest the door. He indicated with a beneficent smile that everybody should sit as best they could.

"Good, er, good morning, er, ladies and gentlemen." He picked up a hinged folder made from tan leather, and opened it flat on the table. There were two pages of heavyweight paper inside, and the old man meticulously laid each sheet on one half of the folder. "I have the, er, sad, and, er, solemn task to read the, er, last will and testaments of Robert Finlayson Newton and Marianne Margot Newton. Umm." He bent low over the wills until his nose was an inch from the type. It was the first time he had read the contents.

The silence weighed heavily.

"The, er, the wills are mirror wills. The, ah, provisions in each will being the, er, same for both Mr and, er, Mrs Newton. Having not survived each other by the statutory, ah, twenty-eight days, I shall proceed and read only the, er, will of Mr Newton." He coughed for what seemed like an age, then finally wiped his mouth with his handkerchief. It seemed that soon one of the junior partners of the firm would be entering the strongroom to fetch another will.

"I, Robert Finlayson Newton, being of sound mind, revoking all previous arrangements, do make my last will and testament."

Heart

Neubauer nudged Margaret, but she was already writing furiously.

"In the event of my death, I leave my entire estate to my wife, Marianne Margot Newton. If she does not survive me by twenty-eight days, then the following provisions are to be made."

Here the solicitor took a deep breath. Neubauer noted that while the man was reading, he didn't hesitate or falter once.

"I appoint John and Miriam Walcott-Green as executors of my will. My estate is to be divided as follows: the drawings by Marianne Newton are to be given to Sheila Barnstable; a sum of £1,000 to be given to Clive Smethwick, and a sum of £1,000 to be given to Patricia Smethwick. The residue of my estate is to be sold and the proceeds given to the Society of Poor Clares, at whichever is their registered offices at the time of our death." The man scratched the end of his nose and closed the folder. "That, er, concludes the reading of the will. Are Mr and, er, Mrs Walcott-Green present? I have forms for probate, that, er, require completing. Thank you, er, everybody."

Neubauer and Margaret waited for almost three-quarters of an hour to snatch a minute with the Walcott-Greens.

"Excuse me," said Margaret, and showed her badge. "May we have a word?"

John Walcott-Green, his suit so sharply creased it could cut fruit, inspected the badge, and showed it to his tailored wife. "Yes, Detective Sergeant Margaret. What can we do for you?"

"I think we're all looking for the same thing."

Miriam Walcott-Green interrupted: "I'm sorry. Your colleague is who?"

"Inspector Neubauer, West German Police," explained Neubauer. "I am just visiting."

"Please," asked Margaret, "help us. We don't know why they were killed."

There on the pavement outside the solicitors, they formed a small knot of discomfort. Despite Mr Walcott-Green's nod of welcome, and the sunshine, it was suddenly cloudy and cold.

Neubauer tried again: "There was something that the Newtons had. It has gone now. What was it?"

"What did they have? They had love. That's why they were killed." said Walcott-Green. He gave a wry smile. "Now I have to sell everything that's left behind. There's nothing I can help you with."

"We can't help you at all," said Mrs Walcott-Green, very matter-of-factly.

Margaret felt embarrassed and ashamed. "I'm very sorry for your loss. We will find those responsible."

"Of course you will, Detective," said Walcott-Green, not believing himself for a moment. "Now, if you please, we have to go."

They turned and walked away down the street, leaving Neubauer and Margaret with nothing.

"That's it, then," she said.

"Walcott-Green is not the sort of person to ever say what it was. It is gone, whatever, wherever, with the Viking. We will never find it."

"Never is a long time, Torsten."

"*Also.* But we have reached the end. Coffee?"

"You buying?"

"I am."

"Okay."

Heart

Part II

Wednesday 11th March to Monday 20th April
1987

Simon Morden

Chapter 8
Wednesday 11th March 1987
Newcastle upon Tyne

Gideon Smith's story

Gideon put his key in the front door and opened it quietly. Kate would be asleep in preparation for her shift, starting at ten that night. He didn't like her working nights; she was just as likely to run into a nutter with a knife in broad daylight, but it meant he saw hardly anything of her. She was awake during the day while he was at work, and in bed in the evening when he wanted to take her out. A policewoman's boyfriend's lot was not always a happy one.

He disliked her absence more the longer it went on. It had surprised him how quickly he'd got used to sharing a bed, and how much he missed her when she wasn't there. He'd heard somewhere that it was to do with the sound of breathing, and he wondered if it were true.

He put down his briefcase in the hall, and hung his trenchcoat, the one she'd bought him for his birthday, on a peg. He untied his shoes and put them in their allotted place.

He padded upstairs, and the treads creaked under his weight, despite his efforts to remain silent. He nudged the bedroom door open, and held his breath. The crown of her head was exposed on the pillow, and ribbons of long, dark straight hair trailed across the dark red covers. The duvet rose and fell in a slow, gentle rhythm. Gideon tip-toed over and kissed her forehead.

The edge of the duvet was tugged down from underneath, revealing her elfin face. She was beautiful to him, everything he had ever longed for.

"Hi," said Kate.

87

Heart

"Hi yourself," said Gideon, and kissed her lips. She smiled, and carried on the kiss. She snaked an arm out to wrap around his neck, and pulled him down. He noticed she was wearing his pyjama top.

"You should be sleeping."

She reached up with her other hand and grabbed his belt. She pulled him sideways; overbalanced, Gideon fell on to the bed. She was astride him before he had recovered. "Sleeping can wait, Gideon Smith. I've something else in mind." She stretched herself over him and pressed her open mouth on his.

"You'll crease my suit," he said eventually.

"You'd better take it off, then. I'm getting impatient." She started to unbutton and untuck his shirt, her hand moving between their bodies.

He laughed. "I love you, Kate."

"And I love you. Clothes off, now."

So it was, half an hour later, that Gideon once again experienced the Little Death, the heart-stopping moment of joy and fulfilment that was the joining of two lovers. Half an hour of tangled limbs, bruised lips and satin sweat.

Kate fell asleep on top of him and, after a while, he slept too.

His dream left him alone that time. He slept soundly.

The phone went, and kept ringing from the downstairs hall. Gideon woke, and found Kate had rolled off him, now curled up with her back to him. The curve of her spine made a ridge down her golden skin. He kissed between her shoulder blades and went to see who was calling.

It was James, checking they were still meeting later.

"Sure, about eight?" Gideon could see the kitchen wall clock through the open door. It read ten past seven.

"Okay. The Baltic?"

"Fine by me. See you there."

The phone went dead and he put down the receiver. He scratched himself, and wandered upstairs for a shower.

He left a note for Kate on the back of the bedroom door.

The Baltic was like a cavern with many chambers, echoingly empty at the start of the week, crushingly full on Friday and Saturday. Wednesday was an in-between time. Students, having had an afternoon off for sport, celebrated by coming out for a few mid-week jars. Real people generally saved themselves for the weekend, but Gideon had never got out of the habit of a Wednesday-night session.

Not that he drank any more.

There had been knowing sympathy from his family. They never pressured him or laughed at him, though they did drink themselves to maudlin oblivion in his company. His little brother had quietly let it be known amongst his friends what had happened to Gideon.

One acquaintance, stupidly drunk, had once started to tell everybody who would hear that only a fool couldn't tell a live man from a dead one. It had taken six people just to hold Gideon back. The lights had gone out in his eyes, and his face had set hammer-hard. No one ever, even in the heights of inebriation, taunted him again.

Gideon's friends in Newcastle were different. Why someone like him wouldn't touch the hard stuff was a mystery, and it wasn't long before he was asked. Rather than blanking out and coming to in a padded cell, he explained how his closest friend had died, and how he'd been too smashed to notice. Word got around, and after six months, no one asked any more. There was no fuss, and he was glad for it.

By the time he arrived, James had already bought him a lemonade and was lurking in a dark corner with it. Gideon sagged into a seat opposite and wrapped his hand around the glass.

As he always did, he raised the drink and gazed through it sadly. "Cheers."

James worked in the solicitor's office next door to Pickett McInly. They'd met one lunchtime by accident, when James was trying to change a flat tyre on his car. It was starting to rain, and the slightly built man couldn't get the wheel off the hub. His suit was getting grubby when Gideon intervened. He'd handed James his jacket and his beef salad stottie, and bent down to grip the wheel with both hands.

It had taken him twenty minutes, and he'd ended up lying in the wet road kicking the tyre so violently that the car threatened to rock off the jack. Finally, it moved, and slipped off the rusted hub as if it were new. Gideon found himself being offered a drink after work as a thank you.

James was small and balding, played football and went to a local church. Gideon was huge, had all his own hair, still played rugby, and wouldn't be caught dead within four ecclesiastical walls unless it was for hatching, matching or dispatching.

They got on surprisingly well.

"How's Kate?"

"Fine, fine. Another week of nights and that's that. Can't say I'll be sorry. They say they can tell at work, you know. I either come in smiling or grumpy."

James snorted into his beer. "I'll just be grumpy then."

"I ought to set you up with one of Kate's friends. We could all go out together if you prefer."

"That, Gideon, is the worst idea I've heard for a long time. I was the short, speccy kid at school, and I never really grew out of it, did I? I'm no oil painting, and that's a fact."

"Lasses don't worry so much about looks. They go for that personality thing." Gideon frowned into the bubbles rising to the top of his glass. "I don't know anything. I'm just happy."

"Good for you, Gideon."

"James, what d'you reckon about me and Kate?"

"Meaning what? Kate's a lovely girl, you're a good friend. What are you getting at?"

"My mother thinks we ought to get married." Gideon sat back in his chair and inspected his left hand, where the ring would go.

"Married?" James squinted across the table, then took off his glasses to wipe the lenses. "You're thinking about it, too."

"Aye, perhaps." He felt a vague unease.

"Getting married because your mam says so isn't such a great idea. Mind you, I've met her, and it'd take a lot of nerve to tell her no."

It dragged a sheepish grin from Gideon. "I would have thought you'd be all in favour, what with your beliefs."

James finished cleaning his glasses and blinked as he put them on again. "Marriage? It's the right thing to do. You just have to find the right person to do it with. I don't have a string of girlfriends behind me, so I don't know why you're asking me for advice. Even my parents are divorced."

"I'm sorry. I didn't know."

"It's all very sad and very stupid. The two people I love most in this world can't even have a civil conversation any more, without it dissolving into 'you did this' and 'you did that'." He finished his pint and smacked his mouth sourly.

"Another?"

"I think so. Look at the happy-clappy Christian, eh?"

Gideon bought two more drinks at the bar and placed James's square on his beermat. "Cheer up."

"I know," he said. "I might have to wait a very long time, but she'll come. One day, Gideon, one day. Anyway, we were talking about you and Kate."

"Well, what do you think?"

"Do you believe in destiny?"

Gideon sat quietly for a while. Then he screwed up his face and asked: "Destiny?"

"Do you believe that there's someone for everyone? If you do, you'll have to discover if it's your destiny to marry Kate."

"I'm not sure that I do. Believe in destiny, that is."

"What *do* you believe in? Marriage is one thing you have to be certain about. Anyone can live together and break up if it doesn't work. They can get married with the same attitude. But if you believe that this is it, you burn all your bridges. Whether you're happy or not, no matter who else comes along, whether you or she gets sick, or crippled; you stay together. That's what it means."

"I didn't know you felt so strongly about it."

"No, neither did I until now. I'd rather you lived in sin than make promises you couldn't keep. Divorce is a worse disaster than you realise. Especially if you have kids." He took a long pull at his beer. "Does that make any sense?"

92

"I think so."

"You know Kate well. You live with her, after all. But you've never talked about what you want happen next. If you ask her to marry you, you have to take the risk of losing her."

Gideon didn't like that at all. "So I shouldn't listen to my mother."

"Don't just marry Kate because she's the woman you live with. Marry her because it's right for her and right for you. Marry her because you want to spend the rest of your days building a life together. Marry her because it's your destiny; for no other reason. And remember that sometimes only sheer bloody-mindedness can see you through."

"That's a lot to think about," said Gideon. He sipped his drink. "Thanks, James."

"Don't worry about it. I just hope I haven't depressed you too much."

It was one of the most personal conversations he'd ever had in his life. His discomfort had reached breaking point. "Did you see the match yesterday?" he said.

Gideon walked home. The night was mild and still. A full moon ghosted its way behind an inconstant cloud cover that shone red from below and white from above. He walked up the steep streets that led from the Tyne to the centre of the city. He stopped for some chips on his way, not because he was hungry, but because of their value as comfort food. He sprinkled them liberally with sharp salt and acrid vinegar, and munched on them with greasy fingers and shining lips. When they were long gone, he continued to carry the empty papers, juggling them from hand to hand.

Heart

He'd another hundred yards to go to his front door, cutting the corner across the recreation ground with its strangely angled football goals, red and rusty under the street lights. As he reached the crossroads with their ever-changing traffic lights, he happened to look down. He jammed the chip papers into the opening of a pocket, and retrieved what lay abandoned on the ground.

As he turned it in his hands, he saw that it was a stack of Polaroid photographs, tied up like a parcel with a length of smooth brown string. He eased the knot to one side and looped the string around his fingers as he leafed through the images.

For a brief moment, Gideon thought he'd stumbled across someone's holiday snaps, the sort that wouldn't get printed in a reputable chemists. Then he saw the needle in the girl's arm, and that the two men wore balaclavas. The photographs told a brief, twenty-five-snapshot story of what must have lasted for hours.

They raped her. They tortured her with knives and pins and clamps. They raped her again. They smeared her flash-white skin with her own blood drawn in symbols and signs, and then they cut off her head.

There was one more photograph to go. In it, the severed head was bald.

Gideon looked at the string in his hand, at the glossy strands it was weaved from. He turned back to the playing field, knelt down, and was violently and agonisingly sick. It took a long time.

"Poor bastard."

Gideon glanced up and saw two plain-clothes types standing at the open door of the interview room. They were referring to him, of course. He quickly looked down again at the trembling surface of his plastic coffee cup: trembling because he was holding it and he couldn't stop shivering. He was cold to the core.

The overhead striplight was a line of ripples, but it was better to concentrate on that than on the thoughts that twisted grotesquely through his mind. He barely remembered staggering through the police station doors into the hostile and impersonal reception area. There had been a uniformed officer behind the glass screen, listening to a sorry tale of car theft. He hadn't been paying much attention, just a "Yes, sir", a "No, sir", and a "I couldn't say, sir" at appropriate intervals.

Then he'd flicked his eyes to the new arrival. He'd cut off the car owner in mid-sentence. "Take a seat, sir. Someone will take a statement from you in a minute."

"But ..."

"Now." He'd picked up the phone, dialled for an internal extension. All the time, Gideon was getting closer and closer to the front desk, holding the fateful bundle of photographs in his cupped hands. He'd rested them on the counter and sunk to the floor, retching and sobbing, crying hot salt tears on to the bootprint-patterned lino.

He'd been helped into an interview room, given a coffee, then been abandoned while someone tried to figure out what the hell was going on. He was regarded from a distance, as one would cautiously look in on a wild but wounded animal, dangerous to approach within striking distance. Like now, with the two men staring at him, perhaps wondering if he'd done it.

"Mr Smith?"

A man, older than the other two watchers, pushed through the doorway. He took the chair opposite and introduced himself.

"I'm Detective Inspector Mildmay, CID." He put a sheaf of forms on the table, clicked his biro and poised the ballpoint over the first sheet. "I need to ask you some questions."

Gideon nodded imperceptibly.

"Can we start with your full name?"

"Gideon Mark Smith." His voice sounded very quiet.

"And your address, Mr Smith?"

He gave his address, including his postcode, and added his telephone number automatically.

"Thank you, Mr Smith," said Mildmay. He put down his pen and patted his pockets. "Sorry, did you want a cigarette?"

"No," whispered Gideon.

"Filthy habit, I should give it up." He tapped out a cigarette and lit it with a tired metal lighter. "Fine. Now, I'm going to ask you to think back to earlier tonight. You came in here at about half past ten. Had you been out?"

"I'd been to the pub with a friend. The Baltic, on the Quayside."

Mildmay was taking notes. "What time?"

"After eight. I was late."

"And the name of your friend?"

"Cook. James Cook."

Mildmay raised his eyebrows, but wrote down the name anyway. "You were in the pub for how long?"

"Hour and a half. About."

"And what did you have to drink?"

"Lemonade."

"That's all?"

Gideon locked eyes with Mildmay. "I don't drink alcohol."

There was a long silence, and Mildmay backed down. "Okay. You came straight home afterwards?"

"Yes," he said, then, "No. I bought some chips. I'd finished them by the time …"

"So you walked?"

"Yes."

"What was your route?"

Gideon told him: up through Gallowgate, past the football stadium and the television centre. He faltered when he reached the crossroads. He started to shake uncontrollably.

"Take your time, Mr Smith."

"Sorry. I can't help it."

"Where did you find the photographs?"

"On the pavement, in the middle. Tied up with the, with the ..."

"Hair."

"Yes, hair."

"Can you say what time that was?"

"No."

"Did you see anybody else? A parked car, perhaps? Someone in one of the side streets, loitering?"

"No. I was the only one there."

"Okay. You saw the photographs on the pavement. What did you do?"

"Picked them up. I didn't know what they were. I looked at them, looked at them all. I couldn't help it. I'm so sorry I did."

"And then?" coaxed Mildmay.

"I threw up."

"And?"

"I walked here." Gideon gripped his hands together. They shook so much.

Mildmay looked over his notes and started to write out a statement in formal English. He asked for James's address, and details of Gideon's work. When he'd done, he read the whole thing out, and asked if there was anything else he wanted to add.

"No."

"Could I ask you to sign at the bottom, please."

Gideon took the statement form and the proffered pen. He tried to sign, but his hand wouldn't obey what his brain was telling it to do. He re-adjusted his grip and made another attempt.

It was no good. He looked up helplessly. "What do I do?"

"You have to make some sort of mark, Mr Smith. You have to show that you agree with what's written."

"I'm doing my best." He determinedly pressed the pen against the thin paper, and dragged it slowly this way and that. It looked nothing like his signature, but it seemed to satisfy Mildmay.

The Inspector looked at the statement, and stood up, taking it with him. "If you could wait here, I'll be back when I've made a couple of phone calls. Do you want another coffee?"

"Please."

"I'll get someone to bring you one."

Ten minutes passed and a WPC brought him another plastic cup with more plastic coffee in.

"Thanks," muttered Gideon.

"All part of the service, pet. Don't I know you?"

"Hmm?" His chin came up off his chest.

"You're Kate's man, aren't you?"

"Yes. Gideon."

"Has anyone told her you're in here? She'd want to know."

"I don't think so."

"I'll see if I can get a message through." She smiled sympathetically. Gideon was left wondering: does she know? Does she know what I've seen?

He nursed his drink for a while and Mildmay reappeared. "Sorry about the wait, Mr Smith." He kicked the door closed with his heel. "You'll understand that we

98

had to check out your story. You didn't mention that you live with WPC Mason."

"It didn't seem relevant."

"No, perhaps not. Anyway, Mr Smith, sorry to keep you for so long. You're free to leave any time you feel up to it."

"Thanks." They stared vacantly at each other. "Inspector?"

"Yes, Mr Smith?"

"Why? What does it mean?"

"It means that there are some sick bastards out there who'll stop at nothing to get thrills; not short of murder, or torture, or mutilation. We'll get them. Eventually."

"Who was she?"

"I have no idea at all. If she's missed, then we might find out."

"Someone has to miss her."

"I'm afraid not. Someone has to care enough to miss her." Mildmay finally sat back down. "Look, I'll explain it to you. We don't keep records centrally of missing persons. Each force has its own files, and sometimes we tell other areas if it's a high-profile case, but in the main we don't. We don't even know how many people go missing each year. It's in the tens of thousands, and we can't follow up each one. We just don't have the manpower to deal with it."

"Tens of thousands?"

"People just vanish, Mr Smith. Sometimes they turn up dead. Sometimes they turn up alive. Mostly, they're never seen or heard of again. If you walked out of here tonight and didn't go home, we'd look for you for maybe a couple of weeks. Then we'd give up. What else can we do? You've not been sectioned and there's no warrant out for you. You're not under sixteen. You've every right to go where you want when you want. I can't stop you from disappearing off the face of the planet."

"I never knew," said Gideon bleakly.

"No. Not many people do. I'm sorry, Mr Smith, I have other matters to attend to. We might be in touch about this, but I doubt it." The legs of his chair scraped the floor as he stood up. "Goodnight, Mr Smith."

"Goodnight, Inspector." Gideon finished his coffee as Mildmay left, leaving the door open; an invitation to hurry up and leave. The empty cup crackled as he crushed it in his hand, and it pathetically tried to regain its shape after he'd thrown it into the metal waste bin.

The analogy wasn't lost on him.

Chapter 9
Monday 13th April 1987
Newcastle upon Tyne

Gideon Smith's story

He stood on a cliff, on the very edge where the land met the sky. His bare toes curled around the last blades of tough grass, and the wind tugged at his naked body in gusty blows. There was nothing but the endless ocean in front of him, waves rising and falling, crests breaking into foam. They crashed into the black boulders at the foot of the cliff, sending spray high into the air and causing the ground to shudder continuously.

His arms were outstretched, as if he was preparing to fly. The wind roaring from the sea caught under his flattened palms and raised them. Perhaps he could fly, if only he had the courage for the next step forward.

It was a long way down to where the water surged against the rocks, dragging clattering cobbles and scouring the seaweed from their holdfasts. The surf boomed and growled, a monster that waited for him with patient hunger.

He had to choose. Whether to jump or shrink back. As he always did, he lifted his right foot and walked out into oblivion. He fell. Blue sky, black cliff and grey sea tumbled into one, and his back broke against the glass-sharp basalt. The waves rushed in and pulled him away with their strong hands, ripping the skin stingingly from his salty body and dragging him down into the dark.

"Gideon, Gideon! Wake up!"

With a gasp he opened his eyes. He was in bed, panting like he'd run a marathon, soaked with sweat. Light licked its way through the curtains, glaring white stripes and dots across the bedroom furniture. Outside, a car engine was turning over laboriously. The dawn chorus was twittering at the window. The dream had claimed him again.

The duvet was on the floor, and Kate was standing next to her side of the bed. "Half past six. Congratulations, you almost slept straight through." She thumped the alarm clock down. "I almost did as well."

Breathing finally under control, Gideon shuffled back against the headboard and let out a long, whistling sigh. "Sorry. I'm sorry. I don't know what's wrong with me."

"Neither do I, but I wish you'd get it sorted out." She suddenly exploded: "It's been every night for a month now, a whole bloody month of interrupted sleep. It's killing me."

"Kate!"

"For pity's sake, Gideon, this can't go on. Go and see the doctor or something. Get some pills." She huffed. "I'm sorry too, but I've had it up to here. I'm tired. I'm always tired. It's affecting my job and you know I have to try harder than anybody else just to stand still. Sort this out, because I'm in the spare room until you get rid of this stupid dream."

He had known that this day would come eventually. He was resigned to it, but it didn't make him feel any better. "I can't help what comes into my head."

"Normal people don't die in their dreams. You sleepwalk through the day and you die every night. It's like living with a zombie." She knelt on the bed and gripped his arm. "For both our sake's you have to sort this out. I can't do this for you. I can't carry you any more."

He put his arm around her and pulled her crushingly close. "I can't stop it, Kate. I wish I could."

"Say you'll see someone. A doctor. Go today, Gideon."

"I ..."

"Please, say you will."

He was tense with nervous energy, stiff and unyielding as a beam of wood.

"Gideon!"

Then he softened with her pleading, and became pliant and malleable. "I'll go. I'll go."

"Today?"

"Today."

Gideon phoned for an emergency appointment, and felt a complete fraud sitting in the surgery waiting room amongst the coughing and dribbling, and painfully moved limbs. Five times he made to get up and go, and each time he imagined what Kate would say if he told her he had got this far and turned back.

"Mr Smith," belched the tannoy, "Room three." It took him a few moments to decipher the garbled message. He only rose from his seat because no one else did.

He shuffled off, guided by the arrows on the walls. He turned this way and that, arriving at a door with two laminate plaques: "Dr Gupta" and "Room 3". He knocked, and an answering call bade him enter. The doctor sat at his desk, writing furiously in illegible script on a patient's card. Gideon took a seat while he dotted the i's and crossed the t's.

"Now," said Gupta, picking up Gideon's medical records, "Mr Smith. What can I do for you?"

Gideon wondered how to pitch it. Too bland and he'd be nodded and smiled at, patted on the head and shown the door. Too intense, and the result could well be the same. "I'm not sleeping very well."

Heart

When he stopped, Gupta encouraged him with a questioning, "Go on."

"I don't know what's been happening. I keep having the same dream; nightmare really. It used to come once or twice a month. Now it's two, three times a night. I wake up screaming. My girlfriend – I live with her – needs her sleep."

"So do you, by the look of you," interrupted Gupta. "I want to give you a physical. Could you take your shirt off and stand up?"

Gideon began to undress.

"What's the nightmare about?"

"I stand on a cliff for a while, and then I throw myself off."

"And when do you wake up?"

"As I die. There are rocks at the bottom, and the sea. It's very real."

Gupta approached him with a cold stethoscope. "It doesn't sound particularly pleasant. Breathe deeply please. And again. And again. Once more."

Gideon felt the chill surface of the stethoscope press against his skin.

"And it's the same dream every time?"

"Yes. And I die every time."

Frowning, Gupta indicted the chair. "Sit down, please." He inspected Gideon's ears, then shone a bright light in his eyes. He unwound a fabric cuff and attached it around a bicep.

It was a thorough medical: heart beat, blood pressure, reflexes. Gupta even checked his tongue. "Physically, there's nothing I can find wrong with you. You're clearly exhausted, and you've a few superficial bruises that look like stud marks. Football?"

"Rugby."

"Illness of any sort can disturb your sleep. But you said you've had this nightmare for a while, and it's only now that it's become frequent. You've no unexplained headaches, alcohol or drug abuse I should know about? ... I thought not. Is there anything you can think of as a particular point of stress? That may be the trigger."

Gideon put his elbows on his knees and his head in his hands. He told the doctor about the photographs.

"You really should have come to see me sooner, Mr Smith," said Gupta. "I'm going to refer you to a psychiatrist."

"I'm not mad," said Gideon, quickly.

"You came to see me to ask for my help. I can only prescribe pills and bandages. You've let this business fester for a month, and you need to talk to someone. I don't have the training for this, but a psychiatrist does." He picked up his pen and began to write a letter. "I'll get you an appointment for the end of the week."

"Dr Gupta, I'm not mad."

"Mad is a relative term. If you continue to suffer in the way you are now, you risk grave consequences to both your physical and mental health. Depression and paranoia aren't much fun. I'll do some phoning around later today. Someone will give you a call, or drop a card through your door telling you where to go and when."

Gideon nodded mutely.

"Forget the Northern Man bit for a while. Get yourself well again."

"Okay." Gideon got up, shook hands and left. He felt cold and numb. He had the suspicion that the doctor could be right, and that he was going mad. He stepped out into the squintingly bright sunlight, and shaded his eyes. As his vision adjusted, his heart stopped.

Heart

She was standing across the street from him, her bare feet on the dusty pavement flags, blue silk dress waving lazily against her ankles. She watched him from under her fringe with her disturbingly brown eyes. People walked around her, looked at her as they passed her by. Her shadow was as strong as anyone's that summer day.

Gideon stared and she stared straight back, her gaze unwavering.

Finally, he could stand it no longer. He remembered to check the traffic before he walked out into the road. She took a step back from the kerb as he crossed, and they stood quite close for a moment. She turned and started in the direction of the hospital. Gideon fell in beside her, and tentatively brushed her shoulder with his fingers.

Her skin was warm. He hadn't known what to expect. Whether he would have been more surprised if his hand had passed through her, he didn't know.

"Don't be afraid," she said.

"I watched you die."

"I am spirit, but I am as real as you." She smiled seriously and said: "Take my hand. We must talk together, say things that are long overdue. This time we will not be interrupted."

Gideon took her tiny hand in his giant's fingers. Her grip was strong and intimate. "In the nightclub. That was a year ago."

"Time comes and goes. It is right that we speak now, and here I am."

"Everything's changed. My best friend died, I had to change jobs, I found those photographs; my life is a waking nightmare. You chose the wrong man to give your sword to."

She smiled at him in his distress, but not for the reason he thought.

"Don't mock," said Gideon.

"I am not. I am trying to comfort you."

"Cold comfort from a dead woman."

"Now who is mocking?" She quietened him with a finger against his lips. "You are supposed to learn from these things, not be defeated by them."

"And how can I learn," he said, "if all I know is sending me mad? I'm talking to a woman a year dead. Shall I put flowers on your grave?"

"If you wish. My body is buried next to my husband's …"

"Stop. I don't want to know where." He broke contact with her and pressed his temples with the palms of his hands. "I can't believe I'm having this conversation."

"Gideon?"

"You know my name."

"My name is Marianne Newton, and I know much that would be useful to you."

"Like?"

"Like how to stop your nightmares."

Gideon found himself at the main gates of the hospital precinct. There was a small garden, with flower-beds and a bench. They sat down on it; the seat creaked once, twice.

Marianne tucked her feet under her, and stroked the bloom of a pink rose with a fingertip. "When you dream, you fall empty-handed. Hold the sword; you will not die."

"It's that simple? I go to bed with a bloody great sword and get a good night's sleep? Kate doesn't even know about the … it; she'll think I've finally gone stark staring mad."

Heart

"You are not going mad, Gideon. You must believe this. You must keep a hold of what is real and what is an illusion."

"Like now, you mean."

In reply, she took his hand again. "Listen to me. Things are not as they seem. Remember that the Devil himself can appear as an angel of light. You must guard the sword. Keep it jealously. It will not betray you."

"I don't understand. It's only a sword."

"You know better than that. It will talk to you if you let it; it talked to me. It wants to know you, and for you to know it."

"Swords don't talk. Look, Marianne, none of this is possible. It's a lump of metal that's as dead as you are."

"You're talking to me."

"You're just an illusion."

She squeezed his hand as hard as she could, and Gideon had no answer, just a question.

"What am I going to do?" he asked miserably.

"Learn all you can and store it all in your heart. When the moment for decision comes, and it will come whether you are ready or not, you must act on what you know."

"How do I know what I'm doing is right?"

"There are no guarantees. Look in your heart and decide."

He shifted uncomfortably. His head hurt; it was full with all her words. "What is this about my heart? You make it mean something different."

"Then listen," she said. "The laws by which the whole universe turns are written in your heart by the Maker of All Things. Most people lock their hearts away and never look to the place where the solutions to all their problems lie. They never feed their hearts with compassion and good learning, and in turn they lack the

108

nourishment of faith and hope and charity that would return to them if they were not so impoverished. They shrivel on the inside and become dry husks on the outside, unable to think and feel as whole human beings. They are tied up with their mistakes and end up trapped by their lives.

"This is why you must tend your heart as a gardener tends a tree. Water it with good water. Feed it with good food. And when the storm breaks, you can take shelter from the wind and the rain under its branches. It will be your only defence, Gideon. You are strong now, but you will become weak. You have a bed, yet you will lay your head in fields and on mountains, and your legs will not rest. Trust those who are worthy of trust, guard the sword against the might of men, and learn the secret of the heart."

Gideon hung his head. "I'm not that sort of man."

"Have courage. I did not choose you to carry the sword; the sword chose you itself. It chose well." She learned over and kissed his lips, warm breath escaping across his startled face. "*Bon voyage, mon ami.*"

She vanished as abruptly as a film-maker's edit, right before his eyes. Gideon sat on the bench and shook gently for half an hour. Then he went home.

He'd hidden the sword in the loft space, between the rafters under a thick layer of fibreglass insulation. Armed with a stepladder and an old pair of Marigolds, he retrieved it.

He unwrapped it for the first time in over a year. It was as blade-bright as it ever was, and it still reflected images that weren't there. Gideon was ready this time, but it was still a surprise to see a pair of pale eyes staring out from a face dyed deep blue.

Heart

"You have to stop that," said Gideon. "I don't
want to see those things."

"Don't be afraid." Marianne, her image cropped
either side and bent by the curve of the blade, held up her
hand to him.

"Stop it! Stop it now!"

And it did. It lay in his hands and behaved like a
sword, not a prison for souls.

Gideon went to his desk and laid out the sword
across the length of the table. He drew the curtains wide to
let the natural light flood into the darkened room he used
as a study. The sword played across the ceiling with
streams and bars of brightness.

He took a fresh piece of paper and a pen, and
began meticulously to transcribe the characters on the
sword. The nib rolled over the page like the waves on the
sea.

"James?"

"Gideon. Good to hear from you. What's up?"

"Are you free at lunchtime?"

"I'll just check my appointments book." He heard
the rustling of pages. "I've a client at half one, but I'm not
free until after half past twelve. Is it urgent?"

Gideon played with a folded sheet of lined paper,
tapping it against the phone. "I don't know."

"Where are you?"

"I'm at home at the moment. I'll come in and
meet you, don't worry."

"I've some files I have to read. Come over at one.
Bring your lunch."

"Okay. See you then."

"So," said James, leafing through a law book
thick with black text with one hand, and cramming a

110

doorstep of a sandwich into his mouth with the other. "What couldn't wait?" Crumbs scattered across his blotter and he brushed them off with his forearm.

"Recognise this?" Gideon passed the folded paper over a pile of manila files and waited for James to take it.

He opened the sheet and frowned behind his glasses. He turned it in his hand so that, eventually, all four edges had processed under him. "Recognise it as what?"

"Writing, I suppose." He looked over the lawyer's shoulder. "I think the dots go on the top of the lines."

"Oh." James flipped the sheet through 180 degrees, and bent low over it to study the shapes more carefully. "Pretty. Where did you get it?"

"I found it."

James looked up sharply. "I'm trained to spot liars, Gideon. And you lie badly. This is your handwriting."

"Okay," admitted Gideon, "but I can't tell you where I got it from. You'd never believe me anyway."

"Try me."

"Not yet. But I'm telling you the truth when I say I don't know what any of this means."

James passed back the page with its alien script. "What sort of trouble are you in?"

"I don't know. I don't know and I need to find out." He paced the length of the room, to the bookcase and back, then looked out of the window to the street below. "Don't mention this to anybody. Please?"

"Unless you're in the process of committing a crime, I keep secrets fairly well." James heaved the heavy book shut and put his half-eaten lunch down on top of it. "I can't not say this, Gideon. You've changed. There's something different about you, something that's not quite right. You've been avoiding me for weeks, then you call up out of the blue and ask to see me. I've left messages for you at home and at work. When I speak to your colleagues, they say to me, 'Can't you do something with him? He doesn't seem to want to be here any more.' You're off sick more often than not. And now I finally get a look at you, you look like a wraith. What does your mirror tell you? What's been going on?"

Gideon didn't know what to say. He shifted his weight from one foot to the other and looked at the pattern on the carpet. For some stupid reason, he felt himself about to cry. He sat down in the clients' chair and stuffed the by now crumpled sheet of paper into his pocket. He helped himself to a tissue from the open box on James's desk, and trumpeted his nose.

"Gideon, talk to me," implored James. The phone rang and he snatched it up. Gideon had never heard James swear before.

"Yes? Early?" He glanced at the wall clock. "He'll have to wait. I don't care if he's the richest man in Christendom, he's waiting until half past. That's when his appointment is and that's when I'll see him. Give him a cup of tea and tell him I'm busy." He launched the handset back into its cradle. "Damn work. It gets in the way of important things."

"I'd better go," said Gideon.

"Stay there. I can't let you walk out of here like this. Take your time." He started to tidy his desk, rebagging his sandwich and filing it in his top drawer. "What does Kate say about all this?"

"Not much. I'm scared I'm losing her."

"A month ago, you were wondering whether to marry her."

"I'm going to get better from now on. Someone's told me what to do to get some sleep. I'll be back to my normal self soon." Gideon pitched his screwed-up tissue into James's green tin bin. "I'm still your friend."

"I'm glad. Look, this writing of yours. Ask at the university; the Languages Department is bound to do translation work, even if you slip a student a fiver for ten minutes' work."

Gideon stood up and claimed another hankie from the box. "That's a good idea. I'll do that."

"You know where I am if you need me."

"You'd better see your client now. Or you'll be in trouble, too."

James rolled his eyes. "Tell me about it." He picked up the phone and dialled for reception.

Gideon gave a half-hearted wave and left. He popped in next door to his office, and told them he would be back in the next day. They didn't look convinced.

Kate slept with him that night. He remembered her sliding under the covers, still wet from her shower. She teased him wordlessly awake with her hands and her lips. When the time came, she pulled him on top of her and wrapped him in her limbs, drawing him along with her passion.

And afterwards, she clung to his heavily breathing body, pressing her damp skin against his. She held him all the way down from his head to his ankles, her chin hooked over his shoulder and her heels over his calves. She ran her fingers down his spin in gentle lines and curves, and lulled him to sleep.

He dreamed.

He was on the cliff's edge again, the sea tearing at the rocks below, the wind grabbing at his outstretched form. He knew he would jump. He looked down at the white surf and the black rocks, and imagined his bleeding body dragged into the dark ocean. He was going to die again.

The sword, tenuous as fog, started to form in his right hand. His feet were anxious for the off, wanting to propel themselves into space. He fought the urge and concentrated hard until he could bear the ground no longer.

He fell, and never landed.

His eyes opened abruptly. He was alone, and he could feel the heart in his chest beating out the seconds. He rolled over and felt with his fingers deep under the bed. He touched a hessian sack and, satisfied, drew his arm back in.

Kate had gone, and Gideon wondered if she had been a dream too.

Chapter 10
Tuesday 14th April 1987
Newcastle upon Tyne

Gideon Smith's story

He had wandered the corridors and taken three flights of stairs both up and down, but he finally found the Foreign Language Department's office. He knocked on the door, opened it and stepped into the room. "I called earlier, about some translation?"

The secretary rolled back slightly in her chair as he approached. Despite a night's sleep, a shave and a shower, Gideon's eyes were still dark pits in his skull.

"I remember," she said, recovering her composure as rapidly as she could. "It's Mr Smith, isn't it?"

"I've got it here." He reached into his briefcase and retrieved the folded paper. He'd ironed it flat that morning.

"There'll be a standard charge based on the complexity of the piece and the wordage. What language did you say the original is in?"

"I didn't. That's part of the problem." He watched her take the paper and start to turn it. "It is the right way up."

She shrugged. "Arabic? That would be my closest guess. I'll see if Dr Ho is in." As she leafed through the internal directory for his extension number, she explained: "Senior Reader in Oriental Languages."

She tapped out a four-figure number on her telephone keypad and explained the problem. After listening to the response, she directed Gideon down the corridor to Dr Ho's office.

Heart

Ho was a willow-thin pygmy with glasses as thick as bottle bottoms held in little metal frames. Every possible space in his office was crammed solid with books, journals and papers; while the bookshelves groaned, there were piles of manuscripts overflowing across the floor.

He stood up as Gideon introduced himself, and in standing, came up to Gideon's chest. "Ah, the young man with the mysterious translation. Please, have a seat." He looked around for a chair, and moved a box out of the way to allow Gideon to sit down.

"This is it," said Gideon.

It took Ho a brief second to decide what it was not. "It is not Arabic." He pushed his glasses up on his forehead and held the paper so that it virtually touched his nose. Distant telephones rang and were occasionally answered. Footsteps squeaked down the vinyl flooring outside. Ho made no sound as he studied the writing.

"You have piqued my interest, Mr Smith. I can categorically say that it is no modern Asiatic language, and I'm relatively certain that it resembles no ancient style of writing either. There is no system currently in use the world over that uses characters of such shape. May I ask where you obtained this?" His glasses slipped off his forehead and back on to his nose.

"I copied them. From, from an artefact."

"Of antiquity?"

"Is it old? Yes, I think it is. I drew everything right."

"I'm sure you did, Mr Smith. It does appear to be a language of some sort. The symbols are collected in uneven groups suggesting words, and these marks above the main characters resemble vowel sounds found within the Semitic group. The body text could be consonants, and the inflections above, yes ..." He trailed off, deep in thought.

After a suitable length of time, Gideon asked: "What should I do?"

"Ah, yes." Ho frowned at the script, and kept glancing at it as he talked. "Leave this with me, if that is possible. I will enquire amongst my colleagues and see if they recognise it. If not, then there will be no fee."

"Do I call you in a couple of days?"

"That would be best. My filing system is, as you can see, idiosyncratic." He opened a drawer in his desk and retrieved a business card. "Here, take this. Today is Tuesday. If you call Friday, I would hope to have an answer for you by then."

Gideon nodded and took the card, dropping it in his briefcase. He hadn't known it was Tuesday. Ho was rising, proffering a hand stained with liver spots. "Til Friday, Mr Smith."

"Til then, Dr Ho." He sincerely hoped that he'd realise it was Friday when it arrived.

Gideon left the building and made his way back to his office. As he was walking, the hairs on the back of his bull neck began to rise one by one, until they were stiff with fear. He stopped, turned around.

For the briefest moment, he saw them; a great crowd dressed in every style from the last millennia and the dark times preceding it. Men and women, young and old, matching him stride for stride up the road behind him, no more than five yards distant. In the vanguard was Marianne, who put out her arms to either side and brought the procession to a shuddering halt. She smiled and curtsied.

He blinked and they weren't there any more.

Except for the figure at the rear of the caravan, who remained a little longer than the other ephemeral shades. Death raised his fist in salute, the voluminous sleeve of his cloak falling back to expose bleached-bone whiteness. His scythe shone dully and under his hood he grinned. Death could have no other expression. It faded, leaving no more than a dark smudge in the air, which was soon gone.

He felt cold, stone cold. He heard the echo of a hundred voices in a dozen tongues, one after another, each different, expressing the same sentiment: don't be afraid. Quite consciously, he thought, I'm possessed.

Gideon turned on his heel, to go anywhere but not back to work. And met hollow eyes like his own, a gash for a nose, a lipless mouth full of yellowed worn-down teeth.

"Don't be afraid," grated Death.

Wednesday 15th April 1987

At first, the doctors thought he'd had a grand mal seizure. X-rays showed no evidence of a stroke, and a neurologist was all for shaving Gideon's head and pasting electrodes all over his shiny pink scalp. Then a computer had found his appointment with a psychiatrist for Friday afternoon and this put everything in a different light.

Alone and scared, lying in his bed in a brightly lit ward, Gideon heard the hustle and clamour of care going on all around him, circling him, sweeping past him, but never actually connecting. What he needed most was for someone to hold him and press his cheek to their chest, to rock him gently and not stop until the demons had left his mind and promised to stay away. It never happened.

He looked up from inspecting the lines on the palms of his hands to see Kate standing by his feet. She was still in uniform, and still had the blank exterior she wore along with it. He expected her to come to him and he held out his hand to her. He would have pleaded if he could have found his voice. But she shook her head and turned away, her heels running down the ward until the door swung open, swung shut.

He was abandoned, cast adrift, and no one knew what to do with his sick, infested mind.

The man next to him died quietly during the night, his life slipping away as unnoticed as a letter lost behind a mantelpiece. He was an old man, ex-miner and emphysemic. The curtains were drawn around the bed, and muffled voices discussed the mechanics of death.

Ignoring his breakfast, Gideon looked around him and all he saw was desperation.

"I've got to get out of here," he muttered.

"What's that?" said the man the other side of him, twiddling with his hearing aid and making it whistle.

"I shouldn't be here." He swung out of bed and wrestled his clothes and briefcase from the bedside table. He walked straight out of the ward and into the nearest toilets. He checked everything: keys, wallet, Dr Ho's business card. He needed to look at a newspaper to find out which day it was. Unknown to Gideon, he was starting to slip through the mesh of the system that was supposed to catch people like him. He was sliding faster and faster, and there was nothing anyone could do about it.

They tried, of course. They discovered he was missing during the morning rounds. He was phoned. He answered the first call, explained to them that he'd discharged himself, that he felt much better thank you very much and, no, he didn't want to attend outpatients for further investigations. He ignored all the other calls, wiping them off his answerphone just after they'd been recorded.

It was as he went to bed that he felt something was wrong. There were familiar things missing. He walked into the bathroom, clicked the light on, looked around.

One toothbrush in the mug.

He ran to the bedroom, threw the wardrobes open: they were half-empty. Half of everything had gone, even half his soul, but he had been too busy being demented to notice.

On the bed, propped up against the pillow, was a letter with his name on it.

He picked it up, then felt underneath the bed. He wriggled his fingers between the base and the floor, and felt the sack. Then he realised what he'd done: he'd checked to see if the sword was still there before finding out why Kate had left him. He started to cry, and he despised what he'd become.

Dear Gideon,

I've gone. You must realise this by now. I'm sorry I couldn't tell you to your face, but I'm scared of you. I used to share my life with a man I loved. For the past month I've shared it with a ghost. You'll never know how much you've hurt me by the way you've behaved, shutting me out like you've done. You were so uncomplicated, so straightforward, then almost at a stroke you became … not you. You changed, and I found that I couldn't love the man you became. I miss the old Gideon, but I don't know you.

Please don't try and look for me, or contact me at work. I'm staying with a friend for the moment. I'll try and redirect most of my post, but if you pile up what comes in by the phone, I'll pick it up when you're out. You should have your key back after a month. Everything I've left you can keep, or throw away, or whatever.

I'm sorry it had to be like this. I just couldn't cope any more.

Kate.

Gideon's fist closed around the sheet of white paper and tried to squeeze it out of existence.

Friday 17th April 1987

Friday finally came, and he waited until mid-morning before calling Dr Ho. It was an object lesson in patience. He spent five minutes listening to the secretary chase Ho across the building, ringing this extension and that, being told he'd just left somewhere, hadn't arrived somewhere else, or had passed en route.

"Dr Ho?"

"Yes."

"It's Mr Smith. Gideon Smith. I brought in some translation for you last Tuesday."

"I remember you well, Mr Smith."

"Have you managed to work out what it said?"

"An attempt has been made," he said enigmatically. "I'm not sure whether it is you playing the joke on us, or that someone is playing a joke on you."

Gideon hesitated, feeling slightly sick. "What do you mean?"

"If I told you that the language you gave me to translate does not exist outside a work of fiction, would you be surprised?"

"Fiction? It's made up?"

"You do sound surprised! Perhaps you are an unwitting accomplice in someone else's game after all. Come at see me at one o'clock, Mr Smith. I'll even buy you lunch."

"It's a game? You called it a game?"

"What else could it be, Mr Smith? I will explain everything later. Goodbye for now."

Gideon was a knot of confusion. He was unsure of everything at that moment, even his own name. Perhaps everyone was lying to him. Perhaps they were all telling him the truth. He doubted his ability to tell the difference.

"Elvish."

"Yes," said Dr Ho.

"And there is no such language as Elvish?"

"That is correct." Ho was relieved that his luncheon companion was no longer shouting at the top of his voice. The Refectory wasn't the place for that sort of behaviour. "Inasmuch as a language for elves of a particular variety has been invented and used in a novel, and the author of your script has used elements of that language in it. Quite an elaborate hoax, I must say."

"Elves." Gideon shook his head to clear it, but it had no discernible effect. "We're talking about the little men with pointy ears."

"Not in this case. Have you ever heard of Tolkien?"

"Heard of him. Never read anything he's written."

"There you and I share a trait. I showed your script to my colleagues, and none of them knew what it was. I went as far as consulting within the Biblical Studies Department, but had no joy there, either. It was one of the graduate students in English who identified it; knew it straight away, in fact. I gave her the piece as an exercise, and this is what she has given me in return." He slid a corner-stapled booklet of paper across the table.

The top sheet was the sword's script, widely spaced and phonetically spelt out beneath it:

nenye ieru albionië
nenye carmetinco
calta ar mendo macuvenye
circenye cal ar mornie
nevanuvië ancoruva morumbar
YHWH esso naemya aman

He turned the page, and was confronted by thick type, explaining what it all meant.

Ho tried his best: "Tolkien was a professor at Oxford earlier this century. I think he died in the fifties or early sixties. He wrote a fictitious history in which elves played a prominent part. He was an excellent linguist, and he made up several languages to go in his books. This one is apparently called Quenya, and was used by his elves. There were others, so I'm told, using the same alphabet but different words. Your script is written in a variant of Quenya."

Gideon was still stuck with the basic concept. "Elvish."

Tapping the paper, Ho shrugged. "It's all in here."

"But what does it all mean?"

"I am at a loss what to tell you." Ho drained the last of his coffee, and centred the cup in the saucer. "You are obviously upset at being duped, that much is clear. From the complexity of the translation, the perpetrator is clever. If it is of any comfort to you, I was caught out by it too. After you have calmed yourself sufficiently, perhaps you can reflect on the artistry involved." Gideon's eye's clouded over. "Then again, perhaps not."

"But it must mean something."

"Most certainly it does. You have it in your hands, and you can read it at your leisure." Ho smiled, the crow's feet around his eyes magnified a hundredfold through his thick lenses. "If it were true, it would be fascinating." He crumpled up his paper serviette and placed it on his plate. "Now I must take my leave, Mr Smith. I have a meeting I must attend. Thank you for sharing your problem with me. I have learnt much."

Gideon rose and shook the academic's hand. "I ought to thank you, though I haven't been very grateful."

"A word of advice, Mr Smith. If you ever discover who is behind all this, please count to ten before you commit murder."

"I'll try because you asked, Dr Ho."

"Goodbye, Mr Smith."

Gideon went to the self-service counter and bought himself another cup of coffee. He returned to his table, and started to read.

nenye ieru albionië = I am (?) [either] the god (God) [or] the one (?) of Albion.

After half a page of intense hermeneutic debate on whether the words chosen could represent the words transliterated, the translator got down to what the words actually meant.

ieru = the god (God). *Eru* (also called *Iluvatar*) is the creator god of the Middle Earth milieu. Since capitalisation is almost unknown in Quenya, "god" is possible, but "God" is more likely. However, *Eru* is linked symbolically with "one", relating to the unique nature of the god. This leads me to believe that the whole phrase gives the word its context. If we translate "*ieru*" as "the one", it could be taken to mean "the first" but more importantly also "the premier, the most important". *Albionië* is not a recognised Elven word of any system. Albion is a very ancient word for the geographic British

Isles, with a first recorded usage by Phoenician (Philistine) traders in the second millennia BC. Its appearance in an Elvish sentence is anomalous, not to mention unusual.

Gideon glossed some of the intervening arguments, his eyes alighting on passages here and there. His language skills were minimal, and he was having a great deal of difficulty deciphering those parts of the report that were written in plain English.

carmetinco = cutting metal. This could be one of two things: *carmetinco* could be a name, and therefore a proper noun (see note on capitalisation *"eru"*). Alternatively, it could be a title – a metal cutter, or a smith perhaps. I have discounted a third option, which is "I was made by a smith/metal worker", since *nenye* is I am.

calta ar mendo macuvenye = [root]light? and [root]direction? ?hand? This could mean almost anything. *calta* has the root *cal*, meaning light, and *mendo* has the root *men*, meaning direction. *cuva* = hand, and *-enye* is a first person present tense ending. This is the least translatable of the phrases, and consequently may well be very important. Sorry.

cirenye cal ar mornië = I cleave (cleft) light and dark. In comparison with the last sentence, this is almost easy. The corpus contains all these words, and I'm certain that this is a good approximation of what is meant.

nevanuvië ancoruva morumbar = ?passing? for/circle (outside?) dark fate (doom?). This sentence is as tantalising as it is confusing. *morumbar* is dark fate, probably closer to the English "doom". The nature of the doom is uncertain.

YHWH esso naemya aman = YHWH, may his name be blessed. Another word from a different language, possible the most powerful four-letter symbol in history –

the Tetragrammaton. Hebrew scribes recorded the name of their God without vowel sounds, causing the pronunciation to be mystified and a taboo being placed on saying the full name of the God of Israel. Nowadays it is translated as *Yahweh*. It appears in the New International Version translation of the Bible as "LORD". The rest of the sentence "may his name be blessed" poses no real problems. "Blesséd be the name of the LORD" would be a more poetic rendition.

He had read enough. There was more, under headings such as 'The relationship of Elvish to Indo-European languages', and 'Mything persons – the need for Elves'. The author had gone completely to town on something that was one big joke played on Gideon Smith.

And yet ... the few facts he knew were true set fire to the whole fake theory. Marianne had died for the sword, died to pass it on safely. If it was all a trick, then she had to be mad, too; as mad as he. If it was all nonsense, why pick a nonsense language? Why not Latin, which could be spelt, pronounced and translated perfectly? The sword was real, as solid as he was. The jewels in the hilt and guard looked genuine enough.

Then there was everything that had happened to him. His nightmares, his waking visions; could he say that his repeated sightings of Marianne, of others, of Death itself were real or imagined? They were real enough at the time.

Discern what is real and what is illusion, she had said, in her soft foreign accent.

Gideon drank his cold coffee, and wandered off, script held tightly in one hand.

Chapter 11
Saturday 18th April 1987
Newcastle upon Tyne

Gideon Smith's story

The phone rang. He was asleep in his armchair, having made himself tea and toast, and not touched any of it. Forgetting his resolve not to answer it, Gideon hauled himself upright and went through to the hall.

"Hello?"

"Mr Smith?"

"Yes." He recognised the voice, but couldn't place it.

"This is Dr Ho. Do you remember me?"

"Strange question. Of course I remember you; I saw you at lunchtime."

"Good. I have had a great deal of difficulty tracking you down, and I wanted to be sure it was the genuine Mr Smith. I apologise for the lateness of this call, but there are many G Smiths in the telephone book."

He was prompted to look at his watch. It read a quarter past eleven; far too late for a social call.

"Mr Smith? Are you still there?"

"Yes," said Gideon, cautiously.

"Are you alone?"

His heart skipped a beat. "I hope so."

"I wanted you to know as soon as possible. Your translation has caused some interest. I was contacted this evening by a man. He asked me for a copy of the report I gave you. I said you had the only copy. Then he asked me if I could remember anything about what was written. I became suspicious and asked for his name and his business. He refused to tell me, and he threatened me! He said it would be better for me if I divulged what I knew rather than keep it to myself. I hung up straight away, as I am not accustomed to such behaviour. Mr Smith, what is this writing? Why is it important to this man?"

"I don't know who it was. How can I tell why? Did he know me?"

"Only as Smith. Your name seems to have preserved your anonymity. What is going on?"

Gideon leaned his head against the wall. "Dr Ho. I can't tell you because I don't know."

"What do I tell the man if he calls again? I have a family, Mr Smith. They must come first."

"I'll try and find out what's so important. I'll let you know as soon as I do. But, please, say nothing now."

Ho hesitated, then acquiesced. "Remember what I have said, Mr Smith."

"I'll remember. I'll call you as soon as I have anything at all."

Gideon dropped the phone back on to the cradle. Next to it, under his house keys was the report. He picked it up, and stared at the curls on the cover. He tried to pronounce some of the unfamiliar sounds they represented.

He turned to the last page. There was a name: Leah Orchard. She was the student who had done the work. If Ho had been approached, what about her? Ho didn't have a copy of the report and little knowledge of what was contained in it. She would have her notes, a full draft, and an intimate understanding of the script. He had to see her as soon as possible.

But it was Saturday night. His only point of contact with her would be through the university, and that meant the earliest he could find her would be Monday morning. She was also an Arts student, where as an undergraduate, she would have been unlucky to have more than four hours of lectures a week. What that meant for a higher degree with no formal teaching appointments, Gideon couldn't guess.

He took the report back to his chair and re-read portions of it. His eyes naturally avoided the difficult and learned passages, and he skimmed until he reached the section marked 'Conclusion'.

He looked at it, then looked again. He realised something very important. Leah Orchard wasn't treating it as a joke. She had written the summary as if Elvish was a real language with real meaning, and not something made up at all. She talked as if Tolkien knew that too, and that he had been a simple compiler of a history so ancient that it had been handed down and rewritten in fragments by many scholars before it had reached his desk in Oxford.

She behaved to all intents and purposes as if it were true. Elvish wasn't fiction at all; just lost. And if that was the case, then how old would that make the sword? Thousands of years. How much would it be worth? Priceless, an object of incredible age with a value beyond calculation. If elves had made the sword and written on it with their seashore script, then civilised people were making steel weapons while others were still struggling with bronze. Archaeology would be turned on its head. Perhaps he wasn't going mad after all.

He did what Ho had done; went to fetch the phone book. There were fruit sellers, a guesthouse and a couple of tea shops. There was no L Orchard. He called Directory Enquiries, but they were no use. She was ex-directory, in a house-share, or just didn't have a phone. He was going to have to wait until Monday, which could be too late.

What Leah Orchard knew was the key that would unlock the door to a new world, the door that Gideon had hidden upstairs under his bed. Someone wanted the secret for themselves, and they knew that a translator of Elvish could guide them to it.

He caught a brief glimpse of the truth, an enormous, terrible truth: he saw a story that spanned centuries, a battle that was carried on hidden from view in deserted places and behind closed doors. The song of eternity reverberated around Gideon's living room and resonated within his heart. It was uplifting and mind-bendingly appalling at the same time. There was sacrifice and treachery, integrity and selfishness, the highest human ideals and the lowest human behaviour.

It struck him that people would think him crazy, these thoughts of lost languages and civilisations, of dreams and visions, that the truth was that the myths and legends of a continent were the closest thing to history that the present day could get. But he was beginning to believe it.

Monday 20th April 1987

Eight-fifty, Monday morning. Gideon was waiting, ready. The porter at the main desk knew Leah, and pointed her out to him as she straggled through the door, trailing a sports bag with badminton racquet poking uncovered out of the half-closed zip.

"Are you Leah Orchard?" He sprang forward to intercept her.

"Yes," she smiled crookedly, her mouth creased by a fine and well-repaired harelip. "You're early."

Gideon caught himself, and paused before he spoke. "I'm sorry. I don't like being late."

"That's okay. Punctuality is an admirable quality." She swung her straight blonde hair over her shoulder. "What can I do for you?"

132

"You wrote this for me." Gideon pulled the report out from inside his raincoat. "Can we go and have a coffee somewhere and talk about it?" He looked over her head and around at the empty lobby. The porter nodded at him as his eyes passed by. There was no one else in evidence.

"You said on the phone you wanted me to write an article."

He thought on his feet. "A bit like this; shorter and less ..."

"Technical?"

"Yes, good." He scanned his surroundings, itching to be off. "Lead on."

She led him back to the Refectory where he and Ho had sat on Friday. The main hall was closed, but there was a snack bar where Gideon paid for a strong black coffee for himself, and a hot chocolate for Leah. They sat just below street level, and through the windows the legs of students passed by in waves, like caterpillars. Faces looked down and in on them, and wished that they were there rather than heading towards a lecture.

She sat cross-legged in front of him, tracksuit bottoms tucked inside her sports socks, and dirty white trainers tucked under each knee. She leaned forward from the waist and took her cup in both hands. She blew the froth to the far side and sipped at the surface.

"Which magazine did you say you were with?"

Gideon put down his coffee. "I'm not the person you were expecting to meet. I had no idea how to contact you apart from your name and where you might work. But I'm glad I got to you first. Someone has been after Dr Ho over this report you wrote for me. They want a copy and they want it badly."

She took another sip and regarded him with caution. "If they want it so much, then where's the harm in it? It's just a silly little exercise in nonsense."

"I don't believe you think that. You wrote this like you were translating something that had meaning, rather than a made-up language from a made-up book. Why?"

Her face coloured up, and she lowered her eyes. "Because I wish it was true. I wish that somewhere, sometime, Tolkien's elves walked through the forests and sailed the seas, and that in the fringes of the world where people don't go, they live on. You've never read any of his books, have you?"

"No. I'm not a great reader."

"You'd know what I was talking about if you had. Some people have it far worse than I do." She smiled wistfully, and dared Gideon with her eyes to ridicule her dreams.

"Where do you think I got the writing from?"

"Dr Ho said you'd copied it from an artefact. I just entered into the spirit of it. Have you found something written by Tolkien?"

Gideon turned to see who was listening. The seats behind him were unoccupied. "No. I think it's the real thing."

She froze, put her cup down. "What?"

"I think your wish might be true. I have an artefact, a sword. It looks new, but it isn't. It has the inscription that you translated over both sides. Whoever made it knew a form of Elvish."

"You're joking, of course."

"Leah. Can I call you Leah? You translated the writing yourself; it's Elvish. It uses words that don't appear in any of Tolkien's books. It borrows words from

134

other languages. It makes sense; elves may have made this sword.

She shifted in her seat. She was shaking with excitement. "I can't believe this."

"I'm not sure that I do either, but I don't think it matters. This man who's so anxious to get your report thinks it's real. I was given the sword by a dying woman who told me to protect it and keep it safe. Someone tried to take it from me there and then, but until a few days ago, I never put two and two together. They murdered her. Leah, you have to destroy your notes. Deny everything. You never saw the writing at all. You don't know what it says. I'm going away for a while. Take a couple of weeks off, go visit your parents, anything. They're after me, but they'll hurt you if you get in the way."

"You're scaring me."

"Good. Don't meet the man you spoke to on the phone. I'm sorry. If I'd have known what sort of trouble I'd get people into, I'd have done things differently. I can't undo what I've done, but I can try and repair the damage."

"But what about the sword? What are you going to do with it?" She moved closer. "Can I see it?"

"You have to forget it exists."

"But the elves!"

"Forget it, Leah. Forget the sword, forget the translation, forget me," Gideon pleaded. "Please."

"You say what I wish for is real, then tell me to wipe it from my mind."

"I know it's hard."

"It's cruel. I'll spend the rest of my life wondering if you're telling me the truth."

"Don't."

"I have to. I think too much."

"I've warned you. Now I need to go. Sorry, Leah. I'm so sorry."

"I don't even know your name."

"Gideon. Gideon Smith. I doubt if you'll ever see me again, but don't think too badly of me." He stood, and as he bent down for the report, the door at the far end of the bar opened. A gust of wind blew through, and the door swung shut. A man in a tweed coat and black gloves stood there, looking at every face in the room.

Gideon saw him, recognised him and knew it was too late to avoid detection. He stepped away from the table, and hissed: "Ignore me."

She started to speak, but turned open-mouthed to see why Gideon was backing away. The man started to stride forward. Gideon span on his heels and ran to the far door. In three bounds he was up the stairs to street level and accelerating away.

The man put his head down and pursued him, banging his way through the door and leaping up the same steps with astonishing agility.

Leah looked down at the table. An almost-empty mug, ringed with brown froth, a half-finished cup of black coffee and a stapled booklet now curling at the edges. She reached over, picked up the papers and jammed them inside her sports bag. She had some tidying up to do in her office.

It was fortunate that one of Gideon's hobbies was running fast over short distances; otherwise, the chase would have ended abruptly.

The man fell behind, and his face became obscured within the crowds of young men and women oblivious to the desperate drama being played out around them.

Gideon turned right out of the university precinct, still running but feeling the strain of it. He eased off a little, darted across the road and looked back. The man had just reached the corner. His arms were moving in short chopping motions as he ran, and he was narrowing the gap between them.

They ran through a park, along narrow paths, past curious people, around the lake with its dozing ducks. Every time Gideon turned, his pursuer was closer.

He was caught three-quarters of the way across the park, near a stand of trees. Two arms reached around Gideon's waist and brought him crashing to the ground. His shoulder ploughed into the muddy grass and he turned over on to his back. The man who now reached into his coat with his right hand was the same man who had tried to wrestle the sword from him a year ago. He had seen him for seconds, but would remember him forever.

Gideon scythed his legs out from underneath him with one swing of his feet, then slammed on top of his fallen body with all of his weight. The man grunted and struggled with his free hand to gouge Gideon's eyes. He batted the hand away, twisting his head to prevent contact. He scraped his instep down the man's leg, kicking hard against the top of the foot. At the other end, he pushed against the man's nose, banging the back of his head into the ground. Unaffected by the ferocious physical assault, the man shrugged his torso, and Gideon was heaved aside and off.

He rolled free, came to his knees, and was kicked heavily in the chest. Off balance, he tumbled over, but somehow he managed to snag the flying leg in one hand. He pulled and twisted the best he could.

The man landed face first in the mud, arms sprawled in front of him. Gideon punched him twice in the kidneys and smashed his forearm down on the back of his neck. With one last desperate effort, Gideon turned him over and caused his massive fist to descend straight on to the pinned man's temple. It hurt like hell and he gasped in pain, clutching his knuckles as he struggled upright.

The man lay still and quiet. Gideon had knocked him out, but he was in little better condition himself. He was fighting for every breath, had legs that were about to turn to jelly, was sweating like a marathon-running pig, and was so bewildered that he wasn't quite sure which direction was home.

"You murdering bastard," he panted, and staggered away.

He hadn't prepared for this. As his shaking hand finally jammed his front door key home, he knew what he ought to have packed. He knew, but he hadn't worked it out until it was far too late.

He cursed his chronic stupidity, but part of him still couldn't believe that the sword was worth killing for. He slammed the door behind him, bolted it top and bottom, put the safety chain on and the catch down on the Yale. He was so exhausted that he retched several times, and fell up the stairs gasping and gagging.

He turned the cold water tap full on in the bathroom basin and plunged his head under the stinging flow. He pressed his hand below the level of the cascading water, and felt new, vibrant pain. His knuckles were cut, bleeding and already swelling.

Gideon let the water run for two minutes over his injured hand, and for no longer. He dried himself off with a towel and stained it red. He dropped it when he'd done with it. He wouldn't be back to pick it up.

138

He took the hold-all from the foot of the bed and emptied it out over the duvet. Clothes tumbled out, followed by his wash kit, and a plastic bag containing his passport, building society passbook, driving licence and cheque books. He snatched at the bag and jammed it into the inside pocket of his coat. He threw himself on the floor and came back up with the sword.

He heard three shots. He ran to the top of the stairs and looked down at the front door. The lock was in pieces, bits of twisted metal hanging from what was left of the screws. The safety chain dangled uselessly, severed. Through the small panes of patterned glass at the top of the door, he could see a dark shape move close in. The wood bulged, but the bolts held.

He went back to the bedroom and grabbed the nearest thing. It happened to be the wardrobe. He tipped it over, dragged it to the landing using short, frantic steps, and cast it down the stairs towards the door that was now rhythmically heaving in and out every few second. The wardrobe slithered away, gaining speed. One door opened halfway down, caught in the banister and was ripped off its hinges. Shirts, shoes and ties streamed out as the wardrobe bucked upright, cartwheeled over and slammed into the front door, lying diagonally across it. The sound of creaking wood ceased abruptly and the shadow left the glass.

Gideon raced to the bed, snatched up the sword and took the stairs three at a time. He reached the bottom and sprinted for the back door.

He caught sight out of the kitchen window of someone climbing over the back wall from the alley. He'd never seen him before, but he recognised the air of menace about him. The man dropped into the yard and drew a gun. Gideon transferred himself to the netted window in the back door, then ducked down, crouching to one side.

Heart

He thought he ought to have a knife, and his eyes narrowed on the cutlery drawer, eight feet away and completely out of reach. Then he laid the sword in front of him, and pulled at the three bows. He unrolled the sack, tipped the sword out on to the floor, and stowed the sack and the string in a pocket. He gripped the hilt in his sweating, aching hands.

The door handle sank, jiggled slightly and returned to horizontal. Gideon caught his breath, steadied the sword. The blade was inches from his face. He saw the door fall, the man step in with the gun and shoot him dead. And again. And again.

The message was clear, even if Gideon hadn't got it already. They gave no quarter.

The glass in the door shattered. The net stopped the shards flying, and they tinkled down by Gideon's side. A gloved hand poked through the hole. It retreated and returned a moment later to feel for the lock.

Gideon unwound his body, span the sword around and lunged out through the broken window. The sword paused as it reached something firm, then carried on. The blade twisted slightly in his grip, and he pulled it back.

There was dark blood smeared across the mirrored surface from the point to halfway along its length. Where it had cut the net, it had left a red slash. He changed his hold to one-handed and wrenched the net away. The man was lying on the path, his discarded gun feet away. His hands clutched at the spreading stain across his chest, trying to stem the flow. More blood started to ooze from underneath his back, staining the mossy concrete black.

Gideon unlocked the door and pressed himself against the wall to avoid the man's touch.

"Please, please," implored the man, reaching out with a dripping glove.

He slid past, and looked back before he used his dustbin as a ladder to help him over his own back wall. The man's face was drained of all colour, all hope, all life and all light.

Gideon dropped to his feet in the alley, and disappeared.

Heart

Lives can be changed with a simple hello.

"Hello?"

"Yessica? Is that you?"

Margaret sat upright on her saggy sofa, almost jarring the coffee from the table next to her. "Torsten! Hi, yes, it's me. Good to hear from you." She was flustered and happy. "How are you? It's been ages."

"I know. I must apologise for my lack of communication over the past few months. Things have been difficult for me."

"Are you all right?" She noted his breathlessness, the tiredness in his voice.

"A long story, Yessica."

"I've got the time."

"Perhaps I could tell you it in person. I am being pensioned off from the police here. They do not require me any more. So, I think to myself, I shall visit my friend Yessica in London."

"That would be great," she blurted, "When are you thinking of coming over?"

"Would this week be too soon?"

"No, no. Whenever you like." She looked around her at the piles of dirty clothing, clean, unironed clothing, mugs and plates scattered across every horizontal surface. "I'll tidy up tonight; the flat's a bit of a tip."

"I was going to stay in a hotel."

"Oh."

"But if it's no bother ..."

Her emotions swung strangely, almost brutally. "No bother at all. It'll be great to see you again."

There was a pause in which the line crackled. It suddenly struck Margaret what an incredible device the telephone was. She could talk in her own living room to someone six hundred miles away as if they were sitting together.

"Do you remember the Newton murders?" asked Neubauer.

Margaret leaned back into the sofa. They were back on police business; time to relax. "Newton murder. Arden never bought the woman's death as deliberate. He's an Assistant Chief Constable now, you know."

"A what?"

"Big boss."

"*Also*. The Newtons. I have come across something. Several somethings, in fact. For a long time I did not know what they meant. Now I think I do."

"You're being mysterious."

"This is not to your liking? I do not think that you will be pleased with what I tell you, Yessica. I have found things that have given me great pain." Again, the shortness of breath.

"You'd better tell me what when you see me."

"I will, all of it. But put such things to the back of your mind."

"Don't think of the word 'elephant'."

"Sorry?"

"Tell someone not to think of the word 'elephant', all they can think about is 'elephant'."

Neubauer mulled over what she had said, and decided that it lost something in the translation inside his head. "I will call you when I have arranged my flight."

"I'll try and pick you up."

"You are very kind."

"You're a friend."

"*Also. Tschüss*, Yessica."

Heart

"Tschüss, Torsten."

Part III

Tuesday 28th April to Wednesday 20th May
1987

Chapter 12

Tuesday 28th April 1987

The Grampian mountains, near Aviemore, Scotland

Gideon Smith's story

Gideon was dying, and there was a storm outside. The side of the mountain was dark and bleak, cold and rain-driven. Black rock flashed white with lightning, and scree shifted with the tearing wind.

The door to the bothy was ill-fitting, gaps top and bottom, letting the wind whistle through the planking teeth. A stone, more a small boulder, held the door shut from the inside. The wood quivered with every fresh blast of the gale.

Gideon twisted feverishly in a red blanket, his skin glowing brightly by the light of a gas lantern. His sleeping bag was open underneath him, soaked through with sweat. By his side was a bucket of vomit.

He cried out in the cold, damp, stone-walled building, his tortured bellow lost in the roof timbers and leaking slates. He no longer saw what he ought to have done. He was crowded in at every side by the faces of people he did not know, but recognised from his visions. A woman with tumbling darkly red hair kissed his burning forehead and he shivered. She talked to him in a strange language and he half understood what she was saying.

There was a pain in his belly like an everlasting fire, and he was consumed by it. He had eaten nothing for four days, and drunk nothing for the past day and a half. In his more lucid moments, he knew he had to get off the mountain, get to a doctor. But the mountain could have been another planet for all the good it did him; he couldn't even stand to walk a step.

The door rattled, moved inwards slightly, pushing the boulder across the stone-flag floor with a scrape. After a pause, the door was fully open. The rain and the wind seized their chance, and crowded through the opening, causing Gideon to whine and writhe helplessly.

The door was jammed shut, and wedged again with the rock.

"Out of the way, everyone." The faces moved back. "I came to find a champion, and what do I find instead?"

Gideon screwed up his eyes, desperate to focus. He tried to speak, coughed, and spewed a thin stream of acid bile over his shoulder. He felt a shadow fall across him, and something wiping the mess away. Even that slight pressure caused him to gasp and pant.

The blanket was pulled down. The action was feebly resisted, as was the pulling up of his sweater and T-shirts. Warm hands palpitated Gideon's stomach and abdomen. The pain flamed into an incandescent pyre and he thought he had died.

"You, my friend, have appendicitis, and you've left it far too late. You've advanced septicaemia, and you're as toxic as a rancid sheep. You're burning so hot I could fry an egg on your face. What do you say to that, eh?" The voice was lilting, almost singing. An Englishman and a Welshman together in Scotland.

Gideon couldn't say a word, for or against the stranger's diagnosis.

"Well, it's no good standing around talking, is it? It'll have to come out."

He heard and understood. He tried to sit up.

"Nah, nah. You lie still. Do you think appendectomy is easy?"

Gideon felt the heel of the stranger's hand press down on his forehead with all the gentleness of his mother and all the force of an industrial press. Something sharp pressed against his abdomen. His back arched, and the pain dulled and spread, numbing him to the feeling of movement inside.

"There! Great grey-purple thing like a haggis, boiled and ready to burst."

The pressure on his head relaxed. His eyes dimly spotted an object being waved at him. It was his bloated appendix.

"We'll get rid of that, shall we?" There was a splash in the bucket. "Now cover yourself up and rest. We can talk in the morning."

His clothing was pulled back down, his sleeping bag folded over him, and covered with the blanket. He heard the bucket clank and the door to the bothy scrape open. Then he heard no more.

Wednesday 29th April 1987

When he woke up, he saw the sky. It was a deep rain-washed blue, streaked with fast-flying clouds of grey and white that seemed so low as to graze the dusty window. The door was open, and a man stood framed by the doorway. He was watching the ever-changing pattern of light and dark on the landscape of the valley. His hair ruffled like heather in the wind, the same wind that sent his heavy coat flapping and snapping in the bright morning.

"Water," Gideon gasped from between cracked lips.

The man turned his head, his face in shadow. "You're awake." He unscrewed the plastic cap on a bottle of water and poured some into an enamel mug. He pressed the mug into Gideon's hands and cradled his head so that he could drink.

Gideon lay back down with a gasp, and held out the mug for more. The man refilled it, placed it on the ground and reached into his coat for a silver hip flask.

"This'll put hairs on your chest, boy." He lifted the flask to his lips and drew breath sharply. "The water of life, they call it. They're not far wrong." He tipped the open flask over Gideon's mug, and a thin stream of golden liquid trickled out. He stopped quickly, jiggled the mug to mix the water and the spirit, and handed it back.

Gideon levered himself up on his elbow and felt the blood drain from his head. He looked at his healer, and saw a tall man with smiling golden eyes and a lean, wise face. "Thank you."

"You're welcome." The man crossed his legs on the ground and sat back. He nipped at his flask again, then sealed it up, placing it back inside his huge coat.

Gideon drank from his mug, and tasted strong whisky for the first time in over a year. He remembered Nick even as the drink coursed down his throat. "I thought I was going to die."

"You were. Another night and I'd be carrying a body off this mountain."

Slowly, Gideon put the mug down. Slowly, he pulled back the covers, unzipping the sleeping bag with a steady rasp. Slowly, he gripped the hem of his jumper, taking a handful of T-shirt at the same time.

He revealed his stomach. It was smooth, without blemish, nothing but a thin layer of fat and, underneath, hard muscle. His hand pressed down on his abdomen and he felt no pain, just a residual soreness. "Where's the scar?"

The man rested his hands in his lap. "What makes you think that there should be one?"

"You took my appendix out! I saw it!" He searched his stomach again with increased urgency. "You showed it to me."

"True."

"So what did you do to me?"

"What do you think I did?"

"You cut me open. Surely ..." He covered himself and lay back down, his eyes wide open.

"Take another drink, boy. Looks like you need it."

In a small voice, Gideon asked: "What did you do?"

"I took your appendix out, just like you said. I reached through your skin and pulled it out. I needed no knife."

"I don't understand."

"You're healed, boy. You should be grateful to the God who gave me the gift."

"You healed me?"

The man laughed freely. "Don't sound so surprised. It happens all the time. Look, boy. Are you still in pain? No. Are you going to die? Not today, at the very least. You're healed. So drink your drink and stop blinking like an owl."

Gideon struggled to a sitting position. "Who are you?"

"Later. I'll tell you later. Get up, put your boots on and I'll make you some food. You'll be hungry." The man took Gideon's meths stove outside and set it up, then came back to get something from his rucksack, the first time Gideon had noticed it propped up in a dark corner of the single room.

He found his boots and laced them on. He got to his feet carefully. He managed to take two steps to the rough stone wall, only to cling on with his fingertips as his ears roared and his vision swam. He breathed slowly and deeply, and eventually felt that he could make it to the door.

A burst of sunlight blinded him. He used one hand to shield his eyes and spotted the man bent low over the stove, stirring with a spoon. Gideon edged to a long flat rock nearby and slumped on to it.

"Not feeling too bright?" The man looked up and smiled.

"Surprisingly, no." The sun went behind a cloud and Gideon looked down the long valley to the loch that glittered like a silver fish. The wind was gusting, tugging at the heather and sending early bees into a spin.

The man tapped the spoon on the aluminium pan and used the detachable handle to grip the rim. "This'll help. Porridge made with milk, sweetened with honey." He brought it over and placed it on the rock next to Gideon. He presented him with the spoon. "Eat up, boy! You'll need your strength."

"Why should I trust you?"

The man forced the spoon into Gideon's hand. "If I'd meant you harm, I'd have watched you die. I had God's own trouble finding you up here, and now I'm cooking you breakfast." He turned his back and looked at the landscape around him. He continued: "Besides, I've seen that there's a new cairn on the flanks of Beinn Dhu."

Gideon's eyes narrowed to suspicious slits.

"When you've been around as long as I have, you get to notice these things. I wondered, why raise a cairn there? Commemorate someone's fall? Fulfil a vow? Or perhaps if I were going to hide something in plain sight, a pile of rocks might be good cover." He looked over his shoulder. "Why don't you tell me what you think it is?"

"You know too much."

"And you know too little. Drink deeply from the well of knowledge or leave it alone. You know just enough to ask all the questions, but not enough to understand any of the answers." He turned back to the mountains, but his voice carried clearly. "You're ignorant, boy; not a condition to be proud of."

His words stung Gideon. "I know about the Elvish."

"But do you know why?" The man countered.

"Because," said Gideon after some thought, "Elvish was a real language used by real people."

"That's not a why. Why means purpose, passion; it means people and places. Facts aren't a why. They're a how, a what, a when."

"Well, sorry."

"Look." He span around. "This is not the time. Eat your porridge." He walked past Gideon and into the bothy.

Gideon was alone with the sky and the rock. After the first mouthful, he wolfed down the entire bowl of sticky white slop and scraped the spoon across the bottom of the pan to gain the scraps. He began to look around hopefully for the man to reappear with something else, but he remained unseen in the stone hut. Next to the stove was an open carton of milk, a bag of oats tied with a sandwich tag and a jar of home-made honey. He thought about it for a second, then picked his way over to the equipment. He quickly became absorbed in the ritual of creation.

He only noticed the man's return when a blanket was draped around his shoulders.

"A bad start, you and I. I was angry with you, but not as angry as I was with myself. I apologise for my shortcomings."

"Forget it," shrugged Gideon. "I am alive, after all."

"I didn't come here to tell you off for your mistakes. What's done is done, and we have to go on from where we are." The man sighed and slapped Gideon on the shoulder. "I wish you'd listened to Marianne, though."

"I thought I was going mad. She was dead."

"Take good advice where you can get it, I say. Yes, her body was dead, but she has a soul that outlasted her physical form. If you'd followed her instructions, you'd still be safe and warm in Newcastle, not huddled next to a camping stove halfway up a Scottish mountain."

Gideon took the pan off the flame, and dropped the lid on to the burner, extinguishing it.

"Still, it's not as bad as it could be. You're safe, the sword's safe, no one but me knows where you are for the moment. The police would still like to interview you, of course." He smiled grimly. "You know what they're saying about you?"

"I can guess. Madman murderer with a sword."

"Oh dear no. That wouldn't serve their purposes at all. You're a drug dealer, boy; that's where all the men with guns come in."

"No one will believe that."

"No one does. But no one believes the truth either, so they don't know what to think. Some people will be put right; James Cook, Leah Orchard. They'll know what's truth and what's false."

"You'll speak to them?"

"Not me. Another seeker on the road. A fellow traveller, if you like. He's an honest and decent man, humble in heart but great in purpose. You'll meet him one day."

"And who are you? You said you'd tell me later."

"You wouldn't believe me if I told you."

"I talk to dead people," said Gideon. "Try me."

"Not yet. You're scared of me. You're wondering who on earth I am and how I know what I know. You haven't got the slightest idea about me. I could be anyone."

"Yes. But I have to trust you anyway."

"Excellent. You've started on the path of wisdom. Listen then, and I'll tell you a story."

Gideon straightened up and put his porridge bowl down on the rock. The man sat beside him, cross-legged.

"Once upon a time, when all this was forest, and wolves and wild boar ran through the valleys and the hills, there was a boy who was born to be king. But he was only very young when his father died. Other men seized the throne for their own wealth and increase. Those were dark days for the boy, for the usurpers wanted him dead. They searched the land for him, from the furthest north to the utmost south, but they didn't find him. He'd been hidden away, fostered by great lords who taught him war and taught him peace; then they taught him which was best.

"All this time, kings came and went, ruling over this part or that, never uniting the people. Invaders arrived and drove the native folk from the land, and claimed it as their own. The new kings, fighting in their factions against each other were never strong enough to drive them out. The people suffered, robbed by their masters and raided by their enemies. They cried out for justice, but no one could deliver it into their hands.

"Then it was time. The boy, now a young man, was brought forward to be anointed king of all. By signs and wonders, and fulfilling ancient prophesies, he was shown to be his father's son. Most would not accept him.

"Some, however, saw and believed. They joined him and he became their leader. He fought the invaders and they sued for peace. He fought the lesser kings and united their people under one banner. There was peace in the land for a while, and when the invaders reneged on their agreement and the minor lords rebelled, he defeated them all, and showed them the cost of betrayal.

"Finally, finally, by an act of treason, he was mortally wounded. No hand in the land could heal him. He was taken from the kingdom, but he promised to return when his people were in direst need. He would return and be their king once more, and reign with truth and justice and mercy.

"The symbol of his authority was his sword. His friends kept it safe, but his enemies wanted it for themselves. It was hidden, passed from hand to hand to hand to protect it and keep it out of the reach of evil men.

"The king never came back, but the sword still passed from one to another; they kept the faith, and sometimes they died for it. The evil was handed on, too, from generation to generation. Those infected by it believed that whoever held the sword would rule absolutely."

"One day, there was an accident. The sword was nearly lost, given at the last moment to a stranger who knew nothing of its history or its importance. He was told that he had to be careful, but he was consumed by what he thought was his own madness. The sword was talking to him, trying to help him, but it only succeeded in pushing him closer and closer to the edge. At last he understood, but only in part. He tried to learn, but in learning told

155

those who wanted the sword for evil, not for good. Because he didn't know enough, he didn't know where to turn. He ran, disappearing from the society to which he belonged, and ended up lost and alone, with no direction and an unclear purpose." The man stopped, and waited.

"That's me, isn't it? At the end."

"That's your story, and mine too. Despite everything, the sword chose well. The mistakes you've made are history. I've made plenty myself. When I was young ..." He trailed off and stared into the distance.

"If the last part of what you said was real, what about the first part?"

"True, all true. Steel yourself, Gideon Smith, because your life will change forever."

"I shouldn't be surprised that you know my name."

"That is the least of the surprises that are to come." The man uncrossed his legs and rose swiftly to his feet. "The king I spoke of was the Summer King, Arthur, Pendragon of Britain, and his sword lies buried under a cairn on the flanks of Beinn Dhu."

"King Arthur's sword? That's ..."

"Cut-metal. Excalibur."

"So who are you?"

The man lifted his arms to the sun and spread them wide so that the wind filled his coat. The leather snapped and roared behind him, and he tilted his head back to cry out: "I am the immortal Merlin Ambrosius, bard to the Pendragon, and I shall never die!"

Later, much later, when Gideon had uncovered his ears and unwrapped his arms from his head, he asked: "Where do the elves come in?"

The man, Merlin as Gideon struggled to call him, smiled a sad smile. "The Faery folk. Survivors from the fall of great Atlantis."

"Atlantis," muttered Gideon. "Right."

"I know it's a lot to take in, but it's only a side detail. A handful of wooden vessels, a couple of hundred refugees; all that was left of the knowledge and tradition of a thousands-year-old civilisation. The natives thought they were magicians and avoided them, until they found that they were able to cure them of disease and heal their wounds. That was done by science, not magic. But slowly they died out, of murder and of sadness. Only the Faery folk could die of a broken heart.

"Some lay with the Britons, and their fey blood still passes down through the generations. My mother, daughter of the Fisher King, married my father, the greatest bard this island has ever seen or will see until Jesu's coming. They bore me, Merlin, and I was blessed with wisdom and power." He finished bitterly. "Much good did it do me."

"Just how old are you?"

"Fifteen long centuries. That's how I knew where you'd hidden Excalibur. The towns and the cities, they change so quickly. Blink and one building has gone, and another sprung up in its place. But the mountains and the rivers, the hills and the valleys, the cliffs and the beaches. I know them like I know the face of a friend. Your cairn was like a new wart on the nose, and I could no more miss it than that."

Gideon pulled the blanket close around himself – for comfort, not warmth. "I suppose you'll be taking the sword with you when you go."

"Me? Lord bless you, no. It's not for me to usurp your destiny any more than it's your place to do my work.

Marianne gave it to you; freely given, freely accepted. You can't change what's passed."

"I didn't know what I was taking. If I had, then ..."

"Then what?" Merlin snapped. "Seconds after you had the sword, you were fighting to keep hold of it. It's part of you now, no less than your eyes or your ears. Would you lose your sight? Nonsense, boy. You took it. Your destinies run side by side from now on."

"And I don't have a choice in the matter?"

"Walk away then, boy. Disappear and live your life in torment and anguish, wondering about what might have been."

Gideon put his head down.

"You can't do it, can you? Of course not. No matter how scared you are, you know you're going to have to see this through, no matter where it takes you."

"So, tell me, what happens now? What am I supposed to do?"

"Do, boy? Haven't you worked it out yet? Don't you know?"

"How the hell should I know what to do? And don't call me boy!"

"I'm over a thousand years old, and you're under thirty! I'll call you boy until you start acting like an adult. By all that's holy, I'd led an army into battle by the time I was your age. There was no one around to tell me what to do. I did the best I could with the advice I was given. And that's all you're going to get from me: advice."

"What do you advise then, great Merlin?"

"Less of the sarcasm, Gideon."

"That's better than 'boy'."

Merlin looked thunderous, then broke into a broad grin. "You're not afraid of much, are you?"

Simon Morden

Gideon shrugged. "Maybe it's because I don't realise how much trouble I'm in."

"Probably." Merlin held up his hands to the sky. "Gideon, you're not going to find out any of your answers by sitting up here. They lie where the people are, down there in towns and cities, and in the villages too. You have to leave here and find out for yourself what's going on."

"But where do I go? I can't walk the entire country looking for something I might not recognise. Besides, the police are more likely to find me first."

"Don't worry about them. You don't see yourself the way I see you. The magic hangs around you like a thick cloak. It moves with you and gives you a certain amount of favour. As to what you're looking for, when you find it, you'll know."

"How? A voice from the sky? A shower of frogs?"

Merlin looked smug. "Because you will and for no other reason. It's your destiny and you will find it; it's what you were created for. The sooner you start on that course, the sooner you'll know."

Gideon laid back on the rock. "Deep down, I don't believe any of this. It's just not possible. But I'll go along with what you say until ..."

"Until what?"

"I prove you a liar or a madman."

"Your unbelief is at the surface. Below that is a core of you that desperately wants to believe everything I've told you. It tugs at your innermost being, calling it to follow and be part of the story. It's the same with most people: the story cries justice and so does your heart; the story cries freedom and passion, and so does your heart. That's why it's so powerful. People want to believe that Arthur will come back and save them from themselves. If Excalibur is the talisman by which the king will be known,

159

what do you suppose would happen if someone appeared with it who was not Arthur."

"There might be trouble?"

"There would be bloody civil war, with neighbours attacking one another, each convinced that they were right. It would be a disaster from which the country would never recover. And all this for a story."

"But you think it's true."

"I know it's true. I've lived it. So have you, deny it all you want. But the enemy, they hate the story; they see only what they want to and deny the truth. They are not part of the story. They merely invade it, rape it and pillage it for what they want out of it, and leave it bleeding and half-dead. They have a determination born of lust and greed, and they never, ever, give up. As one is destroyed by his own evil desires, another falls into the darkness. They're like a monster with many heads, never the same aspect from age to age, but always the same root of corruption inside."

"So how will I know them?"

"The same way you find your friends. Marianne told you how: learn the secret of the heart. It's not something you can be told, it's learnt through experience." Merlin looked across the vast landscape. "Learn this one thing, Gideon, and you'll be a prince amongst men."

Gideon sat up, and tried to see with Merlin's strange sight. "What happens now?" he asked.

"Tomorrow we retrieve Excalibur. The day after, you rejoin your fellow men and women down in the valleys and along the coasts. Today? Today you rest, because you'll do precious little of that in the weeks and months ahead."

Chapter 13
Friday 15th May 1987
London

Torsten Neubauer's story

Heathrow was the world's busiest international airport. On that Friday afternoon, it had nearly collapsed under its own weight. There was fog on the Continent, stretching from the Low Countries up through to the Baltic. An frustrated mob of travellers was encamped in the terminal, staring glassy-eyed at the departure screens, hoping that salvation would come from the skies.

To Margaret, it looked like the aftermath of some great and terrible natural disaster. All the refugees could salvage were a few bags into which they had packed anything that had survived, no matter how inappropriate to their journey. They had then strewn themselves across every floor, into every seat, waiting to be shown the way to go.

The arrivals lounge was much quieter; transatlantic flights were landing without problem, but the bulk of the European flights were either grounded or stacked above Frankfurt. Margaret sat in the café over a ludicrously expensive Danish pastry and pot of tea, and watched the monitors flick up flights from exotic locations she only knew from geography lessons at school. She didn't own a passport; never even been to France on a visitor's permit.

Dubai, Jo'burg, Florida, Buenos Aires. She stirred her tea until she remembered to drink it. Neubauer had taken a flight from Munich to Schiphol, and from the Dutch transit airport connected with a Thai Air flight from Bangkok. It had occurred to her at the time that he wasn't coming from Berlin. She assumed there was a good reason for that. The arrival time had been optimistically put back an hour. She yawned into her plate; she'd slept for no more than four hours after her night shift before getting in her car and driving up the M4 to Heathrow. Two weeks of living like a vampire had taken its toll on her.

She used to take the rotation of shifts in her stride, sometimes not going to bed from one day to the next, filling the hours between clocking off and clocking on with drinking, eating, partying. Now she was shattered and struggling to adjust, just as nights finished and mornings started. She was continuously tired, and had forgotten what it was like to be well rested.

Her head was poised just above the tabletop. She was dozing. A commotion from across the hall startled her. A flight from Kingston, Jamaica, had brought together friends and relatives in the celebration of reunion. It was very un-English, and Margaret wondered at how free and expansive their joy was. She squeezed a second cup from her stainless-steel teapot and found it almost unbearably stewed. But she needed the caffeine hit, and drank it after adding the contents of two of the almost-impossible-to-open plastic milk containers.

People came, people went. Margaret stayed. Finally, the flight landed and, twenty minutes later, she joined the rest of the expectant faces behind the barriers the other side of the Customs gauntlet. A crowd of Indians was waiting, bejewelled and headscarved in gold and green, for the same flight, which had called at Delhi on its way from the East. When their sons and brothers and sisters and wives and aunts and uncles and cousins streamed through, there was such a cacophony of raised voices that she almost missed the little man at the back of the group, the one with the wheeled suitcase and the walking stick.

162

She ducked under the barrier and when she re-emerged she was behind him.

"Torsten?"

He stopped, and turned slowly. He'd changed, almost to the point of being completely different. His hair was cropped close to his skull, no longer flapping about his face. His face had always held a certain thinness about it, but now his cheeks were pinched. His eyes, still as bright as a rat's, glimmered out of deeply shadowed sockets. They held a darkness about them.

She hesitated, at a total loss as to what to say. Eventually, some words stumbled out: "What happened to you?"

He laughed stiffly, smiling the same wet smile he had used at their first meeting. He gave a short bow, uncomfortable and slight, and she could see his incipient bald patch. "And you, you look as beautiful as when I last saw you."

"No, I didn't mean it like that. I meant, I just thought, oh, sorry." She turned beetroot red, and all her imagined moments of greeting disintegrated about her.

"Shall we start again?" he said. He was leaning heavily on the mountain ash walking stick. He seemed to be dependent on it for support. "Hello, Yessica. Wonderful to see you."

"Torsten, I'm sorry. You just look so ... ill. Why didn't you say anything on the phone?"

He shrugged with one shoulder. "You would only have worried. I am here now."

"Are you all right? Can I take your bag?" Her hands fluttered around him, afraid to touch him, wanting to hold him. They collided and she put her arms hesitantly around his thin form. He let go of his bag and hugged her awkwardly back.

"What happened?"

Heart

Neubauer stepped back. "If you buy me a coffee, I shall tell you."

The wheels of the case went click-click across the concourse floor. The rubber shoe on his walking stick made no sound at all.

She sat him down in the café she had recently vacated. Neubauer had no Sterling on him, so she scraped together the last of her change to buy their drinks. Seated across from him, she waited while he unscrewed the lid of a pill bottle and watched him tap one pill out into the palm of his hand.

"One is sometimes not enough. Two will send me to sleep for hours. I think I have slept enough." He flipped the pill into his mouth and skimmed off the top of his coffee, swallowing before he burnt his tongue. "*Also.* I was betrayed. Someone knew where I was and what I was doing, and they did not like it."

"Go on."

"Icons are valuable items outside the Soviet Union. They turn up in places where they ought not - for example, in a container full of antiques in Amsterdam. The Dutch police tell Interpol, Interpol tell us, because Berlin is the best entry point for Russian contraband in Europe. We investigate; we trace a courier and we find that he travels across the border all the time. The next time he comes to Berlin, we follow him. We take pictures of him eating, sleeping, drinking, going to the bathroom. We also follow the people who meet him, many people. We split our people to cover them all. We work around the clock. We have little sleep and bad food. Even inspectors are taking their turn. Have you heard of Checkpoint Charlie?"

"Yeah."

"American Sector. A gap in the Wall. I was with Pieter. He is in the driver's seat, I am in the passenger seat. The car is my own, an old BMW, metallic green. I liked

164

that car. We were waiting with our camera and our radio. The courier was due."

"But he never showed."

"No. Another car drove past. I cannot even remember what it was. Cars were driving past all the time. The window opened, and fifteen rounds from a Kalashnikov hit the car. Pieter was already dead. I was hit in the right side of the chest."

"Torsten ..."

"I survived. I lost my right lung and had two ribs wired together. I am left with a stick, some scars, a pension and a life as a cripple. Pieter left a wife and a six-month-old child. He was only a boy himself. Save your pity for Marita and little Mattius." He looked up from the tabletop. Margaret was silent.

His life had changed beyond all recognition, ever since that volley of bullets had come crashing through the windscreen. He had taken so much for granted, a lifetime and a split-second before. He had reached over and grabbed Pieter by the shoulder, pulling him down and across on to his lap. If he hadn't made that sideways lurch and had looked to his own safety, he could have escaped harm. As it was, Pieter had died when the first bullet to pierce and star the windscreen entered his head just above the left eye. Neubauer had moved into the path of the fourth bullet. It tore its way through his chest, shattering one rib and sending shards of bone spinning through his lung. Bullet five hit the rib below, snapping it in two and boring its way through his back. It carried with it a wave of blended body parts that exploded over the car.

He had scrambled for the door handle and, not realising how badly he'd been hurt, had tried to pull himself clear. He couldn't, of course, and lay head-down over a Berlin pavement. He had been suspended by a corpse lying on his legs, while he watched open-mouthed as his lifeblood drained away.

He should have died. Death could have come then, or in the ambulance, or in the emergency room, or the operating theatre, or in the days when he drifted in and out of a morphine-drugged insensibility. But he didn't die, he just lost everything he had lived for.

"Shall I take you home?"

Neubauer nodded wearily.

Home was a flat in a three-storey terrace. It had been designed as separate apartments; there was a common entrance lobby that was used by all the residents, and an intercom pad with buttons and a speaker grille.

"I'll dump the car here and park it round the back later. Let's get you inside."

She squeezed the Escort into a parking place with practised urban skill. Neubauer undid his seat-belt and levered himself out of the car. He was tired, and felt hot and sweaty. The doctors had told him that he'd get that way very quickly; something about his ability to dissipate heat and take in oxygen. He would exhaust himself quickly, have little stamina. That was something he would have to live with. Now and forever.

Margaret heaved his case from the boot and pushed it on to the pavement, then locked up the car. "It hasn't changed since you were here last. Still the same tatty wallpaper and saggy sofa."

Neubauer looked up and focused in on the first-floor window, left-hand side. A desiccated pot plant poked up from under the net curtains of the anonymous windows. "It is your home, and I always found it very welcoming."

"Sure." She got hold of the strap and trundled the case towards the steps. "As soon as we're in, I'll get the kettle on." Margaret was suddenly very aware of the ambiguity of their relationship and the way they had left it. They had seen each other socially often. They had discovered a deep friendship that she was sure had lasted until Neubauer had gone incommunicado over six months ago. Then she had felt abandoned and deeply hurt, angry enough not to call him. Now, the matter hovered over her and she was unsure of his feelings towards her. Once, she thought that he might love her. All kinds of things had changed since.

She lifted the case up the five steps to the lobby, then fumbled for her keys. Another resident was leaving the building and she caught the door before it swung shut. She held it open for Neubauer.

"I should be doing that for you," he complained as he limped through.

"You shouldn't worry about things like that."

"I know."

He was spent by the time he got to the sofa in Margaret's front room.

"Coffee?" she offered.

"*Ja, bitte.*"

"Do you need anything to eat?"

"*Nein, danke. Ich habe im Flugzeug gefrühstückt.*"

"Sorry?"

He shook his head from side to side, as if there was a bee inside it and he was trying to dislodge it. "I forgot where I was. I have eaten already, thank you."

"You're tired."

"So are you. You have been working since last night."

"I change shifts, thank God, on Monday. Back to days. It also means I get the weekend off. I need to go to sleep now, but maybe we can go to a restaurant later." She kicked off her shoes, flicking each one with her toe into a corner of the room. As she straightened her spine, she could feel the vertebrae crack.

"Could we eat here? I have something else to tell you."

"There's more?"

"My injuries are not important, compared with what I have found out."

Then she remembered. "Elephant. I'll order a take-away." Margaret undid her ponytail and scrubbed her scalp vigorously with her fingernails. She only desisted when her head tingled.

"I am disturbing your rituals."

"I don't mind."

"Go and have your bath. Listen to your opera. Go to bed. I will still be here when you wake up."

She padded around barefoot and got everything ready: a bowl of breakfast cereal, a towel from the warm airing cupboard, her tartan dressing gown; she started the taps running in the bathroom, added the bubble-bath; she presented Neubauer with his coffee.

"You sure you'll be okay?"

"I will be fine."

"If you need anything, either take it or ask me if you can't find it. If the phone goes, ignore it. See you in a while."

She soaked and played and lolled, listened to *Aida* whilst surrounded by the scent of exotic cinnamon and spicy ginger. When she emerged, she found him fast asleep on the sofa, a pile of glossy black and white photographs by his side. The photos were big ten by eights, or the nearest metric equivalent.

Curious, she picked up the first one and tilted it to dispel the reflection.

It was a picture of a typed document, all in German, and stamped with an eagle astride a swastika.

Strangely, there was a label attached to the front of the document that bore a few Cyrillic characters amongst the numbers. The back of the stiff sheet was marked by the trade stamp of a Berlin photographic studio.

She had to let him tell her in his own good time. Margaret looked at the wall clock, which read one o'clock. The day was halfway through and she was already finished. She dared to touch the sleeping Neubauer's head with her lips, then went to bed.

Neubauer was unfamiliar with Indian food and unsure about how he would react to spicy-hot curry. There weren't any Turkish or Greek take-aways in the vicinity that Margaret would trust. They settled on Chinese. They had a bottle of wine, the one that Neubauer had produced from his wheeled case and presented to his host in time to put it in the fridge.

They talked at length, and with great depth and intensity. They discussed Margaret's lack of promotion, compared with the progress of her male colleagues, who were rising like bubbles in the sea while she was stuck like a limpet to a rock. They joked about plans to make the European Community a Union ("Imagine, Yessica, we could be citizens of the same country!"). They were serious while they picked apart politics East and West, and discussed whether Gorbachev could hang on long enough to destroy the old guard of the Communist past before he was brought down himself.

They had eaten all but everything. A few cashew nuts still clung to the bottom of one of the foil cartons. They had ordered too much rice, but Margaret confessed that all English people did that; it was almost a race trait.

She stirred a noodle around her plate with her fork. "Can we talk about the Newtons? It's why you're here."

"I am here to see you as well."

Margaret hid her discomfort with her wine glass. "Tell me about the Newtons, Torsten."

He stood up somewhat unsteadily. Whether it was the effect of alcohol, prescription drugs or his injuries, Margaret couldn't tell. He gathered together his photographs. She moved the debris of the meal to one side and dragged the standard lamp closer so that it lit the table but not their faces.

Neubauer re-adjusted himself at the table. "This comes in many parts. Like a puzzle, each part means little or nothing on its own. Together, they only make part of the picture. But there is enough to permit us to see what the whole could be like. They are in no particular order, so we shall learn about them as I did." He toyed with the corner of a photo, reluctant to begin. "It was all a mistake, at least at first. I had requested some documents from records, about icons. We have pictures of art that has either gone missing or has been found. Every item is catalogued by type, by artist, by age, by many different ways. Our department researcher is Esther. She is old and very wise. I had told her about the Newton Cross the first night I had seen it. I wondered if she had seen anything like it before. She had not, until she retrieved my documents for me. Someone had misfiled. Something caught her eye, and so it began for me."

He handed Margaret five of the big photos. The first she had already seen, but the others showed that it was a series of letters on the same notepaper.

"This is only one side of the correspondence," he explained, "From the Reich's Art and Antiquities Department. They were written in a four-month period over 1943 and 1944."

"Is this Russian at the top of the page?"

"It is. This is part of the Nazi War Crimes trials evidence that the Soviets handed over for Nüremburg. When the Red Army captured Berlin in 1945, they seized many papers and took them back to Moscow. Some they released. Most they have hidden. A few our spies have stolen, but we do not even know what we do not know. *Also*, this is not our story. This first letter thanks the Commandant for item 563-21, and remarks on its unusual design. The clerk who wrote the letter had sent the item to an ethnographer for identification."

Margaret scanned the page carefully, but understood little. Only one word stuck out, in the delivery address: Treblinka. "I know that name."

"It was an extermination camp."

"Oh."

"The second letter was from someone higher up. This person wanted to have all the records relating to the prisoner who had item 563-21 sent to Berlin immediately. The third letter asks the Commandant if anyone remembered the prisoner: all they had was a name, a number, a previous address. I suppose if you are killing six million people, you cannot afford to keep many details on each one. The fourth letter tells the Commandant that anyone with a similarly designed item should be transferred to Berlin immediately. The letter is copied to other extermination and concentration camps. And the fifth letter is in response to a question. The question was why, and the answer is revealing: anyone with a similar article would be a British agent. British, not American or Russian. Very deliberate."

"This item: you're not saying what it was."

"I know." He handed her a sixth photograph. It was in black and white, but it was unmistakable.

"The Newton Cross." Then it struck her. "But this is a tattoo."

Heart

"An extermination camp was a processing centre for death. Everything was taken from the prisoners. Their luggage, their clothing, their shoes, even their hair. They went naked into the Zyklon-B 'showers', and their bodies were carried out by privileged prisoners, Jews also, called *Sondercommando*."

Margaret was silent, and Neubauer carried painfully on. "The bodies were inspected before cremation. Gold fillings were extracted. If there were any interesting tattoos, these were removed and tanned, to keep them from decay." He put his hand on his forehead and stared down at the table. He muttered the next sentence, but Margaret heard him clearly enough. "They turned them into lampshades."

"God, no." Margaret dropped the photographs. One slipped over the edge of the table and on to the floor. It lay there, forgotten.

"Item 563-21 lay above someone's heart before they were killed and it was cut out."

"I feel sick."

"I feel ashamed. My father fought in the war. He was a bomber pilot. He was at the invasion of Crete and later in Yugoslavia, fighting Tito. He won the Iron Cross for bravery. He killed your soldiers for a political ideal that made lampshades out of human skin. This was what he was fighting for. I cannot accept this. I cannot look him in the eye any more." Neubauer tried to get up and turn his back on Margaret's horrified gaze. He stumbled, kicking the table leg. His hand crushed an empty foil container, and he found that it felt very good indeed.

He limped to the window and pulled the curtains aside.

Margaret came up behind him and offered him an excuse. "Your father couldn't have known."

"How could he not have known? Not about the Newton Cross, perhaps. But when the Jews were attacked and their shops closed, he did not say no. When he went to war, he did not care that the countries he fought in already had governments and people who lived there. He knew enough. He was wounded and given a desk job in Berlin at the beginning of 1943. He married his Romanian Gypsy lover to try and hide his Party past as the war was coming to an end."

"Torsten, millions of Germans fought in the war. Your father was just one of them." She so much wanted to touch him, but even as she moved her hand forward, she could feel the field of rage and betrayal that emanated from him. If she made contact, a great fat spark of fury would leap between them and ruin them forever. She twisted her hair in tight curls around her finger instead.

"I know it is stupid, picking on one old man for something that happened over forty years ago. My mother, this Romanian Gypsy who was racially impure and who should have been exterminated along with the Jews, still loves my father. She is angry with me for upsetting him. It is very difficult for me, and for her. Perhaps you will understand the way I feel about this."

"I'll try. Tell me the rest, Torsten."

"As you wish. Shall we sit down again?" He breathed as deeply as he could with one lung, and found the action unsatisfying. He blew the air out again and slumped on to his chair. Margaret took her seat opposite, apprehensively, wondering what was going to come next.

"Esther is my faithful bloodhound. She does not give up. After we talked about the Newton Cross, she kept looking for clues. Since she did not know what the symbol meant, other than it was a cross, she searched through the theological sections of the most complete collections. She must have walked for hours around libraries, talked to hundreds of people. She came up with this."

The seventh photograph was passed from hand to hand. High gothic script jagged its way in stark lines across a greying page. The border of the paper was wide, the edges nicked and curled.

"This is a page from a nineteenth-century book; it does not give its sources, but it translates as follows. 'Some fervent and pious men of Britain drew on their breasts the sign of the Cross, marking themselves that they knew of Christ's return, and had sealed themselves against the tribulations of the end times.'"

"Which times?"

"The end times. The Apocalypse of St John says that the world will suffer war, famine, plague and death before the Second Coming of Christ. But there is more important information here. 'Those men denied His return at that time. They said it would happen in God's good time.' You see, this is a book on the millennial panic that occurred in Europe in AD 999. Those who were marked with the Cross knew the date of the end of the world, and that it was not then. It was at some time in the future: the future in which we now live."

Margaret strained at the thought. "And they're still around almost a thousand years later?"

"If it is the same symbol, then yes. Robert and Marianne Newton knew about the end of the world. Now they are dead. But there must be others like them. I wondered if the Nazis knew about their secret. I suppose they must have done, otherwise the connection would not have been made between the tattoo and the British. Hitler was very superstitious, very influenced by the occult. He had a large collection of occult books and ritual items. He loved and feared secret knowledge. He would have wanted to have known when the end of the world was to be."

"That's ... ridiculous."

"Perhaps. It is not important if we believe it, but it is important that we believe that they believe it. It might be the reason why they were killed. There is a twist to the story. After I was shot, I supposed I would die. I put all thoughts about the Newtons out of my mind. I had no job, no life left. The doctors were healing me, but my will to live had gone. I found that I had nothing outside police work. I was a shallow man."

"Torsten ..."

"No, please. I must continue. I was that man. Esther rescued me. She sent me a book."

Margaret waited for the book to be passed to her, but instead she got another photograph: the eighth and final one.

"The book was too heavy to bring across. It is *Le Morte D'Arthur* by Thomas Malory. It was first published in 1485 and printed by Caxton, the father of English printing. This copy dates from 1909, and is a second edition published as one complete book with drawings by Aubrey Beardsley. Only one thousand five hundred copies were printed: Esther must have been very lucky to find one in Berlin. But it is not the book that is special. It is the picture by Beardsley, and what someone has done to it."

Margaret looked at the photograph. It was difficult to make out what the picture was originally of, for it was crowded with hand-drawn Newton Crosses. Eventually, she could see that it was a black and white block-printed drawing, with a border of vines and a central picture of a man in stylised armour holding his arm aloft. Before him was a grey lake. The knight had cast a sword into the lake, and a hand had flashed out of the water to catch the sword by the hilt. At the back of her mind, in the depths of her memory, she had the idea that she knew what this was. She closed her eyes and remembered. "The Lady of the Lake."

"I did not know the story. I suppose it is a British thing. But it occurred to me, as it had to Esther, that whoever had drawn Newton Crosses on this picture knew that the Cross is not a cross."

"What?"

"Here is the connection: remember after Marianne Newton had been hit by the car, she gave something to the Viking man. Do you remember what that something was?"

Again, Margaret searched the nether regions of her memory. "It was long and heavy and wrapped in a sack," she said finally.

"*Also.* The Newton Cross is a tattoo of a long sword. That is what Marianne handed the Viking."

Margaret had stopped blinking. "How can you be sure?"

"Because of this." Neubauer pulled out one last piece of evidence. It was a cutting from an English newspaper. Written in biro at the top of the thin, rough paper, was "*The Times* 4-22-87".

"What does this date say?"

"Twenty-second of April, Yessica. Read it."

She did. It was a short piece, part of a long column of snippets from around the regions.

Accountant still missing.

Gideon Smith, 28, is still being sought by Tyneside police after an incident at his rented home in the West End of Newcastle on Monday morning. A man is in hospital after being stabbed by what is believed to be 'a double-edged weapon over three feet long'. Northumbria police warn the public not to approach Smith, who had recently been undergoing psychiatric treatment. An accountant with the nationwide firm, Pickett McInly, he is described as six foot four, heavily built, with short blond hair.

Neubauer gave a smile of grim satisfaction. "He is our Viking. He has the sword."

"He's gone mad and run amok." Margaret blinked at last, several times.

"Perhaps. He is not one of them, not a Cross-bearer. I think he is in trouble. Someone killed the Newtons, and if they are after the secret of the end of the world, it may be that they also tried to kill Smith. Yessica, before I came here, I was in Bavaria in a hospital, sent there to sleep and rest. Dachau is nearby and I visited it. I stood in front of the memorial wall and I made a vow: that I would return to Britain, find Smith and learn about the end of the world. On the way, I might meet friends of the Newtons and tell them about item 563-21."

Margaret swallowed hard. "Is there room for me in this vow of yours?"

Reaching across the table and patting her hand, Neubauer smiled at her. "There is always room for you, Yessica. But I need to show that there are good Germans in this world."

"We know that already."

"Perhaps I have to prove it to myself. And to my father."

177

Chapter 14
Saturday 16th May 1987
London

Torsten Neubauer's story

They were eating breakfast, and Neubauer was idly leafing through the Saturday newspaper, getting the corners soggy with butter and what he insisted on calling 'orange jam'. He turned the pages casually, scanning the headlines, glossing the text, looking at the pictures and reading the advertisements.

"Of course, it could be a coincidence," said Margaret through a mouthful of cornflakes.

"People are stabbed with swords every day in Germany." Neubauer flicked a moist crumb of toast off Helmut Kohl and Margaret Thatcher, who were standing uncomfortably side by side. The size difference between the two leaders was almost comical.

"It didn't say there was a sword."

Neubauer looked over the top of the newsprint at her. "Please. A double-edged weapon with a blade a metre long? What would you call it?"

"Okay. But you can't go running around the countryside every time someone writes in a newspaper that they've seen a sword. I won't allow it." She was adamant.

"You will not allow it?" said Neubauer with mounting amusement. "My dear Yessica, I am an adult."

She impaled her bowl with her spoon. "You try it and I'll fight you. You are ill. You've nowhere near recovered enough to go gallivanting around the country. Face it, Torsten, you can't do the things you used to."

Neubauer twitched the paper so that it hid his dark expression. "As you wish."

"I mean it. When you're well, we'll both go. We're not going anywhere this weekend or this month. You are going to take it easy and do as little as possible. You will see a few sights, eat well and not get tired."

The German thought about things for a while. Then he laughed, put the paper down across the breakfast things, and laced his fingers together on top of his head. "I surrender. We shall enjoy ourselves, with no running off to foreign parts."

"Good," said Margaret with finality. She took up her spoon again, and shovelled more cereal into her mouth. The conversation was over.

They went to Kew and spent all day there, sitting and walking amongst the green splendour of the trees. The vast Victorian glasshouses were shining, multi-faceted jewels, toys to be opened and explored. Neubauer found the tropical hothouse unbearable and retreated rapidly, with Margaret shooing him through the Saturday crowd like a mother hen shielding a chick.

He slept in the car on the way home, made it as far as the sofa and slept there too.

Late in the evening, he awoke suddenly, uncertain as to where he was. Margaret sat at the table with a mug of coffee steaming before her. She was watching him like a hawk.

"I should have called the doctor. I'm really sorry. I shouldn't have even taken you out."

Neubauer, still a little grey around the cheeks, waved her apology aside. "No matter. I am learning my own limits, and today I have gone beyond them."

"Are you sure you're all right?" She got up and knelt by his side, her eyes searching his face for lines of pain.

"I am just tired, that is all. I am a bad house guest."

Heart

"No. No, you're not, you're ill. You're allowed to be, you know."

"What is the time?" He fumbled for his watch, but couldn't find it. It was on the floor, next to his shoes. He hadn't remembered taking it off.

"It's a quarter past twelve."

"You're evening has gone. You should get to bed yourself."

"I was making sure ..."

"I will be fine. Go to bed, Yessica. I might read for a while, to make myself sleepy again."

"Okay." She leaned forward to kiss him, then pulled back. She squeezed his hand instead. "Goodnight, Torsten."

Just as she was drifting off to sleep, she thought she could hear voices talking in the lounge. Radio, she surmised, and shut her eyes again.

Sunday 17th May 1987

They went to Greenwich on Sunday; they sat in the park, window-shopped down the High Street and watched the ball on top of the Observatory fall at one o'clock. They had a pub lunch, and walked arm in arm along the banks of the Thames by the Naval Academy.

Neubauer talked about the Rhine, about how the barges ploughed back and forth, carrying everything and anything to and from the heart of Europe.

Margaret insisted that he rested little and often, sitting on this bench or that wall. She fed him at every opportunity, too – sweets, buns, ice creams. Neubauer eventually rebelled and kept his mouth shut as she plastered sticky icing over his face in an attempt to get him to open up.

180

Six o'clock the next morning, she was at her desk, leafing through the night's reports and, by nine-thirty, Torsten Neubauer was on a train from King's Cross to Newcastle.

When she came home mid-afternoon to find only a note, she called him all sorts of names. Some, Neubauer wouldn't have understood.

Monday 18th May 1987
Newcastle upon Tyne

It was colder than Neubauer had anticipated when he stepped off the train and into the great Dobson-designed station with its glass roof and sweeping curve. Perhaps he had got used to the air-conditioning on the train, or perhaps it really was warmer in the south. Neubauer pulled his coat around him and slung his little knapsack over his shoulder, the one he used to walk with in the Grunenwald.

He had hardly heard of Newcastle before, and knew even less about it. He would have been shocked to learn that Jessica Margaret had as much knowledge of events and places north of Watford Gap as he did. Behind him, the huge diesel-electrics of the motive unit whined into life and rapidly became a roar that made the chill dry air vibrate with energy. The last carriage whipped away from the platform with a tornado in its wake. Neubauer's trouser legs were tugged briefly, then he was alone.

He was a traveller, a linguist, used to strange situations and stranger customs. But he felt less confident than he had in the past: his wounds nagged at him, sapping his strength, reminding him of his frailty. If he hadn't had a mission, he would have stayed in his sanatorium in Bavaria and watched the mountains wear down.

Heart

Neubauer availed himself of a map from the tourist information booth, then headed off for the big yellow Metro sign. He paid for his ticket by inserting unfamiliar coinage into a machine, and slid into the bowels of the earth on a slowly moving escalator. The whole system seemed very new and clean: not like Berlin's *U-bahn*, which whilst clean, was old. Even the *U-bahn* was cut in two when the Wall went up. There were stations that had been severed from the network, fore and aft, and guarded by troops.

He was reminded to stand clear of the doors as he boarded the white and cream carriage. Pictures, words and faces blurred past, then darkness. The train jerked, began decelerating and stuttered to a halt at Monument. Neubauer alighted, checked his map for the hundredth time and, after a walk through unfamiliar architecture, found his way to the Central Library.

He was hot and sweaty once again. He sat in the cool of the foyer for a few minutes before braving the lending section.

He asked for, and was given, the week's local newspapers starting from the Monday on which Gideon Smith had disappeared. There were two titles, stable-mates: an upmarket, business-orientated title called the *Journal*, and a broadsheet populist publication, the *Evening Chronicle*.

That was what the men on the street corners had been shouting. He hadn't managed to understand their call, but then again no one did. It was a code, a symbol, like the Newton Cross; it was significant to those who grasped its meaning.

He found nothing in either Monday edition; the print run had been too early even for the evening paper. But, turning to Tuesday, the stabbing was the lead story in both. The *Chronicle* had a grainy photograph of Smith's terraced house, and gave significant details. It was clear from the police account that firearms had been used and a pistol recovered. It was also apparent that none of Smith's neighbours had heard so much as a whisper, let alone a fire-fight, in the house next door.

It was beginning to sound uncannily familiar.

There were at least two assailants, one at the front door and the unfortunate at the back. Nothing could be found of either Smith or the man who had been at the front of the house. They had vanished.

He wrote it all down.

There was some routine police flannel about their concern for Smith, who had been undergoing psychiatric treatment at a local hospital. Neubauer's eyes widened slightly. Perhaps Marianne Newton's choice of person to receive her mysterious gift had not been so wise after all. That Smith was an accountant was mentioned, and that he was twenty-eight. The article in the *Journal* gave the name of the office where he worked, but covered essentially the same facts in a less sensational tone. There was no mention of a wife or girlfriend, relatives, friends or colleagues, and no photograph either.

He put the papers aside and turned to Wednesday. The story had disappeared into the small print. The anonymous stabbed man was in a critical condition in Newcastle General Hospital and was under armed police guard. The consultant treating him gave the dimensions of the weapon used without using the word 'sword' once.

Thursday's byline was 'Police appeal for witnesses'. The man in hospital was still alive, Smith still missing, the local constabulary clueless. There was some speculation that burglars had just picked the wrong house to break into. Neubauer thought that crowbars would have been more useful than pistols.

Heart

He took photocopies of everything he could find, and found that it made a pitiful pile of paper. Men, even thieves, didn't get impaled on swords in a modern twentieth-century city. The story had a high curiosity factor that would be attractive to a provincial reporter. He shuffled his notes into his knapsack and located the telephone directories. Pickett McInly had a listed number, as had the Crime Desks of the two papers. He asked the way to the public telephones, and started dialling.

"Good afternoon. Pickett McInly? I was wondering if someone would be available to talk about Mr Gideon Smith, who is employed by your office? Certainly I will hold." He leaned against his stick and remembered he hadn't had any lunch.

"Hello? My name? Certainly. Herr Torsten Neubauer. No, I am not calling from Germany; from the Central Library here in Newcastle. I do not represent any organisation, no; I am a private individual. Yes, I will hold again." He tapped his foot for a while. "Hello, yes, I am still here. I understand that it is a matter for the police, but I would rather not trouble them with his until I am certain of my information. I will talk to the police, yes. Thank you for your time. Goodbye." The receptionist had been as impenetrable as the Iron Curtain, and just as cold.

He pumped some more coins into the hungry slot, and retrieved his copy of the *Evening Chronicle* story: "Hello, Crime Desk? I wish to speak to Jonathan Cruickshank, please. He is out of the office? Is there someone else I can speak to about Gideon Smith? You had a front page with the story. Have I new information? Perhaps. Have I told the police?" Neubauer looked at the telephone as if it had mutated into pumpernickel; a newspaper telling an informant to go straight to the police? He thought not, and hung up without replying. The *Chronicle* and the *Journal* shared offices; they would have the same editorial policy. He saved his change and went in search of a café.

He sat there with the rest of the late lunch crowd, munching his way through a substantial sandwich and reviewing his notes. He had precious little. Smith was either a dangerous man or a desperate one. It could have been a ghastly coincidence that he'd disturbed thieves while playing with a sword. But Neubauer thought that the two incidents, London and Newcastle, bore such striking similarities that the only link missing was a black Jaguar.

The difference was that the police were silent. No appearances of an Arden clone on the television, no reams of press hyperbole. Neubauer had once asked his superiors to keep a story out of the public domain. It had been done. So he surmised that the authorities were involved and that they were using up all their favours by throwing out such a blanket of silence.

He looked at his watch: two forty-five. Margaret would be returning home about now, he thought, and wondered if he ought to call her. He decided to postpone the inevitable argument until she had had time to calm down.

He checked his train timetable, put it away again and made a decision. He wasn't going to leave the city until someone talked to him. He was still, technically at least, a serving officer in the West German Police and he was damned if the stiff-necked British were going to get the better of him.

He bought a copy of the local street atlas from a newsagent, examined it, and went to stake out Pickett McInly.

There was a low wall opposite the office suite; that was where he sat with a can of fizzy pop and a bar of strange, milky chocolate. People came and went; clients, couriers that screamed up on bikes and tore away again, staff engaged in site visits. Neubauer had all but picked his victim: the youngest, most junior member of staff, who had been sent on numerous errands, returning with papers, pastries, and once a book. He was about to pounce when he was interrupted by a small, thin man coming out from the law firm next door to the accountants'.

"Excuse me?" he said.

Neubauer reverted to his ignorant foreigner persona. "*Sprechen Sie deutsche?*"

"*Nür ein bisschen. Können Sie englisch?*"

Scheisse! "Some. Can I help you?"

"I was wondering if I could help you. I've been up in my office for an hour watching you sitting here, looking at Pickett McInly. Why don't you go in and wait there?"

Neubauer wished the man would go, but rudeness was alien to him. "I do not think I would be welcome. They do not want to speak to me."

The lawyer adjusted his spectacles and glanced about him, almost furtively. "Why not?"

Something made Neubauer narrow his eyes. Nervousness did not become the man. "I want to talk about Gideon Smith, but no one else in this city does. I would like to know why." He offered up the last of his chocolate.

"Who are you?" The man had virtually frozen to the spot.

"Herr Inspector Torsten Neubauer, Berlin *Kriminalpolitzei.* But I am doing this in a private capacity. I would like to know where Mr Smith has gone, and I would like to know what he has taken with him."

"You're not British police." He was clearly relieved.

"No. I take it you have talked to them."

"I might have. Why do you want to know about Gideon?"

He knew him. He knew something about him. The police knew that too. Neubauer was about to risk all in an attempt to get the man to open up.

"I think that Mr Smith is in trouble; he is certainly in trouble with the police and he is in trouble with someone else who wants what he has. I might know what type of trouble he is in, but I cannot get anyone to confirm what I know, to say if it is the truth or a lie."

The man moved closer and sat next to him. He was cold, clammy, guilty. "I can't tell you anything, you understand."

"I understand. You have been told to say nothing to the newspapers, nothing to friends or family, and certainly not to foreign strangers."

The man nodded.

"But you lied to the police, so you are frightened that they will find out. You are a lawyer, no? You could lose your job."

"Keep your voice down, Inspector! I'm scared of everything at the moment. I don't know what to do! I'm told one thing by one person, one thing by another, both can't possibly be true. What are you going to tell me?"

Neubauer toyed with his stick. "What am I going to tell you? Just over a year ago, a woman and her husband were killed. As she died, she gave Mr Smith a sword which might hold the secret of the end of the world. Someone came to kill him for that secret. But perhaps Smith does not know what the sword was or what it meant. I am trying to find those who have that knowledge; people who have a cross tattooed on them, like this one."

He opened his knapsack and retrieved the photograph of Item 563-21. "This diamond is blue, this is green and this top one is red. But it is not just a cross, it is the sword also."

The young man did something Neubauer considered very odd. He opened his wallet and pulled out a business card. Then using a pen from his top pocket, he wrote a hurried something on the reverse. He handed it over with a set of keys.

"Go here. Wait for me. I'll be not long after five."

Neubauer looked at the card and the scribbled address. "Herr Cook?"

"No more now. Get a taxi to that address. If anyone asks, say that you're waiting for me. I share with two lads, Tony and David. Go, now!" He got up and walked quickly away, back into the office from whence he came.

Neubauer looked again at the card and the bunch of keys he was unexpectedly holding. He had seen a taxi rank back in the centre of town. On his way he realised that when he eventually phoned Margaret, he had something positive to report.

James Cook was later than he said he would be and had the unusual experience of ringing his own doorbell.

Neubauer was already ensconced inside at the kitchen table, being circled round by Tony and David like a rolled-up hedgehog by wary cats. He heard voices in the hallway, too low to determine actual words, but of a tone that expressed confusion and worry.

Cook made dinner for both of them after the other two had gone out. Neubauer wasn't too sure whether they had jumped or been pushed.

"I hope the chilli's not too hot for you." Cook rummaged for a cheese grater and applied it to a lump of cheddar. "How do you know so much?"

"Accident," replied Neubauer. "At least to start with. I was in the right places at the right times. Then I started to look a little closer. I have very clever friends, too. I came back to Britain to solve two murders, the husband and wife I talked about before. My priorities have changed since I heard the name Gideon Smith."

He was presented with a circle of rice and a steaming pile of dark red chilli.

"Please, eat. The reason I'm going to tell you what happened is because the police are lying and you are telling the truth. Before, I only had what Gideon told me, but you seem to know more than he did."

"What did the police tell you? I am interested to know." He poured himself a glass of water from the pitcher and eyed the chilli suspiciously. Then he shrugged and dug in with his fork.

"Some cock-and-bull story about being a drug dealer, that they'd had their eye on him for a while and this was some sort of gangland hit."

"You do not believe it."

"Not any more. I didn't want to in the first place. I knew Gideon. Okay, he'd changed in the past month. It wasn't drugs; I just didn't know what it was for sure. He didn't confide in me until, well, it was too late. Even then, Gideon's story sounded just nonsense."

"You have spoken with Gideon Smith since the stabbing?"

"He hid here on Monday."

Neubauer chewed thoughtfully. "Did he tell you what he had done?"

"He told me everything that he'd done. I wanted to believe him, believe that he wasn't an escaped lunatic, but I couldn't." Cook pushed his plate away from him, untouched. "But I didn't betray him. I did what he asked.

189

I've told no one what I saw and heard, despite the fact that it could cost me everything."

"You are a good friend to have."

"I thought he was mad." He swigged his water sourly.

"And now you believe him."

"I wish I could tell him."

"Perhaps I could tell him for you. What does Mr Smith think happened?"

"He was given a sword by a dying woman in London a year ago. He started having dreams and visions he eventually connected with the sword. There was writing on it; he went to get it translated and someone tried to find him through the people who'd done the translation. A man he'd seen before in London, who'd tried to take the sword from him then, found him and chased him home. Gideon was trapped there. There was some shooting from the front door and another man with a gun at the back. It was this one that Gideon had to attack to escape."

"Then he came to you for help."

"I don't know what he thought I could do. He put me in an impossible situation; he wouldn't turn himself in, and told me his story about swords and elves."

"Elves? I am sorry?"

"The writing on the sword. He say's it's Elvish."

Neubauer remained blank.

Cook leaned forward, insistent. "Gideon didn't make this up. He spoke to a couple of people at the university. This is what they told him."

"Did you see this writing?"

"Yes. Never seen anything like it before. I've seen the sword, too."

"He showed it to you?"

The man's eyes misted over in wondering recollection. "It was beautiful, the most astonishing thing I've ever seen before in my life. It shines! Like a mirror! It's like ... solid light. There are three gems, one on the hilt, two on the crosspiece, red, green and blue. Just like the tattoo you showed me. Stones as big as your eye, in settings that would make a jeweller weep." He stopped his gushing, smiling wryly. "It was very beautiful."

"Mr Cook, why do you suppose that the police have gagged everyone? Nothing I have heard or learned so far is dangerous. Unusual, perhaps a little frightening, but not dangerous."

"I suppose it's because of Kate."

"Kate? Who is this Kate?"

"Kate was Gideon's long-standing girlfriend. She broke it off just before the attack, moved out and took everything with her, without telling him. She thought Gideon had gone mad."

"So did you."

"With good reason. He was seeing a psychiatrist and as close to the edge as I'd seen anyone before. You get to see a lot of borderline cases in my line of work. But I'm straying; Kate's a WPC. I doubt that the Chief Constable would like it widely known that one of his officers was shacked up with a psychotic swordsman. Not good for the force's image."

"I can imagine, though it still seems a little unusual to then concoct a story about a drug dealer. Have they issued a warrant for Mr Smith?"

"No."

"No?" Neubauer mopped his brow with some kitchen towel and drank a glass of water. The fire was beginning to build in his stomach.

"No. He's just wanted for questioning so far."

"Odd."

Heart

"Damn right it's odd. He could have killed someone. The police would leap in with both feet normally. Possession of an offensive weapon, wounding with intent. But no, not a squeak."

"And the other man, the one in hospital?"

"Illegal possession of a firearm, attempted burglary. But he's not saying anything." Cook shifted awkwardly in his seat.

"The police have interviewed him?"

"Oh, yes. He says absolutely nothing."

"Does he have a lawyer? He must have asked for a lawyer."

"Inspector Neubauer, I am his lawyer. He, whoever he is, has not uttered one single word since he was taken to hospital a week ago."

"You?"

"Ironic, don't you think? There I am, hiding Gideon in my bedroom, when there's a phone call for me. I'm on call for the duty solicitor rota. It's the police; they want to interview a man in hospital. Sure, I say, tell me some more. They do. I realise it's the man Gideon stabbed. What do I do? I can't refuse because if I do, Gideon is sunk without a trace. If I agree, there's a serious conflict of interest to add to all the other things I was about to do wrong. So I did it. Not that it mattered. No one knows anything about him – name, where he comes from, what he was doing. No reply to any question, legal, social or medical."

"How ill is he?"

"Serious, not critical. But he just lies there, waiting."

"Waiting for what?"

Cook shrugged.

"What did you do with Gideon Smith?"

192

"I drove him to Coldstream at three o'clock in the morning." He watched Neubauer's eyes narrow. "I'll get a map."

He pointed out the small town just across the border with Scotland. "I was back in my bed by five. If Tony or David suspect anything, they've never said, and they've had every opportunity." He collected the empty plates loudly and jammed them in the sink.

"You are angry."

"Why didn't he tell me?" He turned on Neubauer, simply because there was no one else. "We could have worked something out, found out what was going on together, and no one would have to get killed! Now it's swords and elves and men with big guns. What the hell is going on?"

"That's what I am trying to find out," said Neubauer calmly. "Shouting at me will not help."

"Sorry."

"That is okay. This writing, you say it is in Elvish?"

"I'm telling you what Gideon told me," Cook muttered defensively.

"There is a translation."

"A rough one. A woman called Leah Orchard, English Department at the university, did it for him. He said it didn't make sense, but didn't say what it was."

Neubauer tutted, then stifled an involuntary yawn.

"You're tired."

"I am exhausted. I need to find a hotel for the night and go back to London in the morning. I would like one more thing from you. A photograph, if you have it."

"Of Gideon? I can look. Maybe I can send it to you?"

Neubauer took a sheet of paper from his knapsack and scribbled Margaret's address in one corner. "Keep it safe," he warned.

Cook drove him to a city-centre hotel, anonymous and safe, and bade him goodnight.

But before Neubauer let his overpowering weariness take him, he made the call he had been meaning to make all evening. He woke Margaret up and she wasn't best pleased.

Tuesday 19th May 1987

He overslept, missed breakfast completely and narrowly avoided being charged for a further day's occupancy before he checked out. Still tired and a little disorientated, he found an all-day breakfast menu and loaded carbohydrate with typical German gusto.

Fortified, he went in search of Leah Orchard.

It took him a little while, and he found her as wary as a starved and beaten dog. At first, she refused even to listen to what he had to say, and Neubauer was afraid that she might hit him. He was certainly in no condition to defend himself.

"Please, Miss Orchard," he begged as he backed out of her room, "I am an ill man!"

"And I am a busy woman and do not wish to talk to you." She tried to shut the door on his foot. "Go away before I call for a porter."

Neubauer was in an awkward position: forced out into the corridor, attracting unwelcome attention as rotten meat did flies. She'd started to cloud over when she heard the words 'Gideon Smith' and 'translation' in the same breath, and had risen from her seat at the mention of 'copy' with a flood of denial and iron-willed determination to get this man out of her office.

194

"I know about the elves, Miss Orchard!" he gasped desperately.

A head came through the gap in the door, grabbed him by the collar and dragged him inside. The door banged shut and Neubauer slumped breathless into the chair. Leah, her back braced against the door, started demanding answers.

"Who are you?"

"I am Inspector Torsten Neubauer," said Neubauer uncomfortably. Leah Orchard was strong for her size, and he felt bruised and sore. He produced his badge, which she looked over carefully, not because she'd know a fake, but to show she was alert.

"Who's been talking?" She kept the badge.

"Gideon Smith."

"You're a liar."

"I haven't spoken to him myself, but to a friend of his. I know more than you, Miss Orchard. Please let me tell you."

And he did.

Leah Orchard was as good as her word to Gideon. She had destroyed all her notes, deleted her files on the computer, hidden her textbooks and her own knowledge.

But she remembered. She took a sheet of heavyweight art paper from her desk drawer and opened out a calligraphy set in front of her. Neubauer vacated the chair and watched over her shoulder as she twisted the brass nib this way and that, producing line after line of alien script.

"I could do this in my sleep," she admitted.

Neubauer held the sheet up to the light, careful not to touch the wet ink. "It is very good. What does it mean?"

She took another piece of paper, a standard sheet of A4, and began to write with a biro. "This is the best I could do. It doesn't make much sense."

"Is there anything about the end of the world?"

"Perhaps. It's difficult to tell. There's something very much like a warning in it: *nevanuvië ancoruva morumbar. Morumbar* is best translated as doom." She carried on writing. "This will be the only copy in existence, Inspector. Be careful with it."

"Thank you for trusting me, Miss Orchard. I will be careful." He thought for a moment. "Perhaps I could ask you to do something for me." He copied James Cook's address down on a third piece of paper. "This is the name of the man I talked to. He is scared and alone. Talk to him, Miss Orchard. Let him know that he has done the right thing."

They swapped papers, and Leah gave Neubauer his badge back.

"What are you going to do now?"

"I will go back to London and conduct some more research. I would like to help Mr Smith, but I know too little."

"Good luck, Inspector."

"Thank you, Miss Orchard."

196

Chapter 15
Tuesday 19th May 1987
London

Torsten Neubauer's story

"Bastard."

"*Guten Abend*, Yessica."

She stood aside and let him in. "You're ill again."

"I am tired, that is all." His cane tapped down her hallway.

Her dark expression began to soften. "I hope it was worth it."

"I have the sword inscription," said Neubauer.

"The sword exists?"

"I met someone who has seen it. Come and sit down. I will tell you what I have found out."

Margaret watched him struggle along, and she finally relented. "Coffee first?"

"Please." Neubauer collapsed on to the sofa, and felt his eyelids drag down. He'd slept on the train, but still felt exhausted. His scars were raw; both the entry and exit wounds, and the great railway tracks of operation scars the surgeons had created to cut away dead flesh and repair shattered bone. There had been no time for fancy modern stuff, just nineteenth-century hack and slash. It had saved his life, but left him in pain for the rest of it.

He looked through his knapsack for a bottle of pills, cracked it open and knocked out a couple of white tablets into his sweaty palm. He stared at them, then put one back and waited for his coffee.

Margaret brought two mugs through from the kitchen, noticed the concentration on Neubauer's face, the etching of worry behind his wet smile.

"Are you all right?"

"I will be." He sipped the top off his drink and forced the painkiller down before he scalded his mouth.

"I told you not to go."

"I know you did. It was worth it, Yessica." He pulled out a jumble of paper, photocopies of newspapers and lists of telephone numbers, and gave them to Margaret. At the centre was the art-grade card inscribed so carefully by Leah Orchard.

"This? What's this?"

"The sword inscription. It is in Elvish."

"Right."

"It is true. You have a translation there also. Gideon Smith had the sword, given to him by Marianne Newton."

"And now he's gone?" She searched for the translation and began the long descent into a terminal frown.

"Not as inexplicable as the press would have you believe. He was driven to Scotland on the Monday night, after the stabbing."

"They found him. They came to kill him." She looked from the inscription to the supposed translation. "For this?"

"For the sword. The inscription is part of the sword."

"This doesn't make any sense." She turned the flowing script this way and that, even holding it up to the light, as if a hidden meaning could be illuminated from behind.

"I know. It could be anything, mean anything. The translator apologised for her lack of understanding."

"And Smith has gone with the sword. Any idea where?"

"No. North. Mr Smith believes he might be mad, so he may do anything."

"I'm too tired to take any of this in. I need my bath and you could do with more sleep."

"Sleep? I have reading to do." Neubauer held up a plastic bag and pulled out a paperback book so fat, Margaret would have considered using it as a step-ladder.

"*The Lord of the Rings*, by JRR Tolkien."

"With appendices. Look." Neubauer turned to the very last few pages of the book and creased it open at a table of hauntingly familiar design.

Margaret fumbled for the sword inscription and measured up the characters against those in the table. "They're the same. Elvish?" She looked from one to the other. "I'll be damned," she said slowly, punctuating each word with a pause.

"There is a mystery here," said Neubauer.

"You could be right."

Wednesday 20th May 1987

Neubauer woke up in the middle of the night, gasping for breath. When he realised he wasn't drowning, suffocating, or having his back flayed by some limber creature with talons as thin as paper and as sharp as acid, he sat on the edge of his bed and mopped away the sweat with a towel.

There was something he was missing. He often woke like this, when the germ of an idea tickled his forebrain without leaving an impression to grasp. He didn't force it. He padded to the kitchen, past Margaret's open door, and made himself a fruit tea.

Standing at the window, looking out into the sodium night, it came to him, slowly at first, then in an exhilarating rush that left him grinning broadly.

John and Miriam Walcott-Green.

"Yessica? Yessica?"

Heart

"What? What? Torsten? Should I call a doctor?" She thrashed around under the duvet for a few moments more before righting herself. "Are we on fire?"

"The Walcott-Greens."

Margaret made two abortive attempts at turning on the bedside lamp, before succeeding. Neubauer was sitting on the end of her bed, virtually bouncing up and down in excitement.

"Who?"

"The Walcott-Greens. John and Miriam. Remember the Newtons' will? The Walcott-Greens had the keys to the Newtons' house. We knew then! They came for the sword, but the sword had already gone. The Walcott-Greens are sealed with the Cross!"

"Very good, Torsten. You're a brilliant detective. Go back to sleep." Margaret buried her head in her pillow and groped for the cord switch.

They lived in Belgravia, and Neubauer felt he ought to show his passport at every corner, just to prove he was on legitimate business. There were steps, big grey stone steps with an awkward reach and a wide balustrade that was little use in supporting his climb.

At the top was a front door that wouldn't have been out of place on a bank vault. Beside it was a little ivory bell-push that had 'Press' inscribed on it in black. Neubauer leaned on his stick and heard a melodious tinkling from inside.

There were footsteps, slow and deliberate on a tiled floor inside, and the door swung open.

"Yes?" said the balding man in the grey suit.

Neubauer wished he was wearing his jaeger hat, so that he could take it off.

"I am sorry. I was looking for John and Miriam Walcott-Green. Do they still live here?"

200

The suited man softened, half-smiled around his wrong-side-of-middle-age eyes. "You've had a wasted journey, sir. The Walcott-Greens haven't resided here for a year. They moved to Ireland, bloodstock farm."

"Sorry?"

"Horse breeding, sir."

"I don't suppose you could ..."

"It would be most unprofessional of me, sir."

"I understand. Did you used to work for them?"

"I did. A most congenial family indeed. I was sorry to see them go."

Neubauer opened his knapsack and balanced it on the balustrade. "I am going to show you a photograph. All I need is a simple yes or no, to satisfy my curiosity." He pulled out the photograph of item 563-21. "Have you ever seen this before?"

The doorman's eyes flared, his pupils grew large, his skin went pale. There was a trembling of the fingers that held the edges of the black and white image, which could not be attributed to age.

"I can't say I have, sir." The photograph was handed back. The man's eyes were lowered and refused to look at Neubauer's.

His heart surged. He was vindicated. "Thank you for being honest," he said slyly.

"If that will be all, sir." The doorman kept his gaze directed at Neubauer's navel.

"I'm sorry to have bothered you." The door swung shut with the same effortless glide that had marked its opening.

Neubauer celebrated by going into a bookshop and buying *The Silmarillion* and a biography of Tolkien.

Using his newly cut key to let himself into Margaret's flat, he continued the leafing he'd started on the Underground. He was staggered by the history: a creation myth, the making of a new world, the weaving of legends and folklore into a seamless magical whole. Neubauer was in awe of the man's genius, his intellectual rigour and creative blaze.

But how much did Tolkien really know? Was his Elvish some race memory that echoed along the halls of time to arrive warped and dim in a wartime fantasy book? Or could it be the code-breaker's almanac, designed for Leah Orchard to help Gideon Smith and Torsten Neubauer riddle out the secret of the end of the world.

The telephone rang over the dull roar of the kettle.

"Neubauer."

"Torsten Neubauer?" The voice was English, precise and clipped. It pronounced his name badly.

"Speaking."

"Forget about Robert and Marianne Newton. Forget about Gideon Smith. Such things do not concern you."

"Who is this?"

"This is your only warning," continued the voice, ignoring the question as an irrelevance. "Go back home, Neubauer. Do not meddle or things will go badly for you."

"Is this a threat?" Of all the replies Neubauer could have made, he rued retrospectively the one that actually forced its way out. Of course it was a threat. Even a hackneyed "You don't frighten me, whoever you are" would have been better.

The line went dead and Neubauer placed the phone back down on the cradle. He had asked too many intemperate questions in too many difficult places. His name had surfaced like a surprised diver in an underground cavern, and now he was marked, watched, observed even. He had intruded into a private war, and one or other of the combatants wanted him to stop muddying the water. Otherwise, to use the disturbing turn of phrase of his caller, things would go badly for him.

So be it. He was a man without a lung and without a job. He knew too much to stop, too little to satisfy the burning curiosity he felt. He made a coffee and a sandwich, and retired to the sofa with *The Silmarillion*.

He woke up when he heard the front door slam.

"Torsten? Torsten, are you here?"

"*Hier*, Yessica."

She looked red-faced, as if she'd been running.

"Are you okay?"

"Yes."

She swept past him to the window. She scanned the street below.

"What are you looking for?" asked Neubauer.

"I don't know. I hope I'll recognise it if I see it."

"You think you were followed?"

"No." She started to inspect the windows opposite, looking for a face, or the reflection from a camera lens. "I had a phone call, at work."

"*Also*. They called me here, too."

"Torsten, they said they'd kill you if you didn't back off." She pulled the curtains on the spring sunshine.

"Yessica, I used to get these all the time from the Russian Mafia. Please keep a sense of proportion."

"Last time, the Russian Mafia did try and kill you."

"But they did not warn me they were going to try. Threats are cheap, Yessica. What did your message actually say?"

She fluttered and eventually sat on the sofa. She closed her eyes as she remembered. "Your German friend is too inquisitive. Persuade him to leave Robert and Marianne Newton undisturbed in their grave, and leave

203

Gideon Smith alone. If you do, we will not contact you again. If he ignores you, we will reinforce our displeasure at his expense." Her eyes opened. "I wrote it down, then memorised it."

"More of the same from my call. 'Do not meddle or things will go badly for you.'"

"What do we do?"

"Do? What do you want to do? Two people are dead, one is missing. The man in the Newcastle hospital acts as if he were deaf and dumb. We receive phone calls that threaten me. This is not a nice little search for cross-tattooed mystics and an ancient sword: it never was. I will continue; what do you wish to do?"

Margaret fell sideways into the sofa. "I've got enough problems at work with pushers and petty thieves, without having to worry about secret societies trying to kill me at home."

"They threatened me, not you."

"I'm sure they're very careful about that distinction. Torsten, these people, whoever they are, mean business. You don't muck around with the end of the world."

"I will leave if you want me to."

"No, no. Don't be stupid." She cast up a hand to the back of the seat and caught his fingers in hers. "This just isn't what I expected, that's all. I was so looking forward to seeing you again."

"And I brought the Apocalypse with me. Sorry, Yessica."

She patted his hand. "You do what you have to. I'll be here when you need me."

"Have your bath, Yessica." He opened his book and began to look for his place.

"*Jawohl*, Inspector."

Neubauer glanced over the top of the page. "No one says *jawohl* any more. It is like saying groovy."

Dinner was interrupted by a knock at the door. Margaret frowned and her eyes flicked over the montage that was beginning to crawl over the living room wall: photos, copies of newspapers, names written large on strips of coloured paper, pinned to the wall and connected by strands of different-coloured wool.

"If I had visitors, they'd buzz the intercom by the front door."

"Another resident?" said Neubauer. He laid down his knife and fork.

"Perhaps," she said.

"Use the safety chain."

"Cheer me up, why don't you?"

She went to the door, and fixed the chain in its groove. "Who is it?" she asked, her hand on the latch.

The voice travelled clearly through the thickness of wood. "Mr Ambrose, Sergeant Margaret. I'll slide my card through."

She looked down and watched as the white business card poked from underneath her door. She pulled it the rest of the way with her fingertips and read the embossed writing.

"M Ambrose, Esq. Collector and Freelance Historian". That was all it said.

Neubauer joined her, and she handed him the card. He shook his head to indicate he'd never heard of him.

"What's your business, Mr Ambrose?" she called.

"It says on the card, Sergeant." The voice sounded quite cheerful, and slightly Welsh.

"I've never heard of a freelance historian before," Margaret hissed at Neubauer.

Neubauer edged forward. "Mr Ambrose, what is it that you collect?"

"Information, *Herr Inspektor*."

Margaret's eyes grew dark. "He knows us," she whispered.

"All too well. Yet he is not threatening, not like the others." He was puzzled. "What did he say to your question?"

"Which one?"

"What is your business, you said. It is on the card, he replied." He poised the card in front of his face, and flicked it over between his fingers. On the reverse was a hand-drawn Newton cross.

Margaret stepped back against the hallway wall, her hand against her heart.

Neubauer blinked several times. The card was still there. "Mr Ambrose? We are going to let you in now."

"Most kind." The wait appeared not to have dampened the man's enthusiasm.

Neubauer slipped the chain and twisted the Yale. Beyond the door was a man of indeterminate age, with short curls of brown hair and the most peculiar golden eyes he'd ever seen. He was tall, and hid a wiry athleticism beneath an ankle-length coat of battered brown leather. He carried a matching hat in his hands.

"Please, come in."

"Thank you, Inspector. Good evening, Detective Sergeant. A pleasure to make your acquaintance." He offered a hand and she slowly lowered hers from her chest to shake with him.

Ambrose strode through to the lounge, and looked carefully about him with his odd eyes. He took in the half-full plates. "I've spoilt your meal. My apologies."

"May I take your coat, Mr Ambrose?" Neubauer offered.

206

"Nah, nah." Ambrose waved him away. "I have a train to catch and can't stay long." The man's attention was attracted by the wall montage. His eyes ate up the connections and the nodes.

"Good," was his appraisal. "Sparse, but a good start. Congratulations, Inspector. If I might make one slight adjustment?"

He waited for Neubauer's stammered permission, then approached the wall. He teased out the picture from the asylum book and moved it to the far left, where he repositioned it in splendid isolation.

"Much better."

"But, in time, that page is well after the theology book," objected Neubauer.

"Stop thinking chronologically, Inspector. Think symbolically." Ambrose took his card from Neubauer's unresisting fingers and pinned it to the wall in the space vacated by the photograph.

"How can we help you, Mr Ambrose?" Margaret had finally found her voice. "You seem to know everything about us anyway."

"You've nothing to fear from me, rest assured, Jessica Margaret. I wish nothing but every blessing from the Good God on your endeavour. And you can help me in ways even I fail to understand at this moment in time. But this is your quest, not mine, although we journey towards the same destination. I'm here to help you, as unlikely as it seems." He smiled a crinkly, weather-beaten smile and played with the rim of his hat with his strong fingers.

Margaret couldn't look into Ambrose's eyes without thinking of a wolf.

"I'd prefer it if you thought of me as a hawk, Sergeant," he commented, and rendered her speechless and terrified. He tossed his hat on to a chair, raised his arms in a rustle of leather and spoke in his sing-song voice.

"I am the first of Albion, I am Cut-metal.

"Truth and Justice shall wield me, I divide light and dark.

"If I leave, destruction shall follow. Blessed be the name of the LORD."

He lowered his arms, and some of the fire left his eyes. Margaret was still walking backwards, and Neubauer was rooted to the spot. "Search well, search hard. You'll be deflected left and right, but you have to carry straight on to reach your goal. The way will be difficult and dangerous, but the rewards will more than compensate you for your troubles."

He smiled again, retrieved his hat and adjusted it on his head. "That's it; sermon over. I'll be off. Take very good care of yourselves and each other." He bowed slightly. "Goodnight."

He turned, and they heard the door click shut in the hall.

Neubauer put his arm around Margaret and guided her to the sofa.

"He read my mind," she whispered in fear and wonder.

"Sit down, Yessica."

"He read my mind, Torsten. He knew what I was thinking and he replied to me."

Neubauer awkwardly lowered her rigid body down.

"Who was he?" she asked.

"Freelance historian and collector." He was at a loss to say anything else.

"Mind-reader."

Simon Morden

"He knew the inscription. The true translation."
It sang in Neubauer's head. "He knows the Newton Cross.
Perhaps he knows everything."

"He knew what I was thinking," repeated
Margaret, shivering. "He does know everything."

Heart

Part IV

Wednesday 20th May to Monday 1st June 1987

Chapter 16
Wednesday 20th May 1987
Lancaster

Gideon Smith's story

April slid into May, and Gideon became hard: immune to the wind and the rain that wrenched at his clothing and saturated him to the skin. The soles of his feet grew calluses as hard as boiled leather, and he found he could walk from dawn til dusk. Every footstep carried him inevitably closer to the end of his search.

He carried everything he needed on his back and in his pockets. The contents of his rucksack were pared down and pared again, until he barely noticed the weight. What he owned, he needed by necessity, not by want.

Even Excalibur. Merlin had been right. He could not get rid of it if he tried. He was part of the story now, and even if the story proved to be false, it was still worth believing in. The sword sat in its sacking wraps, sometimes tied to the rucksack by straps, sometimes carried by hand. But always a part of him.

In the moonlight, he would unwrap the sword and hold it. He thought he was practising thrusts, parries and sweeps with its liquid silver blade, but in reality he was dancing with it, spinning a pattern on the ground that he would have recognised as Marianne's from the nightclub, if only he had known. He spent hours in a magical celebration of something that was greater than his dreams. The sword talked to him, and he listened without having to hear.

To start with, he avoided people and their places. After a while, he found that he needed them, needed to talk about the weather and the price of fish. Gideon came

Heart

back, and as he talked over garden gates, and in pubs and cafés, he was asked where he was going.

"I don't know; someplace else," he would answer. "I'm looking for something."

It begged the question: "What's that?"

And Gideon would reply, "I don't know. But I've been told that I'll know it when I find it. It's a great secret, but if I keep looking for it, I'll learn what it is."

Sometimes they'd laugh and say: "Come back and tell me what this secret is."

Gideon would shake his head. "It's not something you can be told. I'll come back and I'll tell you where to look."

Sometimes they'd mock him and call him crazy. He'd quietly finish his meal and his drink, and leave.

And sometimes ...

There was a man and a dog, and they were surrounded by what the tabloid press would call youths. There were six of them, shouting and pushing the man backwards and forwards, this way and that. The dog was barking, not angrily, but out of confusion, unable to understand what was going on. The man staggered under the weight of their hands, remaining upright but increasingly disorientated.

"Who hit you? Come on, guess!"

"Leave me alone!"

"Who's he talking to? Is it me? Don't you know it's rude not to look at someone when you're talking to them?"

"Stop pushing me!"

"Ask nicely."

"Can't you see I'm blind?"

"Blind, are you? I couldn't tell, could you?"

212

All this in the middle of a street pavement in a north-west town. Gideon was passing through, unlike the residents who lived and worked there. But only he walked briskly up the road and confronted the mob.

"You lot. Bugger off."

Six against one. Gideon's size cowed them briefly, but they could sense a fight. The dog, with its fluorescent yellow harness, carried on barking but never left her master's side.

"You talking to me?" said the cockiest boy, swaggering forward.

Gideon grabbed him by the throat, span him around and slammed his back up against a lamp post. "Aye lad. I'm talking to you."

The boy gagged and gasped, trying to find the floor with his feet. His hands pulled frantically at Gideon's fingers.

Aware of movement behind him, he called out. "I wouldn't if I were you." The shuffling of feet stopped. He left him dangling for a few moments more, then dropped him. The boy's spindly legs folded up underneath him and he fell into the gutter. Gideon turned around and looked at the five pale faces full of adolescent indecision.

"Still here? You're more stupid than I thought. Look at you, you cowards. One blind old man and his guide dog? Your mothers would be ashamed of the day you were born if they knew about this. If you don't get out of here now, I'll make bloody sure they do."

The boys started to edge backwards.

"And take this maggot with you." Gideon prodded the mewling, whining figure in the gutter with the toe of his boot.

Two came over, picked up their friend and they all hurried away. As they went, they looked over their shoulders, wearing black scowls.

"You all right, grandad?"

"I reckon. I've lost my cap."

Gideon looked around and saw it battered into the corner between the pavement and a garden wall. He retrieved it, knocked the dust out of it and guided it to the man's hands.

The man let go of the handle on the dog's harness and put the cap back over his thin grey hair. He wore blackened lenses in his wire-rimmed glasses and had shaved poorly. He was ancient, his face wrinkled like the skin of a prune, and his whole frame was spare like a scarecrow.

"Lucy?" he called, and the dog came to heel. The man bent down and felt for her harness again. Lucy stood up, her tail wagging and her tongue hanging out. "Thanks lad. A street full of people and only you came to help."

Gideon knelt to pet the retriever. "That's the way of it these days. You know them?"

"Those yobs?" He looked bitter. "I do. To think my friends died to protect the likes of them. It's a bit much at times."

"I can appreciate that."

"You're not from round here, are you?"

"Other side of the Pennines, by the long route. I'm looking for something and I have to walk to make sure I don't miss it."

"So what is it you're looking for. Is it a person?"

"I don't know. I've been told that I'll know it when I find it. It's a great secret, and if I keep looking for it, I'll discover what it is."

"Sounds like a fool's errand to me, lad. Who put you up to this?"

"Someone older than you."

"That would be something. Hah!" He tugged the peak of his cap down over his brows. "This walk of yours. I don't suppose it passes my front door."

"I reckon it could."

"Cup of tea and a slice of cake in it for you. Fortify you for the journey."

"Okay, grandad."

"Jack to you, lad. You got a name?"

"Gideon."

"Let's off home then and get the kettle on. Come on, Lucy. Home, girl."

Home was a one-room-wide terrace house, sandwiched between identical façades on an anonymous backstreet. It was as ordinary as it could be without trying; the paintwork was just as shabby as that of the houses on either side, the garden just as weedy, the path as uneven.

Lucy waited at the gate and Jack opened it. "Shut it behind you, lad. Keeps the other dogs out of the yard."

By the time Gideon had closed the latch and rattled it to make certain, Jack was at the front door, feeding the key into the lock. Inside, he hung up his coat, undid Lucy's harness, and hung it up on the next peg. He moved with such certainty that Gideon would have thought his host sighted except for the fact that the hall light stayed off when the front door was pushed to. Gideon found himself groping in the dark.

"Can I turn the light on?"

"Of course, lad. Sorry, Gideon. I forget, you know. Lose your backpack and make yourself at home. Living room's through that door there. I'll just put some water on to boil."

Gideon frowned, slipping the straps of his rucksack off his shoulders and unclipping the waist clinch. As it hit the floor, it clattered, and he realised that the old man must have heard the noises as he walked. He found the light with its metal switch and bakelite cover, and flicked it on with his thumb.

The hall was as narrow as he expected, with stairs up facing the door, a dog-leg through to the kitchen and a door on his right. The decoration was firmly mid-seventies, all orange flowered wallpaper and avocado paint.

He shucked his coat and unlaced his boots. He put them under the line of brass hooks, then thought better of it and took all his belongings through to the lounge and put them behind the sofa.

Again, everything in the room seemed to be caught in a ten-year timewarp. The closed curtains were sludge brown, and Gideon weaved his way around the heavy furniture to throw them open. The late-afternoon sunlight slanted in, illuminating the sideboard with its dusty arrangement of silk flowers, dark-framed photographs and an old steam radio. A mahogany standard lamp with a pink frilled shade stood in the corner.

On the low table in front of the sofa, there was a thick book made of cardboard. As he sat down, he picked it up. The spine had a sticky label with 'Radio Times' typed on it, and the current week's date. Curious, Gideon flipped the book open. Nothing but raised dots.

"I didn't realise you could get these."

"What's that then, lad? Is the table clear?"

"It is. I was looking at your *Radio Times*. I didn't know they did them in Braille."

"Right handy it is too." Jack placed the tray square down on the table. It was laden with cups, saucers, plates, teaspoons, a great wheel of fruitcake and a teapot shrouded in a vast woollen cosy. "I listen to the radio and the telly a fair bit, on me own as I am."

Gideon looked around for the television and saw the grey screen poking out from behind a chair. "They allow you anything off your licence?"

"A few pound," he laughed, and he felt his way into an armchair. "You can be mother."

They settled back to their tea and wedges of cake. "Baked by a lass down the Legion. She does them in batches and sells them at cost. They're grand, eh?"

"Not bad at all." Gideon looked around the room and its photographs. "You've family."

"A son and a daughter, and five grandchildren. Matthew, and his wife Lydia – that's them on the left of the sideboard. My Mary, that's my wife, she had a dicky fit when he told us who he was going to wed. But Lydia had a lovely smell and a voice like hot chocolate. I took to her straight off."

Gideon tracked down the wedding photograph. Lydia was a black Arab, tall and fine. There were further photos, some in colour, of the two in later years with an increasing number of raven-haired children.

"Did your Mary come around?"

"After a while. Took a few years, mind, but she relented in the end. Now, she wouldn't have a wrong word said about Julian, who married our June. He was oily then and he's oily now. Runs his own business and lots else besides: the golf club, Masonic lodge, other men's wives. His son's no better, a worse crook than his father, I swear, and he's only fourteen. Whenever he came here, he used to move things, furniture and the like, so I'd fall over them."

"I know what he needs."

"A bit late, I'd say. He's set in his ways now. June tried, bless her, but that husband of hers ruined the lad. Funny, really. Matthew and Lydia live in Algiers and visit as often as they can, and I haven't seen Julian or Damien for years, even though they live an hour down the road. June's a good sort, though. She does for me twice a week, most weeks. Aye, she's a grand lass, even if her choice of marriage partner left something to be desired."

He liked to talk, Gideon could tell.

"You got anybody?"

"I used to have a girlfriend, but she left me."

"Was that before or after your mission?"

"Before. She certainly wouldn't have understood what I'm doing now. I had a job, friends and a home. I had to give them all up."

"You don't sound very happy, lad. Why not just go back?"

"All sorts of reasons, some of them not very nice ones. I can't go back. I have to find out what this secret is and see where it leads me. I'm being taken where I don't want to go and shown things I don't want to see. I'm not sad, but I'm not happy."

"It was like that when I was sent to war. Forced to do things, see things that I had no business doing or seeing. There's a photograph hereabouts, of me and the rest of the Company. I think it was on the telly last."

Gideon got up and found the black and white photograph of men in battledress. "I've got it."

"That was before we were sent to the Med. Within a year, they were all dead and I was blind. Ever hear about the fall of Crete?"

"Can't say I have."

"We were to hold the island. Then when the Germans sent in their paratroopers and bombers, we were told to hold the line while our lads were taken off back to Egypt. What line? We were carved up like a Sunday roast, a bit at a time. We could have no more defended Crete than we could have a sandcastle against the tide. I was left with half my platoon, four lads under nineteen, scared witless by the Stukas and all for throwing in the towel. But I was Corporal and I had responsibilities. I had to shout at them to do as they were ordered. I told them I'd see them right, and they'd be having a pennyworth of chips back in Blackburn within the month.

"The Greek resistance found us before the Germans did, which we thought was lucky at the time. They loved us like brothers, and died trying to get us off that island. So did the four young'uns. The dive bomber that blew them up blinded me. I got shrapnel in the face, see. Not so's you'd notice now, the skin's healed, but it hit both eyes as well. By the time they'd got me to Malta, there was infection in them, and they had to take them out to save the rest of me. Last thing I ever saw was this bright flash and my lads cut down. When I got back to Blighty, they told me I was the only one of the whole Company to survive. Perhaps we should have surrendered."

"You had to try."

"Maybe I did. Maybe I didn't. Well," Jack said, rattling his cup and saucer together on the arm of the chair, "they're all gone and that's that." He sneezed and groped in his pocket for a cloth handkerchief.

Gideon looked at the photo again, at all the faces that were unique under their identical berets. Officers and men, lost in dribs and drabs across an island filled with chaos forty-six years ago, and still staring out from behind their glass cover.

The image flickered briefly to show the men and women who had carried the sword. Equally dead, equally lost, forgotten by all except Merlin. Their sacrifice, like Jack's companions', cost everything, and they had vanished as history swallowed them up.

Jack had survived, blind, and Gideon carried the sword, ignorant of the secret of the heart.

Jack sneezed again.

Heart

"Are you feeling okay?"

"I think I might be going down with something." He trumpeted his nose vigorously. "I've been a bit off colour the last day or so."

"I'll pour you another cup of tea. Do you need some aspirin?"

"There's some paracetamol in the bathroom, if you could fetch it down for me. I feel a bit warm."

Gideon stayed that night, after putting the old man to bed and taking Lucy out for an evening walk around the streets. He called in at a corner fish and chip shop.

"What've you done with Jack?" the man behind the counter asked.

"He's in bed with a cold. I suppose I'm looking after him in a way."

They negotiated for a bag of chips, and Lucy looked expectantly at the wrapped parcel.

"Give him my regards, lad," said the man, giving Gideon his change. "Tell him I'll see him in when he's feeling better."

He and Lucy ate the chips on the way back. He slept on the floor, on top of the cushions from the sofa. It was strange, looking up and not seeing the sky.

Chapter 17
Saturday 23rd May 1987
Lancaster

Gideon Smith's story

Jack was three days in bed. Gideon got used to the routine of cooking, shopping and walking the dog. He'd managed to weed the front garden, sweep the path, and scrub down the back yard. He was in the garden, rooting out dandelions from the square of grass, when Jack appeared at the front door in his dressing gown.

"How're you feeling?"

"Not so bad, lad. I reckon I've had enough of laying in bed."

"That's a good sign. Go and sit down, and I'll brew up. June called earlier on the phone. She said she'd be here tomorrow about ten. She would have been round today, but there was something up with Damien; that's the son, right?"

"Aye. I wonder what bother she's trying to get him out of now?"

"She wouldn't say, at least not to me. I'll put the kettle on." Gideon got to his feet and followed Jack down the hall. "Anything on the telly tonight?"

"I'll have a look."

Jack opened the Braille book and ran his finger across the pages while Gideon went through to the kitchen and arranged the tea things on a tray, just like Jack would.

"There's a comedy on at nine. I listened to it last week and wouldn't mind more of the same."

"Sure. Fancy fish and chips for your tea?"

"That'd be grand. You are taking money from my purse for all this, aren't you?"

Gideon jiggled the teapot. "What was that?"

"You heard. What are you doing for cash?"

He brought the tray through and rested it on the table. "One thing I'm not short of is money. The first thing I did when I realised I was never going back was to clear out my bank accounts and savings, and closed the lot. I've a few thousand on me. It'll last a while."

"That's as maybe, but you need to be careful with it or it'll be gone. Dinner's on me, lad. I insist."

They settled down to their fish supper a few minutes before nine. Gideon had pushed the television in front of the fireplace so that he could see it as well as Jack hear it. The programme had lots of word play and wit, with only a few purely visual gags that Gideon had to explain. After it was over, he cleared away the plates and refreshed the pot. The television continued to drone away in the background with a documentary.

"So what's this?" asked Gideon when he came back in.

Jack felt for his cup. "A biography of Lord Golden. He's a government minister in the Lords'."

"Oh aye?" Gideon could feel himself glazing over.

"He says some sensible things sometimes. I take it you don't have much time for politicians?"

"Can't say I've ever given it much thought. Put the cross in the box at the right time and forget about in between. As long as they leave me alone, I don't really mind who's in. Now I can't vote, it doesn't matter at all, even with the election a fortnight away."

"I don't know if I'll bother this time. I don't trust Labour and I don't like Maggie. A vote for the other lot's a waste of time round here. Maybe I'll just spoil my ballot paper." Jack smiled mischievously.

"You're feeling better."

"I reckon."

Gideon was distracted by the television. The narrator had mentioned Crete. "Here, Jack. The man says Golden was on Crete in the war."

"A nice safe posting in HQ, I'll wager."

"No, listen."

The narrator continued, speaking over dusty archive footage of the battle for Crete: "... invasion. Lord Golden, then a young lieutenant, was cut off from the main retreat and forced to lead his platoon into the mountains to evade capture. In the ensuing weeks, German planes and foot patrols scoured the island for British and Commonwealth soldiers that had been left behind. Some were found and taken to PoW camps. Some were never heard of again; unproved rumours of mass graves persist to this day.

"In Lord Golden's case, he was the only man from his Company to escape. While negotiating with the Greek resistance leaders for a boat to take him and his men to Egypt, his platoon was surrounded in the barn where they were hiding. In the fight that followed, the barn caught fire and they were all killed."

"That's just like your story," said Gideon.

The screen changed to a photograph of young men arranged for a formal picture.

"That's just like your picture, too."

"What's that?"

The camera dallied on the men. "It is your photograph. Your Company; he was in your Company."

"What're you saying?"

The picture narrowed and focused on a man in peaked cap, seated in the front row.

"Hush a minute." Gideon snatched up the frame from the top of the television and held it next to the flickering image on the cathode-ray tube. He searched the faces. "That's him."

Heart

The narrator carried on, speaking about the lieutenant's escape from Crete and repatriation in Alexandria.

"Gideon?"

"They showed your photograph on the telly, the one of your Company back in 1940. Golden was in your unit."

"No, he wasn't," said Jack. "No Lieutenant Golden in 2 Company."

"It was the same picture. Golden's in it."

"Hang on, lad." Jack became indignant. "You can't tell me that there was someone in my Company I didn't know about."

"That's what the programme said. Golden was an officer in your Company, and he was the only survivor."

"Rot. I was the only one out, and I was blind."

Gideon sat back on his heels in front of the screen, still clutching the photograph. "Why would they make a mistake like that? Surely Golden should have put them right."

"All I know is that it isn't true. They can't go changing things like this. Where did they say this man was sitting?"

Looking again at the picture, Gideon located the thin-faced man with piercing light eyes. "Second from the left, front row."

"That was Sutton. Lieutenant Sutton. He never sailed with us, mind. He was ill when we left for the Med." Jack's hands had developed a tremor. "What are they going to say down at the Legion? They're going to think me a liar, after all these years."

The rest of the documentary had their full attention.

Sunday 24th May 1987

That night, Gideon phoned the BBC's duty desk and left a message for the senior researcher.

Shortly after nine the next day, the call was returned.

"Mallory Porlock, BBC," said the fruity voice, "A Mr Smith left a message with the duty officer. He said it was urgent."

"I'm Smith." Gideon sat himself down next to the phone. "You did the Lord Golden programme last night, didn't you?"

"I did indeed, Mr Smith." There was a pregnant pause. "What did you think?"

"I was fascinated, Mr Porlock."

Porlock warmed to his subject. "He's a most intriguing character. He's done so much, too; I could have done five hours on him rather than just the one. He was very generous with his private papers. Between you and me, I don't think it's done the government's chances any harm at all."

Gideon steered him back to the point. "You got most of your material from him?"

"Directly and in person. It was a great privilege to meet the man. I checked the facts, of course, as any diligent student would."

"Like his Crete story?"

Porlock hesitated, very much the old hand. "What are you driving at, Mr Smith?"

"Did you check whether or not he'd ever been on Crete? Did you see his name on any MoD records?" Gideon held the photograph up in front of him, to look at it one more time.

"It would have been War Office then. What are you going to tell me?"

"You showed a picture of the 2nd Company, 4th Lancashire Light Infantry. Golden was never in that Company."

"He was in the front row."

"I think you'll find that was Lieutenant Sutton."

There was silence for a good ten seconds. "Who? Mr Smith, can I ask you what you base this on?"

"The man in the back row, fourth from the right, told me."

"Ah, no. Mr Smith. I'm afraid you've been misled. There was no other survivor from that Company. They were all killed in the war. It was on the programme, you know."

"I listened very carefully to what was said. There was only one survivor from Crete, you're correct in that regard. But it was Corporal Jack Bassenthwaite. He escaped to Malta where he spent the next three years. I have in my hand the very same photo you used last night and I can see him with his stripes on his arm."

"But ..."

"Jack was told when he got back to Britain that he was the only one to get out alive. He accepted that at face value, lived with it all these years. Now he hears that someone else takes that claim, and it's someone he's never served with." Gideon bent over the phone. "I wouldn't bother you. It's a politician embroidering his past to make his present look grander. But, for Jack, this is important to him. He's an old man now, and he's upset. He takes the view that it's dishonouring dead men's names."

"This corporal, this Jack. He saw the programme?"

"He heard it. He's blind and has been since Crete. He can name every man on that photograph. Most of them were his neighbours and friends, his foremen and his bosses. Where you said Lord Golden was, he says it was

Sutton, who didn't even sail with them from Southampton. Sutton had pneumonia and had to stay behind. He remembers, Mr Porlock, he remembers everything. He's told people his story, and they're going to think him a liar."

"Yes, Mr Smith. I can see that. No Golden in the regiment at all?"

"He can't say for certain about the whole of the 4th Lancs. But as for 2 Company, definitely not. You've made a mistake."

"This is quite serious, you know," said Porlock. "Lord Golden is a very senior man, and his reputation could suffer severely. Can I come and see this man? Talk to him about this?"

"I'm sure that'd be no problem."

"Where are you?"

"Lancaster."

"Would you meet me at the station if I tell you which train I'll be on?"

"Sure."

"I'll call again tomorrow with a time. Thank you, Mr Smith. I'm certain we can sort out this misunderstanding for the benefit of all concerned, but if you'd keep mum for the moment, I'd very much appreciate it. Careless talk, eh, Mr Smith?"

"What did he say?"

"He says he's coming up to talk to you. He sounded worried."

"So he should," said Jack firmly.

"Tell me about Sutton."

"I didn't know him that well; he wasn't one of the local volunteers. He wasn't a nice man, I can tell you that much, always ready to pull you up for not having your kit in order, or giving a sloppy salute. Sometimes, he'd order you to do something against the rules, then put you on a charge when you refused. He was malicious, but too much of a coward to be brutal. Some of the sergeant-majors could break a man and leave them a gibbering wreck. No, he was just disliked, not hated. A lot of the officers were only young lads who didn't have a clue about leading men to war. Thank God for the NCOs who wiped their noses and tucked in their shirt-tails." Jack sighed. "Some turned out all right, some went completely to pieces. Sutton never made it to the Med, so I can't say how he would have taken it."

"This photograph; when was it taken?" Gideon put it carefully back on the television set.

"Late 1940. October? First week of October, I reckon. It was perishing cold anyhow. We sailed for Athens a week later."

"And Sutton? What happened to him?"

"He was ill when the photo was taken. No penicillin in those days, of course – that came a year or so later. I never saw nor heard of him from that day on. He was in hospital by the evening. We could have done with him, too, even if it was just to get in the way of a bullet. He wasn't replaced, and we were spread as thin as a ration of butter. Never had enough men to fill the gaps."

"Don't get morbid, Jack. June'll be here in a minute."

"Aye, lad, you're right. This whole episode brings back memories, not all of them pleasant. They were good lads, they were. Good lads."

The doorbell chimed.

"That'll be June, Gideon. Could you let her in?"

"Sure."

Gideon went to the front door and heaved it open. Outside was a small, timid woman, laden with bulging carrier bags. Her ash-blonde bob seemed cut specifically to hide her face from onlookers.

"Can I take some of your bags?" he asked.

"If you like," she said, and allowed Gideon to lift a pair of handles from each hand.

"Shall I take them through to the kitchen?"

"If you could."

"Of course I can." Gideon was beginning to think that melancholy ran in the family.

"I met the postman at the gate. There are some letters in one of those bags."

"I'll sort it out. You go and say hello to your Dad."

He rustled his way into the kitchen and deposited the bags on the floor. Lucy appeared promptly and began to nose expectantly at the plastic. Gideon pulled out a can. "Look, girl. Dog food!"

Lucy's tail batted a cupboard door in five-four time.

He found the envelopes in the other bag, then moved all the shopping to a work surface. In the living room, June and her father were exchanging family chit-chat.

"Garden's looking nice."

"Gideon were doing it yesterday, weren't you, lad?"

"No bother. Doesn't take long."

June looked at him from under her fringe. She would have been pretty if she had had the energy to smile. "Thank you anyway. Dad, your post's here."

"Anything interesting?"

Gideon flicked through the pile. "Electricity bill by the look of it. A couple of bits of junk mail, and a postcard."

"Who's it from?"

"I don't know." He turned it over, and stayed silent.

"What?"

"It's addressed to me." He looked at the card long and hard, daring it.

"Who knows you're here?" Jack adjusted himself in his chair, moving forwards. "What does it say?"

Gideon read the short message and kept it to himself. "It's from a friend who promised to keep in touch. Marianne always knows where to find me." He looked at the picture on the front of the card, then turned back over for the caption: St Simeon's, Middleton-cum-Marchbury. "I'll go and put the kettle on, shall I?"

"Aye, lad. I need to tell June about our news."

"What news is this, Dad?"

"There's a television reporter coming to see me."

"What have you been getting up to?" June's face stiffened.

"I'll go and make the tea." Gideon absented himself from the room, but could still hear the voices coming through the open door. He was warming the pot when June appeared by his shoulder.

"I hope that you're not going to upset him."

"It's not me who's upset him. He told you what was said on the programme."

"Yes."

"I'm just helping him to sort it out, that's all." He tipped water down the sink and fetched the tea caddy from the shelf.

"I don't know who you are and that worries me, you being here in Dad's house."

"You think I'm taking advantage of him? I didn't mean to stay this long. I've a journey and I need to get on with it. But Jack was ill, so I looked after him. Then this TV business blew up. I'll go when it's done."

"And in the meantime, you're living in his house and eating his food."

Gideon opened the cupboards. They were full. "I paid for all this. In fact, the only thing Jack's paid for was for last night's fish supper. I've walked Lucy, I've cleaned, cooked, weeded the garden, and if I'd the time, I'd slap some paint around outside. I'm not here for my benefit."

"That's all well and good, but what do you want?"

"Nothing, except Jack's peace of mind. It's good that you're concerned about him, but he's your Dad, not your son."

"What about my son?" She was starting to snap suspiciously.

"Nothing at all. I'm just saying Jack's quite capable of making his own trouble. He doesn't need my help."

She didn't look convinced. They sat in silence as they drank their tea.

"This is daft," said Gideon, putting down his cup and getting to his feet. "I've no desire to come between father and daughter. June, no matter what I say, you won't believe me. I'll take my leave."

"No, lad. This is my home, paid for by the sweat of my own brow. If I say you're welcome in my home for as long as you like, you'll stay put and not get chased out."

June stared at her father; she hadn't seen him so animated for years.

Gideon stood there, watching their faces. June's eyes were probing Jack's impenetrable expression. "I'll take Lucy for a walk in the park, and let you two have it out."

The dog ran around for an hour like a dervish. She retrieved all the sticks that he threw, and nosed around the bases of trees in search of interesting smells. He wandered along, hands in his pockets, content to let Lucy go where she wanted. Then he called her back and slipped her lead on.

June had left by the time he returned.

"Sorry, Jack," he said.

"It's not your fault, lad. She treats all men like they were her husband – untrustworthy. She said she had to get back home, to see Damien, but it was only half the truth. I didn't force it. The little yob's been caught shoplifting again." Jack frowned and dislodged his glasses from the bridge of his nose. He pushed them back up again. "He needs tying up, he does. That Porlock man called. Can you meet him off the nine forty-three tomorrow morning?"

"Sure. Jack, what else is there? You're looking shifty."

"I've never asked before. Are you in trouble with the police?"

Gideon sat down. "June's done well. I could lie to you. I could say that I've done nothing that the police want me for. But that wouldn't be true. I think I killed a man."

"You think? Either you did or you didn't."

"Like I was going to hang around. He was trying to shoot me at the time. There was one at the front door, one at the back. I was outnumbered and scared. So I hid by the back door and ran one of them through with a sword I just happened to have on me."

"What had you done, that these men wanted to shoot you?"

"They came to steal the sword from me. I'd been given it for free, and they were going to take it by force. I'm not proud of any of this. Jack, you know what war's like, don't you?"

"Better than most, lad."

"I've never been in one, until now. I have to hang on to the sword, or one half of the country will kill the other half. That's where this secret comes in, the secret of the heart." Gideon made a decision and reached behind the sofa to his rucksack. He put the sacking parcel on his lap and unknotted the string. "This is what they're after. Hold out your hands."

Jack reluctantly held out one hand then the other.

"It's heavy, but don't worry about dropping it. It's bomb-proof." He laid Excalibur gently across the old man's trembling palms.

Open-mouthed, Jack explored the shape. He rested it across the arms of his chair after checking the length, and ran his fingertips up and down the blade. He traced the inscription with a fingernail, then trailed down the hilt and felt the knots of jewels and metal. He wrapped his bony fingers around the grip and thrust his arm aloft, narrowly missing the light fitting.

Gideon leaned forward and pressed down on Jack's wrist. "Try not to wreck the place."

"This is something else, lad. Beautifully weighted; you could cut down trees with this. It's polished smooth, cut and worked. Real craftsmanship, this."

"Definitely one of a kind."

"No wonder they're after this. Bet it's as bright as a new pin."

"Like a mirror."

Jack waved the sword slowly in front of him. "What does the writing say? It's not in English."

Gideon laughed. "No. A lost language, known only to a few. I've a very rough translation, which doesn't make sense, but it does tell you the sword's name."

"A name? That's a bit odd."

"The name's Excalibur."

Jack put down the sword very quickly and seemed reluctant to touch it again. His hand would reach forward hesitantly, then draw back. "Who told you that?"

"Merlin the magician."

"Are you mad, lad?"

"I wish I was. I wouldn't have dreamed of believing him, but first he put his hand into my stomach and pulled out my diseased appendix, all without the aid of a knife. He knew everything: how I got the sword, what I'd done with it. I'll just have to go along with him until I can prove him a liar."

"He must be a charlatan. Think about it, Gideon!" Jack was outraged.

"I know. It's too much to ask a man to take in. But he explained it like this: if he's wrong or right, it makes no difference. The ones who want to take the sword believe it's Excalibur. You can't dissuade them, no matter what. They'd kill me because they think they're right."

"That's a bit rough, lad."

"That's my lot. I have to deal with it the best I can. It's a bit like being sent to the Front, I suppose."

"Makes this business with Porlock seem a bit tame. I wonder what he'd make of it?"

"He's never to find out. You have to promise me that."

"Aye, all right. Not a word." He ruminated for a few minutes and reached out to stroke the sword. "That postcard you had. Was that from this Merlin character?"

"No, no. That's from Marianne. She's been dead for almost two years, but she gets around a bit. And she tells me things are not as they seem."

Monday 25th May 1987

Gideon met Mallory Porlock at the station on a damp and breezy morning. The train out of Liverpool was late arriving, and he had to stand around for half an hour, drinking British Rail tea.

The diesel trundled in, squealed its brakes to the sound of an apology over the tannoy, and shuddered to a halt. The doors flipped open and about twenty people disembarked; a mixture of suitcases, satchels and carrier bags followed them off.

Gideon held up his make-shift sign, a piece of cereal-packet cardboard with 'Porlock' biroed on. He needn't have bothered, since he spotted the man long before the BBC researcher found him. He was wearing a green velvet jacket a size too small, a yellow cravat of such enormous proportions that threatened to swallow his head whole, and scuffed brown suede shoes. Gideon waved; Porlock lifted his battered briefcase in acknowledgement and weaved his way towards him.

"Mr Porlock?" Gideon transferred the sign and the tea to his left hand, and extended his right.

Porlock had a vigorous shake, pumping his hand up and down enthusiastically. "Mr Smith, a pleasure to meet you. Mr Bassenthwaite's not here, is he?"

"I left him at home. He doesn't mind travelling around, but he's had a cold the past few days and it takes a while to get over it at his age."

"Absolutely understandable, old chap. Shall we hop in a taxi or do you have transport?"

"I came in on the bus."

"Ho to the taxi rank, then. Dear old Auntie's paying, so we must accept all the fruits the licence payers provide, bless them."

They started out of the station and settled in the back of a saloon-car cab. Gideon gave the address, and the driver clicked his meter on as the wheels gathered speed.

235

Porlock leaned over and in a stage whisper said: "The old man. He is all there, isn't he?"

Gideon frowned at the line of questioning. "Apart from his eyes, yes. He's as alert as you or I. He's not even particularly frail, even though he's nearly seventy. Don't worry; he hasn't dragged you up here on a wild goose chase."

"Hmm." Porlock played with his cravat. "Doesn't it strike you as curious, though? This whole episode, that the only man who can gainsay Lord Golden is blind?"

"I don't believe in coincidences, Mr Porlock, not any more."

"Please, call me Mallory. But that's a fascinating view. You're a fatalist, then?"

"I wouldn't know," said Gideon, unsure as to what a fatalist believed. "I think there's a greater plan; if there's a coincidence, it's because I don't understand where it fits in the plan."

Porlock changed the subject. "Your man has a photograph."

"The photograph. They're identical."

"Hmm. I'll have to compare the two, of course. I've a copy with me." He tapped the briefcase on his lap.

"I can't see a blind man spending much time altering forty-year-old photos. Did you do any checking on Lieutenant Sutton? Any records exist?"

"No record at all on the 4th Lancs. They've ceased to be." He gave a tight smile. "Both the regiment and the records."

"Is that usual?"

"No, but it happens. A lost file here, a misplaced record there."

"And a whole regiment goes missing."

"Another of your coincidences, Mr Smith. You do have a first name, don't you?"

"Gideon."

"Well, Gideon, the records just aren't there."

"So it seems." Gideon leaned forward and tapped the taxi driver on the shoulder. "This is it, here. Just set us down on the right."

The driver pulled in, and Porlock paid with a crisp note. He asked for a receipt and was grudgingly supplied with one.

Jack had been listening for a car and had come to the front door. Lucy peered out from between his legs, wagging her tail.

"Jack Bassenthwaite? An extreme pleasure to meet you," called Porlock.

"Mr Porlock," replied Jack. He had put his cap on to come to the entrance of his own house and he tugged the brim.

"Please, call me Mallory. No need for all this formality, is there? Hello, girl." He patted Lucy and shook Jack's hand in the same exuberant manner as he had attacked Gideon. "Shall we adjourn inside? It's a most frightful day out."

"Gideon? Kettle on, lad. I'll show Mr Porlock into the front room."

"Mallory," he was reminded.

"Aye, Mallory." A note of distrust had crept into Jack's voice.

"I don't know about you, lad, but I'm fair exhausted."

Gideon blew out a funnel of air. "Well, he wears me out. What did you think?"

"It came down to this: I was right and he was wrong, no two ways about it. I reckon, at the end, he accepted that. The man in the photograph is Sutton, not Golden."

Taking a fresh cup of tea from the pot, Gideon stirred in some sugar. "So why is Golden pretending to be someone else? What earthly reason would he have?"

"It's obvious, lad. Make himself look better. I always thought highly of him, too. Someone as well respected as him doing something like this. Lying, I mean. That's what it is, isn't it?"

"It's that all right. He must have found out that there were no records and that your Company had been completely lost. He could have his pick of names, and there'd be none to say it wasn't so."

Jack scrubbed at his chin. "I've a mind to ask him what he really did during the war. Or get a reporter to ask for me."

"Which side do you photograph best from?"

"They'd be better off taking a picture of Lucy. Far prettier."

Gideon picked up the postcard from Marianne that was still lying on the coffee table. "Things are not as they seem," he said, and blinked slowly several times. "Jack?"

"Aye, lad?"

"What are we missing here?" He looked at the picture of the church. He'd never heard of Middleton-cum-Marchbury until yesterday.

"What d'you mean?"

"Suppose for a moment that Golden isn't pretending to be Sutton." He tapped the card on the table, edge on. "What if it's the other way round? What if Sutton is pretending to be Golden?"

"Eh?"

His mind was plugging together suspicion and supposition. "What if Sutton is using Golden's name and title? What's just occurred to me is that the picture of

238

Sutton in 1940 looks like Golden does now. If it was a different person, would they look so alike?"
   "Perhaps. Time changes you."
   "It could be a coincidence, after all."

   Mallory Porlock was found dead on a railway line outside Birmingham that afternoon. He'd fallen from the door of his high-speed train, and an inquiry was set up to look into his case and others like it. The inquiry eventually blamed the locks for being faulty, weak under pressure and likely to spring open if leaned on. It had been a tragic accident.

Heart

Chapter 18
Thursday 28th May 1987
Middleton-cum-Marchbury, Warwickshire

Gideon Smith's story

Gideon let his rucksack down on to the platform, then followed it carefully. The surface of the step was wet, and the gap between the train and the concrete kerb of the platform edge was wider than it ought to be.

The station was no more than a glorified bus shelter. There were two signs to give the place a name, and an exceedingly short timetable tied to the gatepost with plastic clips. Once upon a time, judging from the stumps of foundations poking through the ground, it had had a waiting room, a signal box and a ticket office. Now it had been reduced to two prefabricated huts, one on each side of the twin tracks. The train that had stopped there ran twice a day, and he was the only person visible when it pulled away. It sounded like a bus as it chugged away, a thin stream of black smoke whistling from the sooty exhausts.

The sun came out briefly, hot and sharp in his face and made him squint. Then it was obscured by translucent cloud high in the heavens. It was robbed of its power and left a cold moon in a grey sky.

Gideon unzipped a pocket on his rucksack and pulled out a new Ordnance Survey map. He unfolded it under cover of the concrete shelter and pinpointed his position: the black dot that was almost exactly in the middle of nowhere. He'd asked about buses at the last main station and the man in the booth had laughed.

He looked up and judged where north was. He had fifteen miles to go, and it would be dark by the time he got to Middleton-cum-Marchbury. He folded up the

240

map and tucked it away in his coat's long pocket. He
threw on his rucksack and Excalibur shifted. He reached
behind himself to make sure it was held fast.

He started his journey as he always did, by
putting one foot in front of the other and repeating the
exercise until he'd done.

At the crossroads, he was confused. The white-
painted post with three name arrows was wrong. The sign
to Middleton, seven miles, was pointing in precisely the
opposite direction to which it ought. The correct turning
that went down to the valley below through tall-hedged
lanes wasn't indicated at all. Seven miles was a long way
to travel only to find it had been a mistake. Gideon
consulted his map in the dying light, and trusted that
rather than the evidence of his eyes.

He took the right route. With the lights of the
village flickering through the trees in the near dark, he
climbed a fence into a wood and propped himself up
against a tree to sleep.

Friday 29th May 1987

There was a dense, low-lying mist the next
morning that wreathed the tree trunks and obscured the
lie of the land. Gideon set out his stove to boil some water,
and scrutinised his map once more.

He assumed he was by the bend in the road just
before the village proper. He would have to cut across the
fields opposite him and into the woods beyond for a
distance of four miles. There were roads and a long
driveway, but for reasons he couldn't put his finger on, he
wanted his first views of Middleton Grange to be quiet
and unobserved. Later, he'd go into the village and find
some old people, someone who'd been around, who had

known Golden as a young man. They would be able to tell him the things he needed to know.

He made some coffee to the sound of roosting jackdaws, and drank it black. He was used to the feeling when sleeping rough of waking up damp and stiff, and he knew how to dispel it with a hot drink and a brisk five minutes of stretching. He packed up the stove as soon as it was cool, and rinsed out the bottom of his mug.

He checked his watch: ten to seven. It was time to move off. He shouldered his pack and climbed back over the fence, across the deserted road and through the gate in the hedgerow. Shrouded by the fog and hidden by a bramble hedge, he made good time. He passed around the outside of a field of long green grass, and another that contained cowpats and bullocks. They loomed, lowing, from the white mist, staring at the interloper with their huge brown eyes.

Gideon carried on, moving silently, leaving nothing but footprints in the dew to mark his passing. He arrived at a high stone wall, brick with a capping of brown sandstone. The wall was as tall as he, and he guessed that it marked the start of the estate grounds. He pushed his rucksack over the wall, then levered himself up.

He was surrounded by cold, dark, damp trees. Next to the wall, the undergrowth was as tangled as gale-blown hair. It took him several minutes to sort himself out and move into clearer ground, where the trees weren't so tightly packed and the brambles grew in clumps rather than a creeping, knee-deep carpet.

The foliage above and around him deadened all sound, even his own clumsy attempts at stealth. Underfoot, the ground rustled and sighed, but never cracked or snapped. Despite it nearly being high summer, all Gideon could smell was decay and neglect. It might have looked different with the sun dappling the ground

242

with cool shade, but not that morning. It was as still and gloomy as an abandoned house.

It took forever to get to the edge of the wood. Finally, tired and frustrated, Gideon settled down at the treeline between the branches of a large and leafy rhododendron bush. He opened the top of his rucksack and found the binoculars. They were new, still in the shop carrier bag. He opened the case, removed the caps to all the lenses, then put the eyepieces to his face. Twirling the focus with his index finger brought the Georgian edifice of Middleton Grange through the fog.

The house lay on the other side of the valley to him, across open parkland studded with mature chestnut trees. He could make out a formal garden leading down from the house to the river, and a stone bridge crossing at the lowest point. There was the long driveway, coming from his right, and he traced it circling the lawn in front of the main doors to the house. Gravel tracks led off to various outbuildings.

Save for a single spire of dirty smoke rising from one of the ornate chimney pots, there was no sign of activity at all. Gideon glanced at his watch: nine o'clock. He frowned and looked through the binoculars again. He scanned the windows and all the doors, but saw nothing at all to indicate life inside.

Then a big black car nosed around the corner from the stable block and slid silently around the lawn to the front door. Reflections on the darkened windows made it impossible to see in. Gideon steadied his arms on his knees and tried to keep his breathing shallow.

Lord Golden, tall, grey-haired and distinguished stepped out to the car in the company of a stocky suited man. The man opened a rear door and Golden slipped into the back. As soon as the door was shut again, the car pulled away. The man stood for a moment, alone on the driveway, before going back inside. Gideon studied his face, but could see little apart from his comparative youth.

The whole episode had taken less than a minute. In that time, Gideon's attention had been firmly fixed on the front door. Only as he lowered the binoculars to rub his eyes did he see the three dun streaks crossing the bridge below him. He hurriedly refocused and tracked their flight. Black and tan dogs, giant legs eating up the ground, jaws open and tongues dripping. Dobermans.

There could be no doubt of their quarry. They were aimed straight at him. He put the binoculars in the rucksack and thought furiously. There was nothing in his belongings that was worth dying for and nothing with his name on.

He pulled Excalibur out of its bindings and backed out of the bush. Once he'd extricated himself, he crashed through the undergrowth, leaves and twigs flying, thorns catching at his clothing and pulling him back.

There was barking behind him.

Gideon put down the sword and untied the sacking with controlled haste. He took hold of Excalibur and stuffed the wrappings into his map pocket. As he straightened up, he looked into a pair of luminous green eyes.

The dog put its ears back and growled, baring all its teeth.

At the edge of his vision, he could see movement either side of him. The other two dogs started to circle him, shoulders hunched and heads down, looking for an opening past the bright blade. They could sense his sharp sweat and pounding heart. Gideon adjusted his grip and crouched slightly, poised to fight or run. He knew that the dogs would be followed by men, sooner rather than later. He had to act. Slowly, testing each footstep, he started to

244

creep backwards, all the time warding off the dogs with Excalibur's point. Every time he took his eyes off one of the beasts, they nudged closer and, snarling, snapped at his legs.

He took another step and tripped. He fell uncontrollably, his face landing inches from the gaping metal jaws of a mantrap. Then a weight fell on his legs, and pain drilled deep into his shins. He hacked at the dog with a furious sweep. He cut it across the shoulder and kicked it off with his boots.

The other dogs jumped him, and he disappeared under a howling, baying tumult of claws and canines. Gideon went berserk.

When he'd done, one dog lay with its head cracked open in the sprung trap, another tried to crawl away with blood seeping from the slash that marked its entire flank. The third limped pitifully, whining and barking alternately, unwilling to attack, unable to leave. Gideon himself was in tatters: his clothes hung off him in rags and he was stained from head to foot in forest slime. His face was a mass of scratches and his skin was punctured in many, many places. He leaned on the sword, now twice his salvation, and waited for the red mist swimming before his eyes to depart.

Voices penetrated the wood, and he remembered he still had to escape. He turned away, jogging breathlessly into the trees. He gained the wall, but found he barely had the strength to climb over it. It was more of a fall than a jump. He sat there for a moment and looked at the sky. The mist was burning off, and above him he could see blue. He scrambled to his feet and, hugging the line of the hedge, staggered off to find the road.

He was straddling the first gate when the shotguns opened up. Two men had dropped down his side of the estate wall and were even now reloading.

Heart

They were beating for him like they would beat for pheasants. There were now six of them in a long line, sweeping him before them, waiting for him to either raise his head into the line of sight or collapse exhausted at their feet. Every time they spotted him, there was a volley of gunfire that made the half-formed crops quiver with buckshot.

It was as plain as a pikestaff that they were trying to kill him. They'd given him no opportunity to surrender, and their silent pursuit of him was single-minded thoroughness itself. Gideon was pushed forward all the time, with no chance to hide or evade them.

He crept, doubled over, through a field of green corn, his back woefully exposed. He had no strength left to run. He'd endured the chase for over an hour and it was almost at an end. There was a drystone wall in front of him. He dropped the sword over first, then tumbled after it. His distress was magnified by what he saw: he was in a graveyard. But as he looked desperately around for the best place to die, he saw a beat-up estate car backed up to the porch door of the squat Norman church. The door was ajar.

With a last effort, Gideon picked up the sword and made a low dash through the headstones. He slammed the studded oak door shut, and spotted bolts top and bottom. He rammed them home with two heavy concussions that echoed back from the vaulted ceiling. He sank down to his knees on the tiled floor, quite wretched.

He crawled into the nave, pushing Excalibur in front of him, thinking that he had to save the sword somehow. The illuminated saints in their windows looked benevolently down on him, but couldn't lift a finger to help. The sun passed through their haloes and deep-coloured robes, making Gideon's skin glow ethereally.

He cried out. "Please. They mustn't get this. I have to keep it safe. I promised!"

"Who are you? What do you want?"

Gideon blinked, rubbed the sweat out of his eyes. There was a woman making her way slowly down the aisle towards him. She was tall and thin and grey, and her hands trembled as they gripped a small green watering can.

"They're going to kill me. If you believe in anything that this place stands for, help me." He clawed his way upright using the back of a pew. The woman saw the sword and took a step backwards. "Please. If that's your car outside, get me away from here. I'll take your keys if I have to, but I won't hurt you."

"Lord Golden's men?"

"Men, guns, dogs. I need your answer now. Another minute will be too late! They mustn't catch me with this." He held up the sword, almost overbalancing in the effort to keep it aloft.

Her eyes travelled to her left, and looked at a face in the stained glass. Gideon followed her gaze, only to see Excalibur mirrored stone for stone, metal for metal. The angel holding it had his face.

"It's a sign," she said, almost sighing in satisfaction. "Quickly, under the altar. Hide yourself and make sure you don't move the cloth." She stepped forward to help him and ended up supporting a good part of his weight as they shuffled towards the chancel.

"I don't understand," said Gideon. "How?" He was talking about the image in the window, but she thought he was asking a different question.

"The altar is just a wooden-framed table. Lie still and don't make a noise. They'll be here soon." She lifted the front of the altar cloth and pushed him under. There was barely enough room between the thick legs and heavy

247

tabletop. She dropped the cloth back down behind him, and it just touched the dusty stone floor. A thin line of light crept in underneath the fringe, and nothing else. It was dark and quiet. "Now, patience."

He heard the bolts being undone, the big ring latch on the door twisted and pulled. Then there was a minute of soft silence, punctuated only by the sound of frail footsteps.

Shouting woke him up. Startled by his inability to stay conscious, he jumped slightly. Then he recalled where he was, and froze.

"Did he come in here?" The voice was rough and angry.

"Did who come in?" the woman replied.

"Trespasser. Big man, blond haired. Killed three of the dogs, the bastard."

"I can't say I've seen anyone like that. I'm sure I would have remembered.

"Have you left the church for any reason, left it unlocked?"

"Good Lord, no. That would never do. I've been here all the time, doing the flowers for Sunday."

"If you see anything, phone the Grange at once. You got that, Agnes?"

"Quite clear, I'm sure."

"Right. On we go, lads. He couldn't have got far."

Several heavy pairs of boots tramped out, and the door banged once. Gideon held his breath for a few moments longer, then let it all out.

Agnes clicked her way back up to the altar. "You can come out now. There is one distinct advantage in being an old biddy, you know. No one expects you to be a consummate liar."

Gideon inched his way out. "Thank you. I still don't understand why, but thank you."

"How are you feeling?"

"In pain. Thirsty." He lay on his back on the cool marble steps of the altar. "I could just lie here and sleep."

"Drink this." She held out the watering can and he pointed the long spout into his mouth. After choking himself with the first mouthful, he sat up and drank it properly. "We have to get you away, which won't be easy. You'll have to wait until nightfall."

"Can't you just drive me out?"

"They watch the only road. I know a way across the fields they won't suspect. For now, hide in the tower. Hardly anyone goes there. I'll come back for you later, when the commotion has died down a little."

"Please," said Gideon, "can you tell me what's going on?"

"I'm afraid I haven't the slightest idea. But that is you in the window, don't try to deny it."

"How long has it been there?"

"The window? It says on it, somewhere down the bottom. Do you want to look?"

"I ought."

"Don't be afraid. It's only glass." She held out her hand to him.

Rather than pull her over, he got unsteadily to his feet. "Whenever anyone says that, I know I'm not going to understand what they mean."

Together they walked to the window. Gideon looked up at it, open-mouthed. It was him, under the halo and framed by the outstretched wings. The sword was the sword in every detail. The writing at the bottom was gothic and difficult to read.

Agnes spoke the words with her eyes shut. "'Place me like a seal over your heart, like a seal on your arm, for love is as strong as death, its jealously unyielding as the grave.' I often wonder what it means. If you look very closely you'll see a date and a name: bottom right."

He walked down the pew and peered through the dirt. He read: 'M Ambrose 1851'. "I don't know anyone called Ambrose."

"Would you believe me if I told you that, until today, that angel had no face. That's why I helped you."

Gideon put his head against the cold stone. "Merlin Ambrosius," he said. Agnes didn't hear.

"Unfortunately, we can't stand here gawping. We have to get you hidden." She ushered him towards a dark and dusty door at the east end of the side aisle. "I'll bring food and drink when I come."

"I could do with some water now."

"I'll fetch it when you're safely installed." Agnes bent down and reached under the front pew. With a rattle and a scrape, a heavy iron key was brought out. "This might take a bit of effort."

She inserted the key and heaved at it. As she strained, the lock creaked, and finally popped back. She almost fell, and Gideon caught her.

He heaved at the door. It was dark inside and smelled of mice.

"You'll be all right in here. Go up to the belfry; light comes in through the baffles, and there's more air, if you don't mind sharing with a few pigeons. Don't go out on the roof, in case someone sees you. I'll bring your water and put it at the bottom of the stairs, then lock you in."

"I'm Gideon, by the way."

"And you already know I'm Agnes. Now," she pushed him through the door and up the first step, "I must go. People will get suspicious if I don't get home soon. I wouldn't want them to talk."

"Is that bad?"

"Worse. Up those stairs!"
"Goodbye. Thank you."

Gideon slept for hours in amongst the nests and feathers, oblivious to the sound of cooing pigeons. When he woke, he found a large vase full of water at the foot of the stairs. He drank some, then sat watching the village though the slats in the bell tower. He saw a few people walking or cycling, but they never left the village boundaries. They called at other houses, at the shop or the Post Office, or at the solitary pub. It was self-contained, isolated.

A Land Rover rattled past, and stopped by the war memorial long enough to let two men in sleeveless green jackets jump over the tailgate. As the vehicle drove away, they broke their guns and began to knock on doors. Gideon pulled back from the light, even though there was no chance of being detected. The place was strange, and didn't seem to use the rules of normal civilisation.

As the sky grew dark and the stars came out one by one, he watched the lights in people's houses. He was so close he could smell their cooking and it drove him to distraction. It was an hour later when the door at the bottom of the tower was heaved open.

"Gideon?" came the tremulous call.

"Still here, Agnes."

A torch beam pierced the gloom, and the top of the ladder rattled against the belfry floor as she stepped up to meet him. A wicker basket was pushed through the narrow opening, and Gideon took it out of the way. He reached down to help her up.

As she came through, she extinguished the torch. "I imagine it would be safe to move to the roof now. As long as we're quiet, I'm sure it'll be all right."

Heart

There was a further ladder up to the tower roof. Agnes showed him the way by furtively flashing the torch on the lowest rung. Gideon shouldered open the trapdoor, and the night sky greeted him like an old friend. She passed the basket up to him. He slid it on to the stone roof, then rolled out himself. They were hidden by the crenellated parapet and sat with their backs to it. Agnes motioned to Gideon to lean close.

"We'll have to whisper; the sound travels, you know, and no standing up. They're still looking for you, have been all day. Asking all sorts of questions and looking in all sorts of places: sheds, barns, outbuildings of every kind." She delved into the basket and lifted out a triangular tin-foil packet. "Sandwiches."

Gideon swooped on them and ripped open the foil to expose the bread. He crammed one of the doorsteps into his mouth and chewed briskly.

"Why did you come here?" asked Agnes. "No one arrives by accident."

"I wanted to find out about Lord Golden. There was a documentary on the television a few nights back, but some of the things they said about him couldn't be true. Then I had a tip-off from a friend, who told me that things were not as they seemed. She was right."

"What did you want to know?"

"What he did during the war. He says he was on Crete, but I don't think that can be right. He seemed to be pretending to be someone called Sutton. Either that or it's the other way round."

"I'll tell you a story. I'm one of the few old enough to remember it clearly, and perhaps the only one who would tell it to a stranger. But you're in the window downstairs, and that counts for rather a lot." She opened a flask of tea and poured each of them a cup. "They'll find the face at the weekend. Perhaps they'll be wise to me,

252

perhaps they won't. I'm tired of the lies, Gideon. I don't think it matters any more.

"Once upon a time, between the wars, Percy Golden grew up here with his parents, and his brothers and sisters, in Middleton Grange. He was a bright young man and very good looking. I'm afraid I had a bit of a thing for Percy, even though he was a year younger than me. He was twenty and at Oxford when Mr Chamberlain announced we were at war. Percy joined up straight away and we learned he was doing some cloak-and-dagger job for the Ministry." She sighed heavily. "He was away six years and came back a different man."

"They say war does that to people."

"Oh no. You quite misunderstand me. Not that he behaved differently. He *was* different, a different person altogether. He called himself Percy Golden and everybody behaved as if he were. It wasn't him, though. At first I thought it was just me, but we all knew, exchanged looks in public and whispered behind our doors in private. But nothing out loud. You didn't in those days, out of deference. These days, you don't dare."

"But what did his parents say?"

"They died, later. As did all his brothers and sisters. Some said it was unlucky, some said it was a curse."

"But they said nothing? A different son comes back from the war than the one they sent. It makes no sense."

"Of course it doesn't. But that's the way it happened. Lord Golden's parents never said a word. They treated him as their son. When they died, he assumed the title. This is the history I grew up with. But you knew this already; I've just filled in some of the background detail."

He picked at a scab on his arm. "He won't be happy if he finds out what you've done."

Heart

"I've become tired of living recently. I'm worn out like a sock that's been darned too many times. I have a granddaughter, you know. A pretty thing who would be nineteen now, nineteen last Saturday. Elizabeth came to stay with me at Christmas and I put her on the train to go back to her parents before the New Year. She never arrived, and that was that. I often come into the church, on my own, and pray for her return, or any news about her at all. Just to know if she was dead would be a relief. Did you ever have anyone who went missing?"

"Me," said Gideon wistfully. "I haven't talked to my parents for a couple of months. I could contact them, but I'm certain they're being watched. Other people besides Lord Golden want me dead, and I think he's already had someone killed. They said it was an accident, but I don't believe in coincidences."

"The rumour is that he's a necromancer."

"A what?"

"Someone who conjures up the spirits of the dead to learn about the future. You might not pay much attention to rumours, but he knew where you were."

"I have to get back to Jack."

"They still have a checkpoint on the road." She saw his sceptical expression. "Golden's men run this village. Our connection with the outside world is really quite thin. If you're going to leave now, you'll have to go on foot and alone." She got up, still bent over, and shuffled to the far side of the tower. Gideon followed, and looked down her pointing arm at the starlit countryside below.

"Go through the churchyard to the stile in the corner. There's a footpath that runs all the way to the river and a small wooden bridge. Cross that and turn right. Left, and you'll end up at the Grange again. Go upstream

254

as far as you can go. You'll find a road crossing the river. Go left, and you'll be on the road to town."

"How far is that?"

"Twenty miles as the crow flies. It may as well be the other side of the world for all the difference it makes to us here."

Gideon looked for his watch, but it was no longer on his wrist; torn off somewhere between the church and the Grange. "I'd better get going then."

She pressed more sandwiches on him, and some biscuits. What was left of his pockets bulged. As he lay out the sacking on the ground to mask the brilliant mirrored surface of Excalibur, she asked him: "Where did you get it?"

"I was given it freely, and accepted it freely. At first, I thought it was an accident that I had it, but I don't think that way any more. Some say it's Excalibur, the sword of King Arthur. I don't know about that, but as long as they believe it, they'd kill me to take it away." Gideon placed it back in the sack, rolled it up and tied the knots. "I'm ready."

"Then go. I'll cover your tracks here. Please, take this with you." She opened her purse and brought out a small glossy photograph. It was too dark to see of who. "It's a picture of Elizabeth. If you find her, tell her to call her parents, or me." She sounded so sad.

Gideon found a space for it next to his map. "I'll make sure I do."

"Now, off you go. May God go with you, Gideon."

As furtive as a weasel, he stole across the churchyard and on to the secluded path. He met no one and heard nothing. He'd escaped.

Heart

Chapter 19
Saturday 30th May 1987
Leamington Spa

Gideon Smith's story

Gideon changed in the station toilets, into the clothes that he'd bought from an Oxfam shop he'd passed on the way. The entire outfit had left him change from fifteen pounds. He transferred all the things in his pockets into the fawn raincoat, one previous owner, presumably dead. The rags he'd worn he left stuffed in a plastic bag behind the u-bend. He ached all over. He'd inspected his naked body in the cubicle, and there was hardly an inch of flesh that wasn't scored or bruised.

Clutching his ticket, he boarded a near-deserted carriage on a train that was heading in roughly the right direction. He ended up the only person in a compartment of six seats. He slumped down, dust rising in musty clouds from the ageing upholstery. The carriage rumbled and started to move off. He looked at his second-hand watch and set it against the receding station clock.

He patted his pockets for the half-packet of biscuits he knew he had. He removed the map to get at them and the photograph Agnes had given him fell out from between the folds of paper. Some of the dust floating around the compartment settled on the photograph. He held it gently by the edges and blew on it, then brushed the surface lightly with the back of a finger.

She had nut-brown hair falling down her back, and her face was relaxed, confident, eyes clear of pain and worry. He was fated only ever to see her face in a picture. He knew her, but the last time he'd seen her he'd been handing the little stack of Polaroids depicting her torture

256

and murder over the counter of a police station. That had been hundreds of miles and a different life away.

He began his mourning for Elizabeth.

He knew something was wrong before he turned the corner of the street. He could smell the odour of burnt wetness strong in his nostrils. Gideon hurried stiffly along the pavement from the bus stop until he could look down the length of the ordinary terraced street.

Halfway down, there was a soot-smeared shell of a house. Numb, he walked towards it and stood outside, his eyes casting over every last detail. There was blue and white tape tied around the gateposts, warning him not to cross the police line. The garden, which Gideon had so carefully weeded the week before, was strewn with the remnants of furniture and carpets, half-burnt, half-melted, all ruined beyond redemption. The windows were all boarded up and over each of them the red brick was stained with ugly black streaks. The reek of a life's worth of accumulated belongings incinerated hung in the air like a ghost.

A neighbour's door cracked open, and the wife came down the garden path. She was still in her housecoat and fluffy pink slippers. Gideon had talked to her often over the wall that divided the properties.

"Gideon? Where have you been?"

"Mrs H? Where's Jack?"

She unlatched her gate and stood next to him, staring up at Jack's old house. He'd never live there again. "He's in the County Hospital. My Trevor was ever so brave. I know I go on about him, but he was a real hero yesterday."

"Is Jack badly hurt?"

"What did they say? Smoke inhalation or somesuch. Lucy's well, too, so you can calm yourself on that score. But it was terrible! Who'd have thought that someone would want to do such a thing to old Jack?"

"Tell me what happened."

"Well, me and Trevor were in bed. Timmy's got a poorly stomach, so we'd been up and down all night checking on him. We woke up when we heard glass breaking. I thought it was Timmy, I don't know why; must have been half-asleep. But Trevor goes to the bedroom window and looks out, and says 'Bugger me', if you'll excuse my French. 'Someone's throwing a petrol bomb in the street.' So I get up and come to the window, and this man throws this bottle through Jack's downstairs window.

"Well, my Trevor, all calm like, says 'Call the police, love. I'll sort this out.' He puts on his shoes and his old coat and goes round. Already there are flames coming out of the window and the room's well ablaze. Lucy's barking away like a good'un upstairs, so Jack's awake. But he couldn't get to the front door. Trevor fetches a ladder from Tom three doors down and climbs up to the first floor, breaks the window and disappears inside. I'm out in the street by now, along with almost everybody else, and we can hear sirens in the distance. I'm asking where my Trevor is and Tom's saying he's in the house, when Trevor appears at the window with Jack and Lucy. He puts Jack over his shoulder and comes down the ladder like he's been saving people all his life. Tom nips up and wraps Lucy in his coat and carries her down using the arms as a sling.

"The Fire Brigade turn up, and then the police, then the ambulances. It was mayhem, it really was. Took them ages to put the fire out, it did. Our paintwork is all blistered on the party wall, and everything could do with a wash, but they're talking about giving our Trevor a medal! Can you imagine it? He's in bed at the moment, sleeping it off. I don't think I've seen him so shook up in all my life." She returned to her original question. "Anyway, where have you been? You look like you've been in the wars."

He touched his hand to his face. "I've been off on an errand for Jack. Do you think they'll let me see him?"

"I don't see why not. I spoke to June yesterday afternoon. She sounded very upset. Police are coming to see him today."

"Are they?" Gideon could guess what June would tell them; it was all his fault. "Can you get a message to him for me?"

"Of course, but why not tell him yourself?"

"I don't think June'll thank me for turning up. Tell Jack he was right."

"Gideon says you were right," she remembered out loud. "Right about what?"

"Just that he was right. Thanks, Mrs H. I need to go now, and start lifting stones."

"You what?"

"That's what you do when you want to expose the worms and slugs. I'll be seeing you." He started to walk away.

"What's that you're carrying?" she called after him.

"Nothing. Everything," he replied. "Bye, Mrs H."

Monday 1st June 1987
Liverpool

Two nights later, Gideon tracked Golden down in Liverpool. He stood across the street from the conference hall where there would be a meeting on behalf of the local parliamentary candidates. Despite being advertised as 'public', entrance was by invitation only, and he didn't have the connections or the will to part with the hard cash to gain one of the embossed gold-edged cards.

The police were out in force, and they made Gideon nervous. But they seemed content to contain the demonstration to the far side of the road. Weight of numbers and temporary iron railings kept the protestors from the dignitaries and well-dressed party faithful.

Gideon stood surrounded by a crowd chanting and shouting, punching the air with red and black placards. He was quite still, waiting and watching. The television crew balanced on the steps of the hall panned across him and back. He'd give them something to report, later. He was cold outside, hot fury inside, and he'd rehearsed a thousand times what he'd say to Lord Golden when he finally confronted him.

A whispered rumour started to spread: Golden was already inside and had been for three hours. Even now, he was live on the news, mocking the dinosaurs, the Luddites and the Stalinists shouting so many empty words into the dark outside.

There followed a good deal of argument between the organisers of the demonstration. Those who wanted to carry on all night in the hope that their voices would be heard inside conflicted with those who proposed to call it off and disperse peaceably, knowing that they'd tied up a greater proportion of police for the evening and enjoyed useful publicity in the process.

Into the intense debate, a couple of short sentences were injected: "Storm the building. He'll have no choice but to hear us then." Each of the two groups thought that the other had suggested it, but both seized it as their own. An instruction was passed back through the activists: get ready. The mob grew silent and expectant.

The barrier directly in front went down with a crash, and scattered two startled policemen backwards.

Someone shouted "Go!", and fifty tightly packed bodies streamed through a gap only six feet wide. They ran over the police line as if it never existed. A car squealed its brakes as the protestors flooded across the road, and more police hastily linked arms in front of the doorway to the hall.

Some fell by the wayside, brought down by desperate officers or halted by failed nerves. Most gained the steps, swarmed up them like a wave of insects. There was pushing, each new body at the back of the scrum adding extra force at the front. Men and women grunted with the strain, threw punches, beat helmets and shoulders with their placards, and cried out to be let through.

Something slipped. The police fell backwards and the mob fell screaming forwards. A roaring cheer was raised raggedly and they surged forward through the glass lobby doors that hadn't been locked in time.

The carpet was trampled, the décor scuffed. They clattered through the big auditorium doors and into a hall of banked seating, where a tall man with fine greying hair had just stepped up to the podium.

There was a curious moment of silence. Everyone turned to look at the interlopers. Golden gripped the sides of the lectern with whitening knuckles. Stewards and security guards stiffened before racing along the aisles.

Someone shouted: "A minimum wage for the workers!", and on the next breath the chant was repeated from two dozen mouths. Security bundled into them, trying to push them back as a group. The tannoy barked for calm. It looked as if there was going to be a bloody riot.

One voice was raised above all the others, almost lost, but not quite.

Beneath the call for a living wage, another cry could be heard. "Sutton! Sutton! I know who you are,

Sutton. You killed Porlock. You killed Golden. You killed his family. You tried to kill Jack Bassenthwaite. You tried to kill me. Do you hear me, Sutton? Do you hear me?"

Evidently he did. Golden took a shocked step backwards, the colour draining from his face, his mouth opening to form an incredulous 'O'.

"This man is not Lord Golden. He's called Sutton and he's a murderer!"

The man on stage took another step back and was supported by another man who had come out to join him. Golden leaned back into him and whispered into his ear, pointed his hand out over the auditorium, over the heads of the still-seated audience, over the heads of the wildly heaving mêlée, and straight at Gideon Smith.

The second man followed the arm and found his target. He adjusted his tweed coat, flexed his fingers in his black leather gloves and jumped off the front of the stage into the front row.

The man who tried to kill him in Newcastle was taking orders from the man who tried to kill him in Middleton. There were no coincidences left. Two and two suddenly made four in Gideon's mind. He'd carried the sword right to those who would misuse it the most. The man whose face he'd ground into the dirt was on his trail once more.

And he was trapped.

"Get out of my way!" Gideon put his arms down by his side and flung them up. The weight of Excalibur knocked several anoraked Marxists flying, and he used his free hand to fend off one of the stewards who fell into the gap. He was at the edge of the disturbance. Behind him, the police were coming in waves through the lobby, barring any exit there. To the far left and right, there were the glowing green signs of fire escapes.

A badged security guard in blue serge gripped his arm. Gideon threw him into the collapsing ruck and ran for the left-hand exit. No one tried to stop him, although several suited businessmen rose in their seats and called out that one was getting away.

He kicked the bar release on the door and it shuddered open. Beyond were concrete stairs going down: ten steps, a landing and a turn, then another ten steps. They flashed by in a haze of sweat and adrenaline.

There was another fire door at the bottom. Gideon threw himself through and landed in a black side alley, cold and damp and festering after the bright lights and soft furnishings. There were footsteps chasing after him. He held the sword up briefly and apologised for being so stupid, so blind.

Don't be afraid.

Once again, he ran for his life.

He lost himself in the back streets, turning this way and that without method. He had no idea where he was, but from the salt smell of it, he was down by the banks of the Mersey in the old docks. Gideon slowed his feet, and stopped to gasp the air. Cold cobbles bruised his feet as he span around and around. He saw nothing, heard no pursuing shouts or cries. He found a bollard on the quayside and sat on it, resting the sword across his knees and leaning heavily across it. He was tired, weak and confused; easy pickings for anyone who wanted to try their luck.

But those who would weren't after Gideon at that moment. As he sat holding his head to stop his mind falling out through his ears, he heard two noises. One was the Mersey ferry twisting in the swell, the other was a high scream cut off suddenly.

Heart

He turned, expecting attack. There was nothing save a moth chasing around a sodium lamp.

The ferry lights were getting closer, and the sound of its thrumming engines cutting through the water drifted in and out of the wind. He could start walking now and get to the terminal in five minutes. He would be clean away, safe with the sword, and knowing who his enemy was and what faces they wore. It was tempting, very tempting, just to walk away.

He got to his feet and wearily went to investigate. If nothing else, he could detour down the narrow passage between two warehouses on his way to the ferry.

Halogens high up on each building, either end of the gap's two hundred yard length, showed stark, deceiving shadows. The passage was cluttered with all manner of debris: boxes, great steel drums, rusting machinery and huge coils of damp chains, each link the length of Gideon's arm. In the very darkest part, halfway along, there were what seemed to be two teams of two men, engaged in a tug of war. They rocked back and forth, pulling all the time. Only as Gideon picked his way closer over the obstacles in his path could he see that their rope was a woman.

Two held her arms, two pulled at her jeans. She bucked and writhed between them, her head twisting uselessly and her black hair whipping her face. Her mouth was a strip of industrial duct tape.

They had her pinioned on the ground by the time weak light whispered up the naked blade of Excalibur.

"I'll kill you if I have to." Here was a demon to drag them all to hell. His eyes glowed with unearthly luminescence.

The four men were not brave, or they would never have picked on a young Chinese woman who struggled with English as a second language. From kneeling on her wrists and ankles, they started to crawl away on their bellies, white-faced and whimpering.

"Just a bit of fun," one of them laughed. It came out as a whine, desperate to placate the monster that had sprung up in their midst.

"Fun?" bellowed Gideon, sparks exploding from the ground as he lashed out either side of the cringing man. "Enjoying this?"

The would-be rapist grovelled in the dirt and cried. "Please don't hurt me." He felt the fine sharp point of the blade prick his Adam's apple. "Mercy."

The sword bit deeper.

"No! No, don't kill me, oh God please don't kill me!" He soiled himself and, as soon as the pain in his neck lessened, dragged himself away by his fingertips.

"Never do this again as long as you live." Gideon turned his back on them as they ran and fell, ran and fell, shrieking. He laid down the sword, and rested the girl's head in one hand. She had not moved, not even blinked, since he had appeared out of the shadows to save her. "I'm sorry. This is going to hurt."

He picked at her skin until he'd worked off a corner of the tape covering her mouth, then pulled it off in one steady motion. Her lips were puffed and bleeding. Still her eyes, great dark saucers in pools of white, didn't leave him.

"Get dressed. I'll get you out of here." When she didn't move, Gideon picked up her jeans from where they had been thrown and held them out for her. "You can understand me, can't you?"

She nodded mutely, and eventually raised a bruised hand to take her trousers and cover her nakedness. He looked away to spare her further indignity.

Heart

"Please. My shoes?" Her hushed request brought a lump to his throat. How dare they? He scoured the passage for her footwear, but found nothing.

"I'm sorry," he said, "Your shoes have gone." He helped her to her feet, which were tiny compared to his boots. "I'll carry you if I have to."

She leaned against him as he bent to retrieve the sword, and used him as a crutch as they walked to relieve the pressure on her bare soles; there were many sharp objects on the ground, and she winced whenever she trod on one.

"You have family?"

"Yes. Nearby. They will be very worried."

As they emerged from between the warehouses, three more men came into view. Gideon knew them all.

One was held by the scruff of the neck; Gideon had heard his pleading cries for mercy. The man who held him with black leather gloves was also known, and the third man called himself Lord Percy Golden.

"That's him, that's the one!" squawked the man. He was thrown to the ground, discarded as the useless piece of flotsam he was. The tweed-coated man put his right hand into his inside pocket and pulled out an automatic handgun. He cocked it and pointed it at Gideon.

"Mr Smith, a pleasure to meet you at last. Rescuing damsels, I see." Golden had an orator's voice. "I would have thought you long gone, but you seem to make a habit of meddling in matters that concern you not one jot. Surely you must realise the importance of what you carry by now?"

Gideon saw that Golden wasn't looking at him, or the girl, but at the sword with longing eyes.

"I know what you think it is. I know that you should never have it."

266

"Excellent. That will make events much more satisfying. Markham, you know what to do."

Gideon put out a protective arm to shield the girl. The tweed man, Markham, turned his gun on the man on the ground and shot him through the head.

He jerked like a gaffed fish, and sprawled awkwardly. His eyes and his mouth were open, unbelieving to the last second of life.

Gideon had flinched away, and the girl buried her head in his back.

"Now for the sword."

He was desperate. They were going to kill him and the girl, and there was nothing he could do. It would be all over in a moment. "I can't give it to you."

"And why not, Mr Smith?" Golden was smirking, a tiny turning-up of the corners of his mouth showing the intense pleasure he felt. "You're not sealed. I can take it from you any time I want."

"Sealed?" Hadn't Merlin said something about that? Or was it the window in Middleton-cum-Marchbury church? The seal over the heart was Marianne's cross. He was lacking, incomplete, yet he had seen himself in stained glass with that self-same cross.

Markham sighted down his arm and his leather-encased finger tightened on the trigger.

Blood bloomed on Gideon's chest. He gasped and sank to his knees. The sword clattered down next to him. The girl gripped his shoulders and stopped him from toppling over. He put his hand inside his coat and it came out red.

Markham frowned. His round was still poised in the gun's chamber.

Gideon dared to breathe. The pain was receding. He probed his shirt and there was no hole. He ripped the hem from his waistband and exposed his sternum to the night air. Beneath the smear of dark blood was the glimmering of three coloured diamonds and a black tapering line.

Markham fell back as if struck. Golden tottered weakly, his hand clawing at his tie.

Somehow, the sword had sealed him. He gripped Excalibur by the hilt and climbed slowly to his feet. He saw his enemies' horror. They had seen what they had never dreamed they would see against his white skin, next to his heart.

He took the girl by the hand, and backed away until they turned and ran.

He was almost out of earshot when he heard the faint cry.

"It's not over, Smith. I will have the sword. I will have it!"

Simon Morden

Part V
Tuesday 2nd June 1987 to Wednesday 10th June
1987

Chapter 20
Tuesday 2nd June 1987
London

Torsten Neubauer's story

The paintwork was quite ruined, punctured a hundred times by the point of a drawing-pin. Not much of the wall was visible, papered as it was with a *mélange* of paper: photocopies of articles and newsprint, cuttings from the papers themselves, photographs both black and white, and full glossy colour, drawings and writing by hand in more than one language, all seemingly thrown at random on the wall and stuck arbitrarily to it.

Seemingly. Neubauer would wake in the night, cold sweat pouring from him again, reliving the moments of pain as Soviet bullets tore through his skin. Then he would walk shakily down the hall and stare at the patchwork wall. Sometimes he would sit on a chair in front of it, taking in the whole sweep of it. At other times, he would lean against it and press his damp hands on the crisp sheets of paper, his eyes reading the minute print from just one portion of what he had created.

Tonight was such a night. His stomach was knotted with aching nausea and his ribs burned with remembrance. From long experience he knew that sleep would evade him for the next hour, and he rose, levering himself up using his stick. He moved painfully to the kitchen, his bare feet shuffling across the carpet, then on to cold lino. He poured himself a tumbler of water, drank it in four gulps and clutched the empty glass in a tight fist.

As the grip of night eased, he half-refilled the tumbler and took himself to look at the wall. Currently it was dark, in the shadow of the closed curtains, but with one touch of the light switch, all was made clear to see.

270

Part of his fear was that he was wrong. Wrong about Gideon Smith, wrong about the sword, wrong about Ambrose, wrong about absolutely everything. The wall was his monument to how deluded and estranged from reality the human mind could become, and he chased nothing more substantial than the scraps that made up his story.

The wall was his fear; it was also his hope. He lifted his head and stared here and there, threading his way through the impenetrable maze before him: item 563-21, tied by a length of green wool to a picture of Robert and Marianne Newton he had culled from a bank newsletter. The same strand of wool linked a list of names that included the Walcott-Greens, and a snap of Gideon Smith, sent to him by James Cook. In the same envelope, the lawyer had enclosed a picture of himself with his arm around the shoulder of Leah Orchard. They looked happy and relaxed, Leah smiling her shy, misshapen smile.

Neubauer was strangely moved every time he looked at it. He saw two people who were made for each other in a way that he knew he didn't understand and wished he did. The photograph of the pair was joined to Gideon Smith by blue wool, and another strand led to an outline drawing of the sword together with the inscription, both in English and Elvish.

Green for sword-bearers and cross-wearers, blue for the sword itself. And black, of course: black for the dark side of the quest, the shadow that fluttered over everything like a hawk. Look up into the midday sun and miss the hovering bird of prey poised to fall like an arrow to the ground, terrible and swift.

Black wool joined the Newton murders; the thief Gideon Smith had run through, and who had later been found dead in his guarded hospital room, killed not by trauma but by fright; the man who had arranged to meet

271

Heart

Leah Orchard and chased Gideon; the man who had called both him and Margaret with dire warnings.

There was more, not connected in any obvious way; unexplained deaths and kidnappings of normal, bright and loved men, women and children.

Neubauer would snip the details from the newspaper, and store them in a file. So, so many. Those whose deaths revealed that they carried the Newton Cross, went on the wall. They numbered a hundred. The German wondered if anyone in authority had noticed. Margaret had told him that no one collected the numbers nationally. He wondered how a police force could function under such circumstances. It all seemed so divided; manors and parishes, forces and areas. There was a war going on, and no one was taking any notice, except himself and Margaret; a crippled Berliner ex-cop and a woman sergeant whose enthusiasm was being bled dry by heavy-handed and bigoted leadership.

He looked behind him at the dining table. It was stacked high with different-coloured folders, each chock-full of more information to be reviewed, and either discarded or placed on the wall in its rightful place. Too much work for one man, he thought.

But he had nothing else to do, no other pastime with which to occupy himself. He spent his days in libraries and bookshops, his evenings staring at his wall, his nights in fevered and pain-racked insomnia.

The clock on the wall above the dining table pointed its hands at half past four. Neubauer drew back a chair, placed his tumbler on the table in front of him and selected a folder at random. He began to sort through the papers, re-reading each one and sorting them out into piles.

The clock now read half past seven. Margaret's alarm had sounded some fifteen minutes earlier, alerting Neubauer to turn on the kettle, fetch the breakfast cereal and milk from the kitchen, and lay out bowls and spoons on the table. He tidied up his folders; the bin was full to overflowing with discarded scrumples of paper, and a few more inches of coloured wool had been added to the wall.

He made her a pot of tea, himself a mug of coffee, and settled back in his chair listening to the radio news with his eyes closed. Margaret finally stomped up the hall into the room, hair awry, cheeks puffy.

"Good morning," said Neubauer without looking. Normally he would have shaken hands with another German, but he knew it made the British uncomfortable; he desisted.

Margaret grunted and fell into her chair, pulling her nightshirt down over her thighs and rattling her chair closer to the table. From behind his pink-tinged darkness, he could hear tea being poured, milk and sugar added and stirred in. Then the cereal packet rustled in time with the door buzzer.

Neubauer opened his eyes and looked at Margaret. She looked back blankly, and gave a little shake of her head, as if she had a fly inside.

"Shall I get it?" he asked.

She rubbed her face with her free hand. "Okay."

He got up, refastened his dressing gown around his waist, and walked slowly and deliberately over to the door phone.

"Hello?"

"*Herr Neubauer? Herr Ambrose möchte mit Ihnen sprechen.*"

Neubauer's thumb hovered over the entry button. "It is Ambrose."

Margaret suddenly became animated. "I'm getting dressed." She rose hurriedly.

"Why?"

"He can read my mind. I'm not going to let him see me half-naked as well."

"*Herr Neubauer?*" Ambrose's voice was gently mocking.

"*Einen Moment, bitte.* Yessica?" Margaret's heels were retreating through her bedroom door. He sighed and thought the ways of women wondrous strange. "*Kommen Sie herein.*"

A minute later, there was a polite and purposeful rap on the door. Neubauer was poised to open it. There was Ambrose, leather coat and hat, just as last time. The same golden eyes, shining with mischief one moment and deep knowledge the next.

"Please come in."

"Thank you, Herr Neubauer. I apologise for the interruption, but I was in the area, so I thought I'd drop in, see how you were."

"That is very kind of you. Can I make you some tea?"

"I'd be delighted." Ambrose took off his coat and hat, and laid them over the back of a chair. "Will Detective Sergeant Margaret be joining us?" He eyed the abandoned place at the table.

"She wanted to put some clothes on. You frightened her last time. She believes you can read minds." Neubauer fetched a new mug from the kitchen.

"I'll have to apologise profusely, if I see her," said Ambrose in a loud voice, intending it to carry down to Margaret.

"Can you?" asked Neubauer, putting the mug on the table and pouring tea from the pot.

"Can I what?" He smiled disarmingly.

"Read our minds. Milk?"

"Just a touch, thank you." He never answered the earlier question. "You've been busy."

"I've kept myself busy," Neubauer corrected, and followed Ambrose's steady gaze to the wall. Ever since the first adjustment the stranger had made, he'd been dreading this moment. He felt like an unprepared schoolchild faced with an unexpected test.

Ambrose stood there for a long time, even ignoring Margaret's eventual entrance behind him. He looked straight ahead, his attention fixed some six feet through the other side of the wall; neither his head nor his eyes moved. Every so often he would raise his mug to his lips and would sip some tea. There was perhaps a slight rocking on his heels, backwards and forwards, but it was almost imperceptible. He seemed to be sucking in information without reading, feeling the patterns without resorting to the key, taking in not the parts, only the whole.

Neubauer sweated and waited. Even Margaret held her breath.

A thin smile started to spread around Ambrose's mouth. Finally, he turned to Neubauer with a nod of appreciation.

"Good. Very good."

"Is it correct?"

"No. But it's very close. Closer, I think, than anyone has ever come before."

Margaret ventured to speak. "This is true, then. All this, this ..."

"Subversion, subterfuge, suspicion and malefaction. Is it true? No. Truth approaches the true on a tangent, and runs asymptotically towards it. Rarely, only rarely, does our understanding of the truth merge with the true. But what you see before you is truth in double measure, pressed down and added to. This is as close as you're going to get in this world's realm." He offered his hand to Neubauer. "Good work."

He took the cool, rough palm in his own. "Thank you."

Ambrose turned towards Margaret. "Have faith. Believe the evidence of your eyes. You've watched your friend weave this carpet of mystery. You've given him board and bread, every comfort. But you remain sceptical. There is no need. You lack only commitment. Believe, Jessica Margaret, for all this is real."

She toyed with the elastic hairband in her fingers, before gathering together her hair behind her head and threading it through. "If it were true, then it would be terrible. Gideon Smith is on his own, against all this."

"No one said it was a nice truth, a good truth, an easy truth, even. The truth comes in all colours of the rainbow. Accept that this may be one of the darker truths you will learn. As for Gideon Smith, I think you'll find he's not alone."

"Meaning what?"

Ambrose handed her his empty mug, and gathered up his coat and hat. "Thank you for the tea. I must be off."

Neubauer stepped forward. "Please. Explain, Herr Ambrose."

With his hand on the door handle, he turned. "He has you, has he not? Oh, and by the way, you may find it to your advantage to turn on your TV when I've gone. You'll find the spider in the web. Until the next time, friends. God bless you both."

Margaret was already scrambling for the on switch. The television bloomed to life in a hiss of static, and her hand hovered over the controls.

"Which channel? Which one?"

The door clicked shut.

"Torsten?"

"Leave it. If we had needed to change, he would have told us, no?"

"What are we watching?" She looked at the screen, but couldn't make sense of it.

"Breakfast news."

"No, this! What's this report about?" She jabbed her finger at the screen, talking over the commentator who could have told her.

Neubauer had heard about the incident on the radio. "Communist demonstrators at a Conservative Party rally. They broke through the police lines and had a fight inside with the security men."

"Communists? I didn't think we had any left." She sat back on her heels. "Where is this?"

"Liverpool."

"Ah," said Margaret. "Militant. Extreme left-wingers; Trotskyites, Marxists, socialists of the old order and a few anarchists along for the ride."

The camera was aimed at the stage, where the speaker had just mounted the podium to rapturous applause. A commotion off-screen made the picture tremble, and the operator zoomed the camera back, then panned round over the craning heads and straining necks of the assembled masses, eventually focusing on an unruly mob creating mayhem at the back of the auditorium.

"I still don't know what we're looking for."

"*Ruhe*," muttered Neubauer, his full concentration on the phosphor dots. "*Hier*." His finger slowly reached out and touched the glowing glass.

The Reds were shouting in unison, except for one man. What he said was lost to the ear under the uproar in the auditorium and the reporter's serious tones, but he was pointing with a rigid arm down towards the stage.

Heart

Stewards and security guards piled in without a plan. Nervous and unprepared, they mêléed with the protesters. They had expected only to deal with guiding people to their seats. Police appeared behind them and, with more confidence, picked their targets one by one, dragging them away and incapacitating them before coming back for another.

There was a skirmish at the edge of the ruck. Someone, a dark-suited steward, was flung back, and a man in a fawn raincoat burst through the gap. He waved his hand once and, like a conjurer, caused a security guard to collapse, holding his face in his hands, hit by the long cloth-covered object the man held. The man then disappeared out of shot, running like a sprinter out of the blocks. The camera didn't follow, choosing instead to concentrate on the main struggle. The film cut to the last protester being carried bodily away, and the clip ended.

"That was Gideon Smith," said Margaret, speaking over the voice of the reporter again.

Neubauer was rapt. "Did you see it? He had the sword! He still has it!" He gripped Margaret's arm and his eyes shone with strange light. "We have seen it for ourselves."

"What we need to see is a copy of this tape."

"What was he doing there? What was his purpose? Yessica, I need to know." Neubauer turned back to the television, and the scene cut to the studio. A party hack was pouring scorn on the ancient and outmoded beliefs of those who disrupted the meeting.

"We'll get the tape. We'll try and work out what it was he said. Maybe we can work out why." Margaret's whole manner was questioning.

"Pardon?"

"Torsten, it must have occurred to you. He's lost everything. He's killed someone. We know he's seen a psychiatrist. He could be completely mad by now."

"He did not kill that man." Neubauer spoke more mildly than he felt.

"He had a bloody good go! Stop pretending Smith is some sort of hero. You know he's just someone who fell into this whole mess, very much like us. He's an escaped lunatic with a sword. Face it; he may not have a purpose. He could be acting completely at random. This could mean nothing." Margaret threw her hands up in the air. "Nothing at all."

Neubauer sat on the floor uncomfortably and set his face. "Ambrose said this would give us the spider in the web. You are wrong."

"You hope I'm wrong."

"No. Everything here has a purpose. Nothing is wasted. See up there, on the wall? All the loose ends, what you call the dog-ends of information; all the pointless deaths, the carnage? This incident is part of the whole. You heard what Ambrose said: have faith. Believe, for this is real."

Margaret stood up and stalked back to her soggy breakfast cereal. "For all we know he could be setting us up. I don't trust Ambrose. "

Neubauer bit back. "Is that because he can read your mind?"

"I'm not going to talk about that." She spoke more sharply than she anticipated. "I'm late for work as it is."

"As you wish."

They presented each other with their apologies that night, and the gifts that went with them.

Heart

Margaret was very late, and carried her prizes under her arms: a video player and a tape.

Neubauer added his contributions to the haul on the table. There was an awkward silence as Margaret read the writing on the bottle of wine, smelt the flowers and looked at the headline on the *Liverpool Echo*. Neubauer picked up the unmarked video tape and turned it over in his hands.

"I am sorry," he began. "I know you are uncertain. I am too zealous, I know."

"Torsten, I was wrong."

"No, please ..."

"Shut up, sit down and listen to me." She pulled a chair back and, with a firm hand, pushed him into it. She smiled nervously. "I went off-shift and made a visit to the BBC. They were very helpful, especially after I told them some cock-and-bull story about trying to identify foreign agitators in the demonstration. I spent three hours closeted with a video technician, cleaning the tape up, getting close-ups, sorting out the sound, the full monty. Three hours stuck inside a very small and very sweaty editing suite, all for twenty seconds of Gideon Smith. There were two cameras at that hall on the night. One tracked the lefties, the other stayed pointing at the stage. It's not what Smith says that's interesting – although that is a bit of a bombshell – it's the reaction it causes. Uncork the vino and I'll try and set this video up."

It took an age to tune in the player, but eventually Margaret hunted down the test signal. She wasn't sure whether two glasses of high-grade German anti-freeze on an empty stomach had helped or hindered the process.

The player sucked in the tape, and she thumbed the play button on the remote. Big black lines laced the picture and sent her back to the instruction book.

"Tracking," she said under her breath, and twisted a small black knob this way and that until the picture cleared. She rewound the tape to the beginning and played it again.

Neubauer leaned forward in his chair, eyes narrowing. "How long is the tape?"

"About twenty minutes with all the different shots. You want to look at it the whole way through, or just the highlights?"

"I want to see Gideon Smith."

"Okay." She fast-forwarded to the relevant part, then rewound it slightly, pausing it just before the cut. "You have to listen very carefully, but it's audible."

The short blond hair and wide neck of Gideon snapped on to the screen. The shot centred on him, with four or five other heads around him. He raised an arm and pointed; a more deliberate and decisive gesture than the sky-punching of those surrounding him.

Beneath the radical calls, another cry could be heard. "Sutton! Sutton! I know who you are, Sutton. You killed Porlock. You killed Golden. You killed his family …". A shove at the edge of the crowd rippled through the protestors and knocked Gideon out of camera shot. The soundtrack was lost. Then he shuddered back into view.

"This man is not Lord Golden. He's called Sutton and he's a murderer!" He pointed his white-knuckled finger forward, then slowly lowered it, his eyes fixed on something off-screen.

The picture froze. "That's it. That's what he says."

"I know one of those names. Porlock." Neubauer reached behind him and opened up his black file. It was a few moments before he came up with the newspaper cutting. "Here. Mallory Porlock. Researcher for the BBC." He glossed the obituary. "Fell from a train between

Manchester and London. No reason why. And, and, *Mensch!*" His hand trembled as he flattened the creases out of the paper. "*Hör zu.* His last programme, widely acclaimed by the critics, focused on the life of Percy, Lord Golden, the government's senior Home Affairs Minister in the House of Lords."

"Smith said Sutton killed Porlock."

"And that Lord Golden is not Lord Golden. That he is really called Sutton, and he is a murderer."

"Torsten. What have we found?"

They watched the whole tape over and over again. By listening carefully, matching up the edits from the cameras, Neubauer was able to piece together what Margaret had seen in the editing suite: Lord Golden's reaction to what was happening in the auditorium.

Smith was inaudible from the second camera, which had been much closer to the rostrum. There was very little on tape, too.

"I couldn't risk it. I was supposed to be looking for agents of foreign powers, not at Golden. Raising more suspicion at this stage would be plain stupid," explained Margaret.

They saw Golden stepping back from the podium, pale and shocked. They saw him point to the back of the hall, and the man who appeared standing next to him move off purposefully.

"Smith ran when he saw that man." Margaret paused the image. A heavy-set man with a dark browline and a shaved scalp was frozen to the glass.

"Any idea who he is?" Neubauer was as unfamiliar with British politics as Margaret was with the workings of the *Bündesrepublik.*

"None. He's built like a bouncer."

"A what?"

"Door security at nightclubs; big, violent, not necessarily that bright. I've met his sort before."

"It seems that Smith has also met his sort before. But perhaps he did not expect him here? He cannot think that Golden will be without support. That is not likely, is it?"

"No chance. Smith knew, if he'd thought about it, that the place would be crawling with police, stewards, private security guards, the Special Branch even. Yet he bundles in with a bunch of left-wing agitators and confronts Golden directly. He's not scared of all the assembled forces of law and order, he's not scared of Golden, but he's scared of this man. And you're right, he has to have met him before; you can't be that frightened of someone you don't know."

"So where would he have met such a man? Neubauer looked over to the wall, then got up using his stick. He leaned on it as he searched. "Smith fears the man with a fear greater than death. His expression tells us so. He is desperate to escape him. Where has he faced death?"

Margaret joined him, trying to make sense of the web of wool. "Here. Marianne Newton was dying when she handed him the sword."

"And also here, when they came for him in Newcastle. The man who died had a gun."

"There were two men. Witnesses said that there were two."

"The man who tried to kill Smith there ..."

Neubauer finished her sentence in a rush: "Is the same man who killed the Newtons, and the same man who chased after him in Liverpool. But Smith did not know he would be there. When he saw him, he ran."

"That man is in Golden's pay. He takes orders from him. What Golden says, he does. Golden ordered

that man to kill." She was incredulous. "So who the hell is
Sutton?"

"Sutton is Golden. Perhaps not always, but is
now."

"He wants the sword. Golden wants the sword.
He's the spider."

"So it appears. There is something rotten in your
state of Britain." It gave Neubauer no pleasure to state the
bald facts. "Your government has been infiltrated by a
very dangerous man. All we have to do now is prove it."

"At least we know what we're looking for. We
can find out who that man is. We can pin him down; this
girl here." Margaret pointed to a photograph.

"Leah Orchard."

"She was there with Smith. She could tie him to
Newcastle. And the ballistics. If we match the bullets from
Robert Newton with those from Gideon Smith's house, we
solve one murder."

"If we place the same man behind the wheel of a
black Jaguar, we solve another. It was how we saw it at
the very start. Remember that first day? Robert Newton
shot dead in the hallway, Marianne Newton ran to her
death, the tall Viking disappears. We know now what
happened. We have enough to re-open the case."
Neubauer walked over to the table and unfolded the copy
of the *Liverpool Echo*. "This may help us. 'Mystery
surrounds Docklands' shooting'. A man, one bullet to the
head, close range, no motive, no witnesses. We know that
Golden's man chased Smith. Where did they go? I have
checked on the map, and it is not far from the hall to
where the shooting took place."

"More dog-end information, Torsten? I'll check it
out, after you pour me more wine. I think I'm beginning to
believe."

Chapter 21
Thursday 4th June 1987
London

Torsten Neubauer's story

Neubauer applied for a ticket to enter the British Library, and he used all his powers of persuasion to get one. He showed his badge, an outdated letter from his Embassy, even a note from his doctor. By the end of the day he had worn down the librarian, and left for Hammersmith with his prize.

Eight o'clock the next morning, Margaret dropped him off in front of the British Museum building in Great Russell Street. He had an hour to wait.

"You sure you're going to be okay?" she asked.

"This is a library, Yessica. What could possibly happen to me here? People are not even allowed to talk loudly." Neubauer eased himself from the passenger seat and pulled his knapsack out after him. "I'll be home after five."

"Make sure you eat."

"*Ja, Mutti,*" sighed Neubauer and swung the door shut.

He joined the half-dozen others sheltering under the massive mock-Greek portico and waited for the doors to open. Once inside, it was as if he'd entered Aladdin's cave; there was treasure everywhere under the great dome of the Reading Room. He sat at a desk for a half-hour, just marvelling at what he saw. Rows of books, all catalogued by title, author, subject; magazines, journals, maps and newspapers in stiff-backed binders; the perfume of old paper. He resolved to send Esther a postcard of that wonderful place.

Heart

Neubauer put his head down to his darkly varnished oak desk and began to work. He did not raise it again for the rest of the week, which he spent wedded to the library. He became so knowledgeable, his head hurt with all the information inside.

By the Friday, he had read every scrap of writing about Lord Golden in the public domain. He had read every entry in *Who's Who* for the past twenty years, seeing his achievements build up like a great monument. He read the transcripts of his speeches in *Hansard*, watching him rise through the government ranks and cloak himself with authority and stature. He had a biography detailing his life and his works, seven years old. Neubauer found nothing to suggest that the man was anything but what he appeared to be: a hard-working and influential peer of the realm.

All the while, curiosity burned him. It was like searching an empty room; he was missing something that was so carefully hidden as to leave no trace of its existence. Gideon Smith had not only called Golden a murderer, he had called him by a different name. Were they the ravings of a madman, or an accusation learned from bitter experience?

While he waited for another pile of documents to arrive at his desk, he picked up the tiny, self-published *History of Middleton-cum-Marchbury*. Golden's ancestral seat, a great gothic pile of stone, glowered from the cover. The photographs bound inside showed scenes of everyday village life in 1953, the year of publication, timed to coincide with the present Queen's coronation.

He had read it, of course. Middleton had been a feudal gift of William the Conqueror, and mentioned in the *Domesday Book*. Yorkist barons had held the seat during the Wars of the Roses, and a volunteer regiment had been raised from the land to fight at Ypres. The age of steam had passed Middleton by, and it seemed that nothing had happened during the last sixty years to warrant comment.

He heard footsteps approaching, and closed the book face down on the desk. The back cover showed a stained-glass window from the parish church.

"Mr Neubauer? Your books."

He stared and stared and stared.

"Mr Neubauer?"

"*Entschuldigung.*" He cleared a space and the librarian set down the books, neatly arranged with the largest at the bottom, smallest at the top, and with all the spines aligned. "Thank you."

When he had gone, Neubauer picked up the Middleton history and looked again at the first page. There at the foot of the title plate was the legend: "Cover photograph, Middleton Grange, South side. Back cover, west window in St Simeon's, Middleton. Donated by Mr M Ambrose Esq. in 1851, costing the sum of £30 11s 8d."

Neubauer took his stick in his hand and carried the book over to the queue for the photocopiers.

Later, Neubauer asked Margaret a question: "Yessica, how old do you think Ambrose is?"

"No idea. Why do you ask?" She unwrapped the towel from her hair and began rubbing at it.

"If you were to make a guess? Please, try."

She considered the matter. "It's difficult to say. When men hit thirty, they look roughly the same until they hit fifty, maybe sixty. Then they start looking old."

Neubauer held out the photocopy of the church window. "I would say at least one hundred and fifty. Though I concede, he looks no older than forty."

She snatched the paper from his hand. "What is this?"

Heart

"The window is one hundred and thirty-six years old, and was paid for by Ambrose. It cost him thirty pounds, which I suppose was quite a lot of money then. Look at the picture, Yessica. What do you see?"

Margaret squinted, then gasped. The angel was holding a sword in a double-handed grip, high above his head. On his broad, naked chest was the Newton Cross.

"What is even more astonishing is that Golden must have seen this window every Sunday as he was growing up; it is from his own church in Middleton-cum-Marchbury. Ambrose had the window put in seventy years earlier to taunt him. He has a wicked sense of humour."

"I can't believe this. It must have been a relative, or, or a coincidence." Margaret abruptly went to the window. "Torsten, who is he?"

"Ambrose? A prophet as well as a mind-reader. We know the story of the sword is old. We have to face the fact that Ambrose may be just as old as that."

"Torsten, I'm getting scared. What he must know …". She looked again at the picture.

"It is a poor copy," said Neubauer. "The original is much clearer. One thing that you may miss is that the angel has no face." He opened his notebook, and read from it. "This is the inscription beneath it: 'Place me like a seal over your heart, like a seal on your arm, for love is as strong as death, its jealously unyielding as the grave.' I think we ought to be frightened. I think that this is normal and good. But I do not think Ambrose means us any harm."

"What if Ambrose is the spider? What if he's setting us up, and Golden with it?" Margaret seemed to be fighting with herself. Her face went through several contortions. "I don't like any of this. I'm trapped by it, and

288

I hate what it's doing to me. I don't know what's going on any more!"

Neubauer spoke calmly. "Ambrose speaks of love as strong as death. That is what he chose to put around the figure of the angel and the sword. He quotes from a love poem almost three thousand years old." He smiled. "I hope he is not that old. But the point is made. He wishes us only good."

She took a deep breath and steadied herself. "This poem. Where is it? Have you read the rest of it?"

"I did. There are no clues in it for us. It is widely distributed, but rarely opened. Almost every house in the country has a copy. When I asked the librarian if she recognised the words, she found it for me very quickly. She said it was the least-read best-seller in history."

"You're beginning to talk like Ambrose."

"I can see a copy from here." He walked over to Margaret's single bookshelf and pulled out a black leather-bound book. Blowing the dust off the spine, he handed it to her. "Song of Songs, sometimes called the Song of Solomon. Chapter eight." He looked down at the floor. "Now I must go to bed. It is late and I am tired."

"It's okay. I'll be up for a while, I guess." Margaret settled back in her chair and opened up the Bible. Inside the front cover was a highly decorative bookplate, with her name written on it in heavy gothic pen.

"Presented to Jessica Anne Margaret on the occasion of her Confirmation, August 8th 1968." She hadn't opened it since then. There was an index, and she leafed through the foil-thin pages to get to the Song of Solomon.

When she got there, she started reading. She didn't stop until she finished it, flushed and uncomfortable. No one had told her that the Bible contained such passages. Despite being alone in the room, she felt embarrassed. Bibles were for pious words and stern invocations of judgement.

Not sensuality, passion and sex.

She knocked at Neubauer's door.

"*Herein.*"

She leaned against the frame, her arms folded in front of her. "I've read it."

"*Also.*" He was sitting up in bed, dressed in a candy-striped pyjama top.

"Torsten, since the subject's been raised ...". She started playing with her hair and began to blush, but didn't lower her eyes. "Since you came back, you haven't really shown much interest in me, that way. I had hoped that we'd be more than just friends."

"Lovers," said Neubauer plainly.

She nodded slowly and wondered what was coming next.

"I can not."

Margaret was caught off guard by his answer. "You can't? I don't understand."

Neubauer slid his legs out from under the duvet and stood up carefully. The bed was interposed between him and her. "Yessica, *schätzchen*, every night and every morning I look at myself in the mirror. I was not pleasing to the eye before, I know. My smile showed too much teeth and my hair looked like a bird's nest. It is shorter now, of course, but I still dress badly, still am a man who thinks too much and says too much. Women never looked at me. And now, I am ruined." He followed her gaze. "No, not down there. Up here, in my head." He unbuttoned his top, took it off and draped it on the bed.

Despite herself, she flinched. It was as if a shark had bitten a crater out of his ribcage, and a five-year old had attempted a repair with handfuls of red and white marbled putty.

"This is why I use a stick. Not to help me walk because my legs are weak, but because I lack the muscle to keep my body upright. I lean like a drunk man, and it hurts so much that I fall over. I cannot bear to be looked at. I am a grotesque. I should be dead, but the Frankensteins at the hospital sewed me together again. Skin grafts, metal and plastic. Bones plated together with bolts as wide as your finger. Yessica, you are the first ever to offer, and I am happy that someone could love me.

"But I do not love me. If it were not for the sword, I believe I would have killed myself. The days go by, and there is pain without end. I am still weak, still half a man. I would only disappoint you." He picked his top back up. "Please, say goodnight. I find all of this very hard."

She left him, her head held in her hands, staring numbly ahead, not focusing. Her mind raced from point to point and no amount of reason would make it stand still for a moment.

Friday 5th June 1987

In the morning, Neubauer was better at pretending that nothing had happened, if only because he had had longer to prepare for the time when it eventually did.

Margaret fussed around him, offering him more coffee, more toast, a choice of jams or marmalades, first refusal of the bathroom.

He silenced her with two raised eyebrows and the ghost of a smile.

"Oh," she said, and nothing else.

Heart

But before she left to go to Scotland Yard, he touched her gently on the shoulder and turned her around.

"Please. Do not pity me. Pity would tell me I had no use left, and I know that is not true. Rather, work with me. Do the things I cannot do because I am too weak, and I will do the things you cannot because you have little time. If we cannot be lovers, let us love each other anyway."

She gave a slight nod of her head and a tight, thin-lipped smile. She faced the door again, her ponytail bobbing down her back.

"'Bye," she said, and felt unaccountably close to tears.

"Have a good day, Yessica."

Neubauer started looking for Golden's man. Westminster was virtually deserted: everybody who was anybody in politics was grafting away in their constituencies trying to get themselves elected. The working peers were being wheeled around the country, bolstering the foot-soldiers with their rhetoric and rallying cries.

Not knowing precisely how to access the information he needed, he somewhat naïvely placed a call to Conservative Central Office from a pub just around the corner.

"Good morning. I am a journalist with the *Süddeutsche Zeitung*. I was wondering how I obtain an interview with Lord Golden?"

He was diverted to the Press Office, and he repeated his question.

There was the sound of riffling paper. "Lord Golden; hang on a moment. Okay, got his itinerary. When were you wanting to do the interview?"

"The next few days, if at all possible."

"Right. Saturday today. He's in Cambridge all day, dinner with prominent academics. Sunday daytime, Oxford, ditto. Can't have them feeling left out, can we? Monday night, he's back in London because of the rally in the Royal Festival Hall on Tuesday. There might be time on the Tuesday morning to fit you in."

Neubauer gently laid the handset back into the cradle. Monday night. He opened his rucksack and pulled out one of two folders. He leafed through the bits of paper until he came to the *Who's Who* entry. The latest editions of the reference work had deleted the address of Golden's London home, but he only had to go back to 1978 to find what he wanted. He memorised the address, put the paper back in his folder, the folder back in his rucksack. He stepped outside to test the London taxi drivers' famed knowledge.

The cabby prattled on about the election: who he'd vote for, why, what was wrong with the other parties. "Besides, it's a shoo-in for the Tories, innit? Makes no difference who I vote for, does it? I mean, the bloke where I live, he's got a majority of thousands. I could turn up to the Polling Station dressed as a turnip and write 'I am a fish' on my ballot paper, and what would happen? Nothing. Nothing different, anyway."

"If voting could change anything, they would make it illegal," said Neubauer, repeating the anarchists' slogan.

"You're not far wrong. Where you from, mate? Not from round here, that's for certain."

"Berlin." Neubauer wished the man would concentrate on the road, rather than look over his shoulder at his fare.

"Germany, eh? What about 1966?" The cabby snorted. "They think it's all over; it is now."

Heart

"I think you will find we have won the World Cup since then."
Silence descended, broken only by Neubauer, who muttered. "I am more concerned about 1987 than 1966."
Perhaps the driver heard: perhaps he chose to ignore his passenger.
He dropped Neubauer off at the entrance to the Mews where Golden lived when he was in the capital. The taxi departed in a burst of blue diesel, and Neubauer fished around in his rucksack for his pocket camera.
It was a very simple point-and-shoot affair, cheap and cheerful. To Neubauer's mind, it was very quick and discrete to use. He hobbled down the cobbled mews, entering through an imposing archway that soared high above his head and shouted at him that trespassers were not welcome. He became enclosed by tall buildings on three sides of the courtyard, and he looked around for door numbers.
Golden's was three houses down on the left. Neubauer lifted his camera; click, rewind, click, rewind, click. He turned and left, wishing that everything was that easy. He was not challenged; there was no one at home.

He was sitting on the apartment floor, reading through his black file, sifting and weighing, when the telephone rang. He still felt awkward answering it; he half-expected Margaret's parents or an old boyfriend, and then he would have to explain himself.
"Hello?"
"*Hallo, Torsten. Hier ist Esther.*"
Neubauer relaxed. "*Esther. Welch' eine Uberraschung. Was ist los?*"
"*Setz' dich. Ich habe dir etwas schweres zu erzählen.*"
["Okay, I'm sitting down. Don't tell me the pot plant's dead; anything but that."

"What have you been up to?" She sounded dark and reproachful. "Your good name is being besmirched over here."

"Oh yes? By whom?" He settled back in his chair and shut his eyes. He could imagine sitting opposite her in a crowded café, wolfing down a plate of strudel and vanilla sauce.

"Important people, Torsten; spooks I would guess. They're mining your past for information. I can't stop them, either. I tried once, and was taken to task. This is a high-level government enquiry."

"Let them look. I've nothing to hide."

"Of course you haven't. But they're not trying to find out what you've done. They're trying to find out what you're like. Questions of religion, loyalty, sanity. It makes me uncomfortable, Torsten. It makes me think you're in a lot of trouble."

"I think I am. You do realise that there's a good chance this conversation is being recorded."

"What can they do to me? I'm an old woman, harmless. Someone was going to warn you, sooner or later. At least this way, I know I've told you, rather than risk having a letter intercepted."

"I've done nothing they can arrest me for. Not yet, anyway. Don't worry about me, Esther. I'm righting ancient wrongs. I'm actually enjoying it." He let the coiled telephone cord twang.

"Good. I'm glad, Torsten. But go carefully. You've upset some unpleasant people."]

"*Also. Danke, Esther. Du bist eine gute Freundin.*"

"*Du auch. Tschüss.*"

As he put the phone thoughtfully back into its cradle, he heard the key rattling in the front door.

"I think my phone at work's being tapped," Margaret blurted out before the door had swung shut. Her normal pale complexion was red with excitement.

Neubauer patted the settee next to him. "Sit down, Yessica."

"Didn't you hear what I said, Torsten. Someone's tapping my phone." She threw her handbag to the floor and started to take off her jacket, her haste causing her to struggle.

"They are probably reading your mail, too. Please sit down."

Margaret stilled her hands on the back of a chair. "What's happened? You sound like you already know."

"I have just been speaking with Esther. She hears lots of things; true things, false things, some things she is not meant to hear. Someone has been asking questions about me. Not questions like, 'How is Neubauer? I have not seen him for a while,' or 'What is Torsten doing with himself now he is not a detective?' No. Someone knows what I am doing already. What they want to know is how long I can keep looking in those places where I should not, how determined I am, and how much pressure is required to make me stop."

"Does she know who's asking?"

Neubauer moved his head equivocally. "Spies. My government or yours, it does not matter. They will be co-operating. Who do you suppose is powerful enough to get secret agents to look in my direction?"

Margaret balked. "Golden? How does he know? We didn't know about him until a week ago."

"I do not know how he knows." Neubauer looked down at the scattered clippings from his black file. He imagined his own obituary amongst them or, worse, Margaret's. "We can only assume that he knows as much about us as we do about him. Who authorises phone taps in this country?"

"The Home Secretary, and only in exceptional circumstances. That's officially. God only knows what really happens; everybody could be bugging everybody else and I wouldn't be any the wiser." She finally pulled the chair she was leaning on clear of the table and slumped into it. "Golden, of course, is a Home Office minister."

"You think your office telephone is bugged. Please explain."

"I was making a call to Merseyside; the ballistics report on the docklands' shooting still hasn't turned up." Margaret sounded more tired than a day at Scotland Yard ought to make her. "I put the phone down, picked it up straight away because it rang, and I heard myself in the conversation I'd just had.

Neubauer nodded. "*Also*. It is true, then. We should check this apartment for bugs. If we find any, they may already have copies of all my notes, and of the wall." He hung his head. "A lot more people could die because of this."

"What do we do?" Margaret asked bleakly.

"We have a choice: go on and take the consequences, or finish and leave Smith to his fate." He looked at the wall, deep sadness pulling at his face.

"We always had that choice. But instead of common criminals, we're after the people who pay my wages."

He shrugged. "This is your country, Yessica. You choose."

Margaret looked down at her lap. "I'm going to have my bath. I'll tell you afterwards."

"Okay."

Heart

An hour later, she stood at the entrance to the lounge, wet hair shining over her shoulder and her body wrapped in a towel knotted over her breasts. "Torsten? We're carrying on. I don't have a career to ruin, and anyway, this is too important to let go. I'm involved whether I like it or not."

Neubauer smiled, and felt uneasy at the same time; a touch of vertigo, perhaps. "I am glad that this is what you chose. What decided you?"

She ignored the bad grammar. "Ambrose. If we're all that Gideon Smith has, we can't desert him now. I could live with packing it all in and returning to what I laughingly call normal. I may even be able to live with losing you. But Smith's going to get killed, and even though he doesn't know it, we might be the only people able to stop that. I couldn't live with myself knowing that I did nothing." She shrugged, and the towel around her started to unknot. She caught and twisted the ends together in her hand. "Not a hard decision really."

"I would beg to differ, Yessica. Our lives will never be the same again."

Chapter 22
Saturday 6th June 1987
London

Torsten Neubauer's story

It was Saturday morning outside Lord Golden's home.

"I still can't believe I've given up the first free weekend I've had this month to do this."

"You offered."

"I know. It doesn't mean I can't complain about it." She wound down her window and flapped her hand outside. "It's warming up. When London gets hot, it gets unpleasant. If you want to go home, just say so."

Neubauer was already sweating. He rummaged around in his knapsack for a bottle of water. "I understand. I will not be a, what do you call someone who is killed for their religion?"

"Martyr."

"*Also.* One of them." Neubauer unscrewed the cap and drank deeply. He wiped his mouth with the back of his hand and passed the bottle over.

Margaret took the bottle, swigged, then handed it back. "They're coming out." She turned the keys in the ignition and the engine rumbled to life. Her eyes narrowed as the black Jaguar nosed its way out of the mews and paused before the stream of traffic. "I don't suppose I have to tell you what make of car that is."

"No." Neubauer lifted his disposable camera and clicked.

There was the merest of gaps; the bonnet of the Jaguar reached out and took the space as its own, blocking the road until it was fully integrated with the nose-to-tail rat-run.

Heart

"He's going the wrong way!" The car had turned left instead of right, leaving the Escort facing the opposite direction. Margaret watched the limo start to shrink in her wing mirror. "You ready for this?"

"Do what you must." Neubauer braced himself against the footwell and held on to his stick.

Margaret pulled the car out into the road, apparently heedless of the oncoming car. It barely stopped in time, howling to a halt in a haze of rubber smoke. The driver slammed his first down on the horn, further incensed by the nonchalant flick of Margaret's two fingers.

She returned her hand to the steering wheel and hauled it around to a full lock, throwing it perpendicularly across the busy street, blocking it completely. The moment the lane was clear enough for the length of the Escort, she popped the clutch and the car lurched two wheels up the pavement, then banged off back on to the road.

"We're off then," she smiled. She was enjoying herself.

"*Mensch.*"

Golden's limousine was ten cars ahead, but stopped at a set of traffic lights. The lights cycled and everybody moved off.

For half an hour they dogged the black car's every turn and twist. Following was easy: the traffic moved along at a snail's pace, and Neubauer said as much. As if to underline the point, a cycle courier snaked his way between the lines of cars in a blur of spokes.

Eventually, the car disgorged its very important passenger in Parliament Square.

Margaret pulled over and tapped at the steering wheel. "Who do we want? Golden or his man?"

"The man. Golden cannot hide. He is too well known and his movements are public knowledge. Go after the car."

They ended up in Soho, and the driver parked the car at a parking meter in Soho Square. As they drove past, the driver's side door opened. They caught a glimpse of the man.

"It's him," said Neubauer, "The man who chased Smith."

"I'll dump the car."

Neubauer twisted uncomfortably in his seat to look behind. "Be quick. He is locking the car."

Margaret reversed the car into a space Neubauer would have thought could barely have fitted a pram. "Feed the meter. I'll lock up."

"Can we not just go?"

"You can pay the fine then. Out, out! We'll lose him." She checked her wing mirror before opening the door.

Neubauer pulled himself out, and looked around at where he was for the first time. His attention had previously been fixed on the car and not on his surroundings. Not as bad as the *Reeperbahn*, or the streets surrounding Dam Square, but still very familiar to a Berliner. Girls, girls, girls was the same in most language, and XXX wasn't advertising beer.

"Nice place," he said. It had been, once.

"Great Chinese restaurants," said Margaret, twisting the key in the car door and pocketing the jangling bunch. "Can you see him?"

"*Ja*, he's looking in that shop window. What is a pawn brokers?"

"I'll tell you later. Now stay well back, look at anything but him, and don't, whatever you do, get seen."

Neubauer steadied himself on his stick. "Yessica, I know all this. I was a detective too."

She paused briefly to apologise. "Sorry, Torsten. He's off."

Heart

The man, in his heavy tweed overcoat, strolled away from them, craning his neck like a tourist.

"He must be sweating like a pig," commented Margaret. The sun was gaining intensity as the day travelled towards noon, and the air smelled of photochemical smog.

Fifty yards ahead of them, the close-cropped black hair and bullet head turned towards a poster advertising hardcore XXX action. He went in through the cinema door and was lost to their sight.

"Wait," said Neubauer, holding Margaret back. "Perhaps he suspects. He may come straight back out again."

After five minutes of loitering suspiciously, Margaret frowned. "He's not coming out. We need to check what he's up to."

"*Also.*"

In the dimly lit lobby were pictures of naked women in a variety of unnatural poses. Margaret declined to look at any of them. She'd been in these places before and always came out feeling grimy. She put her warrant card against the cashier's glass and steel booth.

"A man came in here; five-eight, five-nine, thick-set, short black hair, big tweed coat."

The middle-aged woman in the low-cut lace dress leaned back in her chair and put the book she was reading down on the counter. Neubauer glanced at it: Proust, in French.

"Can't say I've had much custom today, dearie. When's this geezer supposed to have come in?"

Margaret creased her browline. "Five, ten minutes ago."

"A spotty adolescent about quarter of an hour ago, but it's a bit slack, if you know what I mean."

302

"No one since then? We saw him come in." She looked at Neubauer in confusion.

"You're welcome to look around, dearie. There's about ten in the theatre at the mo, but I can't recall anyone like who you're looking for."

"Torsten, check the toilets. I'll have a scout around. He's got to be in here somewhere. You got a back door?"

"Fire escapes, but they're alarmed. Do you want me to get the manager?"

Margaret waved her help aside. "We won't be a minute."

But the cashier was right; the man wasn't in the cinema. Even in the darkness of the theatre itself, the audience's fevered faces lit only by the cold flickering images on the screen, she could tell at a glance he wasn't there.

She met Neubauer in the foyer. "Nothing?"

"Nothing. Where is he? He cannot disappear."

They emerged, blinking, on to the street. As they stood, Neubauer leaning on his stick, Margaret arms akimbo, they spotted the man on the opposite side of the street.

They both turned away and waited until he had passed.

"How the hell did he get there?" hissed Margaret.

"I do not know," was Neubauer's terse reply. He looked over his shoulder, and watched the man's back. "We should stay over here."

"Okay."

The man walked towards the square, and then turned right along one side, forcing them to cross the road. About halfway down, he ducked into a betting shop.

Margaret and Neubauer crossed over again, and sat on a bench. From there, they could see the door from over the roof of a parked car.

"How are you doing?" asked Margaret.

"Well enough. I took extra drugs this morning."

"He's tricky, this one. You don't think …"

"That he knows? How could he? Perhaps this is his usual routine."

Half an hour passed.

"So tell me," said Margaret, "How did he walk into that cinema and appear ten minutes later behind us?"

"You think he has done it again?"

"I know he has. He's standing on the corner of the street reading a bloody newspaper."

Neubauer slowly turned his head. "How? Yessica, I do not like this."

"Relax, Torsten. We can still see him."

"Perhaps it is only because he allows us." But he muttered this under his breath.

The man folded up his paper and tucked it under his arm. He started to walk away.

"He's moving again. Come on." Margaret helped Neubauer to his feet and urged him forward. At Neubauer's reduced pace, the man started to increase the distance between them.

"We're losing him." Margaret looked left and right across the road, and darted nimbly through the traffic to the other side, leaving the German stranded.

She was off, and Neubauer had to wait for the lights to change again before he could hobble over. "Yessica! Stop. He is playing with us."

Margaret looked back as her name was called, and purposefully ignored Neubauer's warning. She turned again, and began to trot down the pavement. She could barely see the man, just catching a glimpse of him every other pace as she raised herself on tiptoe. She was closing in on him, and in the moment when she thought he should be no more than ten yards ahead, he was gone.

She walked forward a few steps, stopped and span around, half expecting to see him someplace else. A small alley punctuated the rows of buildings, and she walked up to the entrance carefully. It was dark and foul, filled with rubbish and the stench of the night.

Something moved at the far end: a piece of paper flicked up into the air, moved by a fleeing heel. She jogged down the length of the alley as she could see it, to where it turned at right angles to its previous direction.

Above her, a narrow slit of sky; around her, urban flotsam and the steam vents from nameless restaurant kitchens. In front of her, a blank wall. She stalked up to it and pressed her hand against the crumbling brickwork, just to make sure. Out loud, she said: "This is stupid."

A shadow she had passed changed and flowed, creating the shape of a man in a tweed coat. He reached into his pocket and pulled out his matt-black gun. Margaret heard the sound of a shell being chambered and her head snapped around.

Then the man's lips opened and the chanting began.

The sound ground into her very bones. She felt she was being smothered by a heavy velvet curtain, and she was dragged breathlessly down. Her knees buckled first and she slid inexorably to the foetid floor beneath her.

The sights of the gun followed her descent, lining up on the bridge of her nose. If she concentrated hard enough, she could see down the barrel from where her death would spit. The man stopped his incantation. There was a dreadful silence and then the handgun barked once.

The thrown walking stick bounced off his shoulder and clattered against the wall next to him. The man turned slowly, lowering his gun, and looked with narrowing eyes at Neubauer, who was desperately clinging to the corner of the alleyway, hoping beyond hope that his distraction had proved sufficient to deflect the bullet's path.

"Yessica? Yessica?" He called hoarsely. "If you have killed her ..."

The man smiled, and said quite distinctly: "Perverse Teuton cripple." He started to walk towards him with his steady, purposeful gait. Over the course of the next three strides he melted away, growing pale and translucent, until he had vanished before their eyes.

Neubauer felt a brush of air seconds later, and heard a dry, hiccoughing laugh.

Margaret was screaming; pointing and screaming at the top of her lungs, not caring who heard her or if no one heard her. She screamed for herself alone.

Neubauer lost his grip on the wall, and made his way on his hands and knees to where she lay. He gathered her up in his arms and clutched her to him. She began to sob, burying her face in his ruined chest and trying to shut out the world turned upside down.

Neubauer had hurt himself. He had opened scar tissue with his frantic effort, and his shirt had been red with new blood by the time he pulled the near-catatonic woman from the alleyway.

Using the car was out of the question. Neubauer raised his arm to hail a taxi and almost passed out with pain. His vision greyed and he clutched at a lamp-post. "Help me," he called weakly. "Somebody help me."

A Rastafarian called an ambulance, and even when Neubauer told him he was Babylon, he stayed to help. Margaret was chalk white, shivering and muttering under her breath as the paramedics picked her up and laid her on a stretcher. Then they came for Neubauer and found he was less compliant.

He lay on the pavement, curled around on his side, and gagged when they touched him. Gently, they discovered that they weren't going to kill him by moving him. Swiftly and without warning, they hoisted him on to the metal stretcher and into the back of the ambulance. Neubauer could see Margaret staring blankly at him. He tried to reach out for her with his good arm, but the distance was too great.

"Yessica, can you hear me?" The paramedic in the back with them shook his head and tried to move Neubauer's arm back across his chest. "Yessica, say something."

"Come on, now. Lie quietly, sir."

"See to her. Forget about me."

The man turned and frowned at Margaret. "There's nothing I can do for her. Blood and bones, sir. That's what I do. But she's going to need something a sight stronger than a cup of tea." All the same, he took a red blanket and tucked it around her quivering form. "Now please, lie still. You're making a mess of my nice ambulance."

Neubauer forced his head around until he was staring at the ceiling. Buildings flicked by through the windows, and he felt himself weave through the scattering London traffic. "Will there be police at the hospital?" he asked.

"You want to make a complaint of some sort, sir? I can radio ahead if you want."

"No," he said, too quickly. "No police. No more police, that is. I mean, we are police."

"You're not making much sense, sir." The paramedic shone a torch into Neubauer's eyes. "How're you feeling? Dizzy? Nauseous?"

Heart

"I am fine, considering. Please listen; this is important. Detective Sergeant Margaret and myself are working undercover. There must be no fuss and no police. Do you understand?" He gripped the paramedic's arm as tightly as he could.

His grasp was loosened by the lightest of touches. "Yes, sir. As you say, no fuss."

They swung into the hospital and the blood rushed to Neubauer's head as they braked abruptly under the covered entrance to Casualty. The paramedic pushed open the back doors, and two porters helped him out with his human cargo.

He counted the lights as he was wheeled in. A shout of 'cubicle seven' made the gurney he was on twist. The curtain was drawn, and a doctor, stethoscope around his neck, lurched into his field of vision.

"Hello? Can you hear me?"

"Yes," grunted Neubauer. "My name is Torsten Neubauer. You will find a form E111 in my wallet. Seven months ago I was wounded by several rounds from a Kalashnikov AK-47. I have opened my scars. Right torso. That is all."

The doctor, nonplussed, stepped back and regarded his patient. "Thank you for the full history. Medication?"

"Dihydrocodeine. I took one this morning at seven. A painkiller would be helpful."

"Right. Nurse, get his shirt and jacket off. I'll get the on-call plastic surgeon. Mr Neubauer, what can you tell us about your friend?"

"Yessica Margaret. She is physically unharmed, but has had a great shock." She has stared down the barrel of a gun and seen someone disappear before her very eyes. But he didn't say that. He didn't know what else to add.

They sewed him up as best they could, and strapped up his ribs with tensioned strapping. When the injections began to wear off, it felt like he was in a giant vice, his life slowly squeezed out of him.

Two and a half hours later, the hospital said he could go and take Margaret with him. They gave him two sets of forms, one for himself, one for Margaret. They urged him to call her GP as soon as he got home.

He found her sitting on a plastic chair in the waiting room, shivering every few seconds. He stood before her, leaning on two aluminium crutches. Eventually she looked up and, a little while later, she focused on him. She blinked slowly and tears began to well up in her eyes. The salty water streamed over her lids and down her pale face, splashing on her knees. She didn't make a sound.

Neubauer took her home, sat her on the sofa, and arranged for a garage to collect her car.

She would walk if prompted, eat and drink if prompted. Otherwise, she sat, gently rocking backwards and forwards, her shoulders hunched. Her eyes examined the writhing of her fingers in her lap.

Neubauer looked on in despair. Her mind had become as scarred as his body. Their quest was over unless he could heal her, and he knew that was a wish born of lunacy. Golden had won, Smith was as good as dead, and whatever mystery lay behind it all would stay buried forever.

He traced the threads on the wall, and determined to tear it all down. It had nearly killed Margaret, and he had been a fool to ask her to sacrifice herself. She loved him; of course she was going to say yes to him, no matter how mad his schemes.

He threw one crutch to the floor, and reached up a clawed hand. The strapping pulled and it made him angrier still. Strands of wool caught under his nails, flicking drawing pins to the floor. Paper and photographs fluttered like dying birds. His scour came to Ambrose's calling card.

Freelance historian and collector – Neubauer snorted, but stopped his slow destruction. There was a telephone number on the bottom right of the card. He did not recall seeing it there before. It had not been there to remember.

He sat next to the phone, and dialled the long string of numbers. There was a code starting with zero; he was calling outside London. The phone rang four times, then was picked up.

"Herr Ambrose? Neubauer ..."

"I'm sorry I'm not here to take your call," said the tape in slightly accented English, flowing up and down with a sing-song inflection. "Please leave a message after you hear the beep."

Beep.

Neubauer spoke slowly and clearly. "This is Torsten Neubauer. Golden knows. His man tried to kill Yessica. He has scared her so much she is unable to talk, unable to do anything. I ... I am uncertain what to do. Help us, please. We cannot continue like this."

He replaced the handset and sat in his chair. Outside, the sun beat down. Inside, the air in the flat was chilled.

Chapter 23
Sunday 7th June 1987
London

Torsten Neubauer's story

He was standing at the window, squinting at the setting sun and watching the sides of the buildings turn a deep red. A day of despondent waiting had passed him by. He had gone through the motions of washing, dressing, eating, and it had felt like a dream. Margaret had barely moved. She had to be coaxed to drink, to go to the bathroom. At times she had forgotten to breathe, and Neubauer suddenly became aware of a deathly silence that he had had to break with a shouted command.

A motorbike pulled up outside, a huge BMW touring machine, silver-grey with a cluster of boxes anchored to its tail. The rider shook out the hem of his leather coat and pulled off his helmet.

"Ambrose," breathed Neubauer. "Yessica, Ambrose has come. He will know what to do. He knows everything."

Margaret blinked and shivered, shivered and blinked.

Ambrose stowed his helmet in one of the panniers, and took out his battered hat. He batted it twice against his knee in an effort to restore its shape, then jammed it on his head. After a short interval, the entry phone buzzed. Neubauer was standing by it.

"Herr Ambrose?"

"Come down, Herr Neubauer. Bring Sergeant Margaret with you."

Neubauer frowned. "I am not certain that I can."

"I'll wait for you," said Ambrose, and the sound of footsteps receded from the external microphone.

In a game of patience, someone a century old would win. Neubauer put the phone back on the wall and gathered up his crutches. "Yessica? Ambrose is here. He wants us to meet him downstairs."

She looked up, but made no other movement. Her open face was in turn pleading and vacant.

"We are going to have to go to him, Yessica." Neubauer knelt down on the floor at her side and pulled at her feet. He slipped her shoes on and, with her foot on his knee, tied up the laces.

As he struggled back up, he gasped with pain. He should be in bed, unconscious. He gritted his teeth and pulled her to standing. They leaned against each other, swaying gently backwards and forwards as if dancing to a ballad.

He had to guide her. A turquoise silk scarf was draped over one of the coat pegs by the front door. He tied one end to her left wrist, and held the other between his sweating palm and the handle on the crutch. "Follow me. We shall see what we shall see."

They had the lift to themselves.

"I know you do not trust him like I do. But trust him through me. He came when I called, Yessica. That must mean something." Margaret started to shake, and Neubauer damped down the motion by holding her painfully to him.

The doors opened. Ambrose was waiting, sitting on the step outside, catching the last of the sun. He stood up and turned to face them through the glass. His eyes were luminously golden. He opened the lobby door without a key, and held it as they inched outside.

"Good," said Ambrose.

"What is good about this?" snapped Neubauer. "She has gone mad. If she is not cured, she will break like china."

312

Underneath the brim of the hat, the golden eyes narrowed into fierce slits. "You're in this state because you still don't understand, despite the evidence staring you in the face. I have my own purposes to work out, and they're taking up most of my time. I came because you asked, and I can just as easily go again."

Neubauer was startled by his sudden sternness. Jaw jutting out, he replied: "I called you because I have faith in you. A man who is over a hundred and twenty years old must know something worthwhile."

A grudging smile crept across Ambrose's mouth. "Perhaps I do, Herr Neubauer, and perhaps you don't know the half of it yet. Come on, then. We've a way to go."

"I really do not think Yessica is able to walk anywhere."

"Nonsense, man." Ambrose leaned close and looked into her blank eyes. "She'll get there. What about you?"

Neubauer adjusted his grip on his crutches. "We appear to be at your mercy."

"Far from it. It's me who's the servant of all. It just so happens that I've orders to follow from those whose authority outranks yours." He whirled his coat around and set off down the pavement.

He led them on a journey without direction or purpose. They seemed to cross one street several times, appearing out of different side roads along its length. Neubauer called to Ambrose: "This is wrong!" With every step, he was getting weaker.

Ambrose lifted his hand and waved them on without looking back. "Don't fall behind. It's dark, and you're lost."

Finally, a black front door, anonymous and unremarkable, on a Georgian-fronted street in God-knows-where. Ambrose climbed the seven steps up, and opened it without knocking.

Neubauer staggered in on his last legs. Ambrose caught him and held him. "Look you now, Inspector. You'll never complete the race if you run after every shadow. Be single-minded, remember. I told you that right at the start: don't be deflected left or right. It's a shame it's come to this pretty state, but I don't think you'll be distracted again."

"Thank you for your words of comfort," hissed Neubauer. He had no strength left; his head fell against Ambrose's shoulder, and his coat smelled of smoke and rain, of an endless cycle of summer and winter. He allowed himself to lie like that until he recovered.

His crutches found the floor, and Ambrose leaned him against the wall. "You'll live, despite everything." He reached past Margaret and shut the door.

"Where are we? Your home?"

"Good Lord, no. I haven't had a house for a while. Must be years, now. I'm far too busy to be tied to one place." He walked, quite slowly, down a dimly lit corridor with many doors to either side. He seemingly chose one at random. "In here."

They crossed a room tiled with slabs of black and white stone arranged like a chess board. At the door opposite, Ambrose held up his hand for silence, and led them inside.

Neubauer's first impression was one of immense space, like a sudden clearing in a dense forest. There appeared to be nothing above them, and the edges of the room in which they stood were far back in the distance. The illusion was enhanced by a myriad of candles arranged in a wide circle of tall metal stands. Each candle was a glowing point of yellow light that suffused

314

Simon Morden

outwards, touching only what it wanted, not necessarily what it ought.

As his eyes grew accustomed to the shadows, he could make out the forms of people, standing outside the circle. They were not dressed in ritualistic robes of occult office, but in everyday workwear: suits and denims, dresses and overalls. They talked in groups of three or four; their voices did not carry even though they did not whisper their conversations.

At one point in the circle of candles, someone had set up a trestle table and placed on it a simple wooden cross. The table was the only furniture. There were no chairs or pews or rails or pulpits or lecterns.

Then he saw the dull reflection of gold all around him. He strained his eyes, and saw that there were patterns in the gilt, figures of men and animals, trees and hills, stars and planets. "What is this place?"

Ambrose's voice was dark and rich, reminiscent of the time he had quoted the sword inscription. "It is one of Britain's secret places, part of old Albion. Forgotten and lost by all but the faithful, who still gather here as an act of remembrance and an act of hope. Ah, they know their history, and share one vision of the future." He breathed deeply and sighed. "There are other places, here and there, at the far-flung fringes of the land and, at the same time, at the very centre. Those troubled by the mystery of belief are always restless, always searching for wild heaven. They find a taste of it in these thin places, where the distance between this world's realm and the next has all but vanished."

No one from the strange congregation had challenged them, but Neubauer felt unease. "Should we be here?"

"No one finds their way by accident. Each and every journey begins with a single step. You are here because this is where you ought to be at this time. These brothers and sisters know that. They wait for you to make yourself known."

"Yessica. What about Yessica?"

"Ask her to enter the circle. She will follow."

Neubauer took a step forward and felt the pain rip like a wave up his side. He clamped his jaw shut and waited for the nausea to pass. Slowly, he moved forward, Margaret tugged along behind him like a child's pull-along toy.

"Who are you?" said a woman's voice, soft and demanding.

"Inspector Torsten Neubauer, West German Police, and Detective Sergeant Margaret, British Police."

"Who are you?" asked another voice, male; arch and imperious.

"I have told you who we are."

"Who are you?" someone asked for the third time.

Neubauer thought furiously. What he had said was not acceptable; he was answering the wrong question. "We have been looking for the truth and have discovered more than we wanted, but less than we need."

"What do you know?"

Ambrose strode into the circle. "I'll tell you what they know: fragments. They know the who, the what, the where and the when. But they do not know the why." He began to orbit Neubauer and Margaret, and bombard them with words. "What comes first?"

"The picture from the asylum book. But I still do not understand ..."

"Symbolic! What's it a picture of?"

"Newton Crosses."

"No. What is the picture? What's behind the crosses?"

316

"A sword."

"A story about a sword," thundered Ambrose. "Why did the Newtons die for the sword?"

"Because they belonged to the cult that knows the end of the world." Neubauer was becoming dizzy, trying to track Ambrose's circling figure. He shut his eyes.

"Incidental," whispered the voice in his ear. "Why is there Elvish on the sword?"

"I do not know!"

"Because my mother wrote it there. Why does Golden want the sword?"

"You have all the answers. You tell me."

"Because," said Ambrose, "he wants to be king."

Neubauer opened his eyes and Ambrose's breath was in his face. "King? King of what?"

"King of Britain." He took a side-step and pressed his palms to Margaret's temples. "Now all will be revealed. Jessica Margaret, do you know who I am?"

"Yes," she said.

"Then awake! Legends walk the earth once again, and this is no time to be caught sleeping. Who am I?"

"You're Merlin," said Margaret. Colour returned to her cheeks. "You're Merlin the magician."

"And what is the sword?"

"The sword is Excalibur, King Arthur's sword." She smiled. "At last it all makes sense."

"So," said Ambrose, turning to Neubauer. "Sergeant Margaret has become wise. What about you? Do you understand?"

"No. No, I do not." His relief at Margaret's healing was overwhelmed by his indignation. He confronted Ambrose, nose to nose. "None of this makes sense. Who are you?"

"Gideon Smith asked me the same question. He understood when I told him the answer. You know the answer already, but you will not understand. It's a British thing. The story is in Sergeant Margaret's blood, and mine, but not yours."

"Am I inferior then, that I cannot understand your story?"

"Not inferior, no. You have a story all of your own. I will answer your question, but first answer mine." Ambrose stepped about and gestured with his hand at empty space. "We have here a time machine. You have a gun in your hand and it has a full clip of bullets. Inside the time machine, you see that the dial is set for February 1920. The co-ordinates will take you to Munich. From your history books, you know that a certain man will be in that city at that time. He would be defenceless against you. You may even escape the authorities and travel back to your own time." He dropped his hand. "You know who I'm talking about, don't you?"

"Hitler. Adolf Hitler."

"Would you kill him?"

"Without hesitation."

Ambrose suddenly leapt back, shouting. "Why, Herr Neubauer? You pledged to uphold the law in your own country. Why then would you kill an innocent man in cold blood? Are you such a barbarous butcher of human flesh to hold life in total contempt?"

"You know why, Ambrose! He ruined Europe; he killed the Jews, the Gypsies, the Russians, the Communists, the homosexuals, the disabled, the mentally deficient. He was the devil himself, and it would be better if he had never been born."

Ambrose lowered his voice. It occurred to Neubauer that he was being played like a harp; a touch here, a touch there. His strings were pulled one by one, and the resulting tune was less than edifying. "Passionate words, Inspector. The Holocaust haunts you for two

318

reasons. Your father was a hero of the Reich, and your mother an enemy. You yourself represent everything you hate and fear, two sides of the collective madness that overtook your people.

"But history is not for you to rewrite and you know that in your heart of hearts. All you can do is work for a time when all will be made whole and clean and good and true. This is your story, Torsten Neubauer, and the story of your *volk*. I'm not part of it and I can't understand it like you do. Does that make me less? In no way does it diminish me. But it makes it hard for me to understand what drives you to do the things you do. Hard, but not impossible, for I have the experience of many years. I am Merlin Ambrosius, bard, prophet, immortal of days, servant of the Most High God. That is the truth, but it means nothing to you. To Jessica Margaret and to all these gathered here, to every Briton with a living heart, it means everything."

Bewildered, Neubauer addressed the congregation in a strangled cry: "But what does it mean?"

Margaret, to show her understanding, answered for Merlin Ambrosius. "Where Excalibur and Merlin are, Arthur is not far behind. That's it, isn't it?"

"The Once and Future King, Herr Neubauer," said Ambrose. "Ponder these words, for they are mystery indeed."

"Is this not myth? I came seeking the truth and I am given this madness?" The German was moving towards anger, and his words had rancour.

"I am myth!" roared Ambrose. "You say I am one hundred and twenty years old and you are wrong; ten times over wrong. Listen to me, heathen Saxon, and listen well. You are blind until you grasp this. Just because we call it a story does not mean it has no power, no fury. If the Holocaust was just a story, would it not grip you in the

319

same way, make you remember and be willing to battle at the barricades, crying 'Never again'? This is the strength of legend and the inspiration of myth. We would die in the knowledge that we serve the King!"
The congregation bellowed their assent, and the sound buckled Neubauer's knees.
"*Mein Gott.*"
"If we would do this for a story, what would we do if it were true? What would we do if Arthur, our king, had gone away and was coming back?"
"Torsten," said Margaret, "it's the end of the world."
Neubauer looked around him, at the candles and the dimly illuminated faces beyond the circle. "Golden would be king. You have your Elizabeth. Surely the people of this country would not follow another."
"We've had revolutions before," explained Ambrose. "We've even executed our monarchs. Golden would use Excalibur as a talisman of power, as well as its lever. You're wrong to think that people wouldn't flock to his flag. Excalibur would be all he needed."
Neubauer fell into thoughtful silence.
"Do you believe?" asked Ambrose quietly.
"I believe. I understand partly, but I believe the whole."
"Do you have anything you want to say?"
Neubauer cleared his throat and addressed everyone in that holy place. "I have an apology to make. But first I must tell you …". He paused, and his eyes started to brim with tears. "A story; a story about Item 563-21."

"Things have changed." Neubauer was in contemplative mood as he drank his coffee. Outside the apartment, it was night and life carried on. Cars drove past, people ate takeaways from foil cartons, drunks shouted to no one in particular. "I was a democrat. What am I now?"

"A monarchist. But a different monarchy." Margaret sat next to him on the sofa, her feet stretched out in front of her. "I swore allegiance to the Queen, her ministers and officials. It puts me in a difficult position. Freemasons be damned, this is a whole new ball game. Ambrose, Merlin, is organising a coup."

"Not strictly true. Golden is plotting. Ambrose is waiting for what will be; a long-forgotten king from a thousand years ago coming back to claim his throne. I doubt, however, that the authorities will make a distinction. I am now a foreign insurgent planning to overthrow your state. I could get shot for that." He felt the stitches pull as he breathed. "Shot again. I am not comfortable with the idea."

Margaret nodded. "I feel different; somehow surprised. Like I'd received an unexpected Christmas present."

"Christmas was an unexpected present, Yessica." Neubauer sighed unevenly. "Can we talk in the morning. I am ...", he searched for the right word, "exhausted."

"I'm sorry. Do you want me to help you to bed?" She got up and held out her hands to him. "You've done too much today."

"I know. It was worth it." He held on as she pulled him up.

"Thank you," she said. "You carried me, and you were in no fit state even to try. It's my turn to help you." She put Neubauer's left arm around her shoulders and walked him to his room. There, she laid him on the bed and fetched him a glass of water for his pills.

He took two, and she held his hand as he slipped into unconsciousness.

Chapter 24
Monday 8th June 1987

London

Torsten Neubauer's story

Margaret dropped Neubauer off in Soho before going to work. It was early, and there were few people out on the streets. A street cleaner was brushing the gutters free of broken glass and grit. In the distance, a refuse lorry was noisily emptying bins.

He retraced his steps from two days ago. The landscape looked very different in its unpopulated state. The lorry, with its attendant workers, approached. Neubauer hurried as best he could. He beat them to the alleyway, and once inside, he found it damp and clinging. As he turned the blind corner, he saw a little shed made out of cardboard boxes.

He knocked on its roof. There was a muffled shout and what sounded like a torrent of abuse. "Please," said Neubauer, and searched around for something else to say. "Police."

He waited, and eventually part of the corrugated cardboard flipped up. Out popped a wax-white face with cheekbones like axe blades. Her hair was as short as a skinhead's and her expression as pugnacious as a prize-fighter's. Her accent was pure Glaswegian, and she must have been all of seventeen.

"What do you want?"

It took a moment for Neubauer to understand her. "Nothing at all. I just thought it rude to start my search without warning you first."

She scowled. "Warn me of what?"

"Firstly, that I am here and mean you no harm. Secondly, the refuse collectors are close by. They will move you on, no?"

"Thanks," she said, and climbed out of her box. She began to stuff a stained sleeping bag into a plastic carrier.

Neubauer looked at the piles of rubbish and judged his position. He took a few steps forward, a couple backwards, and sighted down his crutch. "Here, I think," he said to himself. He walked towards a collection of black plastic sacks, split into strips by feral cats, their contents spilling out like intestines.

"You talk funny. You're not from down here, are you?" said the girl.

"I am German," he said.

She nodded, and watched him struggle a pair of Marigolds on. "What's wrong with you?"

"In general, or particular?"

"The crutches."

"I was shot by Russians. What about you?"

"Really? Russians? Why?" She avoided the question about herself.

"I got in the way. You must know what it is like, to be in the way."

"Oh aye. Those binmen, the police, security guards. But you learn quick out here, where the safe spaces are."

Neubauer got down on his hands and knees, and laid his crutches to one side. The first thing he found was his walking stick. He rubbed it clean and put it to one side.

"What are you doing?"

"On Saturday, a man tried to shoot a friend of mine. Somewhere here is the bullet." He began excavating handfuls of rotting vegetables and sifting through them. "I believe he has killed before; I would like to confirm it. Knowledge is power."

Heart

"Your world sounds as safe as mine," she said. Her
sleeping bag stowed, she turned to go.
"Wait," called Neubauer. "Perhaps you know this man.
He is heavy, big muscles. He has short dark hair, brown
eyes, a square face. He always wears black gloves and a
thick coat made of black and white tweed cloth."
"Does he drive a black Jaguar?"
Neubauer sat back on his haunches. "That is him. Stay
away from him if you value you life."
She laughed, and the sound was out of place in that
shadowed alley. "That's the problem, isn't it? I don't think
that I do. No one bothers about me except me. Soon, it
won't even be that. You see, you get offers out here. I've
had offers; food, shelter, clothes, booze and drugs. The
girls and boys get into those big, shiny cars, and they
never come back."
"Perhaps they have been taken to Paradise."
"The men come back, like your friend Markham, making
promises about everything if you'll just go with them. It'll
be my turn soon. They'll catch me with my guard down
and I'll go with one of them."
Back with his nose in the filth, he thought he spotted a
bullet hole. Slowly, he peeled back the layers of detritus.
An archaeologist would not have taken more care. He
worked his way down, and there, dull and lifeless, was a
bullet.
He picked it out and dusted it off. The bullet was
complete, not deformed in any way. He ought to thank the
rubbish for being there. As he inspected it, turning it over
in his gloved hands, he saw writing scraped on to the soft
metal. He recognised the sigils as Nordic runes, but did
not know what they said. He wrapped the bullet in a small
square of plastic film, and popped it in a jacket pocket.
"That is that," he said. He peeled off the rubber gloves and
discarded them amongst the scattered rubbish. He reached

324

for his crutches and his cane. The girl helped him to his feet, and the alley was suddenly crowded with municipal employees.

"Aye-aye," said one. "We know your game."

Neubauer squared up to the outsized man in the fluorescent yellow waistcoat. "Think what you will about me, but you will apologise to the girl."

"Oh, lah-di-dah. Ever so sorry, miss." He tugged his forelock, then his demeanour changed abruptly. "Now get out. Working men have a job to do."

Back out on the street, the Scottish girl smiled at Neubauer. "You thought I was important."

"You are. What is your name?"

"Tanya," she said.

"Tanya, listen. A time is coming when everybody in this country will be asked to choose one side or another. You will be asked to follow either a man who will have all the answers, or a legend that only brings more questions. Choose carefully, because one will think that you, and all your friends, are important. The other will not."

"What are you talking about? Are you strange in the head or something?"

Neubauer balanced on his crutches, and pulled out his wallet. "Here," he said to Tanya. He counted out some bank notes. "Fifty pounds. What you do with it is your business. I suggest that you buy a train ticket and go home. Perhaps you cannot go home, I do not know. Buy food, clothing. It will not always be summer." He thrust the folded notes into her limp hand. "I must leave now. Goodbye. Remember me when it is time for you to choose."

Deep in the records room, on a rickety table overhung by a single incandescent bulb, Margaret laid out Robert

Newton's case file. Neubauer sat on the only chair and watched her leaf through the papers in the box.

"Here it is. The ballistics report."

Three bullets, Neubauer recalled: knee, shoulder, head. Three black and white photographs of blunted projectiles that killed a man. He retrieved the bullet from his jacket and laid it on the table in front of him. "They are the same, no? See, the round that struck Robert Newton in the shoulder. It has the same word cut into it. Markham did kill him."

Margaret jabbed her finger accusingly at the photo. "I never saw this until today. I was on the case, and I needed to know this sort of detail." Her voice rose in pitch and volume. "What the hell was Arden playing at? Didn't he realise that there could be other murders we could have linked with this one? Other marked bullets in a dozen unsolved crimes."

"Yessica," said Neubauer, "I think he did realise. When did Arden get his promotion?"

"The bastard knew all along, didn't he?" she shouted. "He knew Marianne Newton had been murdered too, and he wouldn't let us follow that up. He knew about the ballistics, and he sat on it because we'd find a trail of dead bodies the length and breadth of the land. We've wasted a whole bloody year! How many more people has Markham killed? I'm going to have Arden. He's going to get what's coming to him."

"Please, Yessica. Quietly." Neubauer lifted his finger to his lips. "Someone will hear."

"Everybody's going to hear about this. I'll string him up by his thumbs. Do you suppose he knows about the sword?"

"Golden would not have told anyone he did not have to. No; Arden's promotion was reward for his blind co-operation. He did as he was told." He looked again at the bullet in his left hand, the photograph in his right. "No one will hear of this, Yessica. We cannot accuse Arden, or Markham, or Golden. Everything would come out into the open, and that would not be good. We are not here to expose any of them. We are here to save Gideon Smith." He paused and reconsidered. "No, Smith carries the sword. The Newtons carried it once and they are gone. It is the sword we must protect."

She leaned on the table, her fingers splayed and white. "We can send the lot of them down. We've more than enough evidence."

"We cannot do this."

"Torsten, we have no protection! We dig up one layer of dirt only to find another. Now we discover that Markham is a serial killer who preys on homeless kids and that my ex-boss is as bent as a three-bob bit. And they're trying to kill us!"

Neubauer drew breath and started to explain patiently: "The sword is safe with Smith only because Golden does not know where he is. We are not proposing to kill Golden, are we? He will not give up, no matter his situation. Even in prison, he would reach out and crush Smith. The only way to, to confound; yes, confound Golden is to keep him away from Smith."

"You're wrong." Margaret thumped the creaking table. "Golden is the key. We get him and Smith walks free. The sword will still be safe."

"No! Stopping Golden will change nothing. There will be other Goldens, other Markhams, and they will all appear all at once if there is a trial. What would your press do to Smith, the holder of Excalibur? Every madman would know where he was, and so would Golden. Everything we have just promised Ambrose would be broken, finished. The myth would be destroyed and we would have no story. I cannot permit this." He banged the table leg with a crutch, and documents slipped to the floor.

"You talk as if everything was rotten. That's not true. We have our problems here, but there has to be someone to trust, doesn't there? We can't bring Golden down on our own, Torsten. We need help." She stared at her impassive colleague and swept the remains of the file off the desk in a snowstorm of paper. "Answer me, damn you!"

"Of course we can take Golden. We know where he is. We get a gun from the evidence room. You can get through any police line and blow his head clear off his shoulders. That is the only way we can bring Golden down without exposing Smith. But you will not do that and neither will I, because we are decent people."

"You told Ambrose that you'd have killed Hitler if you'd had the chance."

"*Also*. Get me the gun and I will kill him myself."

"Torsten!"

He slapped his hand down. "Then let us end this foolish talk. We cannot do anything to Golden without, as you say, blowing the gaff. We do have people to trust, those who already know the secret. We trust Ambrose, and each other. It is enough, I think."

"Everything's gone. Everything I've worked for, tried to respect. It all means nothing." She was close to tears, her anger blown out like a summer storm. "Tell me what I should do."

"Come with me to find Smith, and see the sword."

"You mean resign."

"Our work here is finished. We must move on."

Margaret took a step back from the table and looked at the rows and columns of slowly ageing files. "It's not that easy, is it? I have to give notice, give a reason. I can't just drop it. I've got the rent to pay, too."

"Give it all up for the chance to save your country from Golden. You will be unrecognised, your name lost forever. There will be no medals, no headlines, no comfortable living afterwards. All this assuming we succeed. Come with me and hold back the darkness." Neubauer held out his hand, and she accepted it.

"Where do we find Smith?"

"I do not know. We start in Liverpool. When we meet, we will tell him our story and he will tell us his."

"I don't know if I can do this."

"Yessica, I will leave without you if you will not come. But I need you to be with me."

"You're going tomorrow?"

"We cannot wait. Everything is ready; if we are going, then we must go. If we stay, then we will miss the moment."

Her voice was small, broken, exhausted. "I'll come."

"Good." He squeezed his fingers together around hers, then let go. "We must tidy up. Can we take this file with us?"

"I can sign it out. Why?"

"Insurance. It cannot hurt."

Margaret bent down to glean the information from the floor.

Tuesday 9th June 1987

The flat had changed overnight. The wall was pock-marked and packed away, the pot plants given a last water, electrical appliances unplugged and the gas turned off.

Margaret came back in through the front door clutching the day's post: a bundle of letters and a small jiffy bag.

Neubauer tapped his suitcase with one of his crutches. "I am ready."

"So am I. I'm just dragging it out, that's all." She flicked through the mail. "Bill, bill, junk, junk, bill. Something from my sister, and this." She pocketed the handwritten envelope and discarded the rubbish. She waggled the brown padded packet in her hand to see if it rattled.

"Yessica," said Neubauer, "What is that on your hand?"

The outside of her palm glistened. It was oily, and smelled faintly of marzipan when she lifted it to her nose. "I think someone's sent me some cake."

"Please?" Neubauer took the packet from her. It was heavy, with high-denomination stamps on the outside. The gummed closure was a shade darker than the rest of the paper where it had been stained by the leaking contents. He sniffed it himself, then touched his tongue to the edge. "Yessica, get your coat and your bag. This is a bomb. The explosives are sweating and unstable."

She took a step forward, then another rapidly backwards. "Put it down."

"Go, Yessica." Neubauer's hand stayed perfectly still.

Margaret hovered uncertainly, then ran to her bedroom. She had a rucksack packed, stuffed so full she could barely lift it. She grunted under its weigh as she threw it on. As she waddled down the corridor, pictures skewed in her wake. They would never be straightened.

Neubauer gently placed the packet on the table. He stood there, staring at the greasy smear.

"Torsten, what are you doing? We have to get out!"

"I am wondering what was going through the mind of the man who made this. Did he intend to frighten us, or kill us?"

"I don't think he really cared. Look, I get nervous around things that go bang, so let's leave now." She turned and hit the wall with her back.

He wheeled his suitcase towards the door. "Still, it is a shame. I had wished to go on my own terms, not be chased out."

"Whatever." Margaret took the suitcase from him and locked the door behind them. "You call the Bomb Squad, I'll get the car."

When she pressed the lift call button, her finger was shaking.

"You car is not in a garage," observed Neubauer.

"No," she said slowly.

"Shall we go by train instead? Better to travel hopefully than arrive in several different pieces." The lift arrived and the doors slid open. Neubauer ushered Margaret in. "Please, after you."

Chapter 25
Tuesday 9th June 1987
Liverpool

Torsten Neubauer's story

Liverpool Lime Street Station; long platforms dotted with waiting passengers, trains idling their engines and filling the space with sooty smoke, the announcer blaring out the departures and arrivals in incomprehensible English.

They walked towards the entrance, Margaret still struggling with the weight of her pack. "Can we hire a car? Please?"

"Only if we pay by cash. I do not know how good Golden is at collecting information. We should use a small company, not a national one." Neubauer handed over his ticket to the collector and passed through the narrow gate.

A small crowd of people stared up hopefully at the arrival and departure board. Margaret went to the newsagents to buy an *A–Z* of Liverpool, and Neubauer joined the taxi rank. After a few minutes, their bags were in the boot of a cab, and they were asking the driver if he knew of any good hotels down by the docks.

"You want the honest answer or the tourists' answer? I could shaft you right here and now, because the docks aren't a place you want to stay. You look like nice people; I'll take you to the Adelphi."

They skittered around the town centre, up one-way streets and back down wide carriageways. Neubauer leaned forward. "Did you hear of the shooting, about two weeks ago?"

"Them's going off every other day. We've a drug war round here, just starting to get nasty. The lad they popped, nothing to do with it. In the way, mate, in the way." He pulled up to a set of traffic lights. "Don't go wandering round at night. Unsavoury people, you know what I'm saying? With respect, the addicts aren't going to worry about whether you carry a cane or not. They'll roll you and leave you lying in the gutter if you're lucky."

"Such a charming place."

"Scousers? Salt of the earth. Wouldn't live anywhere else." The lights changed to green, and the square Victorian façade of the hotel hove into view. "Here you are, mate." Neubauer sat back and exchanged pointed looks with Margaret. She raised her eyebrows, and said: "You knew it wasn't going to be easy."

"He makes it sound like Beirut."

"It'll be fine. I'll fend off the low-life for you."

The cab drew up inside the covered foyer, and the driver heaved the suitcase and the backpack out on to the pavement. Margaret paid him, and a bus-boy came out to carry the bags.

They had an argument at reception involving Neubauer's passport; the hotel wanted to keep it, he told them it was his and he would look after it, thank you very much. To prove his point, he paid for the first two nights in cash, using a thick roll of twenty pound notes. Eventually installed in their twin-bed room at the back of the hotel, they lay on their respective beds and stared up at the ceiling.

"It's still early. Dinner's not til seven," said Margaret.

Resisting the urge to sleep, Neubauer reached over to the bedside table and picked up his black file. "Do you think that talking to your police contact here would arouse suspicion?"

"I don't know. No one knows we've gone yet. Tomorrow, yes. Today, maybe not."

"We need the exact location of the shooting. We need to know the names of witnesses. We need to know where

Smith went. Dare we risk giving ourselves away for this information?"

"Perhaps we don't have to. You stay here. I'll go and ask some questions."

Resting the file on his chest, he said: "Be careful. Do not run into Markham."

"The election's over. He'll be long gone, chasing after Smith." But, to placate him, she added, "I'll be careful."

Neubauer shut his eyes and sighed. Margaret got to her feet and began to leaf through the *A–Z* gazetteer. There were so many unfamiliar streets. She felt as if she was in a foreign country, and in need of a native guide.

"Torsten, wake up."

He blinked, and found himself where he'd fallen asleep. "I had a dream." He half turned on the bed, and swung his legs out singly. He let their weight lever his body to sitting.

Margaret tapped her watch. "It's dinner time."

"*Also.* One moment, please." He ran his fingers through his hair and thought it about time it was cut again. "The dream was strange. I was hiding in a forest and stalked by something that had no form, but cast a shadow."

"Did it find you?"

"As usually happens, you woke me just in time."

"We can save the Freudian analysis for later. I'm starved."

"Let me find my shoes." He straightened his jacket and slipped on his lace-ups without untying the knots. "I am ready, if a little confused. Lead on."

He ordered soup, she chose the gingered melon slice.

"I know where we're looking. I had a good long talk with the concierge."

"The who?"

"The man who stands at the front doors greeting people. They're fixers. They get what you want, and they know who to get it from."

"*Gut*. What does this man say?"

Margaret pulled out the gazetteer, already rolled into a thick cylinder and looking dog-eared. She riffled the pages, turned back the corner of one and passed the book across the condiments. "Square A3. You see the 'Tate Gallery – under construction'? Run your finger to the left until you reach 'warehouses'. Just there, by the waterfront."

Neubauer studied the map carefully. "Is your man sure?"

"We can check, but yes, he's certain. If you turn forward one page, you'll see the conference hall at the top right. Smith must have run and come up against the river. The only way across from there is by ferry."

He flipped the page back and forth, building up in his mind an image of the route. "The man who was shot; the taxi driver said he was a nobody. I do not believe that. He was at the wrong place at the wrong time. I think we can assume that Markham shot him, otherwise you would have your ballistics report by now. Could he have been the witness to something terrible?"

Margaret went pale. "Torsten, what if Golden has the sword?"

"Smith is floating out to sea, and the revolution has already begun. We would be none the wiser." Neubauer played with his soup spoon. "That would be unfortunate."

"What do we do?"

"We make it a priority to find out whether Smith is alive, and whether he still has the sword. It was intemperate of him to bring it to his enemies, but perhaps he had no choice. Who would he leave it with, and not believe them to be in the gravest danger? But this will have to wait until tomorrow. Here comes our food." He put down his spoon and leaned back as the waiter set the brimming bowl before him.

Margaret waited until her melon had been delivered before replying. "Don't you think we ought to get a move on?"

"We must be thorough. If Golden has the sword, then it is too late. If he has not, then we still have time." He sampled his soup and reached for the pepper. He looked up and raised an eyebrow at Margaret's frowning face. "What?"

"Isn't that a bit complacent?"

"What would you have me do? I am tired and hungry. We went haring off once, trying to find Golden and Markham, rather than Smith. If we had acted correctly then, we would not be chasing a trail gone cold. Besides, Ambrose would not have alerted us to this event if, by the time we watched it on the news, the sword had been taken. There is time, Yessica, because no one has told us to the contrary." He slurped at his spoon.

"First thing."

"As you wish. Have you arranged a car?"

"Pete, the concierge, he knows someone who can get us a hire car for cash, no questions asked." Margaret used her tiny fork to spear the first segment of melon. "It'll be registered, but not to us."

"*Gut*. First thing tomorrow morning, we will go and see the scene of the crime."

Wednesday 10th June 1987

Neubauer turned over at the first clatter of her alarm clock without opening his eyes. He had slept poorly, unused to the soft sounds of a woman a metre and a half away in the dark. Sometime after midnight he had finally dozed, but seemed to hover between waking and dreaming. On occasions he found himself back in the forest, lurching from trunk to trunk and casting glances back over his shoulder as a shadow followed him distantly.

The clock was silenced with a long sigh, and he heard Margaret's feet slither out from under the sheets and on to the floor.

"Torsten? You'd better get up."

"*Wie spät ist es?*"

"Um? Oh, half past five." She stretched in the half-light, and some joints popped with the effort."

"*Halb sechs? Mensch!*" He pulled the covers over his head and gripped the edges tightly.

"You agreed – first thing." She padded over to the light and clicked it on. Some of it filtered through to Neubauer.

"Now get up and help me save my country."

With an invitation like that, he didn't feel he could refuse. He exposed his face to the harsh illumination of the bulb.

"Can I have a coffee first?"

"If you hurry." She shook the little kettle to test the water level and clicked it on. She gathered up her clothes in her arms. "I'll be in the bathroom."

He lay there for a few moments, and realised that he would end up in the street in his pyjamas if he didn't get dressed. He struggled out of his nightwear and looked critically at his scars. They were as ugly as they had been the day before. Give them five years and they might begin to mute. Neubauer took his shirt from the back of the chair and hid them.

The kettle rumbled and began to fill the room with steam. He found his stick and hobbled over to the dresser. "Do you want one too?" he called.

"Sure."

He made two cups of coffee, and thought he should buy a pair of decent-sized mugs to travel with. While the drinks cooled, he sat on the edge of the bed and fed his legs into his trousers. He was wrestling with the belt when Margaret re-emerged, hair wet and dressed in jeans and a jumper.

"Which one's mine?"

"Either. They are the same."

She picked up a cup and sluiced in some cold water from the basin tap. "The car'll be out the front."

"Very efficient." He sipped at his coffee and shook out his socks. "How much did all this cost?"

"Over the odds, but not by much. You'd rather Golden found us, I take it." She gulped once, twice, and drained the dregs. "Ready."

"You would be good in the *Stasi*," he muttered and put his cup back on to its saucer. He put on his socks, and slipped into his shoes. "*Also.* I am ready, too." He took a last sniff and swig of his coffee, and picked up his jacket and cane.

Margaret's new-found friend was as good as his word. She picked up a set of car keys from the night porter and jangled them as he let them out of the locked front doors. She scanned the road, then advanced on a silver Ford Sierra parked a little way down the street. The dawn lit the east sky, dappling the underside of the salmon-pink clouds. It was cool and the air smelled of brine.

Neubauer eased himself into the passenger seat and ran his finger over the scuffed interior. "We have a full tank of petrol?"

"I should hope so." She turned the key in the ignition and listened to the engine as it turned over. The needle swung to the top of the fuel gauge and lights glowed on the dash. "Seems fine."

She brought the seat closer to the steering wheel; Neubauer moved his further away and stretched his legs. He received the gazetteer in his lap and assumed he was to navigate.

"I know where we are going. But where are we now?"

338

"Search me." She pulled away from the curb, leaving Neubauer to scan the sides of buildings for road names, complaining how much easier it was in Germany.

After gyrating around the docks for half an hour, he stabbed at the map. "I think we are here."

Margaret parked up and they began a slow walk towards the river.

"This would have been hell at night. It's bad enough trying to find our way around in the daytime," she said. She stepped over the first of a pair of steel rails set into the concrete pier.

Neubauer picked his way over the tracks and looked slowly left and right until he came to the water's edge. He leaned back on the railing. The wind blew from the west and wavelets tapped the pilings beneath his feet. "This is the place."

"How can you be so sure?"

"There is the remains of some blue and white tape tied around that post, just over there."

Margaret turned and saw the ragged end flutter. She also saw the small, slim woman standing by a three-high stack of transport containers. She looked as out of place as they did; no hard hat, no fluorescent jacket, no heavy boots or clipboard.

"Who's that?"

Neubauer shielded his eyes. "I do not know. We are here, she is here. Perhaps we have all come together for the same reason." He unhooked his cane from the top bar of the railing and made his way towards her. As he closed the distance between them, the woman made to go, and he saw that she was young and scared.

"Please, wait. I cannot chase you," he called, and tried to walk a little faster. "I know who you are looking for."

She stopped and dug her hands in her pockets while Neubauer regained his breath. Margaret hovered in the background, unwilling to break the spell.

"You have seen this man?" He opened his wallet and found the picture of Gideon Smith that James Cook had sent him. "He had with him a sword. A big sword."

He pressed the photograph into her pale hands and watched as her almond eyes narrowed.

"You are his friends, or his enemies?" Her English was not as good as Neubauer's, but better than his Cantonese.

"We are his friends, me and my companion. We were police officers." As he said it, she stiffened and he hastened to finish his sentence. "But not any more. Our only job now is to help this man."

"You may continue," she said, and tucked a strand of black hair behind her ear.

"What happened here? A man died for certain, shot by Markham. But where did Smith go?"

She checked her watch. "I should be at home. My parents are still asleep and they do not know that I come here."

"Would it help if we drove you back? We would have longer to talk."

"Perhaps."

He turned and called out: "Yessica? Can we give the young lady a lift?"

"That would be fine." She came over and linked arms. "My name's Jessica Margaret. I used to be a Detective Sergeant. Torsten was in the Berlin police. What's your name?"

"My English friends call me Mary."

"So, Mary," said Margaret as they walked slowly away, "I'm told this isn't the place to be at night. How come you were here?"

"Such a terrible story," said Neubauer. He raised his hand to wave. Mary slipped in through the door of the flat above her father's wholesale shop, and he caught sight of her narrow pale face staring back.

"Poor kid. Attempted rape one moment, murder the next. Golden's a real shit."

"And Smith has gone again. Paid for her taxi and gone." The door shut, and he hoped that her mother heard her. "She should tell her parents."

"Maybe she will, now." She slipped the clutch and, as quietly as she could, pulled out of the bus stop and on to the road. "Smith's gone mad."

"So she says. Perhaps he was mad beforehand, as you have suggested." Neubauer scratched his chest, and wondered if it had felt like being shot. "The sword saved his life, but turned him insane. I wonder what Ambrose would have to say about this?"

"I'm sure he knows already. But if we're to help Smith, we have to find him." Margaret turned left at the traffic lights and found herself on a street she recognised. "They must be serving breakfast by now."

"We should call him. Ambrose." He opened his wallet again and found the business card. The telephone number tended to come and go, and he had always meant to make a separate note of it, although he had the suspicion that a copy would vanish just as mysteriously as the original did. For now, the card displayed the number. "If you order for me, I will let him know where we are and what we have found. I will even ask him where Smith is, although I doubt if he would tell us."

"Part of our journey." She parked opposite the hotel. "Do you really think we can do this?"

"I do not know. We can try, and that is all anyone can ask."

"What do you want for breakfast?"

"Everything. Lots of coffee."

"Right. You get on the phone to Ambrose and I'll grab a table. Torsten?"

"Yessica?"

"Don't forget to ask about Smith."

Simon Morden

Part VI

Sunday 28th **June to Wednesday 16**th
September 1987

Chapter 26
Sunday 28th June 1987
The north Pennines

Gideon Smith's story

No one would have noticed anything wrong unless they had watched him for a good while. Passing him on the road would cause his image to flash by in a sixty-mile-an-hour blur; nothing but a dirty fawn coat and a face that was set like flint in the rear-view mirror.

The only thing he carried was slung over his shoulder: a long, thin sacking parcel, wide at the top, narrow at the bottom, protruding over the head and falling behind lower than the hip. He had no change of clothes, no spare food, nothing. He was stripped down to only what he wore, and that was filthy and bloodstained.

Watch him, watch what he does. He suddenly stops, spins around and faces the opposite direction to that in which he has been resolutely plodding mile after weary mile. His expression remains the same, but he sees something that is beyond mortal sight. He stares for a minute, then turns back to his journey. The man is troubled by what he has seen, and wears a frown. The frown slowly seeps away as the road is eaten by his feet. Each step he takes, he seems surprised: he imagines himself walking off a cliff, and wonders why the sky supports him.

A motorbike roared and revved behind Gideon, slowing and kicking through the gears until the engine was merely muttering. The habit of walking was too great to break, and he didn't miss a step. Eventually, after the bike had trailed him for a hundred yards, it pulled ahead and stopped. It blocked Gideon's path directly. The rider rolled the machine on to its stand and opened his visor.

"Gideon, man. What are you doing here?"
Golden eyes peered out.

He had almost forgotten his name, having spent all his time with ghosts. "I ... I've been pushed here, by them." He pointed over his shoulder.

Ambrose hit the side of his helmet with his gloved hand. "No, you fool! They follow where you lead! They've been as lost as you."

Gideon shuffled his feet around and frowned again at the crowd behind him. They were twenty strong, not always the same faces, but some characters remained constant. Death was always present, always at the back and a little separate from the others. Marianne was not there today; in the vanguard was the ruffed Elizabethan man and the British Tommy, Lee Enfield held by its webbing strap.

"Mr Ambrose, sir, if you please," said the Tommy. He lit a rough roll-up he took from behind his ear. "We're a bit confused as to where we're going. Mrs Newton says to trust him, but I don't know. I reckon he's gone a bit doolally."

"Nah, nah. I'll sort it out." Ambrose pulled his helmet off and cradled it like a severed head. "Gideon, you're nowhere near where you're supposed to be."

"Oh," said Gideon. "Where am I supposed to be?"

"North of here. I would have told you sooner, but there was a crisis elsewhere. The story is being written as we speak, by a dozen different hands. Since it's my task to bend the plot to its most favourable outcome, I've had to become a juggler. Matters are coming to a crux, Gideon." He watched Gideon watching the ghosts. "You've done well, lad. I doubted you; I thought your character too weak to carry the weight of Excalibur. She's chosen you.

Heart

Sealed by the sword and not by human hand, sent by the sword and not by human plan."

"You know about that, then: the tattoo."

"It was going to happen, just a matter of time. Don't be afraid."

"Don't you start."

Ambrose opened one of the rear lockers and fetched out a spare helmet. "This isn't getting the baby a new frock, is it? You have the power to decide the fate of millions of souls, but power without wisdom is folly. You're no closer to learning the secret of the heart than you were at the start of all this, and without that you're almost certain to choose poorly."

"I still don't know what it is."

"You'll never find it here." He handed Gideon the other helmet and put on his own. He held up his hands to the roof of trees over the road. "They've no secrets to tell you. Come with me, Gideon."

Gideon jerked a thumb at the road behind. "But what about them?"

"They're ghosts, man! They'll follow you wherever you go. Now get on, and stop your blathering."

Gideon gathered up his coat so that it didn't catch in the wheel, then squeezed into the helmet. He gripped the U-shaped chrome handle behind him. "Where are we going?"

"North," called Ambrose. "Feet up."

They pulled away. The ghosts looked at each other and started forward. The Tommy slung his rifle over his shoulder.

"How about a song? Pack up your troubles in your old kit bag, and smile, smile, smile …"

Other voices joined his, and on they walked.

Half a day of thundering down minor roads in the back end of beyond, watching the villages and hamlets whip by, dust and debris spinning in their wake.

As dusk drew in, Ambrose throttled back and freewheeled to a halt. Gideon opened his visor and looked around. Ahead of him, previously hidden by Ambrose's back, was a village nameplate. Over the tops of the hedgerows was the first sight of grey slate roofs.

"Where are we?"

"North."

"Yes," said Gideon. He'd had the sun on his back, then over his left shoulder. "But where are we?"

"We're where you have to get off."

Gideon hopped off and unscrewed his borrowed helmet. "You're not being very helpful."

Ambrose regarded him sternly. "I've taken you to where you need to be, so a little gratitude might not come amiss. Two things: Golden is looking for you. He'll use any means at his disposal to find you, trap you and trick you into giving him the sword."

"Any means?"

"Any and all. Nothing is beyond him. Don't be fooled by displays of compassion or contrition. The worm in his heart has destroyed anything worth loving or even pitying, and his soul is damned. He knows it, too, and revels in his filth. You know about Elizabeth, don't you?"

Gideon reached into his coat, and inside his wallet was a bent and battered photograph of a girl with clear brown eyes. "Her."

"They found you through her. You picked up her death images; they guided Markham to your door. They must have sacrificed a dozen before her and a dozen after, trying to tie down your location. Do you understand, Gideon? They'll find you, eventually, and that's just the way of it. Know the secret before they do."

347

Heart

Pressing the photo in his hands against his bearded cheek, Gideon asked, "How many more, Merlin the Magician? Prophesy for me."

"Don't mock me. How old am I? Don't you think I've seen enough killing with my own eyes to despair that this war will never end? All my life the only constant companion I've had was Death."

"My companion, too."

Ambrose relented. "Ah, well. Man was born to die, and the night comes all too quickly."

Gideon hung his head. "Sorry. I've been away too long. Talking to you, it's difficult. The words don't seem to get interpreted, they just come out, no matter how they might hurt."

"You're not mad. A little crazy, perhaps. But you've come to this late, and I expect you to know all the answers." He held out his hand for the crash helmet and Gideon handed it over. "I'll tell her grandmother. I met her once, you know, fifty years ago. She won't remember, but I wanted to see her then as I knew there wouldn't be time now."

Gideon put the photograph back in his wallet, the wallet back in his coat, and his hands back in his pockets. "You said two things."

"Get washed, lad. You stink. You'll never learn anything from anybody if they turn to stone on your approach."

"Thank you."

"I mean it. Now go; seek and you will find."

"I still don't know what I'm looking for."

"You'll know."

Ambrose watched the figure shamble off down the road, shoulders slumped forward, feet barely lifting from the road. He turned his golden eyes to heaven. "Make it soon, Jesu, for all your children's sakes."

348

It was more a small town than a village. It boasted more than one shop and more than one pub. There were a line of sodium street lights down the market square, and a red telephone box outside the Post Office.

There were people, and they were driving through in battered Land Rovers or walking along the uneven pavements. It looked so normal that Gideon almost cried. He dragged himself to the bridge and hesitated by the parapet. In the darkening light, he looked up at the shadowy shoulder of the hill in front of him. He was pulled to it by the urge to scream meaningless curses into the teeth of a gale and feel the sting of the storm-driven rain against his face.

Ambrose had told him that here, of all the places he'd passed through, the secret would be found. It didn't make sense, but there was nothing more to be gained from running. He turned his back on the bridge and trudged down the wide main street. He wondered at each person as he passed them by: did they know the secret? Should he ask them?

He heard music in his head, then, a moment later, music in his ears. At least, that was the way it seemed to him. It was coming from one of the pubs, a large whitewashed building with warm light spilling carelessly from the windows. In a dream, Gideon crossed the road and stood at the doorway.

"You going in, or coming out?"

Gideon stepped aside. "Sorry, I was in the way."

The man was portly, built like a barrel. His jacket was never destined to meet around his midriff. Much shorter than Gideon, he inclined his cap up and squinted at him. "You all right, lad? You look a bit peaky."

"I'm scared to go in."

Heart

They were blunt words, but the man took them in his stride. "Why's that then?"

"Because of the way I look, and smell. I can't remember the last time I washed."

"If that's all you're worried about, forget it. This is farming country – spend half our time treading in muck, the other half shovelling it. Get in there, if that's what you want."

Gideon stumbled up the top step and was steadied by a hand on his elbow.

"What's that on your back?"

"Just a lump of useless metal," replied Gideon. He bought the man a whisky for his kindness, and had one himself. It burned on the way down and flamed in his gut. Ambrose had called it the water of life and used it to revive him on a barren Scottish mountainside. It brought back memories of his great confession, and Gideon shuddered.

The other whisky was tossed down with practised ease. "Cheers, lad. If you'll excuse me, I'll join the boys over on our table." He indicated a group of scruffy gaffers hunched over their pint pots.

The music, which had momentarily stopped, restarted again with a long, slow note on a fiddle. It filtered through a closed door from the second bar. The room was darkened, crowded and smoke-hazed, with most of the young crowd standing and facing a compact stage heavy with speakers and microphones. The tip of the fiddler's bow bobbed up and down over the heads of the audience as Gideon squeezed into a chair in the far corner. The singing strings eased into a jig. Feet stamped, tables banged, hands slapped as the musician whipped his instrument faster and faster. Finally, he could do no more, repeated the final phrase over the next four bars and ended with a flourish.

The applause was raucous and wild. It was intimidating even for a man with a sword propped up by his side. As the noise died back down, there was a another cheer. A crown of dark red-brown hair swung out on to centre stage, and the hollow knocking of a live microphone being plucked from its stand echoed from the black speakers.

The woman started to sing unaccompanied, and all the hairs on Gideon's neck started to rise. He knew the voice and had heard it in his dreams. Her tone was clear, like the ringing of church bells. His breath caught in his chest, as if he was about to panic.

When you find it, you'll know.

He knew.

It took him an age to stand; only when his curiosity overcame his fear did he lever himself upright and look across the tops of the audience's heads.

She carried herself like a princess. Her head was back, her hands holding the microphone almost above her so that she could sing unencumbered. She was not immediately beautiful. Her pale, stage-lit skin was luminous against her high-necked long black dress. Her eyes were as dark and bright as polished jet, and the strong bones of her face cast stark shadows.

He reached out his hand to cover the sword's pommel, and felt such a surge of heat and passion that he was rendered momentarily blind; everything was sharp red, boiling white, solar yellow. It passed. It was not a warning, but both reassurance and omen. He was not mistaken; it was a sign of things to come.

Don't be afraid, said Marianne's whisper. He turned in time to see her fade with a smile on her face. They all came to him in turn: the Tommy and the Elizabethan man, the Edwardian clerk and the nun. Don't

351

be afraid. He shut his eyes as Death hissed the final four syllables. He was not comforted by the inhuman voice.

For Gideon was afraid. Markham could kill his body, but he could lose his soul to this woman. He had to meet her, talk to her, convince her of his sanity and sincerity. There she was, proud and cold, oblivious to his presence. There he was, skulking in a dark corner, brooding, a wild, filthy barbarian cóme down from the mountains.

He stood for the rest of the night, transfixed. The band stopped playing, and the crowd cleared to go home. It left him exposed to cruel scrutiny. A fire exit was thrown open and the back of a Land Rover filled with amplifiers and great loops of cable. The cold wind that gusted through the door caused the woman to throw a green shawl around her shoulders. She laughed and joked with her friends, until the fiddle player pointed out the granite figure of Gideon Smith. She squinted into the shadows and he looked quickly away, casting his eyes down.

She had seen him, and he quaked in his boots. She started to weave around the chairs and tables towards him. He wanted to flee, but he gripped the sword tightly and stood his ground. It felt like the hardest thing he had ever been asked to do.

She had her head at a slight angle, half-smiling, half-frowning. She stopped a bare foot away, holding the corners of her shawl in her folded hands. "Do I know you?" It was said with an Irish lilt; not aggressively, but with genuine interest.

"I ... don't think so."

She had deep green eyes; but he knew she would. She was taller than he imagined, only a few inches shy of his height. "You seem familiar, you know. Are you sure?"

"I would have remembered," replied Gideon truthfully.

"Only I've been told that you've been staring at me ever since you came in."

Gideon blinked. "I'm sorry. I've go to ...". He steeled himself with a deep breath. "I've got to talk to you about something that's not going to make any sense at all." He waited for the arched eyebrows, the step back, the flick of the dress hem as she walked away.

She measured her reply carefully, far more carefully than he. "What's the nature of your something?"

"It's a secret." He realised what he'd said and rephrased himself. "The something is a secret, a mystery. Especially to me."

She looked at him strangely. Gideon had never seen that expression of wondrous anticipation and trembling anxiety before. "Okay," she said, "walk me home. It's a fair way, so you'll have time to say what you need to."

"What?" He met her disquietingly direct gaze.

"I'm going to trust you. I think you wouldn't harm a hair on my head and would die to protect me." Which was an odd thing to say. "You have the look."

"I thought I was mad."

"It's not a minority sport, especially around these parts." She lost some of her seriousness, and smiled. "Come on, walk with me. I need to be up early tomorrow. The longer we dawdle here, the later it gets."

She paused at the fire exit that led to the chill yard outside and looked around at the still-stationary Gideon. "Are you coming?"

Don't be afraid.

He slung the sword over his shoulder and started forward. "I'm coming."

Heart

They walked side by side in silence through the deserted square and darkened streets. Her pace was brisk, and Gideon didn't feel the need to shorten his own mile-eating gait to suit her.

"My name's Ruth," she said.

"Gideon," he admitted miserably.

"A good name, Gideon. It fits you. For someone who wanted to talk to me, you've precious little conversation."

"I don't know where to start."

"How about the beginning? That's usually a good place."

"I'm not sure where the beginning is. I didn't come to this at the start, not even halfway through. I don't know the story at all, that's my problem!"

"Why not tell me what you know? You can't do any more than that, can you? And don't be angry: not with me, at least."

They left the last house behind them, and their footsteps were guided by her knowledge and the starlight.

"I've been told I need to learn a secret," he started, and she interrupted him almost immediately.

"That's not where you came in, was it? No one said to you, 'Gideon, there's this secret ...'"

"No, you're right. I saw someone die. She was beautiful, and there was nothing anyone could do to help her. Her last act was to give me this." He reached over his shoulder and patted Excalibur. "And she told me not to be afraid. I've spent most of my time since being very afraid, for some very good reasons. I never knew such things went on in this country." He turned around and walked backwards for a few moments. The road was very dark and he couldn't tell if his ghostly retinue was there or not. He turned again and carried on.

"I thought I was mad, for a long time. I dreamed the same dream, over and over again, and it nearly killed me. But it was a warning. Someone was after me because of what I now had. I didn't know. I didn't guess until it was almost too late. They came for me and I think I killed one of them. But I'd been told I had to learn a secret that would make sense of it all. It'll answer all my questions. Maybe it'll solve all my problems."

She nodded.

"You know, don't you? You know all this and yet you're making me tell you. Why are you doing this to me?"

Ruth stopped so abruptly that Gideon had gone two yards before he could check his stride. "You listen to me, Gideon, listen to my voice. Listen to what I'm actually saying, not what you think I've said. I understand you, but I don't know anything about you. I'm not fey, despite what people say." She cocked her head to one side. "You've been away from home a long time, haven't you?"

"Too long."

"I understand what you're asking of me, Gideon. Do you?"

"Do you know the secret?"

"I know lots of secrets."

"I'm talking about the secret of the heart."

"I know it."

With the utmost fear and trepidation, he asked her: "Will you teach it to me?"

"If you're prepared to learn it, it's yours." She closed the gap between them, and gently guided her arm through his. "And so it begins," she said wistfully, but Gideon didn't know why.

The sofa was too short for him, but she left him to sort it out for himself. There would be no mollycoddling for him here. He took the cushions off and laid them on the floor in front of the embers of a coal fire. Wrapping himself in a blanket, he lay on the floor, watching the tiny glowing tongues of flame dart out of the shimmering heat.

He could hear her moving around: doors opening and closing, a tap filling a basin and, after a while, the plug being pulled. Then the light went out in the parlour where Gideon lay. He thought he was alone, but Ruth appeared in the dim red glow next to him, dressed in an old tartan dressing gown and her hair wrapped in a white towel.

"I wash my hair at night. It saves time in the morning, and it gets smoky when I sing. It makes a late night, but I prefer that to early mornings."

Gideon rested on one arm and looked up at the ceiling. Having a roof over his head reminded him of being at Jack's. "What do you do?"

"Community nurse. I change dressings, deliver drugs, check up on patients who've been discharged from hospital. It's a good job, a useful job. I get to meet real people and they're pleased to see me, generally. I get as much out of it as I put in."

"I walked, that's what I've done. And run, and hidden. I'm reluctant to trust anyone in case they turn out to be my enemy."

"What about me? Do you trust me?"

"I've got no choice. You know the secret."

She pulled the towel from her head, and her hair fell around her shoulders in a dark, deeply reflective mass of coils. "I have seen you before," she said. "I dreamed of you, months ago. You were wrapped in a white sheet, like a shroud. You looked more dead than alive, so I didn't think it looked out of place. You were like one of those medieval tombs, stretched out. You had a sword lying down the length of you, gripped in your hands. I touched you. You were still warm."

"I saw you then too. It wasn't quite like that for me, but I remember you. You said something to me, but I didn't understand what you said." He remembered her kissing him on the forehead. He glanced at her and wondered if her recollection was filtered by embarrassment.

Suddenly, she got up. "I need to go to bed."

"Goodnight, Ruth."

Gideon watched the hot coals glow and hiss in the grate. He was almost asleep when her voice whispered to him so quietly that at first he thought it was Marianne. "*Síocháin, ionúin.*"

Chapter 27
Monday 29th June 1987
Grasmere

Gideon Smith's story

The fire was cold and the cottage empty when he woke. In a form of wondering panic, he reached out for the sword and found it by unnatural instinct. It lay still and quiet under his hand. She could have taken it if she had wanted to.

It was light. The curtains were drawn back and there was evidence of breakfast on the tablecloth. He wrapped the blanket around his shoulders as he padded in his thick woollen socks around the few whitewashed rooms: kitchen, bathroom, parlour, bedroom. Ruth had gone for the day and left a complete stranger in custody of everything she possessed. There was even a set of keys next to the front door.

It was an exercise in trust, he decided.

He shaved using her razor, and thought it revenge for all the times Kate had used his. He cleaned his teeth with a flannel and used a cocktail stick to rummage between the enamel. He ran a bath so hot he whimpered with pain as he eased himself into it.

He rubbed soap into every crevice and scrubbed it back out again, and felt pinkly clean. All except the small cross straddling his sternum in blue, red and green. Like a cat in a kennel, it was out of place; an incongruity he was at a loss to explain. As a child, Christmas morning had brought shadows under the tree that were heavy with promise, together with an empty lead crystal glass and a few pastry crumbs on a plate. He'd poured the sherry and placed the mince pie on to the best china. Then they had gone, with no human hand involved.

This time, he knew his parents weren't involved.

He stared at the cross for a long while, then pulled his clothes into the bath with him.

He heard the Mini drive up on to the verge and the engine run on for a moment after the ignition had been cut. The handbrake creaked and the door popped. He straightened up with the small weeding fork in his hand and opened the gate for her as she lumbered through with a suitcase of medical supplies.

Ruth looked over the thin strip of garden fronting the cottage, and at the dark freshly turned earth between the plants. "Looks good," she said. "I never get the time."

"It wasn't meant as a criticism."

"I didn't take it as one." She glanced up at his badly cut hair. "I could have done that."

He brushed the top of his head, and shrugged.

"Have you been out here long?"

"I don't know. I lost my watch a while back."

"Do you even know what day it is?"

Gideon looked at the evening sky, which was starting to redden in the north-west. High cloud was layering up on the horizon: it was going to rain in the small hours of the morning. "No. What day is it?"

"Monday."

"Monday the what?"

Ruth put her head down and shook it. "Ready for a mug of tea?"

"Sure." He got back down on his hands and knees, and plunged the tines of the fork back into the ground.

"If you've worked all day without a break, you're entitled to stop." She put down the case and stood with her hands on her hips. "This isn't an endurance test."

"I know." He continued to dig.

"Neither do you have anything to prove to me about your gardening ability, your love of the outdoor life or your stubbornness." She bent down and wrested the fork from his fingers. "You'll behave like a civilised man while you're in my house. You'll have three meals a day and rest whenever you require it. Okay?"

Gideon frowned. "Is this part of the secret? Have I started yet?"

"You started the moment you were born, but you lost your way. Now I have to be hard on you to teach you what you need to know." She stretched out her hand. "It's never to early, or too late, to learn this secret."

He grasped her hand with his soil-stained fingers and was surprised by the strength he found. She pulled him upright, and they stood staring at each other for a while; she in her blue uniform and upside-down watch pinned to her pocket, he in sun-bleached and rain-washed greys and blues.

"Did you clean the bath out?" she asked prosaically.

"I remember doing it. Whether I did it well or not, I don't know."

She led him to the front door, still holding his hand. Gideon wondered how it could be both warm and cool at the same time.

"On these long summer evenings, I like to sit just here, on the front step, and just watch and listen. Will you join me?"

Gideon had never had the patience or the wit for chess, but this was how he imagined it might be: from a neutral start, both sides were evenly matched. Somewhere in the game, one player gained a creeping advantage over the other. Only as the game progresses is the advantage pressed home or lost. He felt himself being gently outmanoeuvred, a tug here, a touch there. She was the teacher, he the reluctant pupil. How could he learn anything unless he lost?

"It wasn't a trick question," she said as she waited for him to reply.

"I know."

"So sit down. I'll bring the tea."

There were sounds of Ruth busying herself inside; a kettle was filled, crockery rattled. Gideon leaned back against the door post. Heavy bees hummed happily around him, birds twittered in the trees surrounding the cottage. There was no artificial noise. He shut his eyes and the evening sun slanted on to his face and warmed his skin with its orange heat.

He was roused by the sound of a laden tray approaching. He slipped easily from sleep, just as easily as he had drifted off. The tray was placed next to him, with its cosied teapot and slabs of dark fruit cake.

"Made with Guinness," said Ruth, who had changed into a long bottle-green summer dress. "My mother sends me them every so often."

"Still in Ireland?"

"Never been away. Odd: planes, ferries, they leave every day, but she won't have anything to do with them. Won't leave the country, and that's that."

"So how come you're here?"

"My uncle's cottage, before he died. He left it to me. Most of my family are great travellers: the Irish often are." She drank some more tea and looked out over the garden. "What did you do with the sword? I assume you've hidden it somewhere."

"In a manner of speaking."

"Meaning?"

Gideon got to his feet and stretched. "I'll show you."

Heart

They walked around the house, following the rough, weedy gravel path to the back garden. The rear of the house was more of a managed woodland, with huge trees that soared from the ground and poked the sky with their crowns. The ground was green with ferns and brown with brambles. In amongst the trunks was a vast stone, a glacial erratic carried down from the mountains and abandoned by the retreating ice.

Ruth looked up. The rock was taller than she, and twice its height in width. On the top was the old black tarpaulin she kept by her back door for no reason but that it was out of the way. Rather than folded flat, it was draped over a tall protuberance, hiding it completely.

Gideon braced himself between the stout thickness of one tree and the solid side of the rock. He clambered up using branches and holds until he was perched on the rounded summit. He lifted the tarpaulin and pulled it to one side.

The sword was embedded point-first two feet into the rock.

"I want to see if you can pull it out."

She held up her arm and put a foot flat on the vertical face of the dark stone. She mounted the rock and stared at the sword. It had turned to gold in the light of the setting sun. She knelt down beside it and touched it reverentially, her fingers tracing the inscription down the blade.

"It's beautiful." She wrapped a speculative hand around the exposed hilt of the sword and used it to stand. Almost without looking, she tugged. The metal was firmly rooted. Her laugh was nervous and short. She took a firmer two-handed grip and gave a sustained pull.

"It's not moving." She relented and stood back, slightly breathless from her exertion.

362

Gideon reached past her and the sword slipped out of the stone as if it were held in place with soft butter.

"I'd say that was burglar-proof." He plunged it back in with a slight rasping noise.

Ruth felt slightly giddy and sat down, her legs dangling free. "That's quite a lot to take in, Gideon. Legends are walking the earth once more."

"I know. But I don't know what it means." He took the tarpaulin and covered the proud hilt once more. "You're supposed to tell me."

"No, I'm not. I'm supposed to show you. That's different."

The sun sank lower, and it grew darker.

Later, after dinner, Gideon made a fire and tended it until it burned brightly and well. Ruth pottered in the kitchen, and he ambled around the parlour, looking at this photograph, fingering that ornament. He came across a sepia-tone picture in a dark wooden frame. Holding it up to the light, he could make out a man in a bowler hat, a woman in a plain dress and holding a parasol; on the chair between them sat a dumpy baby swathed in white lace.

"Who's this?"

"Who?" Ruth came out, drying her hands on a tea towel. "That one? My great-grandparents. The baby's my grandfather on my mother's side. Here." She reached further along the sideboard and took a pewter frame in her hand. "This was my grandfather in Egypt, 1940."

It was a small photograph, brown at the edges and poorly contrasted. A man, vital and bare-chested, squinted at a camera in the height of the desert-summer day. The Great Pyramid of Giza framed his outline.

Gideon brought the photograph close to his face, so that it was almost touching his nose. In the shadows between the grandfather's muscles, and half-hidden by the mat of chest hair was a shape: a tattoo in the form of a cross.

He laid the picture down and stepped forward towards Ruth. His fingers slowly undid the top two buttons on her dress, and he parted the cloth slightly, just enough to reveal a triad of red, green and blue diamonds between the swell of her breasts.

"You're one of them, aren't you? Like Marianne who gave me the sword."

Ruth closed her dress. "It was handed down from my great-grandfather, to my grandfather and my uncle, to me. Sit down and I'll tell you how it happened."

Gideon slumped into one end of the sofa. She sat at the other end, folding her legs under her. She looked down at her gaping dress and redid the buttons.

"My uncle, my mother's brother, recruited me. I was twenty at the time, a student nurse in Dublin. He had children of his own, and the line normally moves from parent to child. He thought I was more suitable. Fey, perhaps; that's what they say now, anyway. He got it from his mother. She married into it by loving my grandfather."

"The one in Egypt."

"And all over. The Republic was neutral during the last war, but my grandfather didn't hold with the government's position. He joined British Intelligence in 1939, counter-intelligence in Palestine and North Africa. My grandmother let him go with her blessing. She could see that being neutral would be no defence in the end.

"He did well for the British, and got a chestful of medals as a reward. They're in a drawer hereabouts. Then they asked him to go behind enemy lines, organise the Resistance. He was parachuted into Poland in the spring of 1943 and he was never heard of again. Left my grandmother with a son and a daughter. That's why my mother has never left Ireland. She was too young to remember, but somehow she caught the mood of it.

"I used to have holidays here, from when I was old enough to travel on my own. I loved this place, and when my uncle died, he left it to me, not his own children. I still don't know why. Before he died, he told me this incredible story. It was the most terrible, frightening, noble story I had ever heard. Then he asked me what I would do if it were true. I told him that I would have no choice but to fight on the side of right. 'No choice?' he said. 'None,' I replied. He unbuttoned his shirt and showed me his tattoo.

"I knew then it was true. I was so scared, I was cold right through and couldn't stop shaking. You do the tattoo yourself, you know."

"Did it hurt?"

"Not for me. I had access to local anaesthetic."

"Tell me the story."

"How much do you already know?"

"Too little." Gideon shifted in his seat and faced Ruth. "The sword is Excalibur, Arthur's sword. There are two groups of people, one protecting the sword, one trying to claim it for their own, and they're murderers. Merlin the magician is around, too. He seems to show a lot of interest in me, but he never tells me anything useful. Like what to do with the sword."

"What you know is true. Who holds the sword holds the whole country in the palm of their hand. So it's for you to do with it what you will." She watched Gideon blink. "Do you know what the inscription says?"

"In part. I had someone attempt a translation. That was how they first found me." He remembered Leah Orchard and wondered what had become of her.

"I am the first of Albion, I am Cut-metal. Truth and Justice shall wield me, I divide light and dark. If I leave, destruction shall follow. Blessed be the name of the LORD." She shrugged. "It's all in the story. I had to repeat it to my uncle until I was word perfect. It's not something you write down. Part of the inscription says that the sword can't leave the British Isles, the boundaries of ancient Albion. An unknown disaster will happen if it does. My uncle thought it would be like Atlantis."

"Merlin said he came from Atlantis. Or was that his mother?" Gideon pinched the bridge of his nose. "I get so confused. Where does the secret come in? Marianne said I had to know it. So does Merlin. Have you met him?"

"Merlin Ambrosius? No. I wouldn't know what to say to him if I did. I think I'd be too frightened to say anything."

"The secret?" Gideon persisted.

"Power immeasurable. The secret of the heart is the secret of creation itself. But I still can't tell you what it is. I'll show it to you, and you'll learn it."

"Are you sure it'll help me?"

She smiled, a big bright smile. "Without it, you, me, everything, is nothing."

Sunday 13th September 1987

Ruth held the secret. He had been told to learn it. Once he knew it, he could act. He would know what to do.

Yet he never believed it. As he watched Ruth carry her case of medicines to her Mini, he railed silently against the whole ludicrous situation. But part of him felt calm and at peace, knowing that in around eight hours' time, he'd hear the engine die and the gate creak, and she would be back. So it began for Gideon too.

She shared her home with him, and more besides. The nuances of her character, her compassion, her temper swift and hot, her ability to say with a word, even a yes or a no, what he was feeling but unable to express.

She dragged him week after week, complaining all the way, to the village church. There he suffered the uncomfortable pews made for a Victorian man seemingly half his size, the slow Victorian hymns cranked out on a wheezing organ, and the readings and sermon plucked from an age before Victoria's grandfather had sat on the Hanoverian throne.

The people there were kind enough, though in their own way. A single man living in a small house with a single woman, they surmised wrongly but with little blame on their part. But they presumed too much.

Leaving the porch one Sunday morning, Gideon finally confronted her. "Why do we do this? They haven't changed in over a hundred years."

"I don't go to be entertained."

"Why do you go then? Why do you insist I come with you?"

"I go because I ought. You go because you must."

Gideon ground to a halt on the gravel path. "Must? What's that supposed to mean?"

"The secret. Listen behind the quaint rhymes in the hymns and under the blanket of Prayer Book language. Jesus never spoke with thees and thous. He spoke like us, with an accent so strong people used to make fun of him. We do our best to hide God in an obscure religion that ordinary folk can't fight their way through. But it's not about religion. It's about faith." She started walking again. "The church is part of the secret, Gideon. Listen to what's said and try and work out why."

They passed a gravestone with a bunch of fresh white lilies resting under the crook of a slate. Ruth said, "Five years ago, my uncle was laid in the ground, next to his wife, just here. A good Irish Catholic buried in an

English Protestant churchyard. Why do you suppose that happened?"

He looked nonplussed at the inscription to Declan and Maeve O'Connell. "Has the subject changed?"

"No."

Gideon strode to catch up with her. "Why don't I understand? Is there something wrong with me?"

"You don't understand because you don't understand. I know that's a circular argument, but one day, you'll know it all and wonder why you never saw it before, because it was in plain sight all the while. Think of it as looking at the way the world works through new eyes. Everything is different, nothing is the same. Not even *Hymns Ancient and Modern.*" She changed, brightened, as she always did when she had finished lecturing Gideon.

Sunday had become the day they had a pub lunch. Twice was a habit, three times a tradition. Ruth always had fish and chips, and a Guinness that she complained about. Gideon never had the same meal twice, and varied his beer every visit. He was cramming in experience like a man who knew he would be hungry again. Today he ordered a steak and kidney pie, and a bottle of imported German lager.

A short, red-cheeked local was staring at him with clear animosity. Gideon felt his hackles rise and his chin jut. As he collected his change, they exchanged words.

"What is it?" asked Gideon baldly.

The man spat on the floor, then turned back to his pint. "She any good?"

The meaning filtered through slowly. "What did you say?"

"That frigid bitch finally got her knickers down, has she? Puts it out for you, does she?"

Gideon looked over to Ruth, who was frowning and shaking her head. She was warning him off. "You'll leave us alone."

"Or what? She going to put a curse on me?" The man looked up. He wasn't afraid of Gideon. He was in the grip of a long-standing madness that had festered like gangrene.

Ruth appeared beside Gideon and pulled him away, forcing him to sit down with his back to the bar. The door to the outside opened, then swung shut with a bang.

"You know him?"

She picked up her stout and drew a finger down the condensation on the outside of the glass. "We have a past."

"Ex-boyfriend." For some reason, the thought made Gideon unaccountably uncomfortable.

"No." She took a long pull from her Guinness that left a line of white foam on her top lip. She cleared her throat. "He tried to rape me."

Gideon played with their numbered lunch ticket. He couldn't think of anything to say. All he wanted to do was go out, find the man and hit him very hard. Ruth put her hand over the piece of paper.

"It was a long time ago."

"I don't like him."

"You have to realise that I wasn't created the day before we met. I was born, went to school, learnt a vocation, started a career, moved countries. Some of it was good, some of it not so nice. I don't doubt that some terrible things have happened to you."

He thought of poor Nick who he had put to bed dead; he shook and looked down into his lap, ashamed. Ruth's hand tightened around his. "Some things I wish I could forget," he said bleakly. He was being chased by ghosts living and dead, and even by Death itself, who saluted him with an upraised fist.

"You will learn the secret of the heart and transcend all your problems. You'll be changed."

"For the better?" It was an honest question.

"No. Nor for the worse. But you will be changed. Gideon, my past has made me who I am. Nurse, singer, sealed. I can regret, I can remember. But I can't alter anything that's happened. Jason, he's part of my past I regret. He wanted me, I didn't want him. I didn't handle things well. I was young and naïve. He tried to take advantage of that and me."

"No excuse," muttered Gideon.

"No. No, it wasn't. Things could have turned out badly. In the end, they didn't turn out as badly as they could have done. I learned a lesson that night. No one will ever touch me without my permission."

It was the way she'd said it. "You've never ..."

"Never." She was hard, like a rock. "In the moment I realised that Jason wasn't going to take no for an answer, all I could think about was the Seal. I couldn't explain it away. I had no alibi prepared. That's when I fought with all the strength I possessed, and some that I never knew I had. He hurt me and I hurt him back. But he didn't come near me again, and I never let anyone else close for the same reason. It's my seal, my Cross, my Sword. No one else would understand."

Gideon's mind was stuck like a needle on a warped record. "Never?"

Their food arrived and, by unspoken agreement, the subject was dropped. Only on their way back to the cottage did he say anything further.

"You've never ..."

She saw the meaning of his hesitant and unfinished sentence. "No," then she said it out loud.

Despite their being alone on the road, Gideon blushed furiously and turned his head aside. "I'm a virgin. It doesn't make me pure of heart. It never stopped me wishing and dreaming. In some respects, I was coerced into it by my sealing."

"I lived with a woman; we shared the same bed for almost a year. Why do I now feel dirty?"

"I don't know." It was said shyly, secretively.

"You don't even have a boyfriend."

"Don't be silly, Gideon. You're here."

"I really don't understand."

She looked at him with her glass-green eyes. "I think that you do. I think you don't want to understand."

She walked a little ahead, and Gideon trailed miserably behind, his senses crowded out by more than the sound of the wind in the trees and the birds in the branches, the scent of woodland and the sight of dappled green.

Chapter 28
Wednesday 16th September 1987
Grasmere

Gideon Smith's story

The Earth turned and swung in its orbit around the sun. Time passed by in the outside world whilst leaving Gideon and Ruth in an asynchronous cocoon that obeyed its own laws. Pass it did, though.

Jason had gone out that Sunday evening. He had met with a man who appeared to have succeeded where he had so catastrophically failed, and his pride was more wounded than if he had been struck with a fist. He got staggeringly, almost incoherently drunk, and made a confession he would later not recall.

The man who had heard the jealous, hate-filled words tumble out slipped away, his face blurred by more than alcoholic haze. Once outside, he adjusted his heavy tweed coat with his black-gloved fingers. It was a warm autumnal evening. The midges swarmed in the air in roiling masses, but they left the man alone. He should have been hot, sweltering under the thick cloth of his coat, but he was cold, so cold.

The Jaguar was parked next to a red phone box. Coins were inserted, the dial spun.

"Markham, sir. I've found them."

Gideon came back from his inconsequential errand. A pint of milk and a loaf of bread nudged each other gently at the bottom of a plastic carrier bag, swinging with each step up the land. He rounded the corner, saw the Mini parked up on the verge outside the front gate and almost missed the dark, sleek lines of the much larger car behind.

372

He stopped in his tracks and dropped the bag. As he ran towards the cottage, a river of milk wound its way across the camber of the road and into the clogged ditch.

"Ruth? Ruth!"

There was no answering cry. Inside, there had been a whirlwind. Nothing was in its place. Chairs were overturned, crockery smashed, books lying like wounded butterflies across the floor. Gideon looked around and felt his heart beat very slowly. He checked the bedroom and the bathroom. They were intact, untouched. The kitchen was a sea of disorder and the back door waved lazily in the breeze.

He stepped to the door, pushed it open to its fullest extent. His eyes carried over them the first time, the tableau of two men and one woman, striking poses and as still as shop dummies.

"Smith."

Markham had his arm around Ruth's neck, pulling her head back and exposing the whiteness of her throat. He had his gun in his other hand, the barrel pressing against her temple. A lock of her hair draped over the black metal, obscuring the point of contact between pale skin and hard weapon.

She was bleeding from her mouth and her nose. The blood was startlingly red. Some of it had coloured her blue uniform with black splashes and streaks. Her eyes were screwed tight shut, but they opened at the sound of Gideon's voice.

"Let her go."

Golden sat on one of Ruth's dining table chairs, set out a yard away from Markham. His thin legs were crossed and his school-tie urbanity was complemented by a smouldering cigarette poised just so between the fingers of his right hand.

"Let her go? Now why do you propose we do that? We've had the Devil's own job in finding you. Hill and dale, every nook and cranny in the country. You'd done a good job at disappearing since we last met. We had to use the most extreme methods to track you down." He smiled. His teeth glistened wetly. The ash fell from the end of his cigarette and he took a calculated drag. "Still, all's well that ends well."

"I know who you are, Sutton. I know what you've done."

Golden looked briefly pained. "Please, Smith. We both know that what you know and what you can prove are two entirely different animals. I am a government minister; you are an itinerant still wanted for questioning by the police. Your credentials as a credible witness are somewhat sullied. So, if you could see your way to maintaining our grand illusion for a little while longer, we can engage in civilised conversation."

Ruth seemed to be having difficulty breathing. She coughed and gagged. Bloody phlegm fell over Markham's arm and down her already stained dress front. Gideon started forward, and Markham drilled the barrel of his gun further into the side of her head with a twist.

"Please," said Golden, "stay where you are. We can negotiate quite easily from where we are."

"What do you want?"

"The sword, naturally." He cast his eyes up to the rock. The tarpaulin had been cast aside, but Excalibur remained.

"What do I get in return?"

"Your paramour here could be returned to you if you wish it."

"I don't trust you. You're a liar."

"Of course I am. I'm a politician." Golden dropped his cigarette on the grass and left it smouldering.

He got to his feet and began to pace in a tight circle around the chair. "But believe me when I say this in all seriousness: she will die unless you hand over the sword. Say the words, give it to me freely and both of you will live. Obviously, I can't take it from you. The bastard Merlin had you sealed. Extortion is well within the rules, however."

"I didn't seal him. The sword did it itself."

Merlin Ambrosius stood at the back door, resting his hands on the frame either side of him. The brim of his hat shielded his hawk's eyes from the sun.

Golden stiffened and gripped the back of the chair with his knotty fingers. "You."

"Me? I suppose so. The time for hard decisions has come, and Gideon needs an adviser. Go and fetch Excalibur, lad." When Gideon hesitated, he added. "Don't worry. I'll keep an eye on things here."

Gideon skirted past Markham. He felt Ruth's eyes follow him as he climbed up on the rock and pulled the sword from the matrix of crystals that held it fast. Golden hissed and greed flushed the old man's face. The envy of possession made him grimace with pain. So close, so close.

Gideon returned with the sword, planted it point down in the grass and covered the pommel with both his hands. It was a deliberately martial stance which hid the nausea that churned inside. He coughed with nerves before he spoke.

"I give you the sword and you'll leave Ruth alone?"

"You have my word."

"You're not the one with the gun," said Ambrose.

"Quiet, ancient fool!" raged Golden. "It is with Smith that I do my business."

Gideon looked from Ruth to Ambrose. "Merlin, what do I do?"

"Do? What do you want to do?"

"Save her." She was beautiful, he realised, even with fear draining every trace of colour from her face.

"Can you?"

"I don't know."

"Who do you trust?"

"You. Her. No one else."

"Not Golden?"

"No." His voice was now a whisper, thin and weak.

Ambrose's was strong and quiet, like a deep river. "So how can you expect him to stick to his side of the bargain? He cares not one jot about your life, or Ruth's. The only thing preventing him from killing you and her is Excalibur. If you hand it over, you lose your protection. You're both dead."

"The old man is filling your mind with poison." Golden had edged closer to overhear. He leaned and leered. "My word is my bond; the sword in exchange for her life."

"Maybe ..."

"Perhaps," interrupted Ambrose, "We should hear Ruth's thoughts on the matter. Gideon doesn't want to believe me. He can't believe you. Let her speak. It's her life that's immediately at risk."

Golden searched for a trick. But as his mind took it, the woman's voice would only serve his purpose, no matter what she said. Smith was emotional, swayed by his passions. He could feel his fingers tighten around the hilt of Excalibur. He nodded to Markham, who loosed his arm. Ruth leaned forward and retched. She rested her elbows on the ground and wiped her mouth on the cool grass.

"Gideon, listen to me." Her voice was laboured, shot through with pain. "You know the secret. You know what you should do. I don't want to die, but ..."

"That's enough!" shouted Golden. Markham stepped up, taking a handful of Ruth's hair and pulling it sharply back. He was astride her, his gun at the nape of her neck.

"Why won't you let her finish?" said Ambrose. "This is Gideon's choice. He needs to be in full command of the facts, doesn't he?"

"The only fact he needs to be aware of is that he will never escape me. I'll hound him the length and breadth of the country until he collapses with exhaustion. Wherever he lays his head, I'll burn. Whoever he speaks to, I'll cut their ears off. He will be the most despised man on these islands and he will beg me to take the sword from him. Now, Smith. Choose! The sword or the woman."

"Dear God, I can't." He wavered, and looked into Ruth's eyes. She gave him nothing; no movement, no nod or shake, no indication of what she would have him do.

"Markham," said Golden, and the killer adjusted his stance. Bracing his feet, he minutely moved his aim.

"Wait," blurted Gideon. He paused for the longest second. "I've decided."

Golden raised his hand. Markham eased the pressure on his trigger finger.

With infinite sadness and infinite regret, Gideon said: "Merlin, take me away. Before I change my mind." He felt numb, empty, like an open coffin. He loved her. He was letting her die.

Ambrose took him by the arm and pulled him along the path around the cottage. Excalibur trailed after him, dragging impotently on the paving stones. Gideon's last sight of Ruth was the sad, slight smile that clung doggedly to her bruised lips.

He was pushed into her car. He hunched around the sword, rocking backwards and forwards. He was mumbling "No no no no no."

Ambrose paused by the driver's door and pointed at the Jaguar. There were four pneumatic whines, and the car settled down on its deflating tyres. He crammed himself into the Mini next to Gideon and tossed his hat into the back seat. He passed his hand over the dashboard and the engine started. "What's the secret of the heart?"

Gideon muttered the answer, and it was hidden under the rev of the accelerator. Ambrose had to make sure.

"Again. The secret?"

"Love. The secret is love."

Finally satisfied, Ambrose popped the clutch and bounced the car into the road.

The gunshot was clearly audible over the piston noise. Gideon shut his eyes and a cry of anguish was torn from the very centre of his soul.

He tried to get out and go back.

Ambrose stopped him, leaning over and wrestling the door handle from him. Despite Gideon's manic strength, he overpowered him. "You can't. She's gone, and you can't bring her to life again."

"I don't care. Let me out!" He was still struggling.

"What good can you do, man? Think!"

"I can get rid of those two murdering bastards!"

"Gideon, you'd force them to kill you first, and you're no use to anyone dead." Ambrose chose briefly to concentrate on not ramming a tree at full tilt, then

378

returned his attention to keeping the passenger door shut. "What are you going to do now that you know the secret?"

Finally, Gideon stopped the unequal battle. "They killed her."

"I know. Everyone dies eventually. I'm sorry."

"I loved her."

"Of course you did. How else could you learn the secret?"

Gideon's anger was all burnt out. "You could have told me this would happen."

"You needed a teacher and Ruth was ready for you. She knew the secret and she was sealed. All I did was bring you together. What happened afterwards, I had no part in, no matter how inevitable it was. You were made for each other, and you were going to love each other, whether I'd encouraged it or forbidden it." Ambrose banged the steering wheel with his fist. "Do you know what it's like? Do you? To see the future and not be able to change a thing? I did the best I could by saving you and the sword. It breaks my heart, because I love you all so very much."

"I hadn't even kissed her. You should have given us more time. "

"I could have. Nothing would have been different. It was a gamble that you'd know the secret by the time Golden eventually found you, and you'd make the decision the way you did. If it's any comfort, Ruth was going to die whatever you said."

"Destiny."

"Yours and hers. Now you have to finish what you started."

"I was told I hadn't started this."

"No, that was Arthur, a very long time ago. But you started when Marianne handed you Excalibur. You have to finish it."

"I have to, do I?"

"Ruth didn't tell you? You're the last, Gideon. It was prophesied long ago, as she well knew. You were chosen by the sword and sealed by the sword. You are the last. Now you have to decide what to do. I can help you with that."

"Do what you like." Gideon was once again hunched over the sword in the footwell.

"You have to trust me. I'll take you to a place where you'll have all the time to make all the decisions you need."

"Where?"

"Firstly, the railway station."

"She's dead."

"We all die."

"Except you."

"Except me. That's my curse."

"And mine is that they all die around me. Friends, strangers. I'm Death's apprentice."

"You know the secret, Gideon. Don't pretend you know everything."

They came quite unexpectedly to the outskirts of a town. Cars and people passed busily in front of their junction.

"They don't know. None of them know that she's dead."

"Don't be hard on them, Gideon. Love them instead." Ambrose threw the little car around a roundabout and pulled up into the station forecourt. He put two wheels up on the pavement, just where the double yellow lines were. The engine died at a gesture from his long fingers.

"I take it we're not coming back," said Gideon.

"Not unless you want to."

"I don't know what I want."

"Then come with me." Ambrose reached into the back of the car. He placed his hat back on his head and pulled the tartan travel rug into the front.

Gideon stared at it. He and Ruth had had picnics on that rug. Tears welled up in his eyes. "I left her to die."

"Put the sword in the rug and come with me." He moved Gideon's hands for him. "I can't pretend to take away the pain. But at least you'll understand why you hurt so much."

Inside the ticket office, Ambrose paid cash for two singles to Oban. "We need somewhere thin," he said by way of explanation. He took him by the arm and guided him out on to the platform, sharing it with two back-packers and a bored British Rail porter.

The sun was at its zenith, and Gideon was cold to the core. He no longer stood like a rock, but a block of sculpted ice. His eyes, always blue, were so bleached of colour they were translucent. All he could think about was what he'd done, and how it couldn't be undone. He'd made the decision he thought Ruth wanted him to make. She was far more at ease with her sacrifice than he.

Had been. Had been far more at ease. Past tense. She was dead.

Ambrose looked at the station clock, and the chug of a heavy diesel engine came and went on the wind. "There's a train to Carlisle due."

The bright twinkling lights of the power unit emerged around the bend in the track, and the brakes began to squeal on the September-damp rails. A cloud of sooty smoke, tasting burnt on the tongue, smothered them briefly. Ambrose grasped the brass handle of one of the doors and twisted. The rolling stock was old, branch-line relegated with dusty compartments and dim, yellowing lights.

"Gideon, it's time to go."

He hauled himself up the three steps into the doorway, and squeezed down the corridor. He slid back the door to the first empty compartment that he found. Ambrose was behind him, and closed them off again.

Gideon slumped into the upholstery, into half a century of sweat, grease and travel. He curled his arms around the rug-swathed sword and, as he brought his head to rest against the muffled hilt, he could smell her. He rocked backwards and forwards, sobbing, "What have I done? Oh God, what have I done?"

"You chose the heart," said Ambrose quietly. "The desire to do right doesn't always lead to right being done. The converse is also true. Listen: you are knowledgeable where you were ignorant, you are wise where you were once foolish. You have a heart of love where you had a heart of stone. You are changed beyond all recognition. A brighter star has never hung in God's firmament that shines there now." The train jerked into life, and the diesel whined up to speed. The station started to recede from view.

"I killed Ruth and let those bastards live. How can that be right?"

"Let us make it right. Sleep, Gideon, dream. Listen to the rocking of the train, feel the sound of the wheels on the track seep into your bones. When you dream you will see, and when you wake you will remember. You will know what has to be done." Ambrose spoke hypnotically, his golden eyes flickering with fire.

Gideon fought his utter exhaustion, but could not fight the enchantment that was weaving around him. In the midst of his grief, he felt his vision cloud and grey, his mind becoming slow, then still. Time stopped …

Chapter 29

Wednesday 16th September 1987

Gideon Smith's story

And Gideon dreamed.

He was standing on a wide, flat beach. To his left, the waves rumbled in from an unsteady sea; to his right, dunes loped off to the hinterland. The tail-end of a gale gathered up loose surface sand and sent it drifting in diaphanous sheets across the strand. The same wind plucked at his unkempt bird's nest of hair and tatty beard.

He was in pain. He lifted fingers roughened by heavy labour to his head and felt an old wound above his left ear. He pulled away a mat of dried blood, and traced the stiff black river down his neck. His right hand was heavy. He had the sword, naked steel in his grasp, a fist so tight that if he had died at that moment, they would have had to break each and every finger to pry it from his cadaverous clutch.

Behind him, a solitary hut was well ablaze. The flames crackled their way through the dry wood and popped the tarred roof. It burned brightly and fiercely, with orange cinders lifted high into the air on the updraft. The wind fanned the flames to ready excess.

Two men watched it closely. They seemed satisfied with the conflagration, and conversed in comfortable murmurings over a body that lay anonymous at their feet. The stockier one shot the body with a bullet from his black handgun, and the dark form jerked a plume of sand. Now it was a corpse. The sound of the shot made Gideon flinch.

"The sword, Smith. Give me the sword." Golden and Markham started a leisurely stroll towards him.

"No." His voice was tired, already defeated.

Heart

"We'll carry on, Smith. Even if we have to kill everyone. Give in. Give me the sword and we won't bother you any more."

"I can't do that." He sounded so miserable, so resigned, he reduced himself to tears.

"Of course you can. Give it to me freely. You don't need it."

"You can't have it." His tears gave way to rage, and he swung the sword about his head. He was unsteady on his feet and the effort made him look ridiculous.

Golden stood a respectful distance away. Markham was crushing limpets on a solitary rock with the heel of his black shoe.

"You make me do it, you know. You defy me, and I have to punish you. Remember the man who asked directions from you? Dead, I'm afraid. The woman who gave you that drink of water? Dead too, eventually. And that sweet, angelic child? Oh, so precious and, oh, how tragic." He shook his head in bewilderment. "Why do you do it? You should have ignored them all. Have you no conscience? Just give me the sword. It's for the best."

An anguished cry tumbled out. "Leave me alone."

"Then give me the sword."

Gideon swung around, started to walk away. His boots, worn flat, sank into the sand and sapped the little energy he had left. "Go away," he muttered.

"You're a filthy, crazed beggarman shambling the byroads of Britain. Everyone who acknowledges your existence, dies. You're the most despised man in the country, Smith. You're hated."

"Hate myself already."

"Give me the sword."

"Can't do that, can't do that."

384

"There'll never be an end. And when you finally die, I'll be there and all I'll have to do is bend down and pick it up."

"It's all you need to do now. It's just a sword. It's just a story. It only matters to you."

"I will have it."

"Never have it." As he walked, the wind dashed the sand against his ankles and erased his footprints behind him.

Carlisle

"Gideon, wake up."

"No!" He came to with a shout. He trembled as he looked around wildly. He clutched at the sword for protection, not comfort.

"Calm, calm."

"I dreamed," he said, his voice hoarse. "I thought the dreams had gone."

"And what did you dream?"

"About what it could be like." Gideon pushed his hand through his hair. It was still short, his face beardless. "It was terrible, awful. Golden carries out his promise. He kills anyone who talked to me. I'd be alone forever."

"It'd be your choice, Gideon."

"My God, it's no choice at all."

"By the way," said Ambrose, "we've stopped. We need to change trains."

"Where are we?" There was another station outside the window.

"Carlisle. We have precisely two minutes to make the connection." Ambrose stood up and drew the shaking Gideon to his feet. "Your choices are three, Gideon. You'll dream them all. Now come on. We can't be late for this."

Heart

He hurried them out of the carriage, across the platform and into the diesel-electric that sat waiting for them. When they were seated, Gideon took over a pair of seats and stretched his legs diagonally across the aisle. Ambrose scanned the station outside the dust-smeared window.

"You can't do your hocus-pocus in here. There are witnesses."

Still staring beyond the window, Ambrose answered: "It's a train. You're tired. You'll sleep."

"Not if I've anything to do with it."

"I haven't lived for over a thousand years without learning something about the way human beings work." Content that they would leave without interference, he settled back and faced Gideon over the table.

"I forgot you were an elf."

"Only half an elf. When the train gets going, swaying side to side, the telegraph poles flicking past with monotonous regularity ..."

Gideon caught himself, his head sliding back on to the headrest. He frowned and sat upright. "Stop that."

Ambrose held his hands up in apology. The train started with a jolt.

He remembered where he was. The landmarks were familiar, but the particulars were different. It was Newcastle, he knew that. But he was bewildered by the changes to the main shopping street. The bright lights and the crowds were missing. Most of the shop fronts were boarded up, and litter stirred fitfully across the dusty paving slabs, driven by an east wind straight off the North Sea. It was dusk: there should have been an exchange of late shoppers with early drinkers, but he was alone with the sleeping lamp-posts and the overflowing litter bins. A

386

pair of scruffy pigeons pecked the ground hopefully a few yards from his feet.

Gideon put his hands in his pockets and walked slowly through the emptiness, wondering. It was too quiet. Even the distant rumble of traffic speeding by on the motorway was absent. The half-moon was set in the sky directly in front of him, and it stared blankly down.

A newspaper blew past and wrapped itself around his ankles. He kicked it free, then caught sight of the tabloid-black headline.

"Britain strikes first."

He chased the paper down the street and snatched it up. He turned his back on the moon and held up the flapping sheet. There were three pictures on the front, full colour and newsprint grainy. The Union Jack was being planted on a French beach. There were bodies of paramilitary police on the esplanade of a conquered seaside town. Squaddies were hunkered down in the doorway of a *boulangerie*. The king was leading his army to victory against a stunned and sleeping Europe.

By the pale light he could just read the bald text. The UN was in uproar. The EC were passing resolutions late into the night even as they packed their files into boxes. All the while, the British army marched on, spreading north and south. They had cut off Brittany and were threatening the Belgian border. Harriers were flying over Bruges. People were dying as they fought to protect themselves, and refugees clogged the roads to Spain, Italy and Germany.

Gideon let the front page slip back to the ground from his numb fingers. The breeze caught it and sent it cartwheeling away.

He was no longer alone. A figure had appeared at the far end of the road, and was striding towards him. All in black, it was no more substantial than a shadow, but each step that closed the distance between them made the world a little colder. The pace was even and fast, violently intense.

It was only when the figure was ten feet away could he see that it was a man with a lean face. His smile was wide, and his eyes were coal black with not a trace of white. Gideon looked for the sword, but he did not have it. Of course not. He had given it to Golden in exchange for his peace.

The man's smile gaped and revealed two sharp and elongated canine teeth. His arms reached out and enfolded Gideon in their irresistible embrace.

Glasgow

Ambrose had to carry Gideon off the train at Glasgow. He pulled him into the station bar, propped him in a corner and arranged two trebles.

As Gideon raised the glass to his lips, his hand was white and trembling. "What does it mean?"

"What do you think it means?"

Gideon took a huge mouthful of whisky, held it in his distended cheeks for a moment, then swallowed hard. He spoke barely above a whisper. "It means the end of everything. I gave Golden what he wanted and he went to war."

"The people, the poor misguided people will follow where he leads, even if it is to their destruction. The war will give Golden an empire to rule, albeit briefly. His star will rise and burn bright." Ambrose sniffed his drink and took a gulp. "Then there will be brighter stars falling from heaven to extinguish his. Their fire will consume millions and strip the land I love bare, and nothing will grow on it for a thousand years. The nation's name will be a curse that mothers will frighten their children with.

388

Behave, or the British will come and get you. They will
spit on the ground and trample that spit underfoot at the
mention of Lord Golden. But that's your choice, not
mine." Ambrose's eyes lost their prophetic glow. He
drained his glass bitterly and slammed it down on the
table.

"Oh God."

"Gideon, if you give the sword to Golden, that's
what will happen. He'll go to war and butcher the country
in the process. You'll have rest, Golden will have the
throne. But after a while, you'll only have despair to show
for your transaction."

"But what was that ... thing?"

"In Golden's Britain, demons will walk the
streets. God's protection will be withdrawn and the nation
will be naked. That's the reality of it." Ambrose tried to
drink from his empty glass, and instead stared at the light
refracted through it. "We'll both have to live through it,
and it'll be the darkest time we ever know. We'll pray for
death, and it'll escape us until we reach the very bottom of
the pit prepared for us."

"You'd still let me choose, wouldn't you?"
Gideon hung his head so low that his forehead swept the
sticky tabletop. "You'd let me send us all to hell. Why?"

"Because it's your choice."

"I'm nothing, dammit."

"You could be king yourself."

Gideon looked up. The barman polished a pint
glass with studied precision. "What?"

"It's a credit to your goodness, lad, that you
haven't thought of it. The sword is a symbol. Golden
knows that he can't be king without it. You have it. You
could claim it for yourself." His mouth twitched with the
ghost of a smile.

"I ..."

Heart

"Time to go again."

"Now?"

"Now. After you, your Majesty."

"Don't talk bollocks."

"Then get moving. British Rail's timetable is entirely outside my control. Finish your drink and take up the sword. We've still a way to go."

For the last time, Gideon Smith dreamed.

At first, he thought he was alone again. He was in a vast empty space, shot through with great drifts of slanting light that threw everything else into black shadow. Motes of dust danced in the air, winking as they ponderously turned.

A single candle flickered before him, and he became aware of people all around him, standing apart from him, and hidden by darkness and stone. He was on a throne and they were his subservient courtiers.

He gripped the arms of his chair and lifted himself clear. The sword by his side scraped along the dais, and he unbuckled the scabbard from his waist. Grasping the hilt, he slid the belt away with a serpentine hiss. He'd be needing Excalibur today.

When he finally spoke, he had walked into one of the pools of light. His voice had a bass rumble to it that echoed between the pillars and up to the vaulting.

"Bring them to me."

There was some distant and unseen slamming of doors, and the slow funereal sound of chains clanking closer. Two men, shackled and bound, were pushed out of the shadows towards Gideon. They were dressed in tattered, filthy rags. One was an old man, the other had a wrestler's physique; but both were bruised and cut, with new blood dried over old. The old man was cold and his bones stuck out. The other man stood straight, but as the light illuminated his torso, all eyes were drawn to his scars, scars on scars, joining and dividing, forming a patchwork of body parts. He had been made, not born. A child of bastard magic.

Gideon circled the pair. "You killed Ruth. You killed Porlock. And Elizabeth. And Robert and Marianne Newton. The number of people you killed would fill this cathedral. Imagine it, Golden. Thousands of accusers, pointing their fingers at you and raising their voices to God for justice." He carried on around the filthy pair, then stopped in front of them. The sword was heavy in his hand. "Finally, you have been captured, and brought before the king, who will judge you for your crimes against the innocent."

"I ... I do not recognise your authority," said Golden. His voice held fear, and the tremulous sound surged through Gideon as sour joy.

"You do not recognise me as the supreme authority in this land, yet you would have had this all for yourself! Did you kill Ruth for something that didn't matter to you?"

Golden pressed his lips thin-shut.

"I hold Excalibur. I am king!" Gideon walked around them again, glowering at them from under his brow. "The king's justice will be done. I left no stone unturned in looking for you. I searched the country twice over to dig you out from your hiding place. I say you are guilty. Guilty!"

The vaulted heights shouted back the condemnation. Golden lowered his head. His whole body slumped.

"The sentence is death."

"Mercy," whispered Golden. He raised his hands, rattling the chains clamped around his wrists. He was confronted by the point of Excalibur hovering an inch from his left eye. He was mesmerised by its sharpness and he sank to his knees, murmuring thin and formless words.

"You dare ask for mercy?" Gideon hit him on the side of the head with the flat of the blade. "Silence! You won't put a spell on me."

Golden did not answer, because he was twitching and twisting on the stone flag floor.

"And you, Markham? Will you ask for mercy?"

Markham stood, staring ahead impassively, unblinking. "Usurper. The kingship is not yours by right. It is my Master's, and I do only his bidding. I have no use for your weak mercy, because I am not ashamed of what I have done. I enjoy killing. I especially enjoyed killing your woman. My only regret is that I will not kill again."

Gideon's jaw set hard. He turned on the ball of his left foot, span and brought Excalibur down from the roof to the floor in a glittering white blur. The leading edge struck Markham in the angle between his neck and his shoulder. It came to a halt on the bone of his right hip. He stepped back under the crushing weight of the blow. Then he lost his footing, folding in on himself in a tidal wave of black liquid. He never moved again.

The backwash lapped against Golden before it stopped moving and started seeping through the cracks between the stones. The wetness startled him, and he turned over to see the ruined body steeping in its own gore.

"What have you done?" he said, looking up at the descending scream of steel.

It was over. Gideon staggered to the doors, forcing them wide open. "No stone unturned," he cried, "I left no stone unturned to find them. I judged them. I sentenced them. I executed them. What now? What do I do now?"

There was nothing to greet his eyes but a sea of rubble as far as the eye could see. The cathedral was the only building still standing.

"No stone unturned! Merlin! Merlin, tell me. What do I do now?"

There was no answer. There could never be an answer.

West Coast Line, north of Glasgow

He was crying as they passed over the Falls of Crianlarich. Water thundered below, and dropped in fat tears above.

"I'm lost. I can't do a thing. Are these my choices? Death, death and death? I can't even be a good king, dammit."

He had an empty drink can in his fist. He crushed it flat then tore it in half. The last few drips of sugary liquid splashed on to the table. "I have no choices. I may as well kill myself so that I'm not entirely to blame for what happens."

Ambrose tilted his head to one side. "It's a thought."

"You bastard!" Gideon slammed the two halves of twisted metal down. People turned to look, then turned to look away, embarrassed and muttering. "You're supposed to help me choose, not help me die."

Ambrose regarded him coolly. "I gave you three choices. You suggest a fourth yourself. It's not without its dangers."

"What? Kill myself? You can't be serious."

"Sacrifice. Your life for others." He tugged a fat book out of one of his many pockets. He tossed it to Gideon, who scrambled to catch it.

Heart

It was a Bible, compact, dirty and moth-eaten. Its Rizla-thin pages were dog-eared and print-packed.

"What's this?"

"Is that a trick question? No. Read it."

"All of it? We've not got the time, man." Gideon was bloody angry. He threw the book back.

Ambrose pushed it back across the table, smearing the spilt drink. "Start at the beginning. Stop when you have the answer."

"You're talking nonsense again."

"The way of Enoch. Watch for it. It's brief, and you might miss it."

Gideon knocked the Bible on to the floor. "Tell me."

"Read it for yourself."

"No."

Ambrose smiled deliberately, and retrieved the book. "You will read it. Trust me."

Chapter 30

Wednesday 16th September 1987

Grasmere

Torsten Neubauer's story

Neubauer looked down at the ruined body, not caring to bend down and check for a pulse. She was as dead as dead could be. There had been a single shot to the back of the head. He turned away, sickened. At times like this, he remembered too vividly the blood and fear and chaos.

"Torsten?"

"Too late. Too late again. I am sorry." Just too late. The red and grey mass that had melded with the white shell of the skull was still wet, still warm. "*Scheisse,*" he said with feeling. He walked unsteadily back towards Margaret who stood at the back door.

She held up a road-stained fawn raincoat. "I think this must be Smith's." She lowered her find and looked past Neubauer, who leaned heavily on his stick.

"Ten, fifteen minutes ago, no more. Golden and Markham were here, Smith and Ambrose were here, the sword was here. Now they have all gone. If we had found this place first time ...". He struggled for the words. He was close to exhaustion, and for once his memory failed him. "We were so close! We were in the town when this woman lost her life! How long must we be always too late?"

"Torsten, I know, I know." She took him inside, righted a chair and sat him on it. "We have to be quick now. Where do you think they've gone?"

"Please, Yessica, can't we just call for the police, an ambulance? We have lost our respect for the dead."

Then she said a shocking thing: "Let the dead bury the dead. We haven't got time to mourn, Torsten. We have to find Smith, and we are less than a quarter of an hour behind him. Where have they gone?"

"I do not know. You have become hard, you do not care like you used to."

She brushed his observation aside and put Gideon's coat down on the kitchen table. She rummaged through the pockets and found loose change, a punched train ticket, a few pieces of string, a photograph of a young woman. She passed it to Neubauer.

He frowned as he looked at it. "I recognise her. She is one of the missing. I cannot remember her name. She is probably dead too." He stared at the dark curls of her hair and her clear brown eyes. "Have we come to this? We pursue Smith and Golden, only to find dead people wherever we go?" He put the photo in his shirt pocket. "*Also.* So be it. The nurse had a car, a Mini. It is not there. Smith and Ambrose must have taken it, but where would they go? Golden has a large powerful car that they cannot outrun. So they have left the car somewhere they can get to some other transport. Smith needs to get away quickly, so they have gone somewhere large and near."

"Windermere. It's big enough. Train station, coach station, ferry. He could go anywhere from there. We'll have to hurry."

"I know. I regret it." Neubauer pushed himself out of the chair. He stood on half a fine bone china teacup. It cracked to dust under his foot.

They took their hire car down into Windermere. There were a smattering of autumn visitors taking advantage of the weak sun that was balanced over the shoulder of the peak across the lake. Townsfolk went about their business, oblivious to the search taking place in their midst. Margaret circled the town centre, but only when the tow-truck pulled up outside the railway station did they spot the abandoned Mini.

"There," barked Neubauer, and Margaret braked sharply. Wheels squealed behind them and a horn blared angrily. Before they could pull across the road, a heavy fist banged on the window.

The driver of the car behind, mouth distended with obscenity, gestured wildly. "What the fuck do you think you're doing, bitch?"

Margaret opened the door hard against his knees, and stepped out over his fallen body. She pressed her warrant card into his red and shouting face. "I haven't got time to arrest you. Get back in your car and count yourself lucky. I'm trying to save you, you animal." She pulled him upright using his collar and heaved him towards his own bonnet. He sprawled like a fly.

Neubauer stared open-mouthed. "Yessica, what are you doing?"

"Perhaps I have become hard, but this is too important to be delayed by maggots like him. Now shut up and let me turn this car around." She grunted with the exertion of twisting the vinyl-covered steering wheel, and span the car into the station forecourt. She heaved the handbrake on without stopping first. "Torsten, go to the ticket office. I'll search the car."

Neubauer was grateful that there was no queue. He searched his pockets for his own identification, and hoped it held some sway. "Please," he said to the cashier, "I am looking for two men who I believe recently came in here. Perhaps they have bought travel tickets? One is very tall and broad with blond hair. The other is shorter ..."

"And has the damnedest yellow eyes?" said the man in the peaked cap.

"Those are the people we are looking for."

"He bought two singles to Oban. Left twenty minutes ago? Call it fifteen. That's what I told the Special Branch man."

"Special Branch?" He tried to remember, and recalled Margaret saying something about them in connection with Golden's protection. "An unpleasant-looking man with dark eyes."

"That's him. Also told him that there isn't another set of connections today."

"*Vielen Dank.*"

"There was something else. You might want to tell your friend I overheard them talking about needing somewhere thin." He shrugged. "For what it's worth."

Neubauer re-emerged from the green station doors. He waited until Margaret had finished searching the interior of the car, which was back on the ground sagging on its suspension.

"Nothing," she said.

"Where is Oban?"

She pointed north. "About four hundred miles thataway. Is that where they went?"

"Both Smith and Ambrose. There are no more trains. We must drive." Neubauer walked to the Sierra. "Markham has asked about them too. They are ahead of us, but behind Smith."

"Get the map out, and work out how to get us on the M6 northbound as quickly as possible." Margaret turned to the patiently waiting recovery crew. "Take the Mini to the police station; it's needed for a murder enquiry. I hope we'll be back to give our explanations."

She got back into the car. Neubauer was threading his walking stick down beside him and making sure it didn't interfere with the seat-belt. "Do you remember where we went to with Ambrose in London, after Markham shot at you?"

"After a fashion."

"He is heading for somewhere similar. He calls them thin places. I think that Golden does not know this."

"Thin? It means nothing to me." She strapped herself in and started the engine.

"Do you suppose that this is it? That this is the last day we have to do this?"

"I hope so." Margaret dropped the handbrake, and the car merged with the traffic on the main road.

The English/Scottish border

Lunchtime, they crossed the border north of Carlisle, passing over the long, low bridge that spanned the Solway Firth.

"Please, we have to stop." Neubauer's voice was strained.

Margaret looked down at the dashboard clock, then at her own watch. "We're making good time. We ought not."

"Yessica, I need the toilet and I need to stretch. I am in pain."

She sighed. "Torsten ..."

"I want to arrive in Oban alive. Five minutes will not make a difference."

"I'm worried that it might." A sign for Services flashed past. They were in the outside lane, doing a steady eighty-five. Traffic was light, but there was no sign of Golden's Jaguar. She looked at her passenger, at his pale sweat-slick skin and gritted teeth. She briefly resented his crippled state, but she knew that they had arrived at this point only through the mind that his ruined body carried so imperfectly. He had saved her life. Her fixation with bringing Golden down had to be watered with compassion.

She flicked the indicator stalk down, and in three separate manoeuvres steered the nose of the car into the slip road that led to the first service station in Scotland. "Five minutes and not a second longer. I'll buy some pop from the shop and meet you there when you've done."

Heart

The car park was half full, with a smattering of coaches
and big-wheeled trucks. Margaret pulled into a space as
close to the main doors as she could. Neubauer hobbled
off gratefully, while she went into the shop. There were
pre-packed sandwiches, shelves of fizzy drinks, trays of
sweets and racks of tourist knick-knacks.
She purchased two cans, some sandwiches and a big bag
of chocolate eclairs. With time to kill, she picked up a
glossy guide to Western Scotland. It was packed with
pictures of dramatic mountain skylines, rugged half-
ruined castles and misty lochs. She flicked through the
pages until she reached the entry on Oban.
When she'd read the text, the caption to the colour
photograph opposite caught her eye. A pink sandstone
church squatted low on the shoreline, the tower glowing
red with the dying rays of the sun. She backtracked and
traced her finger along the words. "A thin place, where
the distance between Heaven and Earth grows small." An
icicle of coincidence dripped down her back and made her
whole body shiver.
"I am ready," said Neubauer at her shoulder.
"I know where they're going." She finally articulated her
thought.
"Sorry?"
"Look here: a thin place. Iona. It's a small island off the
coast. It's near Oban."
Neubauer took the book from her hands, looked at its
cover, looked at the contents, and stared hard at the
picture of the ancient abbey and the strand of white sand
before it. It called to him strangely, touching him in a way
his soul dimly recognised. "How do we get there?"
The tartan-trimmed woman at the till pulled out a fat
CalMac timetable and furnished him with the ferry times
and a tourist map. He reported back to Margaret.

400

"We do not have much time. The last ferry to Mull is in only a few hours."

"Will Smith and Ambrose make it?"

"The ships leave shortly after the trains arrive. They will catch the one before us. If we catch one at all."

Margaret pushed the guidebook back to Neubauer's chest. "Buy this and anything else you think might help. I'll get the car and pick you up by the foyer." She turned and ran.

Neubauer suddenly smiled. He leaned on his stick as he quickly scanned the bookshelves, and picked booklets almost at random. "*Der letzte Tag*," he hummed to himself, "*Der letzte Tag*."

Oban

Late afternoon at Oban harbour: the sun hovered over the western horizon, sending hot light slanting across the bay, picking out the strange coliseum on the hill above the town.

"We made it."

Neubauer sized up the queue of vehicles waiting to embark the ferry. "There may not be room for the car."

"It can't be that full. Not after we've come all this way." Margaret pulled over to the side of the road next to the ticket office, and got out her warrant card. "I'll tell them it's a matter of national security. It always gets them going."

She reappeared from the office clutching a thin card ticket, and waved it at Neubauer. When she got in, she passed it to him to hold. He saw that it was a single, and wasn't surprised.

"Golden's on board already. He was about half an hour ahead of us, but we've caught up." She restarted the car and was waved immediately up to the loading ramp. The gate was lowered behind them; they were the last.

Heart

"We will be first off. I think that is good, no?"

"I don't know. Now we've got him in our sights, I'd rather have him in front of us." As she steered into the space indicated by a crewman, the ramp was raised behind them. They sat in the car as the outside light was blocked out. Floodlights inside the hold reflected off the roofs of the other vehicles, even the black Jaguar four cars ahead.

There was a tap on the window. One of the crew, dressed in a fluorescent tabard over a greasy cream Aran sweater, mouthed an instruction through the window.

Margaret cracked the door open to listen.

"Passengers have to go to the upper deck. Fire regs, I'm afraid." He pulled the door open wider to reinforce his wishes.

Reluctantly, Margaret stepped out and waited for Neubauer to extricate himself from the passenger seat. His cane tapped its way along the metal deck, his footsteps tipping the uneven grilles so that they clanked alternately, up and down. The engines sung a bass note through the whole ship. They were leaving the dock and starting towards the gap in the harbour breakwaters.

"I've never been on a boat before," said Margaret, "unless you count the rowing boats on the Serpentine."

"Not even to France?"

"Believe it or not, this is the first time I've been outside England." She helped him up the stairs of the pitching ferry to the upper passenger deck. A glance through the doors to the cafeteria confirmed that Golden and Markham were already sitting down to enjoy cups of tea while they watched the sea whitetail past.

Outside on deck, it was cold and blustery, with a salt tang in the air. They walked to the stern of the ferry and watched the land recede. A castle slipped into view on their left. Open sea appeared to the right. In the far distance, the clouds merged with the mountains, shading into each other so that one never finished and the other never began.

"It is getting thin, no?" observed Neubauer. "Heaven and Earth are drawing together."

"If we're all that stands between Golden and the throne, it could be Hell and Earth that join."

"We will see this through. This is the last day we will ever have to do this. We will stop Golden, save Smith and the sword, and we can vanish. Our duty will be done and our war will be over."

"Or Markham will put cursed bullets between our eyes and we'll lose. There's no one to help us, Torsten, and I'm afraid. Afraid that we've been too late all the way, and we'll be too late now."

Neubauer leaned on his stick and gripped her shoulder. "Either way. Win or lose, there will be an end to this."

"There's so much I haven't done. If I die now, I'll never get the chance." She sighed. "Are you warm enough?"

"Yes." He watched the wake churn out in a wide white road.

"I'm not." Margaret moved closer to him, and in putting her arm around his waist, drew him closer still.

Mull

Neubauer's directions were simple: west until they could go west no further. The road was twisty and long. It ran a tyre's breadth from the sea at times, and at others was surrounded on both sides by hills high enough to be mountains. There was almost no other way to go: one major turning to Tobermory, a few minor tracks, and the road they were on, which ran from one point of the compass to the other.

Neither of them could pronounce Fionnphort properly. It was a name on the map, and a collection of buildings on the ground that couldn't reasonably be called a village. The road crested over the brow of another hill, and the sea and a concrete slipway was in front of them. The tarmac leading up to the sea was flanked by crouching cottages that seemed to shrink against the sky.

The ferry was just beaching itself on the slipway. It was a flat-bottomed skiff with ramps at both ends and a bridge that arched over the top. The sides were just wide enough to take a walkway above and provide shelter below. The landwards ramp of the ferry rattled down on its chains and splashed into the waves that ran up the slipway.

They parked in the wider part of the road that doubled as a car park, stopping next to a coach from Blackpool. A tractor with a trailer packed with bleating sheep drove past. Foot passengers followed: the pensioners from Blackpool milled about with their ash walking sticks and green knapsacks weighed down with thermos flasks and souvenirs. Through their midst strode a mountain-man, heading for the hills. Behind them all was Ambrose.

He stood, hands in the pockets of his leather coat, hat down almost to his nose. Water raced about his feet, but he seemed unconcerned about any discomfort that he felt. If he was surprised to see Neubauer and Margaret, he hid it well. He raised one arm in greeting and they met halfway. The pensioners were being ushered on to their coach. The backpacker had already left the road and was a shrinking figure against the horizon.

Ambrose smiled seriously, his golden eyes shadowed in his face. For the briefest of moments, he looked his age. "You've done well. You're at the right place at the right time. You've read the signs and followed to where they point. I congratulate you both."

Neubauer looked across the narrow sound to the dark island beyond. He could see the grey of the abbey and the

404

white of the sand. The sun was setting behind Iona. "Where is everybody?"

"Smith has crossed over. Golden is somewhere behind you. He is searching this island, but will eventually realise his mistake. He will come." The first sounds of hesitation entered Ambrose's voice. "Gideon Smith is in a delicate state. He stands on the very edge. He is like an egg, do you see? Give him time, and the egg will hatch into a bird, and the bird will soar. One push will send it tumbling over the cliff to shatter on the rocks. There will be no return."

"This egg," said Neubauer, choosing his words carefully, "how much time will it need?"

"One night, Inspector. Just one night out of a thousand years of nights." Ambrose took Margaret by her arm and gestured over at the tiny island of Iona. It was short, low, brooding, as if the weight of millennia pressed it down. "You think that I know everything, Jessica Margaret. But nothing is set. I see what has been done, and what must be done."

Margaret echoed him. "What must be done? I thought that, if we got here, we would know what to do. Torsten told me that this is the last day of our chase. We have to finish here, don't we?"

"Your friend is a good man. It is not his story, yet he sees its truth and believes in it. He knows what must be done, Jessica. Over there, across the water is an island, a holy place where a man named Colmcaille waded ashore to bring the message of hope and love to a dark and ignorant land. There is a place called the Hill of Angels where Gideon Smith sits. At dawn, he will have strength again. During the night, he will be weak and vulnerable. Lord Golden must not set foot on that island tonight, for if he does we are all undone and everything has been in vain.

Heart

Yes, it finishes here. Torsten Neubauer recognises this, and knows what must be done."

He was silent, and Margaret turned to ask Neubauer what he knew and she didn't. He was not there. He was climbing into the car, on the driver's side.

She slapped her pockets, but the key was missing.

Her fury broke over Ambrose. "You bastard!" she screamed at him, then started to run. "Torsten! Torsten, no!"

Neubauer shut the door, locked it from the inside, and fumbled the key into the ignition. He could see Margaret sprinting towards him. He had hoped that it wouldn't happen this way. He found reverse by accident, span the wheels on the loose chippings by over-estimating the bite on the clutch, and lurched to a halt in the middle of the road.

Margaret slapped her hands down on the bonnet. "Get out of the car."

Neubauer looked at the gear stick and selected first.

She dashed to the door, pulled at the handle and howled in frustration. "Torsten, stop. Don't do this!" She tugged all the harder.

The car jerked forward under his inexpert control, dragging Margaret off balance. He started to move away. *"Ich kann dies' machen,"* he told himself.

Margaret ran beside the car, shouting at him, pleading with him, crying for him.

"Yessica, listen to me. We must do what is right. We must keep our promises. We are in the service of the King." He couldn't tell if she had heard him.

"Torsten, you could die!"

"I know." He pushed the accelerator to the floor, and turned on his lights.

Margaret staggered and doubled over in his wake, panting and weeping. Through her tear-hazed eyes, she saw Ambrose pick something up off the road. It was Neubauer's stick; discarded, not to be needed again. "Ambrose, do something!"

"Do something, Jessica Margaret?" He weighed the walking stick in his hands and snapped it in two across his knee. "It is done."

The road followed the line of the valley, and shortly he found a section that would suit his purpose. There was a turn about a kilometre distant, where the traffic would have to slow. The road dipped out of sight again to cross a river, and only reappeared a hundred metres away.

He turned off his lights and pulled over, at the last moment remembering he should be on the left of the road, not the right. He waited. The stars began to come out one by one, and cold stole in. He kept the engine idling over and turned up the heater. It grew warm around his feet, but the chill bit at his side. He clenched his teeth. It would not be long now. Over a year ago, he had asked a pathologist whether Marianne Newton had been murdered. Certainly, he was told, if the murder weapon had been a car. So now he sat, crippled but still capable of violence.

Headlights picked out the road in the distance. A sleek black car hung on the corner, then vanished from view again.

Neubauer took as deep a breath as he could manage, depressed the clutch and tried to change gear with the window winder. He swapped hands and found first, then released the handbrake. He rolled out to straddle the white line with his front wheels. He picked up speed as he descended into the valley.

The needle nudged forty. The Jaguar flashed back into view. It was coming towards him, filling the road with its bright wide headlights. He put his own lights on to full beam, and stamped hard with his right foot.

There was a terrible moment when he felt that he would wrench the steering wheel around, lock the brakes, lose his nerve. It passed, and a second later he hit Golden's frantically swerving car head on.

Time expanded. Every second held a minute's worth of experience. The Sierra's nearside front wheel turned in on itself as the chassis bent and ripped. The windscreen starred and crazed over. Horizontal and vertical swapped their axes in a tumbling jumble. The roof came up to meet Neubauer's head, and the windows exploded outwards. The rushing wind blew fragments of glass, mud and bracken into his face.

It stopped. All the noise and chaos and motion ceased. Even the engine died. His body hung from the seat-belt like an up-ended puppet, his head pressed against the fabric of the ceiling become floor. There was a moment of peace, and the scent of freshly turned earth mingled intimately with vaporising petrol.

Then he tried to reach up with his left hand to release his seat-belt buckle. He felt, rather than saw, that his thumb was dislocated, bent so far back that it seemed alien and distant. He coughed as he drew in petrol fumes, but there was no pain. Again, he lifted his hand to free himself. Again his arm fell back, uncontrollable, broken.

After half a dozen futile attempts, he stopped. There was more petrol than oxygen in the crushed compartment.

It felt very much like the last day.

Chapter 31
Thursday 17th September 1987
Iona

Gideon Smith's story

The night sky was as crisp and clear as cold September could strive for. Gideon Smith sat on the Hill of Angels, the ancient sword across his lap, and stared at the stars until his eyes dried out. Around the mound of soil and rock were his ghosts, a great congregation of people who surrounded him and looked up with him at the Northern Lights. As the black night swam with ribbons and curtains of green and red and blue, Excalibur sang slow and haunting songs to him. The ghosts whispered in wonder at the sights around them.

As the eastern quarter grew lighter, turning from deep blue to salmon pink, the sky quietened and lost its eerie brilliance. The sounds of a heavy diesel engine throbbing in the Sound between Mull and Iona drifted over the slowly waking landscape. The first ferry of the day was coming and it was time to move. He stood stiffly, and made his own path through the heather and past the lake to a horn of rock overlooking a semi-circular bay.

Below, over a thousand years ago, an Irish monk had cut off one of his fingers and thrown it on to the cobbled beach. His gesture had ensured that he had been first out of the gaggle of tarred coracles to land. History had remembered his Roman name, Columba.

Gideon paused at the top and looked over. The tide was in, and the sea heaved hard against the broken and angular boulders at the base of the cliff. White foam leaped into the air and boomed with the delight of it. He had been here before in his dreams. He had stood, bare toes gripping the last blade of scrubby grass, on the edge of the precipice. He had been dashed against the imaginary rocks and sucked out to sea. He had also fallen, and never landed.

The sun broke over the mountains of Scotland.

"Smith? Smith!"

Two men were making their way up behind him. One walked like an old man, the other limped along, dragging his right foot. Gideon stepped away from the cliff and held Excalibur in front of him, ready for war.

"This is it, Smith. Give me the sword."

"You killed Ruth."

"You wouldn't give me the sword, Smith. Deeply regrettable, but it was your choice." Golden was out of breath, and sported a purple bruise under his thin hair. Markham was close enough for Gideon to see that his face was a spider's web of fine cuts. "I'll show you mercy. You can't run forever, you must realise that."

"Of course I know that. It would be easy to give in now. But I also know I'd regret it later."

"You'd live."

"I'd live knowing that you'd won."

Golden smiled, turning his face into a death's head of taut skin. "We all win if I win. Everything will be greater, more magnificent. When I am king, we will rule as we used to. We will all be kings!"

Gideon wasn't listening to Golden's mad vision. He was watching the three people inching their way painfully up the path that led to the bay. A man was being dragged, his arms around the shoulders of his two companions. One of them was Ambrose, the other a woman he'd never seen before. Ambrose lifted the injured man's head, and tilted it in Gideon's direction.

They studied each other, and wondered what stories each could tell. Everything suddenly became greater, just as Golden had said, but the kings of the land

410

were those who had given up the most. With the image of a shattered body suspended between two friends fused in his mind, Gideon turned and started a lumbering run.

"Smith, where are you going? There's nowhere left."

Gideon stretched out his stride, eating up the ground beneath him. He held the sword poised across his body, balanced and rocking with every impact of every step.

"Markham, stop him!"

But Markham couldn't run as fast as Gideon, thanks to the bravery of Torsten Neubauer.

The promontory narrowed, came to point. Gideon's foot hit the vertice between land and sea and sky. With one final kick he windmilled into the blue. Three words were ripped from his mouth, an involuntary epitaph to his life. "I don't believe!"

And so Gideon Smith left the world with a lie on his lips.

Heart

Jessica Margaret's story

Golden had called the coastguard and the police. An orange-hulled boat swayed in the sea off the rocks, beyond the line of the breaking waves. Down on the shore, men were searching. On the wind-clipped blue-green grass above them lay Neubauer. He was sleeping peacefully, covered by Ambrose's leather coat. Merlin the magician had produced a syringe of morphine from his coat and injected it into Neubauer's limp and broken arm.

Margaret hovered at the cliff's edge, scanning the depths. "Shouldn't we be down there, looking for him?"

"Sit down, Jessica. Sit down with us." Ambrose patted the grass with his hand. When she hesitated, he smiled and said: "Please?"

She eventually perched herself on a rock a little way off.

Raising his face to the morning sun, he said: "Let me tell you two stories."

"But Smith, the sword? What if Golden finds it?" It seemed unlikely. The sea gave up its treasures reluctantly. But she felt she ought to worry.

Ambrose carried on regardless, losing the focus in his eyes. "The first is about Gideon Smith, who wasn't a bad man as the world judges these things. He played hard, he worked hard. He had everything that would make him successful. His outward life hid the fact that he was really the shallowest of men. Then he met a dying woman and she handed him his purpose. In one moment, she gave him what he should have been, could have been.

412

"Her name was Marianne Newton, and her last thoughts and words were not for herself, but for others. Not just her friends, either, but for the strangers she would never know. Imagine the impact that had on blind, selfish Gideon. He would have had no last words or thoughts for anyone. His death would have been as hopeless and pointless as his friend Nick's, dead in a drunken stupor.

"Marianne wanted to tell him what he needed to know. She appeared to him, and told him about the secret of the heart, which he had once known in his cradle and forgotten along the way. He didn't understand. He could have stolen a march on Golden, but ended up telling him where he was. He realised too late. They tried to kill him, of course. To them, he wasn't part of the story. But that was their mistake.

"I found Gideon, gave him a sign and pointed him in the right direction. Finally, after months of searching, he found the secret. His wisdom helped him decide that the three choices he had were only counsels of despair. He could have lived out his days as an indigent wretch, a humiliated weakling or a crazed despot. He had to find a way to take the sword out of reach forever. He couldn't leave the country; the sword inscription warned him not to. How was he to deny Golden Excalibur without seeding his own destruction? It would take a miracle, and he didn't believe in them."

He was silent. A skylark rose and fell, twittering in the autumn sun.

Margaret shuffled uncomfortably on her rock. "Ambrose," she said. "Merlin. What do we do about the sword?"

Seemingly jolted out of a dream, Ambrose blinked. He started his second story as if there had been no pause. "A long time ago, when the world still felt new, there lived a man called Enoch. He, unlike Gideon Smith, was a righteous man, a man who loved God and his neighbours. He cared for friends and strangers alike. If someone was hungry, he would give him bread. If they had no coat, he would give him his own. If they had no money, he always had a few coins for just such a situation.

"Enoch loved to take long walks and, along the way, he would talk to God. They would walk together, and at the end of the day, they would part, and Enoch would go home. Except on this day, they walked far and wide, and ended up on the summit of a tall mountain just as the sun was setting. He wondered how he was going to get home, because he knew there were lions and bears in that country.

"God told Enoch not to worry, because he could come home with Him, and stay in His house. Enoch agreed, and instead of staying one night, he ended up staying forever, because God's house was so full of wonder he never grew tired of it."

Margaret had had enough. "While you're prattling on, Golden could be making off with Excalibur!" She leapt off her rock and started to stamp around. She pointed at Neubauer. "And he should be in hospital."

Flint entered Ambrose's voice. "I thought you understood, Jessica Margaret. This is not about what is possible. Gideon Smith listened to the tale of Enoch and railed against it. He found it ridiculous, nonsense even. Yet look at his actions. He said at the end that he did not believe, but he gambled everything, sword, nation, his own life, for what? He did not believe. He did not know God."

"So why did he jump?"

"Because in his heart he had the slimmest edge of hope. He did not know God, but he ran from the Devil. Was it enough? Was his hope in vain? Tell me, Detective, where is his body? Where is Excalibur?"

414

She looked over the cliff again. She was uncertain as to whether she was right or wrong. "Aren't they down there?"

Ambrose rose from the ground, and to her mind he grew in stature. His eyes were fires and his voice the roar of the west wind. "No they are not! Go look for him if you wish. Go! Find his sodden corpse washed up on the beach. Find the sword glittering three fathoms down. Like Golden, you will search until your skin turns to leather. They are gone, gone forever."

"But I saw him fall."

"Did you see him land? Where he went, you know, though you cannot accept it. Without hope, we all die. With it, even the merest sniff of it in the air, we can perform the most extraordinary acts of bravery. Gideon Smith had hope, hope that he would not be abandoned, that Enoch's way could be his way. Did his courage fail him? Did God fail him?"

He turned away, raising his arms to the sea, then letting them fall back by his side. When he looked around at Margaret, he was just a man again. "Look for him if you want. He is not here. He did not die."

Heart

Printed in the United Kingdom
by Lightning Source UK Ltd.
2656